Good Cop

To Meaghan —
Here's to all the
Dancing & Romancing!
Glad you're a fan
Enjoy —
Liz Kelly

LIZ KELLY
www.LizKellyBooks.com

Also by
Liz Kelly
Countdown To A Kiss
(A New Year's Eve Anthology)

GOOD **COP**

HEROES OF HENDERSON: BOOK 1

Liz Kelly

Published by Kelly Girl Productions
©Copyright 2013 Liz Kelly
Cover design by Tammy Kearly

ISBN: 978-0-9889838-0-9

This book is a work of fiction. The characters, events and places portrayed in
this book are products of the author's imagination and are either fictitious
or are used fictitiously. Any similarity to real persons, living or dead, is
purely coincidental and not intended by the author.

For more information on the author and her works, please see
www.LizKellyBooks.com

This book is dedicated to my "Writer Girls"

Holli Bertram
Colleen Gleason
Tammy Kearly
&
Mara Jacobs

Because without them, there would be no Brooks or Vance
(And I would not be having nearly this much fun!)

With love and gratitude,
Thank you.

PROLOGUE

Brooks Bennett ran a hand through his short copper curls and blew out a long breath as he studied his surroundings. Their favorite college haunt seemed smaller and dingier, though the same stale smells of cooking grease and spilled beer lingered. They'd celebrated their College World Series win right here almost seven years ago. Seven years. Fucking A.

"Hey, Third Base," he said, his mouth pulling into a broad grin. He hadn't called his buddy that in years. Vance Evans' expression also showed a little oomph for the first time in days at hearing the nickname. He stopped picking at the label on his long-neck bottle and started looking around.

"We had a hell of a run. State champs in high school. World Series champs here." He tilted the bottle to his lips.

"That we did," Brooks agreed.

"Though, I gotta tell ya," Vance said, shaking his head. "The team we've put on the field this year? They would have handed us our jocks."

Brooks laughed. "It's true. I know it's true, but please don't tell them that. We'll lose complete control."

"Are you kidding me?" He squinted his eyes and twisted his mouth. "No way would I ever admit that. I parade them by our State Championship trophy every damn day." He smiled then and leaned forward, tapping his finger on the table between them. "But it is damn good fun being their coach."

"That's good, since you're not much of a cop," Brooks teased.

"Fuck you," Vance said good-naturedly and then sat up straight and scowled when he heard their long-lost fraternity brother, Duncan James, hailing the bartender. "Show time."

Brooks appreciated the irritation he saw in Vance's eyes, though he wasn't convinced driving an hour into Raleigh and staging an ambush was the smartest way to handle this. But since the college kids were spring-breaking their asses off in Florida or wherever they went these days, the bar was quiet. Maybe the three of them could calmly talk this out.

"Hey, y'all. Sorry I'm late," Duncan said, sliding into the booth next to Brooks. He wore his big-deal-lawyer suit more comfortably than a pair of jeans. "The call I'd been waiting for all day came in just as I was about to leave. Had to take it."

"Y'all? When the hell did *you* start sayin' 'y'all'?" Vance asked.

"Did I? Must be from hanging around you rednecks too long." Duncan glanced at a menu before setting it aside. He took a deep breath and blew it out as he looked at his best friends. "God, it's good to see you guys. How the hell are you?"

Brooks and Vance exchanged a look before casting their disgruntled expressions on Duncan.

"We're bent," Vance told him.

Raising an eyebrow, Duncan sat back and eyed his buddies again. "Never one to mince words," he said, and nodded to Vance. "What's going on?"

"Annabelle Devine is what's going on."

"Annabelle?"

"Christ, Dunc, it's the end of March. The last time we saw you was New Year's Day."

Duncan's mouth hung open for a moment, and then he snapped it shut. "You do recall that it was the two of you who introduced me to Miss Devine, right? On New Year's Eve?"

"We didn't introduce you. She was the target of our damn bet."

"A bet where I came out on top, in more ways than one."

"Clearly," Vance scoffed. "And since you've hooked up with our infamous 'Keeper of the Debutantes,' you haven't been back to Henderson for one poker night. We can't get you on the phone unless we call your office. For God's sake, we even had to beg you to fill out your NCAA bracket."

Duncan turned wide eyes to Brooks. "Is this for real?"

Brooks clenched his jaw.

"Oh, you too, huh?" Duncan looked back at Vance. "I neglect you two for a few weeks and you drive into town to, what? Stage an intervention?"

"We're just here to save you from yourself, bro."

Duncan laughed at that, and Brooks watched Vance's temper spike. Luckily they were interrupted by the waiter.

"Three more beers, three shots of tequila, three bacon cheeseburgers medium-rare, two with onion rings, one with fries, and bring some extra pickles, if you don't mind," Duncan ordered. He handed the menus to the waiter and folded his arms across his chest. When the waiter was out of earshot, Duncan cleared his throat and leaned forward.

"You two are closer to me than my own brother," Duncan said in a low, no-nonsense growl. "But I am warning you one time and one time only. Tread lightly when it comes to Annabelle. If you have a problem with me, it's on me. You do not now, nor will you ever, find fault with Annabelle Devine."

Dead silence.

"We clear?"

"Clear," Books mumbled along with Vance, each taking a sip of beer to dilute the tension at the table.

The beverages arrived before any of them could find another word. Together they upended the shots and chased them with their beers. Silence fell again while Duncan smoothed his hands over the rough table surface.

"I apologize. Not for blowing you two rednecks off while I spend time with Annabelle, but for not keeping you in the loop. I guess I just assumed...." His voice trailed off.

"That we would figure it out," Brooks finished for him, starting to feel like a real idiot.

Vance slapped his hand on the table throwing Brooks a 'come on, man' look. "Really?" he said. "You're going to let him off that easy?"

Duncan grabbed Vance's arm and shoved it off the table. "Look, asshole. What the hell do you expect? The three of us are pushing thirty. For all your talk over the years about raising your families in your hometown, you had to expect there would come a time when women would actually be part of that equation. Well, I've found mine, and I'm ready to move forward. So if that means missing a few poker nights while I'm trying to seal the deal with Miss Devine, *from Henderson*, I might add, I expect the two of you to suck it up and act happy for me. I mean, Jesus H. Christ! Did you think the three of us were going to adopt kids and raise them together?"

Brooks shook his head, feeling every bit the self-important, spoiled child he was. But he almost laughed when he noticed the expression on Vance's face. There was shock, yes. But also a dawning awareness, as if Vance hadn't considered he'd eventually have to find a mate.

Brooks reached out and tapped the table in front of Vance. "Hey. Third Base. You okay?"

Vance shook his dark head like a wet dog and snapped out of his stupor. "Holy shit!" he said, looking between Brooks and Duncan, starting to laugh. "Are we really almost thirty?"

"'Fraid so," Duncan assured him as heaping platters of burgers, fries, and onion rings were set in front of them.

Vance picked up his beer and saluted Brooks. "Then it's time."

"Time?"

"Time to do what he's doing." Vance pointed his beer at Duncan. "Because we have plans. Big plans."

Brooks looked up from his plate and into Vance's eyes. "We're not thirty yet."

"What plans?" Duncan asked.

"You know! Our plans. Get Brooks elected mayor," Vance said, setting down his beer and ticking off his fingers one by one. "Institute our economic plan to bring new businesses and services to Henderson."

"Which will hopefully stop the mass exodus of young people leaving town," Brooks interjected. "Like our buddy Lewis who has taken his big brain and multi-million dollar App-designing business right up to fucking New York City."

"And like your Annabelle," Vance said. "There is no reason she can't travel from Henderson to do her job taking care of sorority girls up and down the East Coast."

"Except that I live in Raleigh," Duncan protested. "I want her to live in Raleigh."

"You don't know what you want!" Vance insisted. "What *you* want is to move your own Richmond-raised ass out of Raleigh and into Henderson because once Brooks and I start these plans, the town is going to need a good business attorney, fast. You'll have more business than you can handle. What *you* want is to open your own damn firm in Henderson and be your own damn boss."

Duncan turned his head toward Brooks. "Well, thank God *somebody* knows what I want."

"Then," Vance continued as if Duncan hadn't just made a joke, "as Henderson begins to develop, you join Brooks and me in our campaign to get it listed as one of 'America's Best Places to Live.' All this while settling down and having enough kids between us to field a baseball team."

"Those are some big plans," Duncan chuckled.

"That's how we roll," Vance said as he reached for the ketchup. Then he nodded toward Brooks. "You know what this means, don't you?"

Brooks nodded, having already taken a bite of his two-fisted burger.

"We need to find ourselves a woman," Vance said, right before he bit off far more than he could chew.

CHAPTER ONE

Lolly DuVal had not been back inside Henderson High School since the day she graduated five years ago, and she certainly hadn't ever set foot in the boys' locker room. But it was a Saturday in late May, classes had been dismissed for the summer, and she had an appointment with the boys' varsity baseball coach. So here she was, hobbling around on her sore feet, nervously entering forbidden territory, searching for a door labeled 'Training Room.'

Ordering herself not to be tentative, she gave a good rap on the door and was relieved to hear a voice from inside calling for her to enter. Coach Evans, his back to her stood up from a desk shoved against the wall between the training tables and weight machines and turned in greeting, smiling enthusiastically as his eyes registered her appearance.

Holy crap, it is him!

Lolly was immediately glad she'd bothered with her appearance instead of showing up sporting a wet ponytail and athletic shorts. She'd blown her brunette hair dry so that her high ponytail had a soft curl at the end. And since her tiny, kitten-heeled sandals were the only thing her feet would tolerate, she was forced to wear her favorite red sundress that would have been too revealing on anyone with notable cleavage, but fit her body beautifully, showing off her long legs to their best advantage. She'd even put on perfume.

"Coach Evans," she said, moving forward and holding her hand out, her head spinning at the sight of him.

Once big man on this very campus and now one of Henderson's

most notorious bachelors, Vance Evans stood before her in nothing but loose-fitting black workout shorts and a pair of well-worn flip-flops. His naked, tanned, and sculpted chest and the extended length of six-pack abs running below it were like neon signs giving credence to all those sexy rumors she'd overheard her older cousins whispering.

She dragged her gaze up to the top of all that tall, dark deliciousness and willed herself not to drool. He'd improved with age—that strong chin and chiseled jaw defined a man in his prime. His dark hair was overdue for a cut and starting to curl at the ends, making him crazy gorgeous. "Thank you for meeting with me." She couldn't help it. She gave him her most flirtatious smile. "I am Lolly DuVal."

"Lolly," Vance said, taking her hand, his startling emerald eyes twinkling with mischief. "Our graduate student from State. The one who wants to protect our team's balls."

Lolly's eyes went wide. She blinked and then burst out laughing. "Well, that's one way to put it."

"Figured I'd go ahead and break the ice." He reached for a gray T-shirt draped over a weight machine and pulled it on over his head.

"I appreciate that. It's not easy talking about athletic cups when you've never had to wear one."

"Now that is a curious thing, isn't it?" he said, using his fingers to sweep his hair across his forehead. "A female designing a better cup."

"Sounds like you have your doubts."

He shrugged his shoulders as he lounged one hip against his desk. "Surely you'd balk if I, for example, claimed to have built a better bra."

Lolly's lips twitched.

"What?" Vance slowly brought himself back up to his full height. "Go ahead. Say what you're thinking."

A few beats of silence passed before Lolly decided she had nothing to lose. "I…have heard," she started tentatively, "that you, Coach Evans, have a lot of experience with women's breasts." She rushed on, "So perhaps you would be very qualified to create a better bra."

Pursing his lips in an effort to hide his astounded grin, it only took a few seconds for him to respond. "Clearly then, you've had a lot of experience with the male package. I'd love to hear all about your research."

"Hmm." She frowned. "I certainly walked into that." Reaching into her canvas bag, Lolly pulled out what looked like a squishy toy you couldn't wait to get your hands on.

"What the hell is that?" Obviously intrigued, Vance moved forward and plucked the gold-colored gel cup from her hand.

"It's the coming thing! At least, that's what my partners and I hope. As part of the graduate program at the College of Textiles, students from engineering, chemistry, and design form teams to create something new. Since fashion design is more my thing, my principal responsibility to the project is product testing.

"Since your baseball camp starts in a few weeks, we were hoping you'd ask a few of the kids to wear our cup and give us feedback." She shook the canvas bag. "We've made prototypes in several sizes. They slide into a traditional jock strap, but due to the nature of the gel material they should mold themselves better to the body, feel less bulky, and hardly be noticeable. In theory, the gel is designed to go directly against the body, creating a suction cup effect, eliminating the need for the jock strap. But until we get some of your players to try it both ways, we won't know if the suction is effective."

Vance turned the cup over and around, chuckling at the malleability. "Well, it's pretty cool; I'll give you that. But it's already hard enough keeping those boys' hands out of their pants without giving them this on top of it."

Lolly stepped in close to snatch her prototype back, muttering about 'boys and their toys'. She turned it inside out showing him the specifics. "A little heavier than the traditional cup, you've got the protection from the titanium shield here, surrounded by the gel material that conforms to the body. We've done impact tests to make sure it holds up. Now our concern is the sweat factor. These really hug your…well, hug everything snugly. I'm told nothing moves around. That it feels a lot less bulky between the legs and makes running less abrasive."

When she received no response, she glanced up.

Vance Evans was studying something, but it was not her prototype. Her eyes roamed his handsome face trying to decipher what he found so enthralling.

"You smell good," he whispered. "Good enough to eat."

Her breath hitched.

"Lolly DuVal." His long-lashed lids dropped to partly conceal his eyes. And even though they already stood in close proximity, his broad chest and wide shoulders seemed to be moving in, backing her up. "Have I heard that name before?"

"Oh, ah…well, there are a lot of…um, DuVals running around Henderson." She felt as if she'd been spun around one too many times. "In fact…my cousin Henry, he's on your team. He's the one who suggested I contact you."

"Hmm. Is that right? You're from Henderson then?"

"I am," she said, continuing to back up.

"And you're clever. The right height. Too pretty for your own good." He said these things not as compliments, but as if he were ticking off a list. "You busy tonight?"

"I, ah—ooh…." She grimaced, her foot springing off the floor. She reached down to soothe it and bumped her backside into the end of a padded training table.

"You're in pain." Suddenly the coach was all business.

"I ran a half marathon yesterday. My feet haven't forgiven me."

"Let me guess. You made the mistake of wearing new shoes."

"No, same running pair I've always had."

"What do you mean, 'always had'? How old are they?" Without fanfare he picked her up by her waist and plopped her down on the table behind her. He crouched down and slipped off her sandals.

"I don't know. I guess I bought them when I started college."

"Scoot back. How long ago was that?"

She slid back until her legs and feet were no longer dangling off the table. "Five years or so."

Vance's head shot up. "You've had the same running shoes for five years?" he yelled.

Lolly blinked several times, tucking a stray hair behind her ear. "Well, I don't actually run…much."

"I thought you said you ran a half marathon."

"Well, yeah. Yesterday. But before that…I guess I probably haven't run in years."

Vance put his hands on his hips and scowled at her. "You ran a half marathon. Yesterday. With no training."

"A friend of mine needed somebody to run with after her boyfriend injured himself, so I said I'd do it."

His sexy lips hung open and his movie-star eyes shifted back and forth over her face. It was obvious that this was information he found hard to compute. "Look," he said, exasperated, "you can't just go out and run a half marathon."

Lolly lifted her chin. "And yet, I did."

He mumbled something that sounded like 'Christ Almighty' and bent his head over her feet. "I don't see any blisters. Your legs have got to be sore."

He looked like he wanted to run his hands up her legs to check for injuries, but stopped himself. "Do you mind if I check you out? Obviously there's some kind of trauma. I'm not a doctor, but I've had paramedic training. And I'm a runner—a *real* runner," he added in a scolding tone that had her wanting to hide her face. "I've run every day for the past five years so I've had my own share of sore feet," he said more kindly.

"Paramedic training?"

Vance reached under the table and brought out a towel, rolling it up as he spoke. "I'm a cop and a coach. Paramedic training comes in handy. Here," he said, handing her the towel. "Lie down and tuck this behind your neck for support. Let's get your spine as straight as we can. Good. Now, with your permission, I'm going to gently prod around. Let me know if anything hurts."

Lolly closed her eyes as the infamous Vance Evans' hands examined her ankles and calves. She silently laughed at the thought of telling her cousins about this. She hadn't been in the man's company for half an hour, and yet he'd managed to get her on her back and was working his way up her body.

"Obviously, you're in good shape. You've got great legs," he said as a matter of fact. "Good muscle tone."

"I play a lot of tennis. Golf some. Oh, and I do Boot Camp three times a week."

"Still, to run that distance without training—you must be quiet the athlete," he said. "Your ankles seem fine. Your calves too. Nothing hurts?"

"Not like the shooting pain in my feet."

When his hands made their way back to the bottoms of her feet, Lolly immediately jumped and sucked in a breath.

"Shh," he soothed. "Easy now. Try to relax. Your arches are cramping up. I can probably massage some of the kinks out."

"Don't tell me you're a massage therapist too," she joked through a grimace of pain.

"No formal training," he admitted, his thumbs sliding up and down the center of her foot. "But I've had my share. Enough to know what feels good."

"This probably isn't appropriate," she protested…weakly. Because in that pain-pleasure way, this was starting to feel good.

"Why? You got a boyfriend with a possessive foot fetish?"

She shook her head. "Kicked him to the curb."

Vance's focus was all on her foot, stretching it back so her ankle flexed. "What'd he do?"

Lolly stared at the ceiling. "Nothing," she sighed. "He was just a little too milquetoast. Figured I'd set him free so he could find his milquetoast counterpart."

"What the hell does that mean? Milk toast?"

"You know. Bland. I mean, he was nice…safe…boring," she whispered.

Her thoughts drifted to poor Davis. He'd definitely been blindsided by the break up. But there was no easy way to tell him that she needed more fire, more passion. That she longed for someone who would take control and make her lose control. There was no good way to tell a man he just wasn't *doing it* for her.

"Guess a girl who can run a half marathon at a moment's notice needs someone who can keep up with her."

"I guess," she sighed.

The soothing manipulation of her ankle was replaced by a languid scraping of knuckles just forward of her heel. The repetitive motion triggered all manner of fireworks shooting up the inside of her thigh. She sucked in a breath. *Now that's what I'm talking about!*

"Don't want to be accused of being boring," Vance chuckled. "And since you aren't busy tonight—"

"Who said I'm not busy?"

His hands stopped. "You just told me you kicked your boyfriend to the curb."

"Doesn't mean I'm not otherwise engaged."

His hands started again, making sure fireworks were launching up the inside of her other thigh. "Playing hard to get?"

Lolly braced herself on her elbows so she could look down the length of her body at the man with his hands all over her feet. Good Lord, he was crazy sexy. "Really? I'm in a secluded room, in an empty school. Exactly what part of this scenario looks like I'm playing hard to get?"

"When you put it that way, it almost sounds like you're looking for trouble."

"Coach Evans, if I were looking for trouble I'd be suggesting you massage more than my feet."

The deep pressure he applied to the center of her foot ricocheted to her groin, causing a deliciously hungry sensation. "Only an amateur would need more than your feet."

"I am so playing with fire," Lolly said, lowering herself back to the table.

"Close your eyes," he demanded, his voice suddenly rough. "Just let me try to convince you…." She obeyed as his voice trailed off and his fingers went to work. She wanted to moan, but broad daylight and his puffed-up ego held her in check.

Even though they were alone. All alone.

"I'm only touching your feet. Only the soles of your feet." Then his voice went just a little lower, a little sexier. "I'm not going to touch your ankles," he said. "Or your shapely calves."

No he wasn't touching them, but of course hearing him utter the mere words brought on the longing for him to do so. Suddenly her ankles and calves were throbbing as much as the arches of her feet. She struggled to focus on where he was touching her. Both thumbs pressed into the center of one foot, kneading their way out to the edges, devouring the muscles made tender by the run.

His voice went husky and quiet. "Or knees. I promise I won't touch your knees."

Oh, God. Now her knees longed for his hands, his magical

touch. The rumors she'd heard about him must be true. Vance Evans was able to do in five minutes what Davis couldn't get done in a year.

"Or your thighs," he whispered. With her eyes closed she wasn't sure, but she could swear he was leaning over her. "I won't touch the inside of your thighs."

Really? Because she was *this close* to begging him to do just that. In fact, she wanted to say yes to *all* he seemed willing and able to do. Apparently after a long bout with milquetoast she was now craving the whole spicy enchilada.

As his hands continued to manipulate her feet, toes, and ankles, her mind wandered off into a daydream about an infamous Vance Evans affair.

His expert hands began long, deep, penetrating strokes that pushed her forward and pulled her back. She bit her lip, straining against the promising sensations clustering at the juncture of her thighs.

"Come on, Lolly," he encouraged as a lover might. "Come… with me…tonight."

She couldn't laugh because honest to God he truly did have her on the verge of exploding. Touching nothing but her feet! How was this possible? Her brain was scrambled. Her groin was throbbing. Exactly what she'd been craving. And it felt way too good to stop of her own volition. The only thing that could save her now was divine intervention.

So didn't it just beat all when not a moment later, divine intervention walked into the room.

CHAPTER TWO

As the training room door flew open, Vance pulled his hands off Lolly's feet and held them up like he'd been caught mid-crime. Since guilt didn't register in his emotional IQ, he chalked it up to the abruptness of the interruption. Piss poor timing if you asked him.

"Hey there. Oh, sorry to interrupt." Brooks pulled up short when he realized Vance wasn't the only one in the room. Vance watched him do a double take as Lolly rose from the training table and then witnessed the slow dawning of that good-ole-boy grin his buddy was so well-known for. "Lollypop? Is that you?"

"Lollypop?" Vance's head snapped around.

As if in slow motion, Lolly batted those heart-breaking, sapphire-blue eyes at his best friend. "Brooks?" she said in awe, like she was witnessing the second coming of Christ.

"What the hell?"

Brooks stepped up to the training table, offering his hand like he was some fucking Prince Charming, as the one Vance wanted for himself gracefully swung her crazy-long, perfectly muscled legs over the side of the table. Brooks helped her stand with a look of euphoria on his face. "What the heck are you doing here? I didn't think I'd see you 'til tonight."

"Tonight?" Vance felt a little sick.

"I came home early to meet with Coach Evans. I'd like his help gathering research on my graduate project."

"I'm sure the coach would be happy to help," Brooks said, smiling over at Vance like this was the best day of his life. "That right, Vance?"

"That's right. I'm officially offering up my own bat and balls for whatever Miss DuVal may require."

Lolly shot him a look as she stepped into those tiny but provocative heels. "Great. Then I'll leave you two to…do whatever it is you two do," she stumbled. "Coach Evans, thank you for your help." She nodded in his direction. "Brooks, I'll see you shortly before eight?"

"Pick you up at your momma's," he said.

Lolly flashed him a brilliant smile. "I am looking forward to it. Imagine, Darcy getting married."

"Well, it's just an engagement party. Which means she's managed to get Lewis on her hook. It remains to be seen if she can reel him in to the altar."

"Is that any way to talk about your sister?"

"Hey, Lewis might be as rich as Midas, but he's as absentminded as they come. I'm only saying Darcy has her work cut out for her."

"Well, I look forward to seeing both of them tonight. And you too." She blushed, heading toward the door.

"Oh." She stopped abruptly. "My feet!" She spun around and gifted Vance with a look of unadulterated hero worship. "You cured my feet!"

Vance felt his chest puff up like the Grinch's when it grew three sizes that day. "I told you I'm good with my hands."

"Indeed," she agreed, her eyes locking with his. "You are very, very good with your hands."

And with a twirl of that short red sundress, she was gone.

The men stood looking after her even when there was nothing left to see.

"She looks good, don't she?" Brooks turned toward Vance, beaming.

"How the hell do you know Lolly DuVal?" Vance growled.

"What do you mean?" Brooks looked at Vance like he had three heads. "It's Lolly…DuVal." Vance responded with a blank look. "She's a close personal friend of Darcy's. Been running around our house for years." When Vance only shook his head he went on. "DuVal! She's one of Henry's cousin's—Henry, your center fielder."

Still nothing. "Molly and Pamela's cousin!"

"*Molly* DuVal!" Vance hit his head. "I thought her name sounded familiar. Yeah, Molly DuVal with the big…." His hands gestured exactly how big. "And the wild…." He gestured again. Brooks just nodded. "Well, that explains a few things then."

"What things?"

"Never mind. The point is you know who she is and everyone she's related to. How do you do that?"

Brooks squinted. "I've lived here forever!"

"So have I, and I couldn't come up with any of that. That's why you are going to win the race for mayor hands down if you ever stop dicking around. You remember everybody's name."

"Because people are important to me. You certainly remember the people with whom you've done business."

"That's different. That's about making money."

"Exactly. You like money. You appreciate money. You understand money. Therefore it's easy to remember the names and faces and personal histories of those people who help you make money. Money is important to you."

"Of course."

"Well, there's the difference."

"I'm not following."

"Women aren't important to you. In fact, you don't even like them."

Vance laughed. "I think you, of all my friends, are the most aware of just how much I like women."

"Nope. You don't. You don't like women. You don't even like talking to women. You certainly don't appreciate women. And although none of the male species actually understands them, you don't even bother to try."

"What the hell are you talking about? I love women!"

"No. You enjoy the female body. Like you enjoy aged whiskey or a Cuban cigar. But the way you talk about women, the way you treat women? Dude."

Vance tried to find words with which to argue, but nothing came to him. "So, clearly, when it comes to women, I need a tutor. But so do you."

"What?"

"Yeah. You do."

"Really? Because I'm the one with the date tonight."

"Exactly. Your little Lollypop may have been all ooh-Brooks-the-golden-boy-of-Henderson this afternoon. But trust me. There's a good chance she's going to be calling you milquetoast by the end of the night."

"Milk toast?"

Vance eyed him seriously. "Nice. Safe. Boring."

Brooks' shoulders slumped a little. "Well, why the hell do you say that?"

"Because she told me she recently kicked some poor guy to the curb because he was nice, safe, and—"

"Boring," Brooks finished.

"Let's face it, bro. You and I have covered a lot of female territory over the years without much to show for it. And up until now that hasn't really bothered me. But now that Duncan and Lewis are racing to the altar and the big 3-0 is breathing down our necks, I think it's time to take a look at that. I mean, I've always thought I'd have kids and a family. Sort of create the environment I was denied growing up. And as Duncan so indelicately pointed out, we need to find women who will have us. And unfortunately I think our reputations have been cemented. We have become the epitome of good cop, bad cop."

"Me being the good cop," Brooks stated.

"Yeah. So somehow I need to become more like you."

"Whatever. It's gonna be a cold day in hell when I start treating women the way you do."

"Fine. Not crazy about the good cop, bad cop analogy? Substitute safe versus sexy."

"Really? Sexy?"

"Well," Vance said, lifting an eyebrow, "I'm certainly not milquetoast."

Brooks planted his ass on the training table Lolly had vacated, shaking himself all over. "*Brrr!* Just saying the word 'sexy' makes me feel ridiculous."

"Yeah, and like I wanna be this town's Golden Boy." Vance broke into his best Brooks Bennett imitation. "Hey, Mrs. Devine! How's your golf game? Really? Well, you hang in there. And give my best to Tess when you speak to her next, will you?" Vance mimicked.

"That is not how I sound."

"That is exactly how you sound to me."

"Well, you can't be me and I refuse to be you."

"Yes, but we can gain a better understanding of where we're lacking and improve in those areas. I need to figure out how to lighten up and get women to wave at me when I walk through town like they do to you."

"And I need to learn how to make their eyes go dark and misty like Lolly's did when she told you, that you had very, very good hands. What the hell was going on in here, you goddamn son of a bitch?"

"Brooks, buddy. That crap is so easy."

"Not for me."

"Which is why, if you go along with my plan, I will reveal to you the secret of my success. Which I learned at the age of fifteen, by the way. It's certainly not rocket science."

"What plan?"

"We help Lolly with her research and she helps us with ours."

"I don't follow."

"She's the tutor."

"No. She's my date."

"Tonight she's your date. Tomorrow she's our tutor."

"Our tutor, how?"

"Man, I don't know. But what I do know is that she was willing to talk about what she didn't want. So maybe she'd be willing to talk about what she does want. It certainly can't hurt to ask. Who else are we gonna get?"

Brooks shrugged. "I don't know. And I see your point, I really do. But I'm hoping this date isn't going to be a one and done."

"Well then...." Vance spread his arms wide. "What could be better than learning about what women want from the woman you actually want?"

"Huh?"

"Trust me. There's no downside here. Let's just talk to her tonight and see if she'd be willing to help us."

"I don't know."

"All right. How 'bout this? I give you one piece of bad cop advice to use on your date tonight. If it works out well for you, and it will, you go along with me on this."

Brooks looked skeptical. "What's the advice?"

"Do we have a deal? Because this is good stuff and frankly, right now, in this town, you are my stiffest competition. I don't want to be giving you pointers and getting nothing in return."

"Jesus, will you just tell me already?"

"Okay." Vance took a breath before speaking in a conspiratorial tone. "Tonight, when you take the Lollypop home, the moment you hit that top step of her momma's porch you shove that lean body of hers right up against the wall and kiss her like you mean it."

Vance let that sink in before he added, "You can thank me in the morning."

CHAPTER THREE

A half hour before Lewis Kampmueller and Darcy Bennett's engagement party officially started, Brooks' attendance was required for family photos. All the Kampmueller and Bennett family members were assembled, which amounted to a whopping total of eleven people. Two sets of grandparents, two sets of parents, the happy couple, and one odd man out.

It wasn't every day that your sister married your best friend of twenty years…and thank God for that. Brooks was genuinely thrilled for Darcy, and he supposed he was happy for Lewis—if that's who the man wanted for now and evermore, who was he to try to shake some sense into him? But Brooks himself was in mourning. Because having one of your best friends fall in love with your sister meant a nuclear blast detonated inside your social sphere and, although some aspects might remain untouched, nothing would ever really be the same again. *Ever.*

And from the looks of things, Duncan James was getting ready to drop a second bomb any day now. Yes, the 'band of brothers' were moving on and now it seemed that even the lowest among them wanted to get in on the act. What the hell had gotten under Vance's skin? Brooks didn't have a clue. But he couldn't shake the feeling that Vance just may be onto something, and that Lolly was the cure.

Still, Vance being…well, Vance made Brooks want to run all this by somebody else.

"Darcy, I need your opinion on something before I head over to pick up Lolly."

Darcy blinked repeatedly. "My opinion?"

"Yeah. Seeing as you're, you know, a grown woman and all, I was hoping you could help me out with something." Looking around the room full of overeager family members, he took her arm and shuffled her out of the house and into the garage, right by the beer refrigerator.

"Brooks, are you okay?" Darcy asked. "You've never wanted my opinion on anything. Holy crap! You haven't done anything stupid, have you? You know, like taken a bribe or stolen police evidence from the precinct?"

Brooks rolled his eyes. "Of course not. I haven't done anything stupid...yet. So that's why I'm asking. And I'm not getting into any details, so just give me your gut reaction and we'll never speak of this again."

For whatever reason, maybe the fact that she was standing in a garage wearing a white cocktail dress moments before her guests were to arrive, she took him seriously. "Fine. Shoot!"

"First, you aren't my sister. You're just some run-of-the-mill female born and raised in Henderson. Who would you rather go out with, me or Vance?"

Darcy eyed her brother, her brilliant calculating mind at work. "Let me assure you that Lolly is very much looking forward to being your date tonight."

"That wasn't what I asked."

"But isn't that what you really want to know?"

"Well, yeah. Of course. But no, not really. Forget Lolly. Well, don't forget Lolly but say, in general, girls like Lolly. Are they more interested in going out with me or Vance?"

"Depends on the girl."

Brooks slammed his hand on the refrigerator. "Damn it, Darcy. It's the first time I'm coming to you for advice, and you are giving me the run around."

"I'm not," Darcy pleaded, biting back a laugh. "I swear I'm not. It's just that even though you and Vance have a lot in common, and you both rate high in the looks department, you are very different. You are more of a Robert Redford all-around great guy, which a lot of women are drawn to. Vance is more of a dark-haired, sexy, Bradley

Cooper type that women know they should run away from as fast as they can but for some inexplicable reason are drawn to like a black hole."

"Fucking A," Brooks said under his breath as he rubbed his face. "You do know that Robert Redford is about a hundred years old, right?"

"But my point is—"

"I get your point. Fine. Okay. One more question." Brooks took a breath. "Say you're on your first date and it's gone well. The guy walks you up to your front door and sort of manhandles you."

"Manhandles? How?"

"Throws you up against a wall and kisses the shit out of you. Are you thinking that's hot and can't wait to see him again? Or are you calling 911?"

A dreamy smile came over his sister's face.

"Fucking A," Brooks muttered and stomped around her, heading for the door.

Lewis and Darcy's engagement party was staged in the Bennetts' backyard. A beautiful stone patio surrounded the family's in-ground pool where lush floral arrangements of hydrangea and roses floated. Beyond the patio, guests filed in and out of a large tent festooned with balls of hydrangea trailing blue and silver streamers. Food stations offering seafood, meats, and cheeses had been set up inside the tent, along with tall, silver-clothed cocktail tables where guests stood enjoying their fare. The Tiki torches lining the perimeter of the lawn added to the festive atmosphere, and by ten o'clock the place was rocking. Bartenders had trouble keeping up with demand. And even though Mr. Bennett's heartfelt toast to his daughter and future son-in-law had been delivered, no one considered heading home.

Lolly stepped out of the French doors and stood on the large landing atop the stacked-stone steps leading down to the party below. She glanced around for her date and spied him standing with Vance Evans and Duncan James in a tight circle, laughing, knocking each other in the arm, and pointing animated accusations at one another.

They hailed Lewis over, and Lolly watched as the intended groom joined the fray, his back slapped and pounded in happy camaraderie. Even if she'd been unaware that the four of them were the best of friends, the buoyant expression on Brooks' face would have given it away.

But she was very aware of how close they were, because since fifth grade Lolly had spent as much time inside this house as her own. And at first, she wasn't sure which of the high school seniors running in and out was Darcy's brother, since Lewis and Vance were always at Brooks' side.

And then came Duncan James, the Chris Pine-handsome and impeccably dressed lawyer from Raleigh. Lolly didn't know him as well because he'd grown up in Richmond, Virginia. Brooks and Vance had met Duncan at N.C. State where they were all Phi Delts. Lolly thought they probably recruited him to fill the gap they must have felt when Lewis headed north to MIT.

And though Duncan was not from Henderson, he had the town all abuzz this past New Year's Eve when he'd done the one thing no other man in all of North Carolina had been able to do. Duncan James had swept into town under false pretenses and not only gave a speeding ticket to Henderson's most notorious speed demon but captured her heart as well.

Lolly's gaze drifted over to Annabelle Devine, a.k.a. The Keeper of the Debutantes, with her flowing red curls and scrumptious dress in her signature color of white. While Lolly's designer brain pictured that dress strapless and dyed red, she watched Annabelle carry on a boisterous conversation with her two older sisters, Grace and Tess. Their parents, Jody and Harry Devine—who were best friends with Lewis' parents—stood next to them looking as proud as if this engagement party celebrated one of their own children.

Annabelle—only a year older than Lolly—had made her mark on Henderson while she was still in high school. When her oldest sister Tess made her debut, Annabelle thoroughly embraced the pomp, circumstance and old school ideals and single-handedly brought an archaic social function back into vogue with a flourish. Each class of debutantes since enjoyed the benefits of Annabelle's historical research, knowledge of etiquette, and the many blue-blooded contacts she'd made in Raleigh. Because of Annabelle Devine, Henderson—previously known for next to nothing—was now known for its kick-ass debutante parties and the outstanding grace and charm of its debs.

All of this made Annabelle perfectly suited for her present career as a Field Representative for her sorority. All across the Mid-Atlantic, from one university campus to the next, Annabelle Devine offered guidance, put out fires, and handled the scandals of impetuous young women. In Lolly's opinion, Annabelle Devine had it all going on.

Out of the corner of her eye, Lolly noticed the tulle skirt of Darcy's cocktail dress and turned with a quick grin for her childhood friend. "What did Annabelle have to say about this dress? I bet she was tickled."

"Ah, Annabelle," Darcy sighed. "She loved it, of course. I've been channeling my inner Annabelle ever since Lewis finally noticed me in that designer gown New Year's Eve. Unfortunately, my elevated fashion sense has my Visa bills skyrocketing."

Lolly laughed. "Good thing Lewis is rich."

"So true," Darcy said, laughing along with her. "But what about you! You never wear your hair down. And your dress is fabulous. Perfectly elegant, yet whimsically playful with those red polka dots. Please do not tell me that you designed it."

"I did," Lolly admitted.

Darcy whimpered, looking Lolly up and down. "I can't imagine being able to design fabulous clothes."

"And I can't imagine being able to design commercially successful video games, so you have me there." They stood side by side, their gazes wandering the party. "I have to hand it to you," Lolly said. "College in Boston and now New York? You are living your big city dream, Darcy Bennett, and I can't wait to follow in your footsteps as soon as they hand me my master's in eleven more months."

"If you can design a dress like this, then New York City is the place to be," Darcy assured her.

"That's what I keep tellin' my momma."

"So, is my brother showing you a good time?" Darcy asked.

"Mmm," Lolly said while sipping her drink. "I imagine I have you to thank for setting this up?"

"Not me. Mom says Brooks saw your name on the guest list, and the next thing she knew he told her you'd be here…with him."

"Hmm."

"Yes. Hmm."

Lolly glanced at Darcy and found herself under scrutiny. "What?"

"Well? Are you interested in my brother? You can tell me the truth. Brooks is always going to be my brother. You, on the other hand, I definitely want to keep as a friend. So, whatever happens, I'm on your side."

"I'm interested. Of course I'm interested. I mean, who wouldn't be interested? He's Brooks Bennett for goodness' sake. Local sports star and superhero. Savior of dogs and old folks."

"Whoop-de-do," Darcy said, circling her finger in the air.

"Stop!" Lolly laughed. "He's gorgeous and a great guy, even if he was a pain in your neck growing up. Look, I'm wearing the bracelet he gave us when we graduated from high school, remember?" She held up her arm, showing off her Pandora charm collection. "I will never get over that he gave me a gift too."

"He always was nicer to you," Darcy grumbled, fingering through Lolly's charms.

"He really was," Lolly agreed, laughing. "Remember that night he found us hitchhiking back from the lake?"

"Yes," Darcy said, completely irritated. "And although it was your idea, I was the one who got in all the trouble. He didn't tell *your* mom, but he certainly let my parents know how stupid we were. I was grounded for two weeks."

"Yes, but for those two weeks, Brooks showed up everywhere I went with his 'I'm so disappointed in you look.' He made me feel so stupid and guilty that I had zero fun," Lolly said. "Being a cop is perfect for him. He made us follow the rules."

"That's true," Darcy agreed. "The only time we ever got away with anything was when he was at college."

"I know, but remember that time your parents took us to the State-Carolina football game? Brooks snuck us into the student section and let us share a beer. Oh my gosh, that was so much fun. That's when I decided I wanted to go to State."

"All right," Darcy said reluctantly. "I'll give him that. We did have fun at that game. And the tailgate afterwards."

"There were no rules being followed at that tailgate," Lolly reminded Darcy. "I think that's when I finally saw his true personality." *And I liked it.* She was reminded it was also when she'd first started fantasizing about Brooks, but that bit of information she'd kept to herself.

Darcy laughed. "Well, it wasn't baseball season. He could afford to be relaxed."

"Speaking of relaxed, when I ran into him this afternoon he seemed much more open and forthcoming than he's been since picking me up tonight." At Darcy's scowl, Lolly rushed on. "Don't get me wrong; he's been very attentive. I thought maybe I should give him time with his buddies." She nodded in their direction.

"Where did you run into him this afternoon?" Darcy asked.

"I was over at the high school talking to Coach Evans about research for my graduate project."

"You were with Vance?"

Lolly nodded. "He's going to get some of his baseball players to give me feedback on my newfangled athletic cup."

Darcy's mouth moved, but it took a few moments for something to come out. "Your newfangled what?" She shook her head quickly. "Never mind. First, tell me about Vance."

Lolly blushed, causing Darcy's eyes to narrow. "It was all very innocent," Lolly assured her. "I had some cramping in my feet from a run I did yesterday and Vance sort of massaged them out. Brooks came in unexpectedly, and at the time he seemed very happy to see me and very excited about tonight." Darcy eyebrows were so far up her forehead that it made Lolly laugh. "What?"

"Vance massaged your feet?" she asked. She stepped in closer. "I hear he has great hands."

Lolly turned so that her back was to the crowd below and only Darcy could hear her. "His hands aren't the only amazing thing. He had his shirt off when I arrived. I swear to God he could easily be an Abercrombie model."

"Holy crap."

"Yeah. So I can't tell if Brooks is upset about Vance massaging my feet or if our date tonight is simply a casual thing or what."

Darcy stood silently, working her lips. "So Brooks walked in on Vance massaging your feet. Now it makes sense."

"What? What makes sense?"

"Right before Brooks left to pick you up, he asked me if girls in general would rather go out with him or Vance."

"Oh Dear Lord. What did you say?"

"I told him that *you* were very much looking forward to this date. With him."

"Thank God."

"But he was persistent. So I told him it depended on the girl. That he was sort of the all-American superhero and Vance was sexy, dark, and dangerous with the power and pull of a black hole."

Lolly laughed. "Well, you certainly summed that up. And truthfully, right now Vance would be the perfect summer fling because I have no doubt he could take care of my pent-up Davis frustration with two hands tied behind his back. But Brooks?" Lolly sucked in a deep breath. "He's really the dangerous one. Because he sorta stole my heart when he gave me that bracelet."

"You should date them both. I mean, you're stuck here in freaking Mayberry all summer where nothing *ever* happens. You'll need to create your own excitement. So I say date them both."

"I can't date them both."

"Of course you can. Pit them against each other. May the best man win."

"Brooks is the best man."

"Then he'll win," Darcy said with a smirk.

"You are baiting me just to give your brother some trouble."

"Only because he deserves it. It's obvious he's not thrilled about my marrying Lewis."

"Well, that's surprising. Have you asked him why?"

Darcy scoffed. "We may be in our twenties, but we relate to each other like we're children. Little children." She waved that off. "Back to you. Right now I insist you raise your right hand and repeat after me: 'If Brooks and Vance are the two most exciting things this town has to offer, then far be it for me to deny myself the pleasure. I will take them both!'"

Lolly laughed and raised her cocktail glass, mimicking Darcy's cavalier attitude. "If Brooks and Vance are the two most exciting things this town has to offer, then far be it for me to deny myself the pleasure. I will take them both!"

"Uh-oh." Darcy knocked her elbow into Lolly's ribs. Down the steps and standing directly below them were none other than Brooks and Vance.

Brooks with his broad shoulders, his short, curly bronze hair, and piercing crystal-blue eyes was dressed in traditional southern cocktail garb. Light pants, white shirt, bright tie, and blue blazer. But when he glanced up at her and smiled, he defied anything traditional, becoming achingly handsome and movie-star debonair.

In contrast, Vance stood a tad shorter and a little slimmer, with those magic hands tucked into the pockets of black slacks. He sported a blue, slim-cut dress shirt that hung over his waistband. Gold cufflinks secured French cuffs at his wrists and several buttons were left undone, showing off his tan and a small gold chain. With his dark hair and jewel-green eyes, when he grinned up at you like that you knew exactly what he had on his mind.

"Gentlemen," Darcy acknowledged. Both sets of eyes shifted from Lolly to Darcy and then back to Lolly. "Okay then, I'll run along and find my fiancé."

"Darcy!" Lolly implored.

But Darcy simply flounced down the steps, letting the words 'You have fun now' float back behind her.

Brooks held out his hand as Lolly descended. "Something to eat?" he suggested.

"Sure," Lolly agreed, taking his hand and trying not to look too long at either man. Her stomach was tied in one huge knot, the size of which could secure an aircraft carrier. *You have got to be kidding me*, she thought as Brooks tucked her hand under his arm and led her off toward the tent. *Did they overhear me say I'd take them both?* Her head throbbed at the thought. Speckles of light started to appear in her vision. She replayed the scene. No, she assured herself as she took a deep breath. It wouldn't have been possible. She and Darcy were whispering. Just coincidental timing. *Oh please, let it be coincidental timing.*

Brooks handed her a plate and passed one to Vance, the three of them commenting on the crab cakes and the jumbo steamed shrimp, making small talk as they loaded their plates. Lolly's head began to quiet and her pulse began to slow as it became obvious she hadn't been overheard.

Or were they simply being kind enough not to call her on it?

Whatever. She followed Brooks to one of the tall tables and stood beside him while Vance headed off to the bar to refresh their drinks. Her nerves spiked again. Being this close to Brooks Bennett with his height and the enticing way he filled out his jacket was quite a rush. Especially now that she was his date, not simply his little sister's friend.

"Your sister looks beautiful," she commented.

"She certainly does," Brooks agreed.

"Lewis is a lucky man."

"So she keeps telling him." Brooks laughed.

"Are you happy about all this?"

Brooks finished chewing, swallowed, and wiped his mouth on a napkin before speaking. "I'm not unhappy about it," he said honestly. "But my two worlds are definitely colliding."

"Because you and Lewis are close friends."

"Because Lewis is the brother I never had."

"Well, now he'll be your brother-in-law."

He chuckled, picking up a shrimp. "I never thought about it like that. That will be a perk. Lewis at family gatherings."

"What's the downside?"

Brooks lifted his head to consider. "I'm not sure Lewis will be able to continue as my confidant."

"Afraid he'll tell your sister things you don't want her to know?"

"Something like that."

Lolly nodded her understanding and started to eat. She'd never considered Brooks a man of few words, but it certainly felt like he was keeping things close to the vest tonight. There wasn't another word spoken between them before Vance arrived with a small tray.

"Dark & Stormy for the lady," he said, setting down a roly-poly type glass in front of her. "Old Fashioned for my old-fashioned friend," he said with a snicker, setting down a short, squatty glass in front of Brooks, who tossed him a sneer. "And a whiskey on the rocks for yours truly," he finished, placing a similar glass beside his plate.

"Lolly," Vance went on, "what are your thoughts on tequila?"

She heard Brooks suck in a breath as he tossed up his hands. She looked back and forth between the two of them, noting the mounting tension on Brooks' face. Vance seemed oblivious and ventured on.

"You free tomorrow night?" He smiled. "Brooks and I have been talking."

"Back off, Evans." It came off like a warning shot. But Vance kept right on talking.

"Seeing as we are going to help you with your research this summer, we were hoping you could help the two of us with some research of our own."

Brooks' hand hit the table.

Lolly looked between the two of them, not sure what to make of all this. "I'd be more than happy to help in any way I can."

"Great," Vance said. "How 'bout we go out to dinner tomorrow night to discuss it? Just the three of us."

"O-okay," she stammered, glancing up at Brooks, whose eyes had rolled so far up she couldn't see his pupils. "What's this about?"

"Tomorrow," Vance insisted, picking up his plate and drink. "You two enjoy yourselves tonight, and we'll discuss this tomorrow. Until then...." He nodded at Lolly, backing away from the table, leaving her and Brooks alone.

"Brooks?"

Brooks closed his eyes and shook his head back and forth. "It's nothing," he said before opening them and reaching for his drink. "Vance thinks you might be a good sounding board. He wants a female point of view." He sucked back half his drink.

"Well, I am female."

Brooks' hand came around and touched her at the small of her back. "You are that," he agreed. His light touch was far more potent than it should have been. She was immediately aware of the strength that stood by her side. Of the masculinity. But most of all she was aware of the edgy mood he was sporting—as if it were transferred through his touch.

His body turned toward her as he leaned down and placed his

elbow on the table, bringing their heads together. His voice was low and smooth, and his words caused the knot in her stomach to unfurl and transform into something rich and molten.

"I have been looking forward to this date for some time. Yet I have allowed…other things to occupy my mind." He looked directly into her eyes. "I apologize."

She shook her head as the words, 'no need,' somehow found their way out of her suddenly dry mouth.

"Not only do I apologize, but I'm going to do my best to make it up to you." He looked up and over to the far side of the pool where couples had started to dance. "Would you like to dance?" he asked, nodding in that direction.

Feeling starry-eyed, Lolly could only nod her head. Brooks Bennett, Henderson's roving sunshine, had a surprisingly sultry side.

"Let's take our drinks," he directed in the same smooth tone. "We'll come back for dessert." His fingers drifted over her shoulder and down to the small of her back as they moved away from the table. His palm settled into place, guiding her through the crowd and toward the music. He was taking control in a way he hadn't all evening, and her body started to hum under his authority. *Oh my.*

His hand slid from her waist, catching her empty hand, and he twirled her under his arm and onto the makeshift dance floor. With their drinks held aloft, they gingerly moved through the motions of a shag to a medley of beach music, laughing and grinning as they figured out each other's rhythm and found a way to blend together.

Their drinks didn't last long as the warm night air made them thirsty, and the increasing tempo of the music made it impossible to hold a drink and dance. Someone on the sidelines relieved them of their glassware, and Brooks, beaming and back to his old self, took Lolly by two hands and swung her into a high-octane jitterbug. He led her with skill, and Lolly was grateful, having never felt much confidence on the dance floor. Sure, she could run a half marathon with the best of them, but that was straight ahead with blinders on. Dancing with a partner required the ability to follow, keep beat with the music, and offer some sort of effort in the hip area, which did not come naturally to her.

Brooks didn't seem to mind. If his goal was to show her a good time, he was hitting the mark. Fully. And when the music slowed to a sensuous ballad, well, that's when things became serious. Because, like the trained police officer he was, he had no hesitation. His eyes narrowed, zeroing in on her like she was his target. He reached out, clasped her hand, and reeled her in...slowly.

His right arm settled around her waist, his large hand splayed and pressing against her back, drawing her in. His left hand held her palm flat against his chest. He lowered his head and whispered against her ear, "Finally."

It was as if he'd been dancing all night waiting for a slow song to play. That his sole intent had been to put himself in a position where, given the opportunity, he could finally wrap his arms around her.

It made her feel wanted.

"Lolly DuVal," he said, after they settled into a slow, languid rhythm. "I am a foolish, foolish man. Here I've had one thought running through my head ever since I laid eyes on you today, and I haven't put it into words." He pulled back just far enough so he could look into her eyes as he said, "You have sure grown into one fine woman."

Lolly blushed and diverted her eyes, smiling shyly. Brooks squeezed her hand to get her to look back at him. "And tonight, when I saw you in this beautiful dress with your hair down like that, I'm afraid words failed me. The truth is, I am very proud to be the man on your arm tonight."

He pulled her closer and resumed their dance, denying her the necessity of a response. But her heart did its best to beat through her chest and pound against his. And there were bells and whistles going off in places never heard from before, all because of his sweet, sweet talk. Never one to shy away from a budding romance, Lolly DuVal felt a nervous flutter drift around inside her stomach. A teeny tiny bit of concern that this time, she was in way over her head.

At the impromptu bonfire in the backyard where the closest friends of the bride and groom lingered late into the night, it was obvious Brooks had shaken off whatever was on his mind. He was on a roll, entertaining everyone with embarrassingly funny stories about Darcy growing up and the hilarious life lessons he and Lewis learned together from the time they bonded in third grade. All the while Brooks held Lolly in the center of his attention, touching her, holding her hand, or toying with the ends of her hair, until the night grew cool and he finally pulled her onto his lap and cuddled her close in the confines of an Adirondack chair.

Lolly marveled at how crazy this whole scene really was. Back in the day, when they were all kids, Lewis and Brooks paid zero attention to her and Darcy. Zero. And now Lewis was looking at Darcy as if his whole world revolved around her, and Brooks had just kissed the back of her own head for the fourth time. Thank goodness she had kicked Safe and Boring to the curb weeks ago. Trusting her instincts had opened the door to *this*. This feeling of belonging. This feeling of camaraderie.

Even more interesting were the feelings of warmth and security and these really interesting bouts of longing she felt deep in her chest because Brooks had his famous pitching arm wrapped around her. He seemed content to have her snuggled against his chest and, *Good Lord*, she wanted to purr. She wanted to stay like that all night long, begging time to stand still, but eventually the crowd had no choice but to finally head home.

It was close to three in the morning when Brooks pulled his shiny black truck into her momma's driveway. The ride home had been quiet, but comfortably so. Brooks came around to open her door and held his hand out to assist her exit. She took it and stepped toward the back of the truck so he could close the door.

It wasn't a moment after hearing it slam shut that Lolly found herself pressed up against the side of Brooks' truck, his legs and waist leaning against her lower body, his hands moving up into her hair and capturing her head, his lips landing on hers with a low, sexy growl as if he were releasing long pent-up desire.

The longing in Lolly's body leapt at the chance to participate, immediately releasing a series of fireworks that spread out to her breasts, causing a tingling sensation from the inside out. Her arms reached up his back to the top of his shoulders and tightened their grip. Her mouth opened and closed, playing at the game before his tongue slid inside and the real intimacy began.

And the real fireworks.

The kind that drugged your mind and body so you didn't have

a thought as to where you were or how you got there. The kind that sharpened your awareness of what feels...so...good and God if I could just...have...a little more....

His pelvis rocked against her hip, and without conscious thought, her body adjusted to the right and she went up on her toes so that the next time he rocked, it rocked her world.

The squeak she uttered around his tongue did not go unnoticed. Without stopping the worshipping of her mouth, Brooks slid one hand down the side of her body, over her rear end, and down the back of her thigh. He then drew her knee up, up and up and held it at hip level, tilting her pelvis forward. His other hand clasped the back of her head in a firm hold as he spread his legs wider, making himself shorter. Then he bent his knees and rocked his long...hard... erection...slowly against Lolly's most engorged nerve endings.

She tried to pull her head back but Brooks had control, so she moaned through his kisses and he responded by doing it again. And then again. And then again.

Until she exploded.

Shaking, quivering, and strung out by her undoing, Lolly's hands fell from Brooks' shoulders to her sides. She couldn't think, couldn't move. She could only feel as she collapsed against his truck. She felt him release her mouth with one final kiss. Felt her forehead fall to his chest and her breath hitch as she felt each of the aftershocks that kept on coming and coming. She could feel Brooks' hand rubbing up and down the back of her thigh, still held high, soothing her, bringing her back down to earth.

When she was finally able to draw in a long breath, Brooks wrapped both his arms behind her back and gently pulled her around in front of him so that his back was now supported by the truck, and she was embraced in his arms, leaning heavily against him. He tugged her hair a little to get her to lift her face and then he kissed her sweetly, saying her name with awe and reverence.

"Laura Leigh DuVal," he quietly breathed the words. "I am under your spell."

Still undone from much-too-much, she could form no coherent words, which apparently humored Brooks enough to shine his megawatt grin and add an extra twinkle to his blue eyes. Taking her by the hand, he led her up the porch steps to her momma's screen door and opened it. He whispered into the back of her head, "I'll see you tonight," and prodded her to step over the threshold into the foyer before closing the door gently behind her.

Lolly stood alone in the dark, her lips charred, her brain numb, her limbs so spent and heavy she felt like her body was dripping to the floor. An inkling of a thought flashed on the outskirts of her mind.

That was far from safe and nowhere close to boring.

And then that too dripped to the floor.

Brooks sat in his truck with one hand gripping the steering wheel. His eyes were trained on Lolly's back. She was still standing just inside the screen door where he'd left her, her arms hanging loose by her sides. His male pride took immense satisfaction in that. So much so that he couldn't bring himself to drive away. His other hand came up to rub back and forth over his lips. He was already craving her mouth again. Her opening up for him. Responding.

God was that good. His eyes closed as the memory swamped him. That moment where her mouth opened under his. That first touch of her tongue. Man, it had lit a fire in his chest, and he all but consumed her trying to put it out. And she had responded. Oh boy had she—grabbing his shoulders and pulling him in. His hands twitched remembering every long, trim muscle of her body under soft, supple skin. Her arms, her torso, her thigh. Holy fuck. Her thigh.

His eyes shot open. He'd made her come. Right here on the driveway in record time. He hadn't even touched her. She just let herself go, allowing him to take her over the edge. It was crazy. And Christ Almighty, there was something about swallowing her moans that had him feeling powerful and in control. Jesus! He was tempted to climb out of his truck, drag her back out to the porch, and do it all over again.

He could not remember being so turned on. Not that he'd kissed a lot of women lately, but man, this one. This one had flipped a switch.

The fact that she still hadn't moved made him grin. She had been so limp in his arms at the end, all warm and soft and docile. And as he was remembering that final kiss against her tender and pliant lips, the nagging cop in him reared up and threatened to ruin the moment.

The nagging cop had seen too much, and for a split second he imagined Lolly in that same state of pliancy but in far less chivalrous hands. She would have had zero defenses against a date who might press her to reciprocate.

Imagining Lolly being taken advantage of by some idiot yahoo sent a wave of fear rippling through his gut. Brooks shut those thoughts down hard and pushed the cop in him aside. The bachelor in him wanted to enjoy the end of this night. The end of a very satisfying first date with Lolly DuVal.

Lolly, his sister's close personal friend.

Goddammit, if that didn't have him sparking the ignition and backing out of the drive. All the way home, he stewed over this unfathomable breech of his privacy. Lewis, his best buddy, and Lolly, his amazing date, were both intimately connected with his sister, who he sure as hell didn't want to know fuck about his life.

It wasn't that he didn't like Darcy. She was fine as sisters went. But his life was already too much of an open book. Not only did he grow up in this relatively small town, but he had been the lead sports story in the paper throughout high school and college. Everybody, young and old, knew his face and his name. He couldn't get away with one damn thing if he tried.

And now he held a public job in the same damn town, so his private life continued to be anything but. But he loved Henderson and the people who lived here, so he managed.

Then four months ago, *bam!* Without warning, his little sister waltzes into his very small, private, and closely guarded circle of confidants, and so now…well…why the hell not just invite Mom, Dad, and Annabelle's scary old Aunt Helen in as well?

Fucking A. Now he wasn't even able to enjoy his hard-on.

And he couldn't go home and seek solace at his own place because he'd stupidly loaned his newly remodeled house to a half-dozen of Lewis' out-of-town guests. Lewis. Fucking dick. Brooks stalked up his parents' front walk and had to check himself before slamming their front door behind him. He toed off his loafers and carried them in his hand up the steps and down the hall just in time to see Lewis sneaking out of his sister's room.

And the nightmare just kept on growing.

Drawing a breath through gritted teeth, Brooks dropped his loafers and rose up to his full height before stalking forward, grabbing his best friend by the throat, and slamming him up against the wall. He leaned in and allowed the earlier fear he had for Lolly to surface and explode.

"She's. My. Sister!" he snarled. "I do not need to see this kind of bullshit. Ever. Especially under my father's roof."

He released Lewis, who immediately leaned over, putting his hands on his knees to catch his breath. Brooks marched past him down to his old room at the end of the hall and slammed the door as hard as he could.

CHAPTER FOUR

Vance Evans rarely put time and energy into convincing anyone to do anything.

Most of the time it didn't matter to him what anyone else was doing. He focused on what he wanted and went out and did that. He found people who wanted to cooperate with him and left the others behind.

When making money first appealed to Vance, he started a lemonade stand by himself in the new development being built behind his father's property. Construction workers, stuck on a job site got hot and thirsty, and even at the age of ten Vance saw a need that he could fill and profit from. Later, he washed cars, delivered papers, walked dogs, and mowed lawns.

When he was tired of doing one thing, he did something else. When that grew old, he looked for another adventure. And because he was always moving to the next bigger and better job, team, idea, or plan, he didn't have time to spend much of the money he had acquired over the past two decades. He enjoyed the making of money. Spending it was incidental. So when his buddy Lewis needed some seed money to start his business, Vance had been ready and willing. And having made that fortuitous investment, now at twenty-nine years old, Vance Evans was a very wealthy self-made, self-reliant man.

Usually.

But today, and not for the first time, he found waking up next to a woman and not remembering her name reprehensible.

Reprehensible? I think that might be a little dramatic, he scoffed at himself.

Well, it's not like she's some pink-cheeked, dewy-eyed blonde you want to try to make this up to, he thought. He almost laughed at that. No, he didn't want anything to do with this crazy-ass bitch from New York. The one who'd spent the entire party last night touching him inappropriately and dropping hints about how she wanted to teach her cheating boyfriend a lesson.

And he certainly hadn't planned on obliging her. No, he truly hadn't. Even as he watched Brooks dance with his little Lollypop for over an hour, he had no intention of taking Slutty Slutzky home.

And though he kept having to drag his gaze away from Brooks and Lolly holding hands like squirrelly seventh graders, he still wasn't going to give in to Ms. New York's over-obvious come-ons.

But, as the evening stretched out into an endless sprawl, that painfully familiar feeling of utter loneliness engulfed him even as he sat in the circle of his closest friends. The moment Brooks pulled Lolly onto his lap and Vance had to watch her beam up at him like he was her sun, stars, and goddamn moon, he snapped.

"Clearly," he stated, staring out over his cereal bowl, "I have a problem." And the only two options he could see were to request the help of a woman he actually did want to go to bed with or admit he was a sex addict and seek professional treatment.

And the latter was so not going to happen.

He stared at his phone after hearing Brooks' message vehemently stating, "We are not doing this. End of discussion."

Oh, but they were doing this. They had to do this. So Vance prepared himself for a long, long discussion.

Brooks sat at his desk at the police station, holding his cell phone away from his ear and grimacing as his sister ripped him a new one.

He deserved it. He knew he did. Which is why he'd snuck out of his parents' home without speaking to anyone, missing the family brunch before sending the lovebirds back to New York. Good riddance.

"Yeah," he interjected. "You're right…my fault…of course…I'm sorry," were all the words he managed to get in before she hung up.

Man, for someone who was always on top of his game, right now he was way out in left field. This shit was not him. He was struggling with Vance, himself, Darcy, and Lewis, and the reason behind all of it was wrapped up in one set of long, toned legs.

He closed his eyes and drew in a deep breath.

Lolly DuVal had always been too damn young. Too damn young and yet very, very perceptive. She'd read him better than anyone else that night eleven years ago when he won the State Championship—and that had made all the difference. She was just a kid back then, so he stood by and watched her grow up. But now it was becoming just plain obvious that Lolly DuVal had been chipping away at his heart for a very long time.

And where Lolly was concerned, he was afraid of everything—especially of himself. Up until now he'd been able to handle it. Whenever the thought of doing something about it would surface over the years, he'd been able to let it go. He'd dated plenty and fallen in love twice. But when he saw her name on the guest list for Darcy's engagement party, a spark went off, and he figured it was now or never. The two of them were all grown up and timing was everything, right?

And their first date? Aside from a few false starts, it hit high on his top ten list. Right up until the time he was choking his best friend in the middle of the night. Now he had to call Lewis tomorrow and apologize. Right. Like that was going to happen.

Grabbing one of the six Krispy Kreme Doughnuts on his desk and the ancient Jake DuVal file he'd searched for all morning, he gave each his full attention in turn. Yeah, anything to alter the trail of his thoughts, because he just might have to admit that he was beating up Lewis for doing exactly what he longed to do to Lolly, and he was definitely not going there.

Within minutes, the next major issue to be faced landed on his desk. Vance plopped himself right where he always did whenever he came into the station. When you weren't much of a cop, they didn't give you much of a desk. So Vance parked himself on top of the blotter on Brooks' desk, swinging his legs back and forth while Brooks leaned his chair back on two legs, reading over the file.

"Put down the doughnut," Brooks growled, face still in the paperwork, before letting the front legs of his chair fall to the floor.

"You can't eat all six freaking doughnuts," Vance protested, returning the one he'd picked up.

"Three hundred push-ups every day says I can."

"Push-ups are bullshit."

"Running is bullshit. Push-ups are the perfect exercise," Brooks said as he rose. "Weight training and cardio all rolled into one. Real men do push-ups. Pansy-ass spandex-loving freaks run."

"Says the fastest sprinter in Henderson."

"And don't you forget it!"

"Sprinting is running."

"Sprinting is running with purpose. To win a race, to beat the throw at the plate, or to catch a perp. Running five miles is a waste of a lot of valuable time."

"It's good mental therapy."

Brooks looked pointedly at the doughnuts. "You've got your therapy, I've got mine." He turned and headed to the copy room.

"How was last night?"

Brooks glanced back, smiling casually. "It was good. My night was good, thanks." He kept walking.

Vance leapt off the desk and followed Brooks. "So, you and the Lollypop?"

"You got my message, right?" Brooks asked, letting his voice trail behind him.

Vance followed, stopping at the threshold of the copy room. Rubbing his hand over the back of his neck, he said, "Look. We need to do this Brooks."

"We don't need to do it with her."

"Well, who else are we going to get?"

Brooks took the paperwork from the file and tapped it all together. "We don't need anyone. It's a stupid idea. We do fine as we are."

"Bullshit! You bore women to death and I have nothing to offer outside the bedroom. This is not getting us where we want to go."

"Sorry." He shook his head, pushing the copy button and standing back to watch it run. "We aren't doing this."

"Why?"

Brooks slammed his fist on the top of the copier and turned to glare at his friend.

"You like her," Vance coaxed. "Admit it. You like Lolly and want to keep her all to yourself."

"Of course I like her," he said, rubbing a hand through his hair. "What's not to like? But…she's young and inexperienced and fresh and happy, and I shouldn't be messing with all that. And you," he said as he moved forward, poking Vance in the chest, "you definitely shouldn't be messing with that."

Vance knocked his hand away. "Why the hell not? She's the same age as Darcy for crying out loud."

Brooks flinched.

"She's probably had a dozen boyfriends," Vance went on before lowering his voice and getting serious. "Trust me, from the way Lolly talked about her last one, that *woman* knows what she wants and she's probably willing to tell us."

"Well, I'm not willing to ask her."

"Why the hell not?"

"Because it would change everything, that's why."

"Not necessarily—"

"Of course it will. I'll look like a fucking moron."

"Fine. I'll talk to her. Let me at least get some advice from a pretty girl so I never again end up with a crazy Yankee bitch in my bed."

"You did not!"

"I wish I didn't." Vance hung his head in shame. "Come on, man, I need serious help here. And honestly, what are the chances of you and Lolly actually working out anyway?"

Brooks' eyes widened, completely insulted. "Well, I don't know, but after I got my head out of my ass things seemed to go okay. Better than okay, actually." He picked up his copies, stalked past Vance and headed back to his desk.

Vance followed, relentless. "Did you do the move?"

"What move?"

"The bad cop move."

"What bad cop move?"

"Because we had an agreement, and if you did the move and it worked for you, you owe me."

Brooks slammed both hands on his desk. "What the hell are you talking about?"

"You know. The move!" Vance stepped forward and got up in his face. "Did you throw her up against the wall and kiss her like you meant it?"

Lines formed across Brooks' forehead. He'd completely forgotten about the move. "Of course I didn't—"

"She went for it, didn't she? I told you she would. Lolly doesn't want safe, and she doesn't want boring."

"I didn't do the move," Brooks shouted. "I drove her home and helped her out of the truck and then I...." His voice trailed off as he remembered exactly what he did. It might not have been a wall, but he sure as hell had her flattened against his truck. "Fucking A."

Vance's lips twitched, trying to hide his smile. "And how'd that work out for you?"

Brooks paced while running a hand over his head, remembering. Remembering how quickly Lolly had responded to him. How willing she was to have his hands all over her. How fast it all escalated. How hot it all got. So hot she was able to climax in the middle of the fucking street. Was that the power of *the move*?

"I already know how it worked out because it's the only damn thing I do right where women are concerned. You sprung bad cop on Lolly, got her all hot and bothered, and then walked away leaving her panting for more."

Brooks stopped his pacing. He kept his eyes on the floor, stuffed his hands in his pockets, and reminded himself to breathe.

"Or not." Vance beamed like he had just won a prize. "Bad cop gets them every time. You so owe me."

"We are not doing this!"

"Oh, but we are. A deal is a deal, Boy Scout. You took my advice and proved my point. You wouldn't be this cagey or irritated if it hadn't taken you someplace you've never been before. And, okay. Maybe Lolly would have gone on a second date anyway, being as you're the *Hero of Henderson*. But without you upping your game, there's a ninety-nine point nine percent chance she'd eventually be kicking your safe, boring, good cop ass back to the curb. At least *now* you've got her attention."

Fucking A.

"Face it, man." Vance stood, arms open wide. "I can help you with this. And for the love of God and the few things left that I find holy, you have *got* to help me figure out a way to stop having sex with women I find repugnant."

The two of them started to laugh.

"This really isn't funny," Brooks insisted.

"Don't I know it."

"Listen, maybe you *can* help me with this. I still don't see why we have to involve Lolly directly."

"Because clearly I don't have all the answers."

Brooks laughed again and agreed with that.

"What Lolly brings is the female perspective, and my instinct is that she'd actually tell us the truth," Vance patiently explained. "Without that, we don't know if we're hitting the target or just shooting blanks."

Brooks slumped into his chair, trying to think of any way out of this. Or any way to make it work to his advantage. Did he really do Vance's bad cop move? He honestly couldn't remember what he'd been thinking as he'd helped Lolly out of the car. It all just seemed to happen.

Premeditated or not, he had to admit it was the first time he'd ever done anything close to that. And Lolly had not called 911. No, Lolly had responded big-time and given him a memory he would never forget. There was no shooting blanks last night. That move had hit the target dead center. It definitely got Lolly's attention.

"All right," he finally agreed.

"Thank you. You won't regret this," Vance assured him.

Brooks groaned, already second-guessing himself. "Hey! Didn't you promise me the secret of your success if I go along with this ridiculous plan? So what the hell is it?"

"Once we talk to Lolly, and she agrees to help us…then I will hand over the secret of my success."

"Right. You're bullshittin' me."

"Swear to God. And by the way, you have to keep it secret. And I mean it. I do not want this getting out. Ever."

Brooks had never seen Vance look so serious. It was a bit of a shock. "Okay. Top secret. I'm the good cop, remember? I can do that."

"Good. Call Lolly and let's get this party started. I'm not getting any younger sitting around here."

"Why the hell are you in such a hurry to get your sorry ass hitched?"

Vance shrugged. "Been thinkin', that's all."

"Yeah?" Brooks almost laughed. "About what?"

Vance hesitated for a moment before saying, "None of your fucking business. Now make the damn call." He smacked Brooks on the leg and started for the door. "Text me where and when."

Brooks pulled out his phone and then yelled after Vance. "Lolly's mine. You got that, right?"

Vance turned halfway out the door. "Lolly is yours until she's not. Then she's fair game. Which is why you aren't gettin' another move until she agrees to help me."

"Jesus," Brooks muttered to himself, "how many moves does one guy need?"

CHAPTER FIVE

Lolly read the theme for her last collegiate fashion show aloud to her mother. "And it says to 'invoke a kaleidoscope of vivid memories and emotions in the audience.'"

"A kaleidoscope of vivid memories and emotions?" Genevra DuVal repeated before taking a sip of tea.

"Yes," Lolly sighed, folding the paper and running her fingers over the crease again and again. "I haven't been able to wrap my head around it just yet. I was hoping you could help me brainstorm."

Mother and daughter lounged inside their screened-in porch full of white wicker furniture with colorful chintz cushions. Their feet shared a large ottoman, and they each had a tall glass of sweet tea in their hand.

"Are you kidding? I rarely get a chance to be creative like this," her mother said. "So different from the number-crunching business." Genevra had received her degree in accounting when Lolly was a toddler. She'd started doing tax returns for friends and family out of her home. Since there were no accounting firms located in Henderson proper, it soon developed into a small business. When she realized the need, Genevra took the CPA exam and hired on an employee. She took business classes in the evenings and it wasn't long before she opened a small office on the main drag in town. To date they were up to seven full-time employees.

"Who attends Fashion Week? What ages?" Genevra asked.

"All ages. Though I suppose the majority of the attendees will range from eighteen to fifty."

"So let's concentrate on your age group. What was popular when you were a kid? Universally. Something everyone relates to," her mother prompted.

"Hmm." Lolly squinted her eyes and gave it some thought. "Power Rangers. Harry Potter."

Genevra smiled. "Two good ones right there."

"My focus is sportswear," Lolly countered. "How am I supposed to bring the Power Rangers to Wimbledon or Harry Potter to the Masters?"

"Hogwarts was a prep school, Sweetsie. Underneath the robes were nothing but striped ties and V-neck sweaters. And although your focus is sportswear, throwing in a fabulous collegiate robe-styled peignoir set or Ranger-inspired boxer briefs would certainly create some buzz. And isn't that what participating in NC State's Fashion Week is all about?"

Lolly looked over into her mother's sparkling teal eyes and smiled. They shared the same dark brunette hair, but her mother wore it up in a sophisticated twist rather than the ponytail Lolly preferred. The two of them were mistaken for sisters more often than not now that Lolly was twenty-three. Her mother had given birth to her when she was barely twenty and was now in the prime of her life. "I love your ideas. Keep them coming."

Her mother nodded, her eyes focused straight ahead into the backyard. "We'll come up with some good ones before the week is out."

"Which is part of the reason I'm staying home this summer. I need a break from my roommates and no one can brainstorm like you."

"Not to mention they're your competition."

"That too," she smirked. "I love them, but they are my competition."

"Well, I'm glad you needed a break, because I certainly enjoy having you home."

"You do?" Lolly asked. "I mean, I know you do, of course. But I don't want to be cramping your style or anything."

Her mother turned her head and gave Lolly a dazzling I-don't-know-what-in-the-world-you're-talking-about smile. Lolly snickered, shaking her head. "Besides the fact that you were not home when I arrived around three this morning, Uncle Jeb was at the party last night and is pretty convinced there is a man in your life. He says you are not talking and that I need to quickly figure out who it is and let him know."

"He said that?" Her mother looked back toward the yard and smiled.

"He just wants to make sure you're okay."

Genevra reached out and touched her arm. "I know, Sweetsie. All your daddy's brothers continue to take good care of me, and I adore them for it."

When her mother didn't say more, Lolly became incredulous. "You aren't going to tell me?"

Her mother just stared straight ahead, smiled that happy I've-got-a-secret smile, and shook her head 'no.'

Lolly jumped up and sat on the ottoman squarely in front of her mother. "Momma," she implored with a grin, "you have got to tell me…something."

Her mother's eyes shifted to take her in. And then she laughed. "Oh, it's silly, really. I'm just…." She closed her eyes and Lolly knew her mother was truly besotted. "I just want to savor it."

Mother and daughter smiled at one another, savoring it together. "Wow," Lolly said.

"Yes. Wow," her mother agreed.

Lolly itched to ask all sorts of questions. When did this start? Is he older than you? Is this the first time you've felt like this since Daddy died? Or even, did you ever feel like this with Daddy?

No wonder her mother wasn't talking. If these were the kinds of questions she wanted to ask, she could only imagine what three overbearing brothers-in-law would want to know. And they had actually known her father, unlike Lolly, who'd never had the chance to meet him.

Her cell chimed. She sat up straight when she saw it was a text from Brooks. '*Pick you up at 7. Dinner. My apologies up front. Vance is joining us.*'

She texted back with one hand. '*No problem. See you at 7.*' She looked up into her mother's inquisitive smile.

"Brooks is taking me out to dinner tonight."

"A second date already?" she asked, clearly delighted.

"Maybe," Lolly said. "I'm not sure. Might be more of a business meeting. Coach Evans is joining us."

"Coach Evans? The one with the magic hands?"

"Yes." Lolly burst into laughter remembering him rubbing her feet. "Oh My God, Mom, he really does have magic hands. My feet were cured! Maybe he's gotten a bad rap. Maybe he just has healing hands and…" she trailed off smiling.

"And what?"

"I was about to say that the rumors were exaggerated, but then I remembered he had a magic voice too. It's no wonder Molly and her crowd find it hard to stay away from him."

"Oh Lord. Molly. If you think your uncles worry about me, they'd have heart failure if they knew that boy was massaging your feet."

Lolly chuckled. "Well, what about you, Mom? Are you having heart failure because he massaged my feet?"

"Sweetsie, honestly," her mother said, sitting back and offering her a dreamy sort of look, "I love that Vance Evans massaged your feet."

"What?" Lolly laughed, outraged.

"I mean it," her mother smiled. "You've got better sense than I ever had. You're ambitious and smart, you work hard, and I know you have big plans for yourself. So if a man like Vance Evans wants to massage your feet, I want you to lie back and enjoy it. Trust me. This time in your life won't last forever."

"Mom!" Lolly sputtered. "Where is the woman who warned me about boys, sex, pregnancy, disease, and heartache back when I was sixteen?"

"At sixteen you needed those warnings. Now that you're twenty-three, well, all those boys have grown into men. Hopefully they know what they're doing. And if you're involved in designing athletic cups for your graduate project, I'm assuming you know what a condom is. As for the heartache…." Her mother took a deep breath and let it out. "If I've learned one thing, Sweetsie, it's that you can't do much to protect yourself from that. And trust me, being lonely is far worse than trying to avoid it."

Lolly reached out and hugged her mother tightly. "I'm sorry that you've been lonely, Momma. Whatever is going on, you truly do have the right to savor it."

⸻ ❧ ⸻

Just before seven o'clock, movement outside the house drew Lolly's attention.

Her nerves had started unraveling an hour earlier as she prepared to see Brooks again. Where this morning her body had woken in a state of unadulterated bliss as she languidly remembered all the highlights of her date with Brooks, as the day wore on and her memory belabored the very potent, very shattering end to their evening together, embarrassment started to rear its ugly head.

How was she supposed to act when she saw him? The man had given her a magnificent orgasm kissing her goodnight. Was she supposed to ignore that? Pretend it didn't happen? Leap into his arms and beg him to do it again?

To compound things, the conversation with her mother reminded her of Vance and his hands and the two of them alone in the training room. Of all he'd said in that ridiculously seductive voice. Of how she'd been so turned on that she was daydreaming about an affair with the Dark Lord at the end of the massage table.

And now she was having dinner with them both. The one who'd turned her on and the one who'd finished her off. She sucked in a breath at the thought. Holy crap!

So when the movement out front caught her eye, Lolly hid herself to the side of the bay window and snuck a peek. She was eager to lay eyes on Brooks, hoping to calm her nerves before meeting him at the door.

Only it wasn't Brooks. Her surprise and curiosity had her moving front and center in the window to get a better look. Down at the end of the drive she saw Vance leaning against the back of his daddy's vintage orange Corvette, which was parked along the curb on the side of the road. His arms were crossed over his chest and he had one ankle crossed over the other. He wasn't looking toward the house. He was staring at something straight ahead. Concentrating. Lolly followed his gaze, right to her mother's bright yellow two-seater,

Spyder Convertible.

She looked back at Vance and continued to watch. Eventually, he pushed himself away from the Vette and strolled up to the back of her mother's car. He stopped, staring at it. Then he circled all the way around, inspecting the car as if he were interested in buying it.

Maybe he was. His dad was into cars; everyone knew that. He had built a special garage in recent years just to house his collection. Lolly heard it had lifts that would allow one car to be stored above another. Maybe Vance was a car guy, too.

She turned in search of her little clutch purse and glanced at herself in the mirror over the buffet. Her mother would never sell that Spyder. *She loved it way too much*, Lolly thought as she checked her teeth, makeup, and hair. She'd left her hair down, but pulled it back from her face with a wide red headband. She'd layered a red silk tank top over a tight white one, tucked them both into a short but full red skirt and cinched her waist with a black patent leather belt that matched her low-heeled sandals. She grabbed up her white sweater and popped open the screen door just as Vance was about to hit the porch steps.

He looked up and stopped in mid-stride.

Whatever emotion had been etched on his face dissolved into a playful grin as he took a step back and stared up at Lolly, his hands spread to his sides. "On time and looking fine, Miss DuVal. Where have you been all my life?"

Lolly blushed, her hand still on the screen door. "I thought Brooks was picking me up."

"Change of plans. Unfortunately for Brooks, a call came in right as he was getting off duty. A pit bull roaming around the elementary school. Brooks knows the dog and the owners so he thought he should handle it. I told him to take his time. That I'd pick you up and we'd meet him at the restaurant."

"Oh. Okay. So he's all right with this?"

"Oh, hell no!" Vance laughed. "This is his worst nightmare. But being that he is the town superhero and all, what choice did he have? However, he has forbidden me to talk to you about anything regarding our research before he arrives." He held out his hand as she descended the steps. She took it, nodding her thanks. "So of course, I'm going to tell you everything."

CHAPTER SIX

Vance watched as Lolly's mouth hung open in shock right before she let out a genuine laugh. "Vance Evans, you are a bad, bad man."

"So they keep telling me," he grumbled, leading her down the drive. He didn't drop her hand but kept a casual hold on it. With Brooks claiming her as his own, he wasn't going to get many chances to touch her, so he was taking advantage of this one. He was having trouble shaking the day-late-and-dollar-short feeling that kept nagging at him ever since he'd realized Brooks had asked Lolly to Lewis and Darcy's engagement party.

"This is one of my daddy's pride and joys," he explained as they approached the car. "None of them gets driven a whole lot with him out of town so much, so he insists I take one out for a spin whenever I can." He opened the passenger door. "Frankly, I prefer to drive my truck, but according to Duncan James it screams redneck. I figured a pretty girl earning a graduate degree might appreciate riding in a Corvette."

Lolly turned to face him before sliding into the bucket seat. Her sapphire-blue eyes flirted outrageously while her pouty little lips formed a set of words that shot straight to his groin. "As long as I eventually get to ride in your pickup," she said.

Now what the hell was he supposed to do with that? Because what he wanted to do was snatch her up in his arms and kiss that dirty mouth of hers.

"Get in," he ordered. Because a ride in his truck meant full-on, hot, sweaty sex and as young and innocent and blah, blah, blah as

Brooks insisted she was, there was no way she didn't know that. Not if Molly DuVal was her cousin.

Lolly moved fast, wiggling her shapely little ass into the leather seat and then swinging those long, long legs of hers, which he was now imagining wrapped around his waist, into the car. He slammed the door shut.

As he walked around the back of the car, he noticed the yellow Spyder again. He moved into the driver's seat asking, "Is that your momma's car?" He started the ignition.

"It is. She loves it. She won't sell it, if that's why you're asking."

He shook his head, pulling into the street. "I've just seen it around," he said quietly. "Didn't know who it belonged to, that's all."

Lolly nodded. "I guess being a cop, you like to know everybody's car."

Vance shook his head again, then snickered. "I'm not much of a cop. Not like Brooks. He's into it. He's good at it."

"You're not into being a cop?"

He shook his head one more time.

"So you're more into coaching? And being a cop pays the bills?"

He shot Lolly a short grin. "I like coaching. And being a cop is interesting. People are nuts. Get themselves in all kinds of stupid situations. Fortunately, around here most of it is harmless. We're lucky, you know, to live in a place where most people don't even lock their doors."

"Yeah, my roommates and I are a little more security conscious in Raleigh."

"Good thing."

"So you find being a cop interesting, but you're not really into it."

"It's part of a bigger plan," he said, turning onto the ramp for I-85 South.

"Where are we going?" Lolly asked, amused.

"Brooks didn't tell you?"

"No. He just texted me that he'd pick me up at seven."

"He texted you?"

"Uh-huh."

"Are you telling me that Brooks, Golden Boy Bennett did not

call you up and properly ask you out for dinner? That he just texted you a time?"

Lolly nodded.

"He's worse than I thought."

Lolly laughed. "I was fine with it. Really."

"Really? You were fine with it?" Vance pressed. "A nice, safe, boring text."

When Lolly reiterated that she was perfectly fine with the text, Vance gave her one long oh-really look before punching the accelerator and shifting his father's Corvette into the next gear, tossing her back into the seat. He repeated the process twice, blowing the speedometer well past the one-hundred-miles-an-hour mark.

All it took was a quick glance to see Lolly's eyes shining over a big I-love-to-go-fast grin.

"You do realize we're breaking the law right now," he said.

He glanced over to see her nod, nervous laughter tinkling out of those heart-stopping lips.

"Not really a nice thing to do, me being a cop and all," he said while easily maneuvering the Vette around a car they'd cruised up on in the fast lane. "Probably not all that safe, either, considering the speed limit is seventy-five." Then he shot across the three-lane highway and up the exit ramp, downshifting quickly as they flew to the top, gliding to a stop at the very last second. Vance turned his head and stared hard at the woman whose hand was at her throat, whose breathing was rapid, and whose eyes sparkled above a dazzling smile. "Not. Boring."

Lolly fell back into her seat. "Definitely. Not. Boring."

When the call came in at 4:57 that afternoon about Mrs. Darley's pit bull, Pansy, running loose around the elementary school, Brooks figured it would take no more than a half hour to lure Pansy to him with one of the dog treats he kept in the trunk of his patrol car and deliver her back to the Darleys. Pansy was just a puppy, as sweet as sweet could be, but she was big and muscular, and that breed struck terror in the hearts of some no matter how often you reassured them that all pit bulls weren't killers.

Pansy turned out to be the least of his worries. Once she was back on a leash, all the kids who'd run away screaming, climbing up fences and onto playground equipment to get away from her, now wanted to pet Pansy. So he used that opportunity to talk to them about what to do when confronted with any stray dog.

On the way back to his patrol car, ninety-year-old Dottie Lewis waved him over to her old gray Cadillac to thank him for taking care of that incident with her paper boy. This created a traffic jam he needed to unfurl because she'd stopped right in the middle of the street to do it.

When he finally got Pansy up to the front door of the Darleys', no one was home. They were probably out looking for their dog, so he strolled Pansy over to their long-time neighbors, the Craigs, hoping they would take Pansy off his hands so he could head home and shower before picking up Lolly.

The Craigs said they'd be happy to puppy-sit Pansy but while he was there, would he please take a look at something going on in the backyard?

In disbelief, Brooks used his cell to call the fire department while staring at a wire so live it was spewing sparks and had already burned up half an oak tree. It was then that he made the decision he was now starting to regret.

Instead of calling Lolly and explaining the situation, he called Vance.

It was a snap decision made because he didn't want Lolly left hanging. Since his house was already halfway to the Magnolia Grill, he'd head home for a shower while Vance picked her up. It made a lot of sense when he'd first thought of it—what with the tree burning down in front of him and all.

But now the thoughts running through Brooks' head resembled something akin to a Stephen King horror flick.

Over the better part of the last hour, his imagination had run rampant. It started with some very pleasant highlights of Lolly from last night, snapping to an image of her on the training table in Vance's office, and then back to last night and her falling apart in Brooks' arms. Then he saw her misty-eyed gaze as she commented about Vance's freaking hands.

Fucking A.

He loved his friend, Vance. He truly did. He'd given up a lot for him, in fact. But where women were concerned, well…he'd seen it happen enough in the bars or at a party. He or Duncan would be talking to some cute babe and make the mistake of blinking their eyes only to find that Vance had stolen her attention right out from under them. Next thing you knew, his hands would be massaging her shoulders or sliding over her ass as his body moved in for the kill. Around women, Vance turned into something predatory and dark, something totally different from who he really was. Like a werewolf when the full moon hits, he didn't think Vance could control it or was even aware of it. But it was there.

And all that might make him sexy and alluring to a lonely female. But what they didn't know about his buddy is that Vance did not like women. At all.

Intentional lovin' and leavin' might not be against the law, but Brooks suspected Vance found it a very satisfying way to punish the female population. And Vance was Commander and Chief when it came to that rally cry.

You didn't have to be a psychologist when it was all so obvious. Though Vance had never once discussed the ugly part of his childhood, it was there, deep inside him. And just like that full moon, the hurt Vance suffered turned him into a dirty dog where women were concerned.

So the visual in Brooks' head causing his blood pressure to spike as he opened the door to the Magnolia Grill was of a fangs-bared Vance leaning over a torn and tattered Lolly in a booth, in the back, in the corner, in the dark.

A tinkling of laughter brought back the light.

Seduced by the sound, Brooks headed into the well-appointed bar area. There stood Lolly, sweet and fresh, not a bite mark on her, talking with Vance and Annabelle Devine's crazy Aunt Helen who he'd never, ever seen crack a smile. But tonight she was beaming a grin and chatting merrily as Brooks approached.

"Officer Bennett," old Aunt Helen greeted him by name. "Did you wrestle that beast, Pansy, to the ground? Haul her into the pound and lock her away for good?"

"Something like that." Brooks nodded, taking the wrinkled old hand held out to him. "I see you are holding court as usual."

"Well, someone has to warn Miss DuVal about Officer Evans, for goodness' sake. And what in the world are the three of you doing fifteen miles outside of Henderson?" She leaned in and lowered her voice, her flinty eyes squinting above a pursed and wrinkled set of lips. "Are the three of you planning a ménage à trois?"

Brooks couldn't help himself. "We'd be happy to make it a foursome."

"Oh you…." She shook her finger at him as they all laughed, then she tapped his cheek with her hand. "Go on and get. All of you. You're going to scare off my date. He'll be thinking I brought my grandchildren along."

Lolly, Brooks, and Vance headed off toward the dining section, wishing Aunt Helen goodbye before turning to each other and making gruesome faces. "A date?"

"Is she serious?"

"She's got to be a hundred and twenty years old."

"Maybe she's an undead. They're in the news a lot lately." They chuckled about that as the hostess ushered them to a quiet table in the back where they would not be overheard. Exactly as Brooks had requested.

Lolly scooted into one side of the luxurious booth and Vance into the other. Brooks followed Lolly and felt her hand on his leg as he settled himself next to her. He looked over and she smiled at him. "Hi," she said shyly.

"Hi," he said back. Their eyes met and held, hers dark blue and happy. His gaze lingered, taking in her smooth skin, flushed cheeks, and pink lips. If Vance weren't across the table, he'd have kissed them. Instead, his hand moved over hers and squeezed it. "I'm sorry I'm late."

Lolly shook her head as the waiter arrived. He was dark-haired and young. Lolly's age probably, with an engaging grin and a name tag that said 'Harry.'

"Harry?" Brooks and Vance said at the same time.

"You were the bartender at Henderson Country Club on New Year's Eve," Vance went on.

"And you two were the cops who had to watch what they drank."

"Which is why we are here and not at the Club," Vance smirked. "So bring us a round of tequila shots with a beer chaser and then a good bottle of red when dinner arrives." Vance looked over at Brooks, who gave a shrug of acquiescence.

"You sure?" Harry smiled under twinkling eyes. "Last time I served shots of tequila, your buddy Duncan fell in love with Annabelle. And seeing as there is only one rose sitting between you thorns, this may not be a good idea."

"How the hell do you remember Duncan and Annabelle?"

"Because they were sitting at the bar New Year's Eve while you two kept sending trouble their way."

Brooks looked over at Vance, grinning. "Damn. We did do that, didn't we?"

"We sure did," Vance answered proudly.

Brooks turned to Harry. "You have a heck of a memory. You ever considered becoming a cop? We could use a guy with a memory like yours."

Harry simply smiled indulgently—almost as if Brooks was a dumb-ass—but it was impossible to take offense. There was just something about Harry.

"What are the chances?" Vance said with a touch of bewilderment as Harry moved away.

"Guess he was just helping out on New Year's Eve." Brooks shrugged. "Must work here regularly."

"He's cute," Lolly chimed in.

Both male heads turned to stare at her. "Cute," she insisted, her eyes darting between the two of them as she tried to backpedal. "Like a puppy."

"Like a puppy?" Brooks questioned.

Lolly shrugged. "I'm just saying." She ducked her head and took a sip of water.

Brooks laughed. "You're the one who's cute," he insisted, bringing his hand up and running a thumb across her cheek.

Vance cleared his throat. "Do you mind? How 'bout keeping your hands to yourself while I'm sitting right here?" He looked over to Lolly. "It's hard enough swallowing the bitter pill that he asked you out first," he said with a wink.

Lolly blushed and gave a short giggle. Brooks smiled at the sound. Like the color of her eyes, it held happiness.

Harry and his magic tequila shots arrived and were set before them with great flourish. Each had a lime wedge tucked on the rim of the glass. A salt shaker was set in the middle of the table and then tall, glistening pilsner glasses filled with a cold amber brew were spread amongst them. Harry eyed Lolly with a flirtatious grin. "My car is out back," he offered, "if these two become too much trouble. Now," he addressed the table at large, "is everyone having steak?"

Brooks checked in with Lolly, who nodded readily. "Steak it is," he said.

"Trust me," Harry said. "I'll take care of it."

"I bet he will," Vance said as Harry sped away. "A toast," Vance offered, picking up the salt shaker and licking his hand. He applied the salt, handed the shaker over to Brooks, and then lifted his shot glass while removing the lime. "To the accumulation of knowledge and insight," he toasted, eyeing Brooks.

Lolly glanced between them before following along with the salt, shot, and lime ritual.

"Okay," Vance said as he licked his lips before slamming his shot glass down on the table. "It's time to get down to business."

CHAPTER SEVEN

Lolly's stomach gave an eager little twist. What with the narrowing of Vance's eyes and the captivating stillness that descended over Brooks, she could not wait to hear what all this was about.

"Lolly," Vance started. "We thought we'd better discuss this outside of town, just to be sure we wouldn't be overheard. What we want you to do for us is a little out there. Can we count on your discretion?"

Lolly blinked a couple of times. "You don't want me telling anyone about this," she clarified.

"Exactly. Not that my reputation would suffer because it's crap already. But Brooks has aspirations of running for office one day, and well…we don't want anything…you know, to jeopardize that."

Lolly looked at Brooks. "You want to run for office?"

"Mayor," Brooks clarified.

"So," Vance went on, "it's important we have your word that whatever takes place between the three of us stays between the three of us."

Lolly felt herself nodding her agreement as her brain latched on to the words "between the three of us" and started spinning them, making her woozy. The three of us. The three of us. The three of….

Oh shit! Every fiber in her body tensed and went on full alert. *They did overhear me tell Darcy I'd take them both!* She couldn't move. She couldn't think. She couldn't hear. She was aware that Vance's lips were moving, but in her panic she was only picking up words here and there.

"You know…telling me…milquetoast boyfriend."

Oh, no. No, no, please no. She was mortified. She felt her cheeks burning up. *Oh My God. What must Brooks think of me?*

"Occurred to me…you might be willing to…."

She reached for her beer.

"Do…Brooks and myself."

Lolly tilted her beer up and chugged three long pulls. *Oh My God! Are they seriously asking me to do a three-way? Crazy Aunt Helen was right. And my mother! My mother said she wanted me to have fun, but this? Dear God, Dear God, Dear God. What am I going to say? Okay, okay. Focus.* She took a deep breath, set her glass on the table, and tried to concentrate on exactly what Vance was saying.

"And let me say right up front that Brooks is here somewhat under duress. I mean, after your date last night, he's really not all that interested in sharing you with me. Can't blame him. But he knows I need this, so he's agreed to go along with it, as long as you are up for it."

Two sets of eyes—one blue, one green—were trained on her, expecting a response. Instead of calling them kinky bastards, she picked up her beer again and tried to drown herself. She really wasn't comfortable with this. She knew girls who would be, but she'd never imagined herself in this kind of scenario. Would she regret saying 'no'? The two of them were so gorgeous and—

A hand on her arm stopped her train of thought. "Lolly? Are you all right?" Brooks had her hand and was bringing it and her beer glass back to the table. She snuck a peak at him and his face was full of concern, like she was losing it for no good reason.

Are you kidding me?

She released her glass, put both elbows on the table, and put her face in her hands. She couldn't look at either one of them when she said, "I've never done a three-way."

"What the fuck?" Brooks exploded, as Vance slapped a hand on the table and convulsed into laughter.

"Jesus, Lolly! What the hell did you think Vance was asking for?"

Lolly popped her head out of her hands and took in the scene before her. Vance was beside himself with glee. Brooks was appalled. With her?

"I'm sorry," she cried. "I guess I got nervous with all this talk of secrecy and my imagination ran away with me. But it definitely sounded like you…wanted me to—"

"No! We definitely do not want you to do that," Brooks insisted, cutting her off.

"Well, hell, if it's up for discussion, I'm all for it," Vance said.

Brooks leveled Vance a malevolent stare. "It is not now, nor will it ever be, up for discussion," he threatened.

Vance threw up his hands and collapsed back in his booth. "A three-way would be far from boring," he sang. Brooks' fist landed on the table. "I'm just saying!" Vance added.

"Well, obviously whatever you were saying has confused Lolly. So, how 'bout I take a crack at this?"

"Be my guest," Vance offered, folding his arms across his chest. "I can't wait to hear the good cop spin."

Brooks turned to Lolly, only to find her expression caught somewhere between hysteria and mortification.

"I am so…embarrassed," she said quietly and then placed her forehead gently on the table.

"*You're* embarrassed?" Brooks said as if he were the one suffering mortal humiliation. His large palm rubbed a gentle circle over her back. "Lolly, please forgive us rednecks for being so obtuse."

She turned her head slightly, blinking at Brooks. "I'm not sure actual rednecks use the word obtuse." She lifted her head and sighed, unable to look at him. "There is nothing to forgive. It's my fault, I assure you." She took a deep breath. "Gratefully, I assume I am covered under our prevailing state of discretion, so the fact that I jumped to that ridiculous conclusion will not leave this table?"

Both Brooks and Vance nodded. Vance's face sported a rather overzealous smirk.

"Then," Lolly went on, "obviously whatever it is you do want me to do, you are now fully insured and assured that I will keep it confidential."

Harry arrived at the table with large wedges of lettuce covered in blue cheese dressing and sprinkled with pieces of bacon, tomato, and red onion. He also placed before each of them a fluted wine glass and then proceeded to open a bottle, describing the vintage, the winery, and what they were supposed to taste. He looked over at Lolly and winked.

"Stop that," Brooks scolded. "She already thinks you're cute. She knows your car is out back. And with the way things are going, I'm worried she'll run off with you before you bring out the steak."

Lolly laughed. Harry smiled and bowed out gracefully.

"Okay, then." Brooks turned to Lolly. "Let me see if I can clarify where it is Vance could use your expertise."

"My expertise?"

"We'd like a female's point of view. Vance said you might be willing to share yours since you were willing to talk a little about your ex-boyfriend. Why he became your ex-boyfriend."

Lolly blushed and turned her attention to her salad.

"Vance." Brooks indicated with his hand. "Doesn't like women."

"I love women," he protested around a mouthful of salad.

"Vance has zero female friends," Brooks continued as if Vance hadn't spoken. "He doesn't talk to them. He doesn't listen to them. He doesn't like them playing pool with us, or shooting darts, or playing cards, anything. He simply does not enjoy a woman's company unless the bar is getting ready to close."

Lolly watched as Vance's eyes shifted between the attack he was putting on his salad and the attack Brooks was putting on his character. She noticed his eyes narrowing and his jaw tensing, but she also noticed he didn't deny anything being said.

She cocked her head. "Is this true, Vance?"

Vance looked at her, dropped his fork, and leaned back from his plate, chewing his food. He wiped his mouth with his cloth napkin and settled it back in his lap before he spoke.

"Two days ago, I would have denied it." He took up his wine glass and sipped. "But since Brooks delivered this news to me yesterday, I've been thinking about it." He folded his fingers together over the table, shook his head, and then eyed her directly. "There is a lot of evidence to support what he says." He took a deep breath. "I want you to help me with this." He eyed Brooks before coming back to her. "I need you to help me figure this out."

He was serious. So serious that Lolly's heart ached for the darkly handsome man in front of her. Ached so sharply she didn't trust her voice. So she nodded her head quickly, silently swearing to do what she could. There was a long, awkward silence as the three of them ate their salad.

"We're turning thirty soon, Brooks and I." Vance's voice was making the statement matter of fact.

"Thirty?" Lolly smiled, glancing between the two. "You are old," she teased.

"How old are you, Lolly?" Brooks asked.

"Twenty-three. Same as Darcy." It hit her then…Darcy was marrying a man seven years older. They seemed like a perfect couple, yet…seven years?

"Age is just a number," Vance insisted. "Obviously, my emotional IQ would register closer to that of a twenty-year-old. It's all relative."

Lolly agreed with him to an extent. But from the body language Brooks was throwing off, he was not agreeing at all. She touched his leg just as she had done when they first sat down. But that seemed to cause him to pay even more attention to his salad. She pulled her hand away.

Lolly spoke nonchalantly. "I suppose seven years might be a big difference when we're talking about a three-way."

Vance choked on his wine and Brooks steered every ounce of his attention her way, just as she'd hoped. "No one is talking about a three-way," he growled.

"I know." She smiled brilliantly into his scowl. "I just wanted to get your attention," she said patting his leg. He rubbed his hand over hers in reward.

Vance sat grinning across the table. "Clearly she has what it takes," he said. He pushed his salad plate aside and leaned his forearms onto the table, addressing her directly. "My turn," he said, his expression full of mischief.

"My buddy here," he said, pointing to Brooks, "good cop. In all things, he's the good cop. Which is going to work out well for him when he runs for mayor. But I'm afraid, after our conversation on the training table yesterday—you're cute when you blush, by the way—I'm afraid that when it comes to women, Brooks regularly falls into the milquetoast category."

Lolly's mouth worked, but nothing came out. She was indeed

blushing. How the hell was she supposed to respond to that?

"He needs your help. Desperately. And I realize this may be a bit awkward since the two of you had a big date last night, but trust me, without your honest input and a few of my secrets to success, you are headed toward a dead end with this one."

"Trust *me*," Lolly piped up. "Nothing about our date last night was milquetoast."

Vance spread his hands out and lifted his brows in a proving-my-point gesture.

Brooks dropped his knife and fork and glared at his longtime friend and teammate.

"Just keeping it real, man," Vance said in apology.

Brooks rubbed his forehead and muttered something like 'kill me now' as Harry arrived, just in time to save the evening from utter disaster. Unsure of what was really going on around her, Lolly's nerves were strung out and fraying at the ends. As she watched Harry clear the salad plates, her eyes pleaded with him to bring another round of tequila. Like magic, within mere seconds Harry the Gifted was back granting her wish—laying down artistically prepared shots as if he'd had them on the ready, awaiting just the right time for delivery.

Lolly didn't hesitate. She took the shaker, licked her hand, doctored it up, sucked the salt, slung the shot, and bit the lime. When she noticed Vance and Brooks staring at her she shrugged. "Don't judge. I was starting to feel more comfortable with the idea of a three-way."

They both chuckled and lifted their shots. "To Lolly," they said in unison.

The porterhouse arrived on a sizzling iron pan, sliced and set in the center of the table. Harry expertly used two spoons as tongs to place slices of both the tenderloin and the strip steak on their plates, scooping up the essence and pouring it over their meat. Next he doled out portions of creamed spinach, hash brown potatoes, and sautéed mushrooms. No matter what the topic of conversation, mouths couldn't help but water. Lolly dug in with uncharacteristic gusto.

While they ate, commenting only on the delicious food, Lolly reviewed what she had heard. "I'm not a psychology major," she said, out of the blue. "I'd like to help you, Vance, but I'm not really qualified to figure out why you don't like women."

Vance finished chewing, but held his knife and fork at the sides of his plate. After a brief glance toward Brooks, he looked across the table at her, his eyes darkening, his expression earnest. "My mother walked out on my father and me when I was ten. Left us for another man and his daughter. My father and I were both so devastated we couldn't find the words we needed to discuss it. We grieved in silence. Sitting together on the front porch every night, wishing she'd come back. Eventually, my grandmother moved here from Barcelona to care for us, but she spoke only Spanish. She had plenty to say about it, but I couldn't understand a word."

"Vance, I'm so sorry," Lolly said on a breath.

"Oh, it gets better," he said, pointing his knife. "While all this was going down, I went to school every day. I mean, I was there, but I wasn't there because I was so numb and dazed. No one was talking about it there either. My entire world had picked up and moved out. And no one was acknowledging it. Not the teacher or the school nurse or the principal. I felt fucking invisible. But there was this one girl in my class who, out of the blue one day, comes up and takes my hand. And holds it.

"To this day, I remember exactly what that felt like. That human touch. "I simply turned to her and told her everything. I told her my mother had left. That I wanted her back. That I couldn't understand my grandmother but knew she hated my mother. On and on and on. And she *listened* to me. And then…then she told me that she would be very sad if her mother left her, so she was going to share it with me. The sadness. That while she was being sad, I could play and feel better for a while. And then while she played, I could be sad again. That we would take turns being sad, together.

"So we did. I don't know why it worked—I was probably so tired of being sad that I needed to feel better now and then. And she made it possible. I remember her sitting by herself one recess. Somebody asked her to play and she said 'no,' that it was her turn to be sad. I was playing catch or something and I remember smiling because I was free to smile while she held vigil for my mother.

"And every morning she'd meet me first thing and let me tell her what was on my mind. About how I hurt. About how I didn't like the food my grandmother fixed. About how much I missed my dad when he was away on business." He shook his head in bewilderment. "She became my lifeline. My support system. Which is a lot to ask of a fellow fourth grader," he said as he smiled.

"And then…." Vance's eyes closed briefly and he shrugged. Putting knife and fork to work, he went back to his steak.

"And then what?" Lolly asked.

Vance spoke directly to his plate. "Then her father got transferred or something and her family moved away."

"Jesus," Brooks said.

Lolly touched his arm. "You didn't know this?"

Brooks shook his head while Vance explained that he hadn't ever talked to anyone about any of it. "Not Brooks, not Duncan, not Lewis. Guys don't discuss this shit. I mean, they all obviously know that my mother hasn't been around, and they probably figured out that my issues with women stem from that, but…." He shrugged and took a sip of wine. "What are you gonna do?"

Lolly couldn't find words to speak, and apparently Brooks was just as tongue-tied because the silence stretched on and on until Vance's cutlery clattered to his plate and he exclaimed, "Come on, y'all. This is ancient history. Do not let this ruin our evening. I just figured I'd spell it out so that you know you don't need a degree in psychology to figure me out. And I'm not going to any freaking counselor so don't bother going there. I need to learn how to be friends with a woman. You're a woman. And until you kick this one to the curb, we can be friends and nothing more. So, will you do it? Will you be my friend?" he said mockingly. "Will you teach me what there is to like about women so I can stop abusing them and myself at the same time?"

Lolly's eyes widened. "Wow, you really are self-aware."

Vance smirked. "And it only took a good thirty years."

Harry materialized at the side of their table. "Gentlemen, I hope you brought your wallets because I have another bottle of wine to finish off your meal," he said, starting to pour. "It also goes brilliantly with the chocolate soufflé I've ordered for the table. *Goce.*"

"What?" Lolly asked as he left the table.

"He said *enjoy*. In Spanish," Vance offered. "Was he standing there listening to every word I said?"

"I just think he's a mind reader," answered Brooks, "because I was definitely thinking about more wine."

"And the chocolate soufflé sounds amazing," Lolly agreed. "So you two finish off the rest of that steak because I'm going to sip my wine and save room for dessert." She pushed her plate to the side.

Lolly leaned back and watched the Heroes of Henderson refill their plates. She was relieved when the two of them started discussing some faulty ESPN commentary on a random Major League baseball game. Random to her, but clearly a life or death situation for these men.

These men. Her mind trailed back to middle school and the year she and Darcy had become inseparable. It was that spring that Brooks and Vance were seniors and co-captains of the Henderson High baseball team. Lolly went to every game to keep Darcy company. She learned a lot about baseball since the team was undefeated and the town did nothing but buzz about them winning their league and moving on to the state championship.

She'd paid attention to Brooks only because he was Darcy's brother, and she liked sharing Darcy's pride of his baseball prowess. She remembered Vance being at the Bennetts' house so much that she'd asked Darcy if she had another brother.

Back then she and Darcy were nothing more to Brooks and Vance than impediments to be maneuvered around on their way to the refrigerator or back out to their cars. She never imagined she'd be sitting here with the two of them now. And what? Become Vance's friend? Make sure Brooks didn't turn milquetoast?

She was in way, way over her head with these two.

Since the day Brooks called and asked her to the engagement party, she'd done nothing but fantasize about a summer fling. And now—now she had the perfect opportunity and a chance to alleviate her pent-up sexual frustration after a year of nice, safe, boring Davis. Because Vance was wrong. Brooks might be the good cop, but he was no milquetoast. The reality was that he'd be the one doing the educating.

It was all so surreal. She needed to digest it.

Not only digest it, she thought, *but figure out what it would look like to be Vance Evan's friend.* The man practically seduced her in the first ten minutes of their meeting. And she'd allowed it! Could she and Vance really become friends?

Friends had common interests, spent time together, shared confidences. She didn't play baseball; she wasn't a coach or a cop. She…could run. He said he ran every day. Maybe she could run with him. They could talk while they ran. Train for some sort of race at the end of the summer. Friends did that. They could do that.

And he was working with her on the athletic cup research, so they'd be interacting there. He was helping her. Friends did that for each other.

What else?

"Excuse me," she said when there was a lull in the conversation. "Vance, do you play tennis?"

He had finished his meal and was swirling his wine. "I have, in the past, played some tennis. Yes."

"How 'bout golf? Have you ever played golf?"

"I'm a baseball player. How hard could golf be?"

Brooks chuckled while Lolly rolled her eyes. "Perfect," she said. "Listen. What time do you run in the mornings?"

"Six o'clock."

"Would you mind if I ran with you?"

"Not as long as the first place we run to is Tenderfoot to get you new shoes."

Lolly laughed. "Deal."

"I don't work until the afternoon tomorrow. Meet me at Tenderfoot at nine when they open and we'll run out from there. We'll take the old railroad trail and keep in the shade."

"And with a short detour, we can run to the Club and sign up for the Mixed-up Mixed Doubles Tennis Tournament and the King and Queen Golf Tournament. Maybe a little coed sports competition will show you there is more to appreciate about women."

"Done." Vance swallowed the last of his wine. "I'll let the two of you enjoy the soufflé while I head to the library and pick up a book on tennis."

"A book on tennis?" Lolly asked bewildered.

"I'm assuming you want to win these tournaments."

She nodded and smiled. "Go forth and conquer."

"Indeed." Vance stood, pulled out his wallet, and tossed his credit card to Brooks. "Split it down the middle and make sure you take care of Harry."

Brooks nodded. "Will do. Be safe."

"You too," he nodded. "Lolly. Nine sharp. Tenderfoot."

"I'll be there, and thank you for dinner. Tell your dad I like his Corvette."

"He'll be pleased to hear it." He smiled, nodded, and turned to go, leaving Brooks and Lolly alone.

CHAPTER EIGHT

Like magic, Vance disappeared and in his place stood Harry taking a small silver scraper from his pocket and running it over the table cloth gathering crumbs. That's when Brooks noticed an odd tattoo on the waiter's wrist. A quiver with four arrows.

"And how did the first part of the evening turn out?" Harry asked.

Brooks knew the question was directed at Lolly even though Harry hadn't looked in her direction. So he turned his head, curious for her answer.

"I think the first part of the evening went well," she said. "Considering...."

"Considering you're with two complete morons who believe you're the answer to their waning youth?"

Lolly's mouth hung open, but the comment made Brooks burst out laughing.

"Harry! What the hell? Is this table bugged?" Brooks started running his hands underneath the edges of the table. "Who are you? CIA?"

Harry shook his head. "You wouldn't believe me if I told you. Now, if you'll bring your wine glasses and follow me please."

Brooks and Lolly looked at one another with raised eyebrows and then followed Harry out the back of the restaurant to a small deck where a lone, cloth-draped table for two glistened with votive candles. A full moon and smattering of stars shone bright in the night sky above a weeping willow planted just off the deck. The deck itself was a miniature Garden of Eden with ceramic pots of all shapes and sizes planted with everything from bamboo to gardenias. The surrounding scent lent even more enchantment.

Brooks held out a chair for Lolly while Harry nodded his approval and filled their wine glasses with what was left in the bottle. The soufflé, fresh from the oven, arrived as the last drop was poured, and Harry scooped it onto their awaiting plates with a flourish, adding a dollop of fresh whipped cream. He bowed and turned, disappearing without a word.

Brooks and Lolly stared at one another, wide-eyed.

"How do you know him?" Lolly asked, picking up her spoon to delve into the molten chocolate.

"I don't," Brooks insisted. "I met him one time at the Country Club. New Year's Eve."

"Then what is all…this?" Lolly circled her spoon, indicating their surroundings, the entire evening.

"I wish I knew," Brooks said. "Annabelle Devine told us he was magical. I don't get it, but he'll definitely be getting a darn good tip."

"This is delicious," Lolly moaned, licking her lips and sighing at the experience of pure chocolate bliss.

Brooks grinned, enjoying having Lolly seated across from him so he could study her expressions and still be close enough to touch. He reached out at the thought and rubbed a finger over her cheek.

"What?" she wondered, taking her napkin and wiping the place his finger had grazed. "Chocolate on my face?"

Brooks shook his head. "No…I just…." He turned his attention to his own dessert. "Lolly, I hope I haven't put you in an awkward position. Vance got this idea in his head and…well, as you might guess he's a tough one to talk out of anything."

He glanced up to see Lolly studying her dessert, shaking her head vehemently. "I'm happy to do what I can for Vance. After hearing his story I feel terribly under qualified." She put her spoon down and her eyes met his. "How much did you know?"

"None of the details," Brooks said. "I didn't get to know Vance until high school. We were the only two freshmen to make the varsity team and were hazed unmercifully. We bonded pretty quickly."

"You were hazed?"

"Big time. We were constantly being snapped with wet towels. They forced us to eat goldfish after a win. Brutal stuff I can't even get into. I had no idea that kind of shit went on. Almost made me quit the team. But Vance kept saying, 'Dude, we are gonna live through this. In the grand scheme of things, this is nothing.'

"I thought he was nuts until it dawned on me he'd been through worse. When I realized *he* was the kid whose mother had walked out, I figured he was right. Having to swallow a couple goldfish was nothing. So I sucked it up.

"That's when I introduced him to Lewis and the two of them got along right off the bat, talking about…stuff." Brooks shook his head. "Frankly I'm not sure what they talked about; it was all over my head. The three of us played a lot of video games, but those two are bookworms and I'm not…so they bonded."

Lolly sat back in disbelief. "Vance Evans? That Vance Evans, is a bookworm?"

Brooks chuckled and nodded.

"So when he said he was going to the library to get a book on tennis?"

"He's going to the library to get a book on tennis."

"Can you even learn to play tennis from a book?"

"Vance says you can learn anything from a book. Which is why he majored in English."

"He majored in English?" Lolly squealed.

Brooks sat back and laughed. "I know," he said throwing his arms wide. "Right?"

"Well, what's all this about his not being much of a cop?"

Brooks flashed his broad grin. "Ah, we love to tease him about that. He started out being full time, but over the past few years being a cop has become more of a pastime for Vance. But he's still got some special talents we rely on."

"What kind of talents?"

"He can speak Spanish, so he volunteers as a court interpreter. Actually, he's an interpreter for the precinct whenever we need one, which is more and more these days. He's one of the best shots on the force—"

"Better than you?" Lolly interrupted, smiling, goading him.

Brooks scoffed. "Now you're just being ridiculous."

Lolly laughed. He liked making her laugh.

"He's good, but he refuses to carry a gun," Brooks went on. "And he started the bicycle unit. Probably because he can't stand being inside, sitting still, or driving under the speed limit. He still contributes, but he's a coach first, an entrepreneur second, and a cop a distant third."

"An entrepreneur?"

Brooks shrugged. "Apparently the guy's been making money since he could talk. All I know is that he had enough stashed away five years ago to give Lewis seed money for his crazy App business. Which turned out to be a brilliant investment. Vance is probably as rich as his dad, but he still drives the same beat-up truck he bought when he was sixteen."

"He told me that he had paramedic training," Lolly added.

"Yeah, well we've all had that. But I will tell you this…." Brooks said, getting serious as he captured her regard. "He's kind, Lolly. Every Tuesday night he teaches English as a second language. Doesn't take a dime for it. He does it as a way to honor his grandmother. I know he's a snake when it comes to women, but that's because his mother left with his heart. He's either punishing the women he takes to bed because of her, or he's too afraid to let himself want more than sex. But now that he's facing thirty, I do believe he's trying to make a change. You may not be able to help him. I'm not sure anyone can. But I…" he hesitated, "I appreciate that you're willing to try."

Lolly simply nodded, chewing her lip.

"Lolly. If you spend time with him, he's going to hit on you."

Her eyes widened.

"He considers me his brother. I'm close to all he's got. And he'll still hit on you. He won't be able to help himself; it's how he relates to women. And I am probably asking you to do the impossible because I have never once seen a woman turn him down. But for his sake… and yours…."

Brooks went back to eating his soufflé.

"Why did you ask me out?"

Brooks' head shot up. That question came out of the blue and it was a direct one. *Why did I ask her out? Wow.* He carefully placed his spoon on the side of his plate, took his napkin from his lap, and wiped at the side of his mouth.

He could easily come up with several reasons that would be adequate. Instead, he decided not to lie.

"I don't want to tell you."

She smiled a quick smile like he'd made a joke. "You don't want to tell me?"

He shook his head. "Not tonight."

She opened her mouth but apparently couldn't think of anything to say. So she closed it and sat back from the table, letting both hands fall to her lap, still holding his gaze. He could almost see the calculations happening through the brilliant, blue gems of her eyes.

"You and I worked on a baseball statistics project, remember? I was a freshman in high school and you were a junior in college. You happened to come home for the weekend and got roped into helping me."

"It was a father-daughter team project. Darcy and Dad were on top of theirs. You needed a teammate. I'm a good teammate."

"You're the best teammate. I probably didn't even thank you, but I never forgot it. We got an A, by the way."

"You thanked me. You sent me the graded paper. I laughed when I opened the mail."

She cocked her head to the side. "So, considering our next team project, do you agree with Vance that most of the women you date would classify you as nice, safe, and boring?"

"I haven't dated anyone in close to a year."

"That's not what I asked."

He swallowed. He wasn't going to look away. And he wasn't going to lie to Lolly. Ever. "It would not surprise me if nine out of ten of the women I've dated since college would put me in the milquetoast category."

"Since college."

He nodded.

"What about high school?"

"I didn't date in high school. I was a late bloomer."

She didn't smirk or smile. "Okay," she said, leaning forward and picking up her spoon.

"Okay, what?"

"We can do this."

"Do what, exactly?"

"The Golden Boy of Henderson should never be classified as milquetoast. It's just…disappointing."

"Jesus," he muttered.

"And now that I'm aware you have aspirations to run for public office…well, I can understand how your reputation in all things is a concern. Carrying that dead weight into a date might make you seem a little milquetoast."

"You don't know the half of it."

Lolly gave him an empathetic smile. "You've been watching everything you say and do for a very long time, haven't you?"

He wasn't aware it was evident. Of course, considering who he was dealing with. "I…ah…." He let out a long breath and leaned back in his chair. This was Lolly. He wanted her to know the whole story. "For whatever reason, way back when, the press took to me. The first article came out during my freshman year. My parents were so proud and I thought it was great too, right up until some kid asked for my autograph."

"I don't understand."

"Well, as I looked at that kid and asked him his name, I remembered *being* that kid. I remembered being that age and looking up to Tucker Mayfield, a star on the varsity team at the time. Tucker had it all. He could hit, run, field, and pitch. He was smart, good-looking, got good grades—the girls loved him—hell, the whole town loved him.

"He was in the press all the time. Got a scholarship to fucking Princeton. Tucker Mayfield was *the* guy. He was the player I wanted to be. He was the son every parent wanted. And then…then he got caught selling cocaine the same night he'd beaten up his girlfriend and left her out by the lake."

Lolly's breath caught.

"Exactly," Brooks said, pointing at Lolly. "There I was signing my first autograph when Tucker Mayfield flashes before my eyes. In a split second, I remember my utter disappointment. My complete devastation. I remember how the entire town felt let down finding out their shining star was nothing but a drug-pushing bully. I remember my momma crying over the article in the paper. Worrying about Tucker's parents and what they were going through. I realized then that I didn't just have a responsibility to myself and my team to be the best player I could be, but now I had a responsibility to be a role model for this kid who held my autograph. I decided right there and then that I was not gonna let him down. I was not letting anybody down."

"And you haven't."

"Not yet, anyway."

Lolly leaned forward. "That fear. That stress I see all over your body. We are going to take care of that," she promised.

"How are you going to do that, exactly?"

"By promising that I will abstain from voting when and if you run for public office."

"How's that going to help?" Brooks asked, throwing up his arms in exasperation. "Sounds like I just lost a vote."

"It will help because you won't have to censor yourself around me. Whatever we discuss, whatever we do stays between us." She gave him a firm, I-swear-to-God nod before picking up her spoon again.

She glanced down at her plate and then back at him. "Actually," she blurted, holding up a finger, "I might want to get input from my girlfriends at school. I'm only one woman and not all women like the same things. If I'm going to help you and Vance, I'm going to need to do a little research to give you the full spectrum of the feminine perspective."

"Lolly," he interrupted.

"Yes?"

"I'm not interested in what other women want or think. I'm only interested in what you want. What you think."

Well, that shut her up, Brooks thought as her mouth hung open in the sexiest little O. He watched as Lolly took a deep breath and reached for her water glass, her midnight-blue eyes never leaving his.

"Remember a few years back when you and Darcy turned twenty-one and you and your wild bunch came into the Club for your first official drink? Well, I was there and...." *Just the basics, just give her the basics.* "And it occurred to me then that after you graduated from college and moved back to town, it'd be a good idea to ask you out."

"I graduated a year ago."

"Sort of."

"I still haven't moved back to town, really."

"I'm well aware."

"I might never move back," she whispered.

His heart constricted at the thought. He couldn't pull his gaze away from her eyes. "That's a chance I'll have to take."

When Lolly didn't respond, he broke eye contact and picked up his spoon, pretending to want another bite. "So here's *my* promise. I'm sure there will be plenty of reasons to kick me to the curb at summer's end, but I'm going to do my best to make sure nice, safe, and boring aren't three of them."

CHAPTER NINE

Vance enjoyed driving the Corvette. The Corvette suited him. It was fast. It was lean. It showed well. Plus, there was a lot going on under the hood most people wouldn't comprehend.

He drove past the library in a time-wasting, fruitless endeavor. He knew the library wasn't open on Sunday, but a drive-by of the traditional stone building hiding a surprisingly large and modern library always felt good. And even though he wasn't much of a cop, he did like to make sure no teenagers were roaming around looking for trouble.

He headed home, planning to hit Amazon and order a book on doubles tennis. Swinging through the red brick gates of the estate's main drive, he coasted over to the long detached garage, artistically designed to look like a stable. He parked the Corvette in its spot and surveyed the rest of the fleet. Nothing safe or boring. Lolly would appreciate them all.

He headed up the slope toward the pool, noticing lights coming from the back of the main house. He could see his father and grandmother standing at the kitchen island, laughing. Laughing?

Without conscious thought, he bore a path to the French doors and tapped briefly so as not to startle them when he opened the door and stepped inside.

His father, Hale, all of fifty-two, didn't look a day over forty, which made sense because his grandmother at seventy-eight rivaled Sophia Loren. Both were stunning to look at. His father with his square jaw, short-cropped dark hair, and constant day's growth of beard rivaled models half his age, while his grandmother exuded old-world grace and beauty, her red-to-brown hair always in an updo and her slim figure outfitted in upscale and appropriate fashion for a woman her age. Vance realized in that moment that his own looks and style paled in comparison to those of these previous two generations.

Their jovial mood broadened as he entered, love and appreciation shining from their faces at the unexpected family gathering. The joy directed at him caused two polar reactions at once. While it soothed the long-standing ache in his chest to a good degree, it also struck a raw and sensitive nerve. How could he live up to that kind of love?

He couldn't. But he could do his best to return it. "Abuela," he acknowledged with a wide grin and a kiss on both cheeks.

"Dad," he laughed as he caught his father's outstretched hand before being reeled in for a rare hug. "No early morning meeting in the outlands tomorrow?" It was his father's standard operating procedure to fly out Sunday evening to wherever his private equity business was improving some long-standing family-owned business. That or to wherever he was scouting out future investments.

With a brief glance at his grandmother, his father responded with a satisfied, almost exuberant smile. "I've found a potential opportunity right here in town. It looks like I'll be sticking around here for a while. Hope that doesn't cramp your style."

Vance simply stared at him, unable to stop smiling. He couldn't put into words how he'd longed for something to capture his father's attention enough to keep him home. But the words that did tumble forth came without premeditated thought. "Does this have anything to do with a certain yellow Spyder I've seen parked conspicuously close to your car whenever you're in town?"

His father's grin told him more than he'd bargained for. "Really?" Vance's eyes went wide. "Is there something you want to tell me?"

Hale cleared his throat and looked to the marble flooring below his feet. "Well, I just let Mama in on this." He snuck a look at his mother before fastening his dark gaze on his son. "So I may as well face all the inevitable prying questions now. Yes. That little Spyder is not only my next equity investment. The owner of the company and I have…." He looked flustered. "Well, let's say, we've been developing a personal relationship as well as a business one. We've kept it under wraps, not from the two of you so much as from the town in general. You know how the gossip hounds like a good story and never get the facts right. The Spyder has some complicated relationships that aren't worth inciting if we don't hit it off. Why borrow trouble?"

"Agreed, but I want to meet her. I'm sure Vance does, too," Emelina insisted in her heavily Spanish-accented English. "A woman who has captured this much of your attention after so many years is someone I am very eager to meet." She reached over and knocked invisible lint off her son's shoulder, as warm a gesture as she was capable. "Especially if she is going to do the impossible and keep you in town for more than two days in a row."

Hale laughed and Vance couldn't take his eyes off his father. He'd never seen him like this. Happy? Yes. His dad looked happy. Young. Fit. Energetic. Dynamic even. In a good way. Not the usual tightly wound Type A persona he'd grown to respect. No, this man in front of him was a version of his father he had yet to meet.

"I will extend an invitation, Mama. And we'll allow the owner of the yellow Spyder to accept or decline as she sees fit."

"It's Lolly's mother," Vance declared.

His father's head popped up in surprise before he smiled a slow, shy smile. When did his father become capable of shy? Vance watched as Hale's mouth twisted, clearly wrestling with the decision to let them further into his secret. Unable to play the game, Vance blurted, "I saw the car. When I picked up Lolly tonight. I asked if it was her mother's."

His grandmother gasped with alarm. "You aren't dating this woman's daughter, are you?"

Vance didn't take his eyes off his father's face, but he shook his head in the negative. "We are endeavoring to become friends," he answered his grandmother. Then to his father he quietly stated, "If she's anything like her daughter, you've won the lottery. Don't screw it up."

Hale grinned as if life had bestowed on him an embarrassment of riches. "Her name is Genevra." He said it with great awe. "Genevra DuVal. I have not had the pleasure of meeting her daughter. And I don't know when Genevra is going to tell her about us. So, if you wouldn't mind—"

"Discretion is my middle name," Vance assured him.

His grandmother huffed indignantly. "Not from what I hear," she scolded underneath her breath. "Leave your father to the DuVal ladies if you will. We don't need more scandal raining down around us."

"Abuela, you wound me. Do you have any idea the kind of energy it takes to create and sustain a reputation worthy of the Evans name? Frankly, it's about time Dad jumped in here and helped me out."

Hale rubbed his head in waning enthusiasm. "Yes, well, it's entirely likely I'll be soaking up the limelight when the news breaks. I'm mostly concerned about Genevra's in-laws. All those DuVals. They don't know me. It could go either way with them. And even so, our little Spyder driver has kept to herself for a very long time. It's bound to be news."

Emelina snorted inelegantly, causing both masculine heads to turn in her direction. "Get your heads out of your asses, will you? Henderson is going to be mad for this. They all think you are gay!" she shouted at her beloved son. Then she flung her hand toward Vance. "And they think you are trying to make up for it with all your tomcatting around."

"Gay?" Hale and Vance shouted.

"What the hell are you talking about?" Hale followed up.

"Well, of course," Emelina said, clearly exasperated. "When your wife up and leaves you and you spend the next twenty-five years rebuffing the advances of every woman in town, single or married, well…what do you expect?"

"Gay?" Hale said again, rubbing his hands through his hair. "Shit!"

Vance was laughing so hard he could hardly make a sound. His eyes were tearing, his face was squinched up in glee and he held his stomach because he could barely catch his breath. "Oh, this is classic!" he squeaked out through his mirth. "No wonder you can't get a regular game at the Club."

"Shit. Shit. Shit. Why didn't you tell me?" Hale yelled at his mother. "I would have endeavored to dispel the rumors had I known."

She shrugged with a how-was-I-to-know-you-weren't-gay face.

"Are you insane?" he said in disbelief. Vance bent over in hysteria.

"Well, darling boy, it will all come out soon enough," his mother assured him. "Hopefully Mrs. DuVal isn't as discreet as she seems. A few innuendos to her best friends and the word will spread. You'll be back to being heterosexual toot sweet."

Hale groaned, sliding the palms of his hands up his forehead and over his hair. "Again! Shit!"

"What?" his mother implored. "What is with all this cursing?"

"I have yet to give Genevra a truly intriguing reason to throw innuendos around."

"Well, why the hell not?" Emelina yelled, while tears of mirth slid down Vance's face.

Through unrelenting and almost painful laughter, Vance squeezed out, "Oh, this just keeps getting better."

"We've been taking it slow," he yelled. "We aren't adolescents like the boy here, for God's sake. I've been…romancing her," he admitted more quietly.

His mother granted him a genuine smile. And Vance did his best to choke back his riotous laughter. "I'm sorry, Dad. It all just struck me as ridiculous," he said, wiping his eyes and simmering his amusement.

His dad broke into a short smile and then smirked. "All of Henderson thinks I'm gay. Well, that explains a lot, I suppose." He rubbed his forehead. "But what do I care, really? As long as Mrs. DuVal is willing to stick around long enough for me to prove otherwise."

❧

Brooks entered his home that evening with a returned sense of optimism. The night had gone better than anticipated. Thanks to Harry's magic, he felt like he'd been on a second date with Lolly rather than a co-ed group assignment led by Vance.

Lolly.

His mind went a little fuzzy at the memory of her tongue against his. He stood inside his refurbished ranch home allowing the feeling to drift over him again as he relived the kiss. All the little ones that led to the long one. And the long one that led to her itty-bitty moan in his mouth. That led to his hands finding their way to her ass, which led to her running her fingers through his hair and saying his name, which led to him pressing her against his erection....

God, she was hot. Hotter than he anticipated and man, didn't that jack this shit up another hundred notches.

He opened his eyes—unaware that he'd closed them—and looked around his home, seeing it through Lolly's eyes.

Fucking A.

He pulled out his cell and phoned his sister as he walked down the hall to his bedroom, unbuttoning his shirt as her phone rang.

"You haven't apologized to Lewis yet."

Motherfucker. He didn't have time for this shit, he really didn't. He took a deep breath. "Is Lewis there?"

"Yes."

"Put him on."

"Hey," came Lewis' voice.

"Sorry! Now put Darcy back on the phone."

"Right. Okay then," Lewis said, his anxiety clearly relieved. Brooks smiled.

"You've got to be kidding me," Darcy scolded.

Brooks interrupted. He had to. Because if he didn't, he'd just hang up on her, and if he hung up on her this wouldn't get done. "Darcy, you were right."

Dead silence.

Brooks looked at the phone and then smiled. "Man, if I knew it would get that kind of reaction I would have said it a long time ago."

"What am I right about?"

"My house. It looks like a man-cave. Which has been fine and what I wanted...up until now. Now, I need that—" *Fucking A* "woman's touch you were—" *blathering,* "educating me about. Can you do it?"

There were three heartbeats of silence. Three heartbeats where this deal teetered on the brink of life. Because if his sister said one wrong word, this conversation was over. Gratefully she offered the only words Brooks could stand to hear.

"Give me your credit card information. I'll take care of

everything."

"Thank you," he said on an exhale, pulling out his wallet. He read her the credit card number and expiration date and agreed to new bedding for the master and guest bedrooms, along with art, throw pillows, and accessories for the great room. His sister seemed to know when to quit, so when he thanked her again, he really meant it. "And you'll make it look…like me, right? Not New York."

"It will be you, only better," she assured him.

Me, only better. Well, he figured, that was the least he could offer Lolly DuVal. Which reminded him….

"Darcy, why are you and Lolly so dead set on seeing Henderson in your rearview mirror?"

"Hmm, let me try to put this into words you'll understand. Henderson is not New York or Boston or D.C. It's not even Richmond."

"Great places to visit if you like that kind of thing. But to live life day-to-day? How can you not see that this town is a Field of Dreams? Once Vance and I put our economic plan into effect, it's going to be *the* place to live, work, and raise a family in the mid-Atlantic. Mark my words. And frankly, I'm starting to take it personally that you won't move your business here and show a little support."

"I don't own my own business, Brooks."

"Well you could, that's for damn sure. Your video game is still a top seller. Quit working for somebody else and start your own damn company. And bring that ungrateful fiancé of yours with you when you do. His company alone could employ half the town."

"Listen, if you want Lolly to come back to Henderson, you need to convince her to do it."

"I'm in no position to convince Lolly to do anything."

"But that's what this conversation is about, isn't it?"

"Yes and no."

"How much yes and how much no?"

Brooks rubbed his chin. "It's all part and parcel of what I want for this town and my life, and there's no denying Lolly's wrapped up in that good."

"Well…you have good taste. And it's only going to get better now that I have your credit card," she assured him before hanging up.

Getting into bed that night, Brooks found a dog-eared, rag-tag paperback novel on his pillow. There was a Post-it note covering the title with Vance's tell-tale scrawl. *'As promised, my secrets of success. (And I am dead serious.)'*

Brooks ripped off the Post-it and read the cover.

His Wicked Ways by Samantha James.

Fucking A.

CHAPTER TEN

Monday morning, Brooks sat at his desk looking over three Youth Protective Ordinance violations involving the same fifteen-year-olds caught hanging out past curfew last month. He'd offered to meet with the boys and their parents this time and chuckled, thinking he should take Vance with him. A bit of their good cop, bad cop reputations might serve them well during this visit. His cell vibrated in his pocket.

It was a text from Lolly. *'Ran with Vance. Kept his hands to himself.'*
He texted back. *'Glad to hear it.'*
'Does he own Tenderfoot? Acted like it. Bossy.'
Brooks laughed, texting back, *There is a high probabvility.* Then he texted a new message. *'Enjoyed last night.'*
And as he sent that off, Lolly's came in. *'Still reeling from the kiss last night.'*
Brooks about split his face smiling. *Damn woman doesn't beat around the bush much.* He texted back. *'My point exactly.'* But he didn't think she'd appreciate knowing he'd woken up early this morning thinking about that kiss and had to take himself in hand to be able to make it through the day without a perpetual hard-on. His idea of taking it slow where Lolly was concerned was not going to be easy. Especially with the whole nice, safe, boring thing hanging over his head like a guillotine. Where the hell was he supposed to draw the line between being a gentleman, respecting Lolly, and not being classified as nice, safe, or boring?

And a paperback titled *His Wicked Ways* probably wasn't going to help him figure that out. Fucking A.

Vance arrived in his running attire, sweating and breathing hard. Bent at the waist, he took a few deep breaths and offered, "I didn't touch her."

Hmm. "Did you want to touch her?"

Vance stood erect, squinting as sweat fell into his eyes. He swiped a hand across his brow and then used the bottom of his shirt to wipe his face. "Who wouldn't want to touch her?"

Brooks smiled at that. What could he say?

"She's built for running. Long, long legs. Lean. Tiny ass. Firm," he said, before sucking in another deep breath, grabbing his foot from behind and pulling it up to stretch his thigh, "Not a lot of cleavage going on that she has to worry with. I tell you her body—"

"Enough!"

"Oh. Sorry. Yeah. I was just, um, admiring the running form. Seriously. I…you know."

"Whatever. Shut the hell up."

"Done." Vance hopped on Brooks' desk like he always did.

"Do you own Tenderfoot?"

"If by own, you mean do I have controlling interest in the place, then yes."

"Isn't that the type of thing your dad does?"

"Sort of. Yes. I figured with as much money as I spend on running shoes and apparel, I might as well be buying from myself. Plus, I make sure they stock what I like."

"Right. So, what the hell is this?" Brooks slapped the dog-eared paperback he'd found on his bed onto his desk.

Vance covered it with his hand and looked around quickly. "Christ, I told you this was top secret. What the hell did you bring it here for? I do not want this getting around." He grabbed a file folder, dumped out its contents, and stuffed the book inside. "I've got a mind to take it home and keep it under lock and key."

"Please tell me how a stolen library book with a ridiculous title could possibly be your secret weapon."

"Just so you know, I felt very guilty about stealing that book. But…I took care of it."

Brooks cracked a grin. "What do you mean, you took care of it?"

"When I became an officer here, I replaced the copy anonymously and left a hundred dollar bill as a bookmark. You know me. I love the library. Plus, let's face it. That book has garnered me a lot of lovin'."

"See, that's what I don't get. How is that possible?"

Vance leaned closer and talked in a low tone. "Back when we were freshmen, maybe right after we met, I was hot, hot, hot for one Marla May Higgins." Brooks squinched up his nose. "I know, she wasn't the cream of the crop, but she sat next to me in algebra and back then proximity was all it took. So one afternoon—at your house as a matter of fact—I overheard women talking in the kitchen. You had run upstairs to grab your mitt and I was waiting there. I don't know if it was your mom or not, because I didn't know her well enough then. Anyway, one of them said that if a man really wanted to know what a woman wants, he should read *His Wicked Ways*. Since I had no idea how to even talk to Marla May, I figured I could use information like that. So I repeated the title over and over in my head until I couldn't forget it. It took me two weeks to find the damn book in the library and then there was no way in hell I was gonna check out a book with a cover and title like that. So I stole it."

"Right. So you're telling me that you read this book, and from this work of fiction, you've managed to seduce countless women over the past fifteen years?"

"Correct. Got to second base with Marla May. Which I gotta tell you was so easy I decided to set my sights higher. Worked like a charm. Now, I'm not saying I was the ruiner of virgins. I'm just saying by the time I hit college, having read this book a half-dozen times and practiced on a variety of females, I could charm the pants off most anyone I wanted."

Brooks stared in disbelief. "Because of this book?"

"Well, I'd like to think it's because of my good looks and charm, but yeah, the book allowed me a glimpse into what women want. How they want to be treated. What their fantasies are. And it answered the age-old question: How the hell is it possible for a dork to end up with a hot babe?"

"I don't believe this."

"In truth, this book got the ball rolling. Once I figured out the basics, I started reading up on all kinds of…you know, skills."

"Skills?"

"Bedroom skills, idiot." Vance hit Brooks over the head with the file. "Which is all well and good and makes boring sex better, but… the key to getting to the bedroom in the first place is romance." At that, Vance shut up abruptly and appeared lost in thought.

"And this book teaches romance?"

Vance blinked and then rolled his eyes. "This book shows the proverbial romantic hero in action. Back in the day. It's your job to translate yourself into Lolly's modern day romantic hero."

Brooks wasn't even sure what that meant, and his face must have shown it.

"Just read the damn book. This whole conversation never should have happened." Vance shook his body like he was getting freaked out. "But I've got something else I want your opinion on and…well, let me just tell you everything. Then you give me your gut reaction. I don't want to…you know, discuss it, okay? Just tell me what you think and we'll move on."

Brooks sat back in his chair, crossed his arms over his chest, and indicated Vance had the floor.

Vance ran a hand through his hair, looking around the room and making sure no one overheard him. Then he placed both hands on the desk and looked at Brooks in earnest. "That girl I told you and Lolly about last night. The one in fourth grade."

Brooks nodded, his gut tightening as he thought about how Vance had suffered.

"Well, I've sort of found her. I used the resources available to me here to get her full name, her parents' names, et cetera. And then I Googled her. Turns out she's an attorney in Raleigh. Just an hour away. Apparently her dad got a job in the Research Triangle, and she's been living just down the road all these years. I was wondering if I should call our lawyer pal, Duncan, and see if he has a contact at her law firm. See if he can, you know, find out if she's married or whatever."

"So you want to contact her if she's not?"

"I'm thinking about it. I've been thinking about it for a while now. She's just…you know…someone I haven't forgotten. I know we were just in fourth grade, so it's squirrelly. But, whatever."

Embarrassed, Vance hopped off the desk and started to move away.

Brooks understood—in fact, all too well. He slid his chair closer to the desk, moving his hands nervously above the surface while he debated exposing more than he wanted to about his situation with Lolly. Finally he forced himself to call out, "Third Base!"

When Vance turned, Brooks looked him in the eye. "If someone had made that kind of difference in my life, I'd do whatever it took to find her. And then I wouldn't let her go."

When the silence stretched out between them, Brooks lifted a brow. "Besides. It's romantic." Then he reached across his desk and grabbed the file he'd copied the day before. "Read this at your leisure and then tell me what you think."

"What is it?" Vance came forward and took the file in hand, opening it and scanning the contents.

"It's a very old file on Jake DuVal."

"Jake DuVal? Is that…?"

Brooks nodded. "Lolly's dad."

Genevra DuVal drove her sporty little yellow Spyder home from work with the top down. It was a top-down kind of day, and if she wasn't worried about being overheard she'd be singing along with the radio as loud as she could. She absolutely loved having Hale Evans in her office. And that thought made her smile as she cruised to the curb and put her Spyder in park.

She laid her head back against the black leather and closed her eyes, smiling—relishing the feeling of having Hale in her life. The fact that their personal relationship was still a secret had her laughing out loud and popping her eyes open. The two of them working in the same environment and not raising eyebrows was becoming more and more challenging. Even though she adored keeping what was blossoming between them quiet, the sexual tension was currently hitting 7.5 on the Richter scale and heading higher. Pretending they were only business associates was getting trickier by the day.

She turned her head and eyed the mailbox. Hale had hinted about another letter. She stretched her arms over her head, grinning into the sun and basking in anticipation. She pictured the growing stack of ecru-colored Crane notecards, each neatly tucked back into its envelope. After he'd sent the fifth one, she'd spent her lunch break picking out the perfect satin ribbon with which to tie them together. She hid them in her lingerie drawer. The man was such a romantic his letters deserved to be treated likewise. But in truth, these brief notes—that always told her more than Hale himself could voice—were her most precious treasures. And that thought had her chest tightening and expanding all at the same time.

The first one had arrived a few days after they met. A business lunch was already on the calendar but this note—written in beautiful penmanship and undoubtedly with his ever-present Monte Blanc pen—made her pulse leap.

> *I'd like to take you to dinner. Somewhere out of town.*
> *Nothing business. Just personal.*
> *-Hale Evans*

The next one had arrived the day after dinner.

> *You looked so beautiful, I was tongue-tied.*
> *Allow me the opportunity to show off my conversational skills.*
> *7:00 Friday night.*
> *-Hale*

And then the note that arrived tucked into two dozen yellow roses.

> *These remind me of the way you make me feel. Thank you.*
> *H-*

And then they kept coming. Some were just a sentence. Others were funny or poignant. All caused her heart to soar and her hormones to tingle. And oh, God, did that feel good. So. Very. Good. And yet, they'd taken things slow. So. Very. Slow.

After a dozen dates, countless notes, numerous business meetings, and working together side by side as Hale invested money, time, and energy into her tiny accounting firm, her hormones were raging far more than they were tingling. And now she seemed to be in a constant state of tingling anticipation for *when*. When was Hale Evans finally going to make his move?

She shook off the surge of sexual tension and got out of the car with her sights set on the mailbox. *Please let there be another note.* Something more to feed her starving libido. She pulled down the flap and glanced inside, finding catalogs and flyers and a few bills. But, gratefully amongst all of it, she spied the treasured stationery on which Hale wrote his personal notes.

As she headed up her porch steps, she pulled the envelope from the rest and held it to her nose, hoping to get a whiff of his cologne. Opening the screen door, she stepped inside and heard the whirl of a sewing machine. Guiltily she gave in to the desire to read Hale's note alone and quietly moved up the stairs, hoping Lolly wouldn't realize she was home. She was acting like an adolescent, but she didn't care because her whole body felt adolescent. Young. Healthy. Vibrant. Alive! Sensations she'd given up on long, long ago for Lolly. Because of Lolly. And even though she wouldn't want it any other way, she was so grateful and relieved to be getting another go at it all now.

Hale had changed her life for the better the day he walked into it. And if he chose to walk out tomorrow, she would always think of him kindly.

Think of him kindly, she thought—dumping the rest of the mail on her desk and throwing herself on the bed with his note clasped to her heart—but do her best to drag him kicking and screaming back into it. She laughed at the thought and then carefully opened the envelope, slowing down and savoring the moment.

> *I think it's time you met my mother.*
> *She's invited you to dinner at your convenience.*
> *-Hale*
> *P.S. Rest assured, I am not gay.*

What! She sat up and read the line over and over. *Gay? Gay! Why would I think he's gay?* She most definitely did not think he was gay. *There was no way in hell Hale Evans was gay.* She rolled off the bed and grabbed her cell from her purse, planning to text him. Then stopped and smiled. *Oh, why not have a little fun with this?*

She moved across the room to sit at her desk, pulling the box of elegant stationery to her. She lifted the lid and folded back the stiff tissue that covered the pale yellow notes. Pink was too obvious, and this color reminded her of his roses. She'd never responded in writing before but bought these when she'd searched out the ribbon to wrap his letters in, just in case.

Now seemed like as good a time as any to break in her correspondence skills. She searched the drawer for her favorite pen.

> *I look forward to meeting your mother*
> *and will gladly arrange my schedule around her pleasure.*
> *Thank you, Gen*
>
> *P.S. Prove it!*

She smiled as she read the note back, wondering how the business tycoon in her life was going to react to the blatant challenge. She was just tingling to find out.

CHAPTER ELEVEN

On Tuesday morning, Brooks received a text from Lolly telling him that Vance tried to hold her hand while they rested on the ground after a hard sprint. When Vance arrived at work, he headed straight toward Brooks and said, "I tried to hold the Lollypop's hand. She blew me off." Then he walked away.

Brooks smirked.

On Wednesday, Brooks' cell beeped indicating a new text from Lolly. This one made his eyebrows raise. *'Kissed me. TRIED to kiss me. I took care of it.'* Vance must have jogged over to the station before going home because he arrived in his running clothes covered in sweat. "I tried to kiss her," he said without preamble. "She kneed me in the balls." Brooks broke out in boisterous laughter and didn't have time to find out more details before Vance took off.

On Thursday, Brooks started looking forward to the text message updates on Lolly handling Vance. *'Pulled my hair then ran away. What? Are we in fourth grade?'*

It seemed Lolly was going to be able to handle herself around Vance, so Brooks stopped looking for reasons to be jealous.

When the text came in on Friday, his eyebrows rose halfway to his hairline. *'Smacked me on the butt. I deserved it.'* When Vance arrived at his desk late that morning he held up his palms and said, "She deserved it." The look on Vance's face told him that he was none too happy about whatever had transpired, so Brooks let it drop.

It was almost the end of the day on Friday, and Vance knew if he put the call off any longer he wouldn't be able to sleep over the weekend. So he stood outside the precinct, leaning against his beat-up old pickup truck and dialed Duncan's work number. Thankfully, the receptionist said he was there.

"Duncan," Vance started, "I need a favor if you can do it."

"You got it."

That made Vance smile. "Thanks, Dunc," he said a bit shyly. After the way he'd given his buddy such a hard time over his girl, this was akin to crawling on his knees begging forgiveness. He should have figured Duncan wouldn't be an ass about it.

"Are you familiar with the law firm Collins & Reese?"

"I am. They are litigators. Completely different from what we do here."

"There's a girl who works for Collins & Reese. I'm not sure what she does, but she's a lawyer and her name is Piper Beaumont. She and I were in fourth grade together and…well, here's the thing, Dunc. It's going to sound crazy, but she pretty much saved my life back then. Her father moved her out of town after school let out, and I never heard from her again. So lately, I've been thinking. Just wondering where she ended up, you know. And it appears she is right there in Raleigh. Working for this Collins & Reese. I was wondering if you might happen to know someone there and if you could do a little research for me."

"What do you want to know?"

What did he want to know? Hell, he wanted to know if she remembered him. He wanted to know if she was still as sweet as she was back then. If life had been kind to her. There wasn't anything he didn't want to know.

"Ah. I'm not exactly sure."

"Why don't you just friend her on Facebook?"

"Well, for one, I'm not thirteen. And two, clearly you've forgotten the nightmare I had on my hands during the two weeks I did have a Facebook page. I literally considered changing my name."

"Oh, yeah. All those girls, finding out about all those other girls. Yeah. Facebook is not for you. Okay. Well, let me do a little checking around. Off the top of my head, I don't know anyone there personally. But maybe someone else here does. I'm sure there's a small degree of separation somewhere."

"Thanks, Duncan. I appreciate this, man."

"No problem."

"Listen. You and Annabelle play tennis right? How 'bout coming up and giving Lolly and me a game? We need practice. She's got me roped into this doubles tennis tournament at the Club and I don't want to let her down. How's this weekend? We could have lunch or dinner?"

There was a bit of hesitation before Duncan responded. "Sure. We'd love to. Let me talk to Annabelle and I'll call you back."

"Great. Thanks. And, ah...thanks," Vance said before hanging up. He looked at his phone and shook his head. "I am such an ass."

Whenever Brooks Bennett's cell phone rang while he was driving, he did the same thing he cautioned all the kids to do. He pulled off the road, put the truck in park, and then answered his phone. And wasn't that just the biggest pain in the ass. But he did it because the one time he didn't do it, he was sure someone would be snapping his photo and selling it to the *Henderson Daily Newspaper*. As a cop, he had to practice what he preached. As the Golden Prince of Henderson, or whatever Vance was calling him these days, he had to be seen doing it. And, as the hopeful future mayor, he wanted to do it. Wanted everyone to do it.

So when his cell started ringing on his way to Lolly's Friday evening, he turned into the corner gas station and pulled up by the air pumps to answer it.

"Hey, Duncan! How's it going?" The phone calls from Duncan were rare these days, and he didn't even mind being a little late for Lolly now that he knew who was calling.

"Brooks! Everything's good on this end. How 'bout you?"

"Couldn't be better," Brooks responded in his typical fashion.

"Okay...so why the hell is Vance playing tennis with Lolly?"

"Oh. That." Brooks chuckled. "Well, that's a little experiment we are running here in Henderson. The 'Vance Can Be Friends With a Girl' hypothesis."

"I'm not sure that's going to hold up. Why are you allowing Lolly to be the guinea pig?"

Brooks' enthusiasm for the conversation dwindled. He sucked in a breath and tore a hand through his hair. "Listen, Dunc. As a result of that conversation we had back in March, Vance has decided to make a change. Lolly has gone into this with her eyes wide open and I've got her back."

"All well and good, buddy, but who's got yours?"

Brooks' heart stopped. Stopped because Duncan had just stomped all over it while wading into his worst fears. Duncan expected Lolly to fall for Vance.

"I had no choice."

"You always have a choice. But, hey…maybe I'm out of line. Maybe way off base. I saw you and Lolly together and just thought there was something there. Something more. I kinda liked the idea of you and Lolly."

Brooks did too. "You aren't off base. Your concern is duly noted and appreciated. I can only tell you that I've been as up front with Lolly and Vance as I can be. And I'm staying on top of the situation as best I can."

"All right. I'm backing you up on this. If we need to kick his ass, let's be pre-emptive. Now who is Piper Beaumont and why does Vance need to add her to the mix?"

"Oh!" Brooks smiled, his mood lightning significantly. "Well, that's good news if he called you about Piper. And better news for me if you can find this woman and she's single."

"Who the hell is she to him?"

"Oh man, Duncan. This girl was like the only person there for Vance when his mother left. He was just a little kid and no one would talk to him about it. This Piper Beaumont did, apparently. And then her father moved the family out of town over the summer…."

"Yeah, that's pretty much what he said, though I didn't know it had anything to do with his mother. We've never talked about that."

"No, we haven't. Which doesn't say much for us but says a lot about this fourth grade girl. Frankly, I'd like to know what happened to her."

"Okay. I'm on it. Really on it. I'll find her one way or another."

"And if you hit a dead end, Vance and I have a few connections in the police department over there we can hit up."

"Well, if she works for Collins & Reese it should be easy. I'll keep you posted. Oh, and Annabelle and I are driving up tomorrow to play tennis with Vance and your girlfriend."

"What the hell?"

"I know! Right? Unless you are planning a threesome, this has trouble written all over it."

Brooks squeezed his eyes together. "Don't mention a threesome. Vance is all over that idea."

Duncan laughed. "I'll just bet he is. Don't worry, bro. I'll find Miss Beaumont, and we'll drag her hopefully single and shapely ass back to Henderson and get Lolly off the hook."

"The sooner, the better, Dunc. The sooner, the better."

Brooks disconnected the call and sat staring out his windshield at nothing at all. He'd be hard-pressed to find words to make Duncan understand all he had riding on this deal with Vance. Because he was just beginning to comprehend it himself.

Yes, the deal appeared catastrophically idiotic—he'd give Duncan that. And perhaps, in the end, that's exactly how it would turn out. After all, Vance was getting to spend time with Lolly every day while Brooks was stuck reading a romance novel and had acquired only one, albeit quite effective, bad cop move.

But it was Friday night and Brooks was the one picking Lolly up for a date. A date where he held insider information, thanks to Vance pointing out that the key to Miss DuVal was being the antithesis of nice, safe, and boring. For that alone, he figured he owed Vance big.

Plus—ultimately and selfishly—Vance was Brooks' right arm when it came to implementing the plans he had for this town. And he'd really, really like to have a healthy, working, and reliable right arm. Since Duncan and Lewis were no longer day-to-day members of their band of brothers, it had fallen to Brooks alone to put out the fires of Vance's occasional mood swings and to mend fences where Vance's wrath had let loose and laid low.

Brooks knew it was nothing short of a miracle that Vance was now interested in adopting a more sociable attitude toward women. Whatever Vance's own endgame, if Lolly could help Vance change his standard operating procedure where women were concerned, this bargain they'd struck would be worth all of the risk.

It might look like a threesome, but one way or another, adding Lolly to his life meant she was implanted into Vance's life as well. By doing it this way, the risk was obvious. He could lose the one he wanted most to Vance.

But the reward was great. He just might get to keep them both.

CHAPTER TWELVE

It had been five long days since Brooks had set eyes on Lolly.

During the work week he'd texted her, chatted with her on the phone, thought about her a lot, and worried about her a little. Work was hectic and kept him busy, but he'd carved out time each night to read Vance's ridiculous novel—his secret weapon—in hopes of having a better understanding of what women want.

Ultimately, he had no clue. No clue at all. How the hell was he supposed to glean any kind of real information from a fictional tale involving a Scottish chieftain from the early 1200s?

He stepped out of his F-150, deciding to give up the effort of understanding Vance and the book when he heard a screen door slam. His head popped up and his heart sputtered to a brief halt. Fluffy brunette curls drifted down over bare shoulders and onto a strapless white eyelet dress which had a ruffle at the top, a ruffle at the bottom, and not a hell of a lot of material in between. His eyes took in a good length of exposed thigh that turned into sweet little knees and just a little lower an un-Lolly-like surprise: a pair of red cowboy boots.

"Hey, Cowgirl," he called, taking in the entirety of the pretty picture she made.

"Hey, Sheriff," she cooed, tilting her head to the side and putting a hand on one hip.

"Ready for a rodeo?" he asked, starting slowly up the stairs. He ached to put his hands everywhere. On her waist. On her shoulders. On her thighs. Jesus, under that dress.

"If a rodeo is what you've got in mind," she said, grabbing the center of his shirt as he stepped onto the landing.

"You sure look pretty," he whispered over lipstick-red lips, tucking a strand of hair behind her ear.

"I have a big date," she whispered back playfully, batting long lashes over the deep blue of her eyes. "But first, Momma would like to meet you, if you don't mind."

"Nothin' I'd like better," Brooks assured her.

But they both continued to stand there, eyes locked, hands touching, smiles full. Brooks considered five days of not seeing each other might have worked out okay. She shrugged and gave a quick giggle, turning and leading him into the modest and cheerful cottage home.

Brooks admired her hips, her ass, and the backs of those silky thighs as he followed those cowboy boots through the house and onto a screened-in porch the size of a family room. It was charming with cozy wicker chairs and ottomans, side tables, lamps, and rugs. There was a long folding table set up on the far side loaded down with a sewing machine, fabric, and other assorted creative debris. A mannequin in the corner caught his eye, but his attention was pulled away as Lolly's mother stood in greeting.

Holy Mother of God....

Genevra DuVal was a Brunette Bombshell, to coin a new phrase. Comparing her with a dark-haired Marilyn Monroe occurred to Brooks for many reasons, one being the retro-styled navy and white sundress she wore. Mrs. DuVal was a knock-out. A knock-out surely dressed for a date because no woman should be sitting alone in her house looking like this. His eyes shot between Lolly and her mother as they stood side by side. They looked like sisters, he thought. *Mrs. DuVal looks just like Lolly but with a fuller...a rounder...Jesus Christ.* Brooks swallowed.

"Brooks Bennett, in the flesh," Genevra said in a charming southern-belle accent. She was radiant with her hair piled up in a hot mess and her aquamarine eyes shining over a warm and engaging smile.

"Hello, Mrs. DuVal," Brooks said as he clasped her outstretched hand, hoping against hope his eyes weren't bugging out of his head.

"It's a pleasure."

"The pleasure is mine. While your sister, Darcy, is practically my second daughter and I know your parents as well as just about anybody, you, the favored son of Henderson, have proved as elusive to my acquaintance as any town hero ought to be."

"Simply biding my time, waiting for Lolly to grow up," Brooks said, smiling. "And it's good to finally meet her momma."

"Well, you're as charming as everyone says. Do you have time to sit for a minute?"

"Absolutely," Brooks nodded, seating himself in a comfortable white rocking chair across from the women. He crossed his legs at the ankle, glad he'd worn a new pair of flat-front khakis and the turquoise polo shirt his mother said matched his eyes.

"How do you like working for the police department?" Genevra asked.

"I enjoy it very much. It allows me an insider's view of our town and its citizens."

"I'll bet," Genevra smiled. "I'm sure more than a few give you a run for your money."

"That they do," he said, nodding a smile. "But it's a great opportunity to see where we excel as a community and where we fall short."

"And here I assumed y'all were solely focused on giving out speeding tickets."

"Well, there is that…." He smiled. "Which I have to admit is a lot of fun on most days. I know so many of the people I pull over that it's hard to keep a straight face as they try to worm their way out of a ticket. I've had the opportunity to pull my mom over more than once."

"You pulled over your mother?" Lolly said, shocked.

"Sure did. That woman has a lead foot. Always has."

"You didn't give her a ticket though, did you?"

"Of course!" He winked. "But the biggest part of my job these days is keeping a lid on the teenagers. Now that school is out, they don't know what to do with themselves. So the police department is determined to keep a large profile in an effort to keep them out of trouble."

"Are you worried about vandalism?" Genevra asked.

"A little bit, but in a rural community like ours where we have the farms and the lake, it's more about safety. The kids have a lot of freedom and there's always the potential for fires starting and boats tipping over. On top of that, most kids around here have learned to drive a tractor or a boat long before they are eligible for their driver's license. So we get a lot of underage drivers cruising through town while their parents are unaware." He gave a short laugh, looking down at his feet and then back up to meet her eyes. "To tell you the truth, it hasn't changed much since I was that age."

"I swear, Lolly's dad was one of those boys you'd be sitting on tight." She laughed. "He and his brothers were rule-followers by day and hell-raisers by night. If Emma DuVal ever had a clue what her precious sons were doing back then, she'd have packed them up and shipped them off to military school."

"Now there's an idea." He smiled. "I've got an entirely different perspective now that I'm tryin' to uphold the law."

"And now they all have cell phones, so the word spreads a lot faster than it used to. You don't have to go around hunting for parties like back in my day."

"That's exactly right," Brooks said, moving his leg up to cross an ankle over his knee. "Technology is a wonderful thing. I just wish the thirteen-year-olds didn't have access to it."

"Thirteen? You have problems with thirteen-year-olds?"

"They are the worst offenders," he insisted. "I'd like to round them all up and lock them away for a year. Most of their parents would let me, I imagine."

"Is that going to be your platform when you run for mayor?" Lolly joked.

Brooks grinned at her. "That's an opinion I'll probably have to keep to myself."

"Mayor?" Genevra asked, but was immediately interrupted by the ringing of her cell. She looked over to the table next to her, smiled a shy smile, and picked it up saying, "Excuse me a moment, won't you?" She got up and headed to the kitchen before answering.

Brooks lifted an eyebrow. "A hot date?"

Lolly nodded, her gaze having followed her mother. "I think so."

She turned to Brooks. "Actually, I'm sure of it. Though she is not talking."

"What do you mean, not talking?"

Lolly leaned closer. "She's seeing somebody. But she's not saying who. Not even telling me. Says she wants to sa-vor it."

"Sa-vor it?"

"Uh-huh. Saaaa-vor it!" Lolly stressed again. "Brooks, I've never known her to date. Well, at least not like this. And I have no idea how long it's been going on. If I hadn't come back for the summer, I would have no idea about it at all."

Brooks' brows drew together. "Why the secrecy?"

"You're aware of my uncles, right?"

Brooks thought about Jeb, JB, and Jimmy DuVal. All big men around town with large personalities. Those guys led the charge when it came to coaching the kids, refereeing the games, and selling concessions—making them the backbone of the community. *No doubt they'd been hell-raisers growing up,* Brooks thought, *because they were hell-raisers now.* The DuVal brothers had their collective nose stuck into everything, with strong opinions they didn't mind sharing. Brooks had no doubt they'd want to know who their brother's widow was seeing. God help the poor son of a bitch.

"Understood," he said. They both listened intently for a moment, unable to make out anything being said.

"Come on," Lolly whispered. "Use your cop skills to figure this one out for me. I am dying to know who he is."

"Maybe he's from out of town."

"Could be. But then why not tell me?" She shook her head 'no.' "I think it's somebody right here in Henderson, and they are being very careful about keeping it under wraps."

"You can't blame them. Your uncles aside, people are going to have their opinions and probably voice them. My mom has always held your mother in high regard, and she's just going to love hearing about this. Whoever it is, he's either going to be a hero or a goat. Because this town wants to see your mother happy after what she's been through."

Lolly opened her mouth. Then closed it. She leaned even closer and lowered her voice further. "Brooks. The thing is, I don't know what she's been through."

"What do you mean?"

"Well, look around. You see any pictures of my parents? I know it's been a long time since he died, but you'd think she'd have one around. There's a picture of my daddy in my room and a few over at Momma DuVal's. But when I asked to see their wedding album, Momma couldn't locate it. She and I have always been able to talk about anything, yet she's consistently hesitant to talk about my daddy."

"Well, from what I understand—"

"Sorry about that," Genevra called out before she sailed back into the screened-in porch. "Now, Brooks Bennett, what is this I'm hearing about mayor? I'm intrigued."

Brooks shot Lolly a baleful look. "Mrs. DuVal, I wish Lolly hadn't said anything. It's just something I'm thinking about. If you wouldn't mind keeping that a secret for the time being, I'd be obliged."

"Oh, she's good at keeping secrets," Lolly insisted. "Right, Momma?"

Genevra blushed slightly but otherwise looked completely composed. "Trust me not to mention it to anyone, Brooks. But I am curious why you'd even want the job."

"My buddy Vance Evans and I are tired of watching our contemporaries move away from Henderson. We'd like to create an environment appealing enough to draw the young people back."

"Well, you've got my vote," she said pointedly as she looked over at Lolly. "And I have to say, I sure would love to be a fly on the wall the day Mayor Stevens finds out he's actually got some competition for the job."

"Mayor Stevens has done a great job for Henderson," Brooks said.

"Spoken like a true politician," Genevra laughed.

Trying to cover his wide grin, Brooks motioned to the mannequin tucked into the corner of the porch. "What's this, Lolly? Are you planning to outfit the Gryffindor tennis team?"

"I am!" Lolly cried as both women clapped and chirped their delight. "That's exactly what I want you to think when you see that tennis outfit."

Brooks looked the design up and down and couldn't help but grin at Lolly's obvious talent and ingenuity. The sexy tennis dress with its V-neck halter top somehow screamed Harry Potter with its bold left chest emblem and the Gryffindor House scarlet and gold striping at the hem.

"It's for Fashion Week. I need to evoke vivid memories and emotions in the audience, while showing functional and technical appeal," she recited. "The fact that you thought of Harry Potter helps me know I'm on the right track."

"So you just …what? Came up with the design of this dress… from nothing?"

"No. I sat in front of movies three, four, and five and sketched a lot of the costumes. I was able to get an idea of the repeating shapes and structures, not only in the clothing, but in the architecture as well. Lots of triangles showed up. Severe lines. So the V-neck was a good place to start. Of course, adding the colors and the crest helps to trigger the mind. I'm working on the men's version now."

"How many items do you need?"

"As many as I can make. I have to submit my designs for approval. The more I submit, the better chance I have of something making it into the show."

Brooks' head spun from design to designer. "You have to produce the garments before you're approved for the show?"

She shrugged. "In theory, you only have to submit your drawings and fabric samples. But the competition has become so fierce that most everyone submits finished prototypes. The judges like it because they can see the quality of your craftsmanship and are assured the design will be complete for the show."

"That's a lot of work without any guarantees," he observed.

"Which is why I moved home for the summer. Fewer distractions and no fashion students looking over my shoulder. Not to mention Momma is brilliant at brainstorming ideas and is, more importantly, my primary investor."

"Money well spent," Genevra said, reaching over and taking her hand for a moment. The affection between mother and daughter was palpable. It made Brooks smile even while his gaze darted briefly to the floor.

"So this is what's keeping you busy after you run with Vance."

Lolly nodded and grinned. God, those sapphire eyes were lit up with excitement. This was *her* passion, he realized. This was what she was born to do. Like playing baseball and revitalizing this town was to him. She was a designer. And a good one at that.

It was then that Genevra took a quick glance at her watch and popped out of her chair. "You two are probably in a hurry to get out the door and I've held you up."

"No, Momma. We're fine," Lolly said, winking at Brooks. "We're in no hurry, are we, Brooks?"

"Not at all," he said, playing along. "Maybe you'd like to come with us?" he offered.

"As if you'd want your date's mother along," she scolded. "Up! Both of you. Out!" She clapped her hands. "Time to go."

Lolly burst out laughing as she and Brooks rose to their feet. "Momma, are you throwing us out?"

Genevra drew in a deep breath, held it as she looked between the two of them, and then squeaked out, "Yes."

"Yes, I'm so sorry," she apologized, "but you two have to go. Now." She ushered them through the kitchen, into the dining room, and to the front door while taking continuous glances at her watch. "And Brooks, if you wouldn't mind driving out the road to the right, I would appreciate it." She bit her lip as both Lolly and Brooks looked at her as if she'd lost her mind. She squeezed her eyes together. "I know. I know! Please. I'm sorry. Just…just give me this one thing and I promise I will come clean soon. Very soon."

Lolly stood with her mouth open, gaping at her mother. "Oh. My. God," she said slowly, in complete disbelief.

Brooks recognized desperation when he saw it, and right now it was all over Mrs. DuVal's face. He was not interested in standing around while this pleasant interlude unraveled, so he grabbed Lolly by the hand and drew her out the door.

"No problem, Mrs. DuVal," he called over his shoulder, dragging Lolly into a run to his truck. He picked her up and shoved her inside, waving to her mother as he sprinted around the cab and sprung into the driver's seat. He started the engine without buckling his seat belt and spewed gravel in his haste to back out of the drive. He swung the tailgate out to the left and shot a glance in his rearview mirror. His eyes popped wide when he spied the approaching vehicle. They needed to get out of here now.

He threw the gear shift into forward and punched the gas. Lolly's arms flew out, bracing herself with one hand on the door and the other on the dash. With one eye on the country road ahead and one eye in the mirror, he was pretty certain that the tell-tale royal blue Maserati with its convertible top just turned into Lolly's drive.

Mystery solved.

Genevra DuVal watched the close call unfold in horror-struck amusement. Holding the screen door open with one hand and pressing fingers to her lips with the other, her eyes glistened with tears of mirthful embarrassment as she watched her daughter driven from the scene in haste, just as one very slick, very sexy sports car turned into her drive.

Releasing her anxiety from the almost-meeting, the breath she'd been holding hitched again at the sight of the driver. Slick and sexy didn't even begin to describe that one. The one she'd fallen so desperately in love with over the past several months. The one who had appeared out of nowhere, determined to make her every wish come true.

Her heart skittered wildly as he angled to a stop, captivating her with a nod and that *Top Gun* grin even before he put the car in park and turned off the engine. He didn't look away as he exited the car with his dark shades, dark hair, tanned skin, and gorgeous clothes. Lordy, the man knew how to dress. And his body was masculine perfection, she thought, as he sauntered to the bottom step, stopped, took off his sunglasses, and held them in both hands in front of him. He cocked his head to the side, studying her as he always did with that oh-so-sultry half smile. When he spoke, he invariably spoke gently, as if she were skittish and he didn't want to scare her off.

"Great dress," he acknowledged with an appreciative look up and down. "What did I miss?"

Genevra shook her head letting out a breath along with a choked gurgle of laughter at her own foolishness. It was long past time for everyone to know just how she felt about Hale Evans.

"I lost track of time talking with Brooks and Lolly and therefore made a sensational fool of myself hurrying them out the door." She looked toward her feet and wrung her hands together as he came slowly up the stairs.

"It all seems so ridiculous now," she said as he stood two steps below her, leaving them eye to eye. She raised her chin and met his gaze. "Hale, I love you." The surprise registered in his face as she reached up to touch his cheek. "I do," she said as his arms slid around her waist. "And I am ready for everyone to know."

A long breath eased out of Hale as he drew her close. His eyes closed as their lips almost touched. "Thank God," he breathed above her mouth. He hugged her to him, squeezing her securely. "Thank God," he said again, tucking his chin and kissing the back of her neck.

Genevra rubbed her hands up and down the raw silk over his back, amazed at his relief. How could he have doubted her feelings? "I love you, Hale," she said again, her heart full and free. This time he released her enough to slide his lips across hers, kissing her tenderly and gently before moving his mouth to her ear.

"You will never, ever regret this," he told her right before his arms tightened around her waist and he lifted her off her feet, moving them both inside. They let the screen door clap shut behind them. "I think I've loved you from the moment we met," he said between eager kisses. "Christ, I'm certain of it. And oh! Dear God!" he said, pulling them apart. "If my mother wasn't expecting us for dinner…."

He let the words trail off as he pushed a hand through his short hair, looking around her foyer as if unfamiliar with his surroundings. Suddenly, his dark eyes narrowed and he brought his gaze back to rest on her smiling face. "Prove it?" he shouted.

Genevra startled at his uncharacteristic explosion. A giggle escaped as Hale began backing her up.

"I receive this beautiful stationery, doused in some tantalizing scent. A handwritten letter from the woman I adore agreeing to have dinner with my mother and me."

Genevra held out a hand to keep him at arm's length, but he kept stalking.

"And then, there at the bottom are the two dirtiest words I have ever read."

"What words?"

"Prove it."

Genevra laughed nervously. "Hale, how was I supposed to respond? 'Rest assured I'm not gay'?" she repeated from his note. "No woman could possibly mistake you for gay. I certainly don't think you're gay."

"And yet, you want me to prove it."

She stopped. "Well, yes." She eyed him sincerely as he kept coming and stood looming over her. "I...." Oh My God, was he going to make her beg him for sex? "I'm...ready when you are," she said primly, feeling like a damn fool but unwilling to back down.

"Woman," he vowed, pulling her against him, "I was born ready."

She laughed right in his face then, and he responded with a dazzling smile. He stepped back and ordered her, "Pack a bag. You won't be home for a while."

"What?"

"Three and a half months I've waited to get you into my bed. I'm not sure how fast I'm going to be letting you out. Now, please. You have five minutes to pack up any feminine accoutrements you may desire, and if you own a bikini, you may want to toss that in as well. My mother is waiting."

"For me in a bikini?"

Hale looked a tad exasperated that he had to explain. "My mother has worked herself into a state of anxiety over the meal she is preparing. She hasn't talked about anything else but you since I spilled the beans. So, please. I can't begin to 'prove it' until we get through introductions and dinner with my mother. The bikini is for my benefit. Later. Much later. I have a beautiful swimming pool and a Jacuzzi."

"Oh Lord," she pleaded.

"What?"

"I'm just remembering your mother lives with you."

"And?"

Genevra shook her hands rapidly. "Well, I know we aren't teenagers or anything." She squeezed her eyes together. "But...are we just going to say goodnight after dinner and walk down the hall together to your room? In front of your mother?" Her voice rose toward hysteria.

Hale came forward and gently grasped both her arms, bending his legs to look her eye to eye. His soothing voice and demeanor were all back in place. "Genevra, my love. My mother has her own wing of the house. She will certainly be the one to say goodnight first and waltz one hundred and fifty feet in the opposite direction from my room."

"One hundred and fifty feet?" she asked numbly.

"Aside from that, you may as well know that my mother seems to be as eager as you are for me to 'prove it.'"

"She is?"

"Apparently she believes the rumors."

Genevra blinked wide-eyed. "Well then. I'll be ready in five," she agreed and hurried up the stairs.

～ço～

Brooks sped away from Lolly's home, banking curves and shooting down straightaways like he was Tony Stuart in the Daytona 500. And he was enjoying it too, right up until the moment Lolly said, "Wow. Vance would be proud of you."

"What do you mean by that?" he said, just before he caught air over a sneaky bump on a downhill stretch. And by the time he landed, he knew. He was the good cop, damn it. And that thought had him hitting the brakes, moving their speed down to a much saner, if not completely legal, number.

Lolly reached over and rubbed the length of his arm as he bemoaned the joy ride. Good cop had to be an example for the fine citizens of Henderson. *Good cop was a pansy-ass sucker,* he thought, and sometimes he just wanted to kick good cop's ass.

"I shouldn't have said anything," Lolly apologized. "That was fun. You were having fun, and I took it away from you. I'm sorry." She leaned over and kissed his bicep. Which, he admitted to himself, was almost worth having her be able to read him so well.

Of course, that was what had brought her to his attention in the first place all those years ago. Lolly DuVal felt his pain, his anxiety, and his moods better than any other person on the planet. And she had no idea what that meant to him. His mother, whom he loved dearly, could not come close. His dad was forever oblivious. Lewis, the boy wonder of the technology age, didn't have a clue. Even Vance and Duncan, with all the time they had spent together over the last many years, didn't read him as well as Lolly did. Lolly had always been his own Harry-the-bartender.

He laughed at the thought, reaching out to rub her thigh lightly, letting her know he was okay. "I thought we'd head to the Club for dinner."

Lolly turned toward him so fast he had to glance her way and almost choked on the realization that she wasn't wearing her seatbelt. Then he looked down and noticed *he* wasn't wearing his seatbelt.

"I would love to go to the Club any other night, Brooks, truly I would," she pleaded. "But with all the running I've done this week, I am dying for a big, fat, greasy cheeseburger at The Tavern. Attila the Hun, a.k.a. Vance the Bossy, ran me ragged. He took four pounds of flesh off my hide and I'm aiming to get them back."

Brooks cruised to a stop at the first red light entering town. He leaned over, pulled Lolly to him, and kissed her lips. "Your wish is my command," he said, before settling back into his seat and driving on.

"Well," Lolly stuttered, her eyes gone wide. "This date is starting off rather well."

Brooks laughed. "I agree."

"Except for that whole thing with my mom."

"What do you mean? I enjoyed talking to your mom."

"No, I mean her throwing us out so Mr. Mystery wouldn't find out she has a grown daughter."

Brooks hit the break a little harder than he'd planned, throwing them both forward. "Okay. Seat belts," he ordered. And once they were secured he said, "Lolly, that is not the reason she is keeping this affair secret."

"Affair?" she shouted. "Do you think she's seeing a married man? That would explain everything, but oh…oh, oh, oh, this is going to be so bad when word gets out." She shuddered. "I'm going to have to move back to Raleigh."

She didn't seem to appreciate his laughter, but he couldn't help it. "Lolly. Your mother is not dating a married man."

"How do you know? It makes perfect sense why she'd claim she wanted to *savor* it. Hell, she won't get a moment's peace when this sordid story breaks. And neither will I."

Brooks grabbed up one of Lolly's floundering hands and brought it to his lips, scraping his teeth along her fingers and following up with his tongue. From the quiet that ensued, he was pretty sure he had her attention. "Trust me," he whispered into her palm as he continued to drive toward The Tavern with one hand. "All is well."

CHAPTER THIRTEEN

Brooks enjoyed watching Lolly try to get her fists around The Tavern's Big Foot Burger. Getting her mouth around it was something else altogether. Eventually she gave up and used a knife and fork, which Brooks thought was a shame. Some foods were meant to be eaten with your bare hands.

His bare hands were aching to get ahold of something just as juicy and satisfying after he'd touched her thigh in the car. And now, sitting here facing Lolly in the back corner booth, chosen specifically because he'd know every third person who walked into this place on a Friday night, he was tempted to swing himself around the table and plant his ass on her side and make it even more difficult for her to finish that burger.

Yep, he'd swing her right into his lap, press them both into the corner, and play with her hair and other particulars while she ate. It had not slipped his notice that she wore her hair down. For him. Dark and full, it had a way of cascading down over her shoulders and ending with a little curl right at the most interesting place. He licked his lips, imagining running his hands up into her hair while kissing her, then moving his tongue and teeth down to her chin…to her slender neck…to her shoulders…her collar bone…and then dipping his tongue right down between—

Lolly's words 'come clean about what happened with Vance' pulled at Brooks' attention."

What? "Sorry, what did you say?"

She wiped her mouth with a third paper napkin and dragged

a french fry through a dainty pile of ketchup while she spoke. Her demeanor was relaxed and unguarded but her words caused his spine to straighten.

"You know we've spent quite a bit of time together this week and…."

Way too much time.

"He told me you were drafted by the Orioles' organization when you graduated from college."

"Oh! Okay. Yeah. Well, that's pretty much common knowledge."

"Yes, but he told me why you didn't sign."

He tensed. "There were a lot of factors that went into my decision."

"And Vance said as much. But he believes the real reason you stayed behind was because he didn't get drafted."

Brooks opened his mouth to speak but could conjure no words. He fisted his hands absently on the table top and swished his thumb over his middle fingers.

"I can't believe you would do that for him. Not follow your dream."

Brooks sat back and sighed. "If I thought that I had a good chance of getting to the Majors in a reasonable amount of time, I would have signed."

"If Vance had also been drafted, would you have signed?"

Yes. "Probably."

"So it's true. You stayed for Vance."

"It's true that Vance was a factor in my decision. But I want you to be very clear on one thing. I did not stay behind. I chose to live in Henderson. To pursue a life and career in my hometown."

"Because of Vance?"

He eyed her patiently. If it had been anybody else, he would have brushed them off. But this was Lolly. Lolly was asking him. Lolly wanted to understand. And if there was anyone who could, he figured it was her. So he chose his words carefully and told her the truth.

"If Vance had been drafted, then the two of us could have shared the experience of the Minor Leagues. Not on the same team, but we would have been able to commiserate. It would have been easier to give up three, four, maybe even five years to pursue a dream that would likely have ended without throwing one pitch in a Major ballpark."

"How do you know?"

"How do I know what?" He grabbed one of her fries.

"That you wouldn't make it to the Major League."

"Of course, I didn't know for sure. But it was an educated guess. I was a very good college pitcher. Not a great college pitcher. We won the College World Series because of the energy our team created together. Those specific guys, at that specific time." He broke into a big grin remembering. "I can't really describe it. But we all felt it. We could not lose."

Lolly's regard held such appreciation and joy. It was as if she could feel what he was feeling, and it unlocked him.

"I was given this amazing gift twice in my life, Lolly. Twice I was on a team where we…we loved one another. Where we didn't work at baseball, we played the game. We played with heart and enthusiasm and we played for each other as well as ourselves. We won and won and won and shared in something that most people will never have the opportunity to even glimpse. Never have the chance to experience. And Vance, Vance shared that experience with me both times.

"If I had felt in my gut that I had a shot at the Majors, I would have taken it. But statistics and my own personal understanding of the game and my abilities indicated otherwise. I was given the choice of relishing my baseball experiences and working to pave the way for more kids to do the same, or taking the chance of turning my love of the game into work and frustration and possibly have all the shine tarnish. I'd had a good long run and I was content. I decided it was time to move on."

Lolly's lips parted for a moment, and then a grin blossomed forth in a most becoming way. As did the triumphant feeling in his chest as she reached across the table and grabbed his hand with both of hers. "That's the best sports story I've ever heard."

"Well, now." He swallowed, falling head over heels. He brought her hands up first to his lowered forehead and then to his lips, forcing himself to look into her sapphire eyes. The grown-up Lolly did not disappoint, and his head agreed right then and there with what his gut had told him all those years ago.

Laura Leigh DuVal was the girl for him.

"So," he said as he drifted his tongue across her knuckles. "Anything else you need to come clean about?"

Her grin began fading by degrees. Her fingers twitchy in his grasp.

Fucking A.

"It was a rhetorical question, for Christ's sake. Lolly?"

She pulled her hands from his and pushed her plate away, reaching for her water. "Well, I need to tell you why Vance spanked me this morning."

"Spanked you?" Brooks said, feeling his head go slightly dizzy as he folded both arms over his chest. "Your text said he smacked you on the ass."

Lolly blinked. "There's a difference?"

"Right now my mind has conjured up two very different pictures. One where he swatted you on your *derriere* in appreciation of a good run. The other where you are turned over his knee."

"Yeah. This was pretty much the latter."

He held his tongue but couldn't stop himself from sucking in a deep breath.

"Now, try to understand," she explained slowly, like he was someone who rode the short bus. "Remember, this is Vance. Who is learning how to be friends with a girl. All week he's vacillated between being my coach with a lot of very bossy yelling and taunting, and trying to get me in bed with outrageous flirting and inappropriate comments. Now on Monday and Tuesday, I was able to nip all this in the bud and gently explain when and why he went off base. On Wednesday and Thursday, he seemed to be getting it, and his comments and behavior were more appropriate—for the most part. I was happy about that because my body was starting to wear down trying to keep up with him on the run. I didn't have the energy to get in his face about every little thing. But today," she insisted, "today I snapped."

"You snapped."

"Yes. I snapped!" she said, throwing her arms wide and falling back in her seat. "I couldn't take it anymore. I was hot, I was tired, I was in pain from this brutal week of training that I didn't ask for and I was brain dead from trying to deal with all his yackity-yack-yacking, so when he started in once again about his magic hands and how they could bring me release, I finally told him to put up or shut up."

"Put up or shut up."

"Right. And then I threw myself at him and kissed him."

"You what?"

"And that's why he literally turned me over his knee and spanked me. Hard."

"You. Kissed him?"

"Ah-huh."

"Jesus, Lolly, now *I* want to spank you!"

She looked at him slyly. "If *you* spanked me, I'd probably like it."

"Holy shit," he groaned into his hands before rubbing them up into his hair. "You did not just say that."

She had the audacity to shrug. Like he wasn't furious about her kissing Vance. Like he hadn't been tamping down incessant jealousy all week because the two of them were spending time together. Not to mention that he was now fully hot and bothered over the very idea of putting his hand on her ass in any form of passion.

"I swear to God, you and Vance are going to be the death of me."

"Well, I'd feel worse about it if you could name one other woman who has spent ten hours with The Great Seducer and not ended up in his bed. And I only kissed him because he made me insane. It was clearly a case of temporary insanity."

"It seems very foggy to me. How 'bout the two of you stop all this running around together?"

Lolly gave him a quick grin. "Cute. But it's already taken care of. I will never, ever run with Vance Evans again. I have made myself clear on that point. Besides," she said, turning to fumble around in her purse, "we start tennis tomorrow." She slapped a paperback book on the table. "He has ordered me to read this in its entirety. Tonight."

Brooks looked down at the book. *The Art of Doubles: Winning Tennis Strategies and Drills* by Pat Blaskower. "Yeah. That's not happening," he growled as he took the book and tucked it under his arm. He hailed the waitress. "Come on. Let's get out of here."

He paid the bill and tugged Lolly out of the booth. When they reached the parking lot, he stalked straight toward the dumpster and threw the book in.

"Oh, man," Lolly said, eyes aghast at what he'd done. "There's going to be hell to pay for this."

He grabbed her hand and hustled her over to his truck. "Not after the little chat Vance and I are going to have."

"No, really," she said as she buckled her seat belt. "He's ultra-competitive. I mean, I've been playing tennis for a long time, but he was using terminology I'd never heard before."

"I'll take care of it."

"He's going to expect me to know the strategies in that book." Her voice was getting all hushed and shaky.

"Lolly, I'll take care of it."

"And when I don't know them, he'll make me do laps around the court." Her voice was on the edge of hysteria.

"Lolly!" Her face snapped toward his. "He's not your father, and he's not your damn coach. You're the one who's training him, remember? You're the one in charge. Act like it."

He turned the key in the ignition and threw the truck into reverse, pulling out of the parking spot.

"Easy for you to say," she said under her breath.

Brooks sighed as he put the truck in drive and headed out onto the main drag. This was such a bad idea. He'd known it from the beginning, but as Lolly was finding out, Vance was a master in relentless badgery.

"This isn't about tennis," he said as he drove them through town.

"Oh, it's going to be all about tennis tomorrow," Lolly murmured.

"Well then, remind him. Remind him that it's not about running, or tennis, or golf, or whatever. It's about being a good friend. Not treating you like you're one of the kids he's coaching or someone he's trying to lure into bed. But rather establishing trust, offering support, and joking around. A little! A little joking around. If he says something disrespectful or inappropriate, you've got to call him on it. It's the only way he's going to learn."

"Of course," Lolly agreed. "But, still. I mean…if we're going to play tennis…we may as well try to win."

"Oh, My God!"

"What?"

"You want to read that book! That's what you're upset about. You want to read the goddamn how-to-win-at-doubles-and-make-Brooks-crazy book."

"No. No. I mean, it's not like I wanted to read it tonight. I might have wanted to browse through it though. I'm a little curious about what I might be able to learn."

"You're as competitive as Vance!"

Lolly shrugged and looked out her window, mumbling, "You say that like it's a bad thing."

Brooks growled as he turned away from town and took the country road heading to the lake. "You know. It's all coming back to me now," he said, glancing in her direction with lifted brows. "Darcy would come home and be furious with you for not picking her for some team. She couldn't understand why her best friend would leave her standing there to be the last one chosen."

"Oh stop! Your sister is brilliant in many things, but motor skills isn't one of them. She was terrible at sports and as captain, it was my duty to put together the strongest team I could."

"In middle school? You," he accused, "are a female Vance!"

"I am not!" Lolly was horrified.

"Are too."

"You're crazy."

"Crazy is thinking you can keep up with a guy who has run every day of his life for the last five years! Why the hell would you even attempt to do that if you, too, weren't ultra-competitive? That's why you're in pain. That's why you became temporarily insane. You just had to prove that you could do it. Whatever he said, all week long, you just went right along with it even though it practically killed you. Because was no way you would back down. No way you would give in, even though your body was screaming for you to stop. You pushed yourself further than you could actually go. You are *that* competitive."

"Okay. So maybe I am a little competitive. But have you forgotten that it was you who registered me for that first softball team?"

"Somebody had to help you channel all that combative aggression."

"You know what? That's probably one of the reasons you asked me out. I understand competition. Just like you, oh Great Boy Wonder at Center Mound. Don't tell me you aren't extremely competitive."

"I am competitive. But with compassion. With a little common sense. It's not all about winning. It's about participation and enjoyment and pleasure and—"

"Right. Which is why Vance is head coach and you're just an assistant."

"—good sportsmanship. I cannot believe you just said that!"

"If the shoe fits."

"Oh My God, you really are the female Vance," he said under his breath as he turned and headed up the steep climb.

"I am not the female Vance!"

"You so are."

"Am not!"

"The running shoe fits!"

Lolly whipped her whole body around to face him. "If I were the female Vance, I would have had you in bed on our first date. I am *not* the female Vance."

"All it would take from you is one come-hither look, and any guy would tumble into your bed on the first date."

"My point exactly! I don't do come-hither. I couldn't if I tried. I have zero feminine wiles."

"Oh, you have wiles."

"I have no wiles." She ran her hands down her body. "Nothing to wile with."

The truck came to an abrupt stop. Brooks threw the gear shift into park and leaned over into Lolly's face. "You have plenty to wile with. Trust me."

"Where are we?" Lolly asked, nervously looking around, seeing nothing but dark.

"We're on the ridge overlooking the lake."

Lolly looked flustered. "But it's already dark."

"I know." Brooks opened his door, exited, and then slammed it shut.

Lolly scrambled out of the truck. "Why are we overlooking the lake when it's too late to see the lake?" She moved toward him tentatively as he opened the tailgate, her face awash with uncertainty. "Brooks. You didn't drive us out here so you could spank me, did you?"

Brooks sighed, turned, and propped his hip on the tailgate. "No, Lolly. I did not drive out here so I could spank you."

"Okay then. But it's a little dark and isolated. I mean, no one would hear me scream. F-frank-lly," she stuttered, walking away, "if I wasn't here with a cop, I'd be a little nervous."

"You sound like you're a lot nervous."

"Well, um. Let's see. First, I kissed your friend, whom you adamantly warned me about. And then, in my fervor to win an argument, I'm pretty sure I insulted you. And just now I was sort of…shouting…at you. So yes, I'm nervous you've decided I'm more trouble than you're up for, and you might leave me out here handcuffed to a tree."

Brooks, who was now sitting on the tailgate, stared across the twenty feet of darkness Lolly had put between them. With deliberate intent, he stood up and crossed the distance. The gravel crunched beneath his feet, but there was only silence when he stopped and faced her dead on. He reached around, took hold of a long length of hair at the center of her back and tugged it gently so that her face tilted up to his and he could be sure he had her full attention.

"Let's get one thing straight," he said. "If I had wanted to be head coach, I would be head coach."

Lolly's head nodded. And then she licked her lips and nodded some more, sending a jolt of longing through his chest and his belly. "I know that," she whispered, appearing more afraid than before. "I know that. Vance said as much."

Of course he did. Good Ol' Vance.

"You want me to take you home?"

"No."

"Then stop looking at me like I'm Jack the Ripper."

"Sorry."

He released her hair and she paced by him toward the truck, turning before she got halfway there. "I am competitive," she admitted, throwing up her hands and stomping back. "To a fault! If I'm playing tennis or golf or even if I'm running with someone for exercise, I want to win. I'm not one of those people who can simply enjoy being out in the fresh air," she mocked. "Screw that! I want to win or at the very least make a good showing. It's a competition, for heaven's sake. There is always a winner and a loser."

"I get that," Brooks said, moving toward her slowly. "I do. It feels a whole lot better to win." And he knew better than anyone that sometimes that wasn't even enough.

"So you understand that if Vance and I are playing tennis in a tournament, the two of us are going to want to win."

"I get it. Just keep in mind it's not the primary reason you two are playing together." He took both her hands in his and leaned over to kiss her lightly on the nose. "Now, I am declaring this a Vance-free zone. No more discussion of the Dark Prince."

"Dark Prince," she snickered. "He'd probably love that."

"Without doubt."

◦⌁◦

Lighthearted relief bubbled up inside Lolly now that she and Brooks were back in alliance. So the words 'Did you bring me up here to watch the submarine races?' fell out of her mouth before she had a chance to filter them. Nothing like begging a guy to make out with you.

"The submarine races started at nine," Brooks said, pulling her behind him toward the pickup. "But there's another show that starts in about ten minutes," he said.

"I thought you might be taking me to see your house." Her eyes were adjusting to the dark and she could see a small cooler in the back of his truck. He pulled out a patchwork quilt from behind it and handed it to her.

"Waitin' on a few finishing touches," he said, taking hold of the cooler. "My house isn't quite ready for you, Laura Leigh, and you aren't quite ready for it. Besides," he said, pointing in the direction he wanted them to go, "we would have missed out on this."

Lolly followed him through the small, graveled lot and down a grassy slope before Brooks set the cooler down. "Here," he said.

He took the quilt from her arms and together they spread it out, making sure there weren't any rocks or sticks underneath. Lolly sat in the middle, her bare legs stretched out in front of her. The night was warm and humid, so the icy bottle of beer Brooks handed her seemed like the perfect accompaniment. She kicked off her boots while pointing and flexing her toes in a nervous flutter as Brooks' long, strong, and oh-so-masculine body stretched out beside her.

He tilted his bottle in a toast against hers and then took a long pull on his beer.

"You didn't have a beer at The Tavern," she said.

"I'm driving."

"And now?"

"Now?" He leaned onto one elbow facing her. She felt the rough pads of his fingertips rub back and forth across the back of her hand. "Now it's a perfect night and I'm sitting under the stars on the quilt my grandma made for me. On a date I've been looking forward to all week with a beautiful, albeit ultra-competitive girl who just admitted to kissing my best friend…."

"Ah!"

"And then tried to cut our date short to go home and read a book about tennis…."

"I did not!"

"So *he* wouldn't be upset with her…."

"Brooks!"

"And then she hurt my feelings by belittling my status as assistant coach. I think I deserve a beer, don't you?" He laughed as he thwarted her attempt to smack him.

Lolly rolled to her back in defeat. "Oh, Lord. When you put it that way…."

Her voice died off and she felt the exhaustion of a long week settle over her body. She noticed as it seeped into her limbs, and the weight of it settled her against the earth, pulling her down almost into the ground beneath the quilt. She lay there quiet and comfortable, her eyes cast up into the night sky where she noticed more and more stars revealing themselves.

It was at the very edge of her vision. A flash. A streak. Something. She tilted her head and it was gone. Another streak of light to the left had her turning her head back just in time to witness the entire flash-path of a shooting star directly overhead in the center of the sky.

"Did you see that?" she said, pointing.

"Uh-huh," Brooks said from beside her, now flat on his back with one arm bent under his head.

"And there?" She pointed to the right.

"Yep."

"Oh, and another. Brooks!" The sky was coming to life before her eyes. She no longer needed to watch her peripheral vision or wonder if what she'd captured in a fleeting moment was real. The shooting stars hurtled one after another until the frequency increased, and they appeared to dance together like the Bellagio Fountains. The magic of glimpsing one shooting star could have filled Lolly up, but this…this was a miracle happening before her eyes. And her awe was so great it took her breath away.

At some point, Brooks reached down and entwined his fingers with her own. She squeezed his hand in response, unable to speak. He brought her hand up to his lips and kissed it before letting their hands fall between them once more.

When she found her voice, she asked, "What is this?"

"A meteor shower."

"You knew about this?"

"Uh-huh."

"How?"

"The news. They said it would be a perfect night to see it. No moon. No clouds. I figured this would be the best spot. Away from any lights and no trees to block our view."

"You planned to bring me here?" she whispered.

"I didn't want you to miss it."

She was humbled. By the Universe's display and by this man at her side. The swell of emotion that grew in that moment tightened her chest and rode on a tide of gratitude and longing and regret and worry and joy. Each one rolling and pitching over the other, combining and separating and heaving up from her chest and into her throat, damming itself up at the edge of her eyes. Had she been alone, she would have wept out loud, allowing the emotion to move up and out. As it was, she silently gulped air to bank the tears and disperse the emotion. She didn't want to have to explain. She wouldn't be able to find the words if she tried.

"Lolly," Brooks whispered, turning his head to stare at her. She couldn't look at him. Not now. She squeezed his hand.

"Lolly," he said, rolling on his side and inserting himself into her turmoil. His hand cradled her face, allowing his thumb to feel an errant tear. He whisked it away as he placed his other hand to her opposite cheek, both thumbs following the same line of protocol. All she could think was that he was missing the star extravaganza above him, which made her feel worse and caused a tiny sob to escape her chest, push through her throat, and then burst from her lips.

"Laura Leigh, talk to me," he pleaded. His forehead came to rest on top of hers, his breath becoming a gentle caress. His hands cradled her head and he began to kiss her tears away, which only made more erupt in their place.

She wanted to speak. To tell him it was much ado about nothing. But with the turmoil of emotion lodged in her throat, she knew any sound she made would likely release the flood gates to a point that no amount of words would be able to explain. So she tilted her head back and placed her lips under his.

CHAPTER FOURTEEN

Genevra stood in Hale's opulent kitchen holding a chilled glass of buttery chardonnay staring across the large ornate swimming pool to the estate grounds beyond. Next to her, Hale was pointing out various landmarks and chatting proudly about all they surveyed. She couldn't hear any of it.

She'd known Hale Evans was wealthy. Everybody in Henderson knew that. But she'd never imagined such wealth accumulated in one spot. And it was all so beautifully, beautifully executed. Her mind stumbled around for words to describe the red brick gate at the entrance and the stabled garage. The mansion itself, inside and out, was tastefully exquisite in every detail. It was lush, yet inviting. Extravagant yet comfortable. From the dining room to the pool's stone patio, not one thing was overdone. It was all simply done to perfection.

"Ah! Madre. At last." Genevra turned at Hale's words and a genuine smile came unforced at the sight of old world grace and elegance. "Emelina Flores, may I present Genevra DuVal. Genevra, my mother, Emelina."

"Mrs. Flores," she said, moving forward to shake her hand.

"Emelina, please," she insisted. "And may I call you Genevra?"

"Of course," she said, beaming. Hale's mother took up her hand in a double grip and held it close to her heart.

"We are so fortunate to have you in our home. I have been so eager to meet you. You must tell me everything that my son has not shared, as we are destined to be very good friends, are we not?"

"We are indeed," Genevra agreed, grateful for the immediate approval.

"Ladies, it's such a beautiful evening. Let's enjoy our drinks poolside," Hale said, directing them out the open French doors and to the umbrella-covered table beyond. "Madre, shall I pour you a glass of port?"

"That would be lovely," Emelina said, slipping her arm through Genevra's and walking her through the doors. "He's a wonderful man, my son," she said quietly as they strolled over the patio to the awaiting table. "Forgive me, but I will say this now while he cannot hear. He has not been happy in so long, I forgot what he is like when his spirit is carefree. It is because of you he has returned to himself. I thank you for that. In my heart, I thank you for that."

"Mrs. Flo—Emelina, it is through your son's carefree spirit that I, myself, have found happiness again. I hope that our…tardiness in confessing our relationship has not upset you greatly."

"Don't think a thing of it," she said, waving it away before indicating the seat Genevra should take. "I am honored to be included at all," she said as she sat in the comfy patio chair.

"Included in what?" Hale wanted to know as he arrived with the port and a glass of wine for himself. "Lilabeth is bringing out a cheese plate in a moment."

"I was telling Genevra I am honored to meet her, hijo, and how happy you've been of late."

"It's true." He nodded to Genevra. "I'm extremely happy. Especially now that my two favorite women have met. Ah! And here comes the boy. Right on time."

Genevra glanced over to watch a hip-looking Hale Jr. emerge from the wood-and-glass pool house and move toward them with a determined stride and easy grace. His hair was as dark as his father's but worn long enough so it curled into a flip at the back of his neck. Tan and sporting a ready grin, he wore an expensive pair of light-colored slacks over a basic pair of flip-flops. His white linen shirt was open at the collar and hung casually over his waistband. It took all of five seconds for Genevra to forgive her niece, Molly, for the trouble she'd put her father through. Lord, the son was almost as distracting as his father.

"Genevra, my son, Vance. Vance, this is Mrs. DuVal."

Vance came forward and shook her hand. "Mrs. DuVal," he said before twisting his lips into a devilish grin. "Mrs. DuVal, if you've gone ahead and thrown your hat into the dating ring, I'd like to ask you out myself. The two of us have to be much closer in age than you and my father."

"Dear Lord," his father grumbled as his grandmother spit her port back into her glass.

Genevra slid her hand from Vance's and moved it to her throat. "Oh my! Your reputation doesn't begin to do you justice."

"And no one warned me how hot Lolly's mother is." He shot his father a look suggesting that it was all his fault.

"Vance Evans, you are my favorite bad boy ever. I do hope you plan to join us for dinner so I can get to know you better."

"I wouldn't miss it," he said, pulling out her chair so she could reseat herself. "Abuela, you okay over there?" he said, slipping his grandmother a sly grin. "I'll fix myself a drink, get you another port, and be right back."

"No hurry," his grandmother scolded. "Genevra, I apologize...."

"For what?" she insisted. "Emelina, you've no doubt received hundreds of compliments from younger men. Please don't stand in the way of mine."

With that Emelina laughed. "Okay, then I won't. I won't stand in the way of yours."

"Hale, you've told me so very little about your son."

"And now you know why," he said, taking a seat. "The thought of his being old enough to be my competition is setting off a migraine."

Genevra reached over and took his hand. "He's darling," she said, "but even he can't hold a candle to you."

He brought her hand up to his mouth and kissed it. "And, Mother, now you know why I am in love with Mrs. DuVal."

Emelina clapped her hands and then toasted the two of them. "To young love. At any age."

"Here, here," Hale said, clinking his glass to his mother's and then to Genevra's as Vance arrived with his own drink and set an artfully arranged cheese plate before them .

ﺔﺟﻮ

Cocktails, dinner, dessert, scintillating conversation, and after dinner drinks—it all flew by in one happy blur for Hale. The hours sprinted past as he lived out one of his latest fantasies, that of entertaining Genevra in his home.

Of course his mother and son loved her. How could they not? And she was as gracious and solicitous toward them as he could have possibly hoped. It all seemed so easy. So why hadn't he insisted on this sooner? He would kick himself if he weren't so damn happy.

And now he was sitting at the side of the pool in his brand new swim trunks, waiting for the love of his life to make an appearance. God love his mother for giving them some time alone before it got too late. And bless the boy who ventured off after pulling him aside and assuring him he would not be back before two in the morning, just in case they wanted to use the pool.

The pool.

He hadn't bothered to put a toe in his own pool in five years. And that thought snatched a little of his joy.

Grateful to have his thoughts derailed, he turned his head as he heard the sliding door to the master suite open and watched an angel step from the light, into the night. Her pale pink bikini matched the polish on her fingers and toes. It was a color she wore often and it suited her. Feminine. Quiet. Beautiful in its simplicity. In an effort to tamp down his mounting lust at seeing all those feminine curves revealed, he made a mental note to research pink roses. He'd choose the shade that reminded him of her the most and have them delivered to her office regularly.

He watched her approach shyly, combing stray wisps of hair behind her ears. Yet, as she drew closer, he noticed an eager little smile on those perfect pink lips. He lifted his hand and she took it, sitting beside him without hesitation, letting both her legs dangle in the pool next to his.

Feeling young and giddy, he playfully bumped his shoulder against hers. "You ready to take the plunge?" he asked.

She stared at the water, her brilliant smile reaching from ear to ear. "Anywhere," she said. "Anything, Hale. With you, I'll do anything. Tonight has been…." She bit her bottom lip and sucked in a mouthful of air, before saying, "Pure joy."

"I was thinking the same thing," he said, touching her cheek with a fingertip and running it around the back of her ear.

She turned her head and looked him up and down, still smiling, still biting her lip, swinging her legs back and forth in the water. He leaned in and kissed her then, putting an arm around her back. Slowly, gently, he eased them both into the water, his back first with her chest pinned to his. He pushed off the side with his feet, and they floated together sharing laughter and small kisses until he found purchase in a more shallow area. Sliding his arms over her silky-smooth skin brought on his hunger so once his tongue teased her mouth into opening, he tilted his head and dove in.

She smelled of honeysuckle and tasted of wine. His blood heated from the center of his chest, traveling out to his arms first, then over his shoulders and down his back. It crept back around his ribcage, down his abdomen, and into his legs. The feel of her weightless in his arms, softened by the water, slippery and silky, was heightening his senses at the same time it was numbing his thought patterns. With her arms around his neck, his hands were free to loosen her top. The feel of her bare chest sliding against his own brought a shock of such intense pleasure that a vulgar word escaped out of his mouth without him having any cognitive ability to filter or stop it. His body was on autopilot, his hands moving with a will of their own to rid them of the little bit of clothing that dared to come between them.

He held her to him with his left arm around her waist as his lips and tongue were busy staking claim to her mouth. But he let his right hand travel over the present he'd just unwrapped. Starting at the back of one knee, he felt his way up the tender skin of the back of her thigh. Then he moved up to the curve of her bottom, causing his tongue to plunge a little deeper and his other hand to grip a little tighter.

He turned their bodies and floated toward the expansive underwater staircase. His right hand made its way up from the small of her back to the curve of her waist and then up to the silky smooth skin under her arm where his thumb could slide easily over her full breast, bottom to top. Her nipple stiffening at his touch, he eased his knee between her legs and supported the two of them with one foot grounded on the pool's floor and the other higher and sturdier on a portion of the stairs.

Her fingers wound themselves together at his nape, so when he released her lips there was enough space between them for his hands to come around and fully cup her lush breasts. He opened his eyes, taking in the sight of her perfect body, wavy and distorted under the crystal water and limited lighting.

"Genevra, you are magnificent," he whispered, watching his hands move over her breasts and then slide down her stomach and over her hips to her rear end. He kissed her again, turning with her in his arms and moving them up in the water so he now sat on one step. When the lower half of her body floated back to his, he guided her legs to the outside of his own and pulled her down on his lap.

Her hands spread to his shoulders and her head rolled back just enough to cause him to lose whatever phantom control he thought he had. His mouth took that tender spot on the base of her neck hard, sucking in the delicate flesh at the same time he spread his legs, placed both hands on her hips, and guided her body none-too-gently onto his erection. It all happened so fast he hadn't realized what he was doing, and once the deed was done, it felt too good to apologize or, God forbid, pull out.

At the sound of Genevra's gasp, he placed both arms around her, pulling her chest tight against his. He eased his mouth from her neck but remained buried to the hilt inside her beautiful body. One hand rose to the back of her head, and he cradled her to him, whispering in her ear.

"You feel so damn good. All of you. I couldn't help myself," he said as he began rocking. He felt her legs wrap around his waist and considered that a good sign. "Genevra?" he pleaded.

He felt her teeth sink into the tendon along the top of his shoulder.

"So fucking right," he said as his cock twitched and her muscles contracted around him in response.

"Holy hell," he seethed, trying to hold on to his control. But his body had waited too long to have its say and his baser reflexes took over, causing his hips to pump. His hands dropped to guide her hips in the effort.

Her body became slick in no time, increasing the sensation and allowing him to pull out further before plunging back in. "Your body…. Th-he fit…" he stammered. His head bent to her shoulder as he increased the speed of his thrusts. "Perfect…" he grunted through gritted teeth. "Damn perfect," he groaned before taking in air and then holding his breath as he delivered a final series of thrusts, releasing himself into the woman he loved.

For all he knew, he'd passed out, because his awareness came back in the midst of kisses being placed all over his face. He smiled like a drunken sailor, then placed a hand on either side of her face so he could look into her eyes. "I will so make that up to you," he swore, then released her as his arms collapsed back to the water. He allowed the kissing to go on for whatever reason she saw fit. He didn't care. She wasn't running away from him, thank God. He couldn't even be embarrassed, he felt so good.

⚜

Genevra relished the feel of him. And she indulged in the luxury of mapping out his body with her hands while he was depleted of energy, lounging with his arms bent up on the step behind him and his legs floating underneath her own. She could still feel him inside her, and when she squeezed those muscles his body jolted in response. She smiled. That may have been a wicked thing to do, but he deserved it. He'd jumped the gun on polite lovemaking the moment he'd stripped her naked in the family pool.

Her body had pitched with excitement at the first dirty word that had slid from his lips. And when he bit her throat as he rammed himself deep inside? She was ecstatic he had lost himself, because now maybe, just maybe, she would be allowed to do the same.

Eventually she drifted back, separating their bodies and floating away from him under the night sky. It was then she witnessed a series of falling stars. So caught off guard by the sight, she wondered for a moment if she were dreaming. It was all too terribly good to be true, after all. And now the sky itself had decided to celebrate the incredible changes in her life by putting on a show for her benefit while she just happened to be floating naked in a magnificent pool.

A splash alerted her to the fact that she was not alone. She felt Hale's hands pull her under and spin her to him. They came up sputtering, smiling at one another, treading water together as she pushed wet hair from her face.

"Look up," she said, pointing.

Hale followed her lead and after a few moments announced, "Meteor shower. Come on." He pulled her to the side of the pool where they climbed out and wrapped themselves in fluffy white towels. He took her hand and guided her to a full-length lounge chair where he sat first and then pulled her down in front of him. He eased her back against his chest and wrapped his arms around her. Together they stared up in wonder at the night sky.

~✺~

Brooks could kiss like nobody's business.

And thank God for it, because it helped the well of emotion dissipate and returned Lolly's ability to speak. So she did. Right against his lips.

"I don't deserve you."

Her mouth was directly under his, giving him complete and total access. She spoke around the kissing, wanting him to know how she felt. "After all the trouble I gave you...you still brought me here...to this perfect place...on this perfect night."

"Lolly," he said, levering his long body over hers and allowing intimacy where his weight settled against her. It felt good. His weight.

He kissed his way to her chin and then slid rough-and-tumble kisses down her throat. "Lolly," he said again, stopping the kissing and bringing his head up to look into her eyes. "It's only perfect because you're here," he said, smoothing her hair back from her face. "Besides, sparring with you has been the best part of my week. Now look at the stars." He waited until her eyes shifted from him to the heavens. "That's good," he kissed her neck again. "Tell me what you see."

Lolly opened her mouth to describe a double shooting star, but her breath caught as she felt Brooks' hands shift, settling at the sides of her breasts. "Touch me," she whispered, so low she wasn't sure he heard her. But she was rewarded regardless as his hands ran up and over her breasts while his teeth nipped at the arch of her shoulder.

"What do you have under this dress?" he asked against her skin, his fingers molding themselves into her.

"Very little," she replied.

And suddenly, everything stopped. The kissing, his fingers—his entire body froze and she thought she heard a very quiet 'fucking A' pressed into her shoulder. She bit her lip in an effort not to smile and then wiggled herself loose, scooting out from under him. She stood at the top of the blanket looking down on his prostrate body, his neck craned up so he could see her, his eyes searching. "Lolly."

She reached behind and unzipped the white eyelet, wiggling it down over her hips and allowing it to drop to the ground. It was dark, so she wasn't sure how much she revealed, but she supposed it hardly mattered when he drew up his knees and crawled toward her. His hands slid over her bare feet before he leaned down and kissed her instep, sending rockets of desire straight to the only place covered by clothing.

Brooks' talent for kissing went further than she could have anticipated. He took his time kissing her ankles while his hands slid around to her calves and stroked those muscles with his thumb and forefingers. They slid up to the backs of her knees and tickled the skin there while his mouth worked its way around her right knee and the inner slope of her thigh.

All of a sudden, he clasped her around her knees with one arm and around her back with the other. She pitched forward, catching her hands on his shoulders as he swung around, placing her back on the patchwork quilt with her head pointing downhill.

He kneeled over her, hands on her thighs, breathing heavily. He was as disheveled as she'd ever seen him. His shirt was pulled out of his pants and hanging crooked over one shoulder. His pants hung low and his belt and shoes were gone. She didn't know where they were and couldn't remember when he'd removed them. He stroked her right leg from her thigh all the way down to her ankle, a long, slow trail of his fingers over her skin. She choked back a response.

"Lolly. I need to hear you," he said. He dragged his hand up the inner part of her leg using the edge of his fingernails to tickle her as he went. She sucked in an audible breath, gasping when his hands reached the juncture of her thighs, stopping just short of what was now crying with need. "Better," he said.

He leaned over her belly and kissed the spot just above her panty line, moving his tongue in a circle. He stopped for several seconds, his lips hovering above her skin. She was scared he was going to stop whatever he'd been heading to do, so she said, "Brooks, that feels really, really good."

He seized up and took a deep breath. Then he brought both hands to her hips and slowly let his fingers get caught in the sides of her lacy underwear as he inched everything down her legs, past her knees and over her ankles and feet.

"Lolly," he said as he lifted her left ankle to his mouth. "Every part of you tastes so good," he whispered as he kissed her ankle and the inside of her calf. "Your legs are so firm," he said, kissing his way up the length of it. "Your skin so soft," he said as his mouth reached her inner thigh. He draped the rest of her leg over his right shoulder.

"Laura Leigh," he growled, "I'm gonna put my mouth on you." She reached down and grabbed at the arm he'd shoved under her bottom and squeezed it hard. "And remember, like you said, no one can hear you scream."

Lolly's shoulders rocked off the ground. With his left hand splayed between her breasts, Brooks held her down and showed off his kissing technique in a place where it really counted. He didn't have to use his hands; the position he'd put her in opened her up and allowed him access to all he could have wanted. Her pelvis rocked against his mouth and he took the time to praise her by saying, "That's good. Show me what you like," before swirling his tongue around the desperate bud at the very top.

Lolly panted and rocked. He kissed like he was French kissing her mouth and she moaned, her hands grabbing onto the quilt. "Do you want more?" he asked as he pulled his right arm from under her. And although his mouth went back to work, his hand stalled, waiting for a response. But by this time she was lightheaded and almost on another planet.

He asked her again in between intimate kisses. "Laura Leigh… do…you…want…me…to…?"

"Yes," she responded. "Yes, yes, ye—!" She gasped, her shoulders coming off of the ground as his finger slid inside. He held her down with his left hand, teased her with his right and used his mouth in such complete orchestration that her breath seized as she hit her climax. She tried to keep silent but Brooks growled against her, demanding she let him hear, so she gave in and groaned long and hard, ending up limp and replete.

She lay there panting and spent, expecting Brooks to disrobe, but instead he circled his arms around her legs and said, "You're not done, baby. Not by a long shot." Then he rolled them both, his back hitting the quilt. Lolly's knees ended up on either side of his head, her arms shooting out to catch her upper body. When she realized how intimately she was positioned against his mouth, she tried to scramble off, but his grip tightened and held her in place.

"What are you doing?" she yelped, appalled. His hands began moving her hips, rubbing her over his mouth. It felt like he wanted her to use him to...to.... "Brooks!" she cried, aghast at what he was making her do. *Oh God.*

"Brooks," she pleaded even as the sensations began twisting and pulling her body into following his lead. "Brooks," she whispered, horrified that he'd made it too good, and she began...*humping* his face voluntarily. And when he added *more* it was like being taken from behind.

"Ah, God," she whimpered. "All right," she panted, unable to stop herself from riding him. "I get it...it's so..." she squeaked. "So...." She gulped in air, screwed up her face, and held her breath as the intensity mounted. Finally, on a burst of breath she cried, "I can't believe you're making me do this," as her body began to buck and writhe. She shattered way harder and way further than the first time. Every muscle in her lean, taut body strained against his mouth and into the orgasm, so that when she came down, she came down hard, rolling off Brooks and onto her back. Flat out. Done.

Brooks lay beside her, his own breathing off-kilter and erratic. But he didn't wait long to clean himself up and gather her in his arms, tucking her head against his shoulder and putting his chin on top of it.

"I am not speaking to you," she said.

She felt him grin and it pissed her off.

"You're a wolf in sheep's clothing, you know that?"

"What?"

"You are not good cop. You're...you're rogue cop. Oh! You're

Dirty Harry! That was so wrong and so embarrassing. And you *made* me like it."

"Laura Leigh," he growled, "if you stand up and take your dress off, expect things to get a little dirty."

"That was a lot dirty," she harrumphed.

He was on her in a flash, his broad body aligning all major body parts perfectly while his hands secured her wrists over her head. "Oh, it was dirty," he said. "And I think you'll agree that nothin' about it was nice," he growled.

"And you probably didn't feel completely safe," he said, rocking his erection against her. "And from the words that came out of that sexy little mouth," his voice softened just a touch as he smiled his approval, "I'm fairly certain you did not find it boring."

He released her wrists, wrapped his arms around her back, and rolled her on top of him.

"There will be no kicking me to the curb at summer's end, Laura Leigh," he warned before he staked his claim with a rough, passion-filled kiss.

Eventually, Lolly pulled her hands up to capture his face beneath hers. "You're completely dressed," she whispered onto his lips.

"An insurance policy."

She pulled her head back and blinked. "For what?"

He laid his head on the ground. "So I won't get carried away."

"Don't you want to make love to me?"

He stared at her—his expression stony serious. She could feel his hands skimming up and down her sides as she waited for a response. Finally his hands moved over her back and she felt him shift slightly.

"I've wanted to make love to you since you were eighteen years old," he said quietly.

"Wha—? You said you saw me on my twenty-first birthday and decided to ask me out."

"That's true." He tilted his head and ran his hands over her back. "But the idea started on your eighteenth birthday. You were at our house, and you had on a tight pink shirt and some very low-riding jeans. There was a lot of skin showing," he smiled. "You and Darcy were having dinner with us and told my parents that you were meeting a big group at the movies. Which was complete bullshit by the way."

"Oh My God. How do you remember?"

"I mentioned the low-riding jeans, right?"

"Brooks. You paid zero attention to me and Darcy back then."

"I paid zero attention to Darcy. You, I had my eye on."

"Well, why didn't you just ask me out?"

"Lolly. I was twenty-five. It would have been slightly frowned upon. Besides you were heading off to college and I was already starting work. It wasn't the right time. But when I saw your name on the guest list for the engagement party, I remembered."

"Remembered?"

"Remembered your eighteenth birthday. And your twenty-first birthday. After biding my time, the perfect opportunity finally landed in my lap."

His hands had drifted down to her naked rear end.

She crawled up his chest and kissed him on his lips. "So why are your clothes still between us?"

He moaned. "That's a conversation we're going to have another time."

"When?"

"Well. For starters, sometime after you stop kissing Vance."

"I'm serious."

"So am I."

"I can't believe you are holding that against me," she said as she pushed herself off his chest and rolled onto the quilt. She stood, swiping her dress up and pulling it over her head. Muscled arms came from behind and pulled her back against him.

"I'm not holding anything against you," he said into her hair, rocking her gently from side to side. "I swear, I'm not," he promised. "I just need you to be sure it's what you want."

He spun her in his arms and tucked a finger under her chin. "I intentionally left the condoms at home so tonight wouldn't be about sex. And then, well…." He ran his hand over the top of his head. "Things just got away from me. Keeping my clothes on was the only way I could protect us both."

"Well, had I known that, I could have at least…touched you."

He smiled and slipped in a quick kiss. "If you'd touched me, I would have lost control."

"Oh, you mean you might have surrendered to desires of the flesh and done any number of embarrassing things?" She threw up her hands and turned a half circle. She pulled up her hair, indicating he should zip her up. "The truth is, Brooks, I haven't had much experience with this sort of thing."

"Strange how I don't find that particularly upsetting."

"All you have to do is touch me," she said, her voice trembling, her face flushed with heat. "My God! What you made me do. What you had me saying."

"Baby," he whispered over her bare shoulder. "If you had any idea what hearing you say those things does to me." He sucked in a breath. "And maybe I coaxed you into doing something you haven't done before, but that's because I was so into it. I was right there with you every step of the way. There's no need to be embarrassed."

She turned into his arms and spoke directly to his chest. "It was amazing. I'm just sorry you…got nothing."

"I don't know about that. I had the voice recorder on my iPhone turned on."

"You did not!" She pushed him away.

He stepped back and laughed. "Only because I didn't think of it until now."

"Thank God for that."

During the drive home, Lolly reviewed the evening's conversations. It took her a while to work up the courage to reopen the proverbial can of worms. "Why don't you just ask me not to play tennis with Vance?"

"That would certainly make it easier on you. Make it easier on me too, no doubt."

When he didn't say anything more, she realized why. "You'd never do that would you? Is that a good cop thing?"

"Lolly," Brooks sighed. "Either you're going to fall for Vance or you're not. You may as well figure it out sooner rather than later."

Her gut twisted. "So this is a test."

"It's not a test."

"Really? It seems a little bit like a test."

"I'd never tell you who you should or shouldn't play tennis with. I'd never try to run your life like that, nor would you stand for it over any length of time. I trust you. I trust Vance. Sort of."

"Sort of?"

Brooks pulled his truck into Lolly's drive and turned off the ignition. "If I were Vance, I'd be hard pressed to keep my hands off you," he said as he picked her up and pulled her onto his lap. "I've told him in no uncertain terms that for as long as you are willing to date me, you're mine and he should respect that."

"So you'd give him an ultimatum, but not me?"

"Do you need one?"

"I don't think so."

"I'm happy to hear it."

He kissed her then. Distracting her. And the disconcerted feeling she'd developed eased and didn't rear its head until a few hours later.

CHAPTER FIFTEEN

With the night sky falling around them and Hale's arms circling her securely, Genevra drifted into a state of bliss. And then things improved from there.

"I gathered from our dinner conversation that you've never been to Europe," Hale said quietly. His arms shifted her against him as she laughed.

"Hale, I've never been out of the state, much less the country."

"I realized this evening when I couldn't remember the last time I swam in my own pool that I've been working pretty much non-stop for a lot of years now. If the two of us were to ever plan something like a honeymoon, I would take a full month off. We could tour Europe. And not like the kids do with backpacks and Eurail passes. We would do it Four Seasons style."

Genevra blinked a couple times and then tilted her face to the side so she could see him. "Hale? Are you asking me to marry you?"

"Only if you're going to say 'yes.'"

"Oh! Okay." They both grinned at each other. "We need to tell Lolly we're dating first. Tomorrow. First thing."

"Second thing."

She smiled. "Okay, second thing."

"And then on Monday, we'll tell everyone at your place of business that we are not only partners, but that we are dating as well. And we'll ask them to keep it confidential. Which means by the Fourth of July the entire town will know about us."

"Oh, Hale, that's perfect. We'll make July Fourth our first public date."

"I'll reserve a large table at the Club. We'll get Vance and Lolly to invite their friends to join us. We'll take my mother, and you can include whomever you'd like."

"Everyone who is going to have something to say about us will already be there."

"Right. That means the brothers-in-law can each take a swing at me, or they can all jump me at once. Either way, all the messy stuff we've been eager to avoid will all be over and done with by the end of the night."

"Hale. You really have no clue, do you?"

"I assure you, I don't."

"If you're serious about marrying me, then you best plan on a very large affair. Because after we make an appearance on the Fourth of July, the only way we're ever going to get our lives back is to invite everyone to the wedding."

"And then take a month-long honeymoon."

"And then sneak back into town."

"Why don't the two of us sneak back into the house and I'll acquaint you further with the master bedroom," he whispered into her ear.

Wrapped in towels, the two of them padded across the pool deck on bare feet. As they entered the house, Genevra turned to Hale with a request. "You know that beautiful wine cellar you showed me earlier tonight? Why don't you wander down there and take your time picking out something delicious."

He bent his lips to hers for a tender kiss, rubbing his hands up and down her arms. "You want some time to yourself."

"I do."

"All right, then. I will take myself off to the wine cellar."

He did that and then some. When Genevra stepped out of his luxurious marble bathroom twenty minutes later, she found candles emitting soft romantic light on a corner table and the bed linens turned down invitingly. On the upholstered bench at the foot of the bed, a tray sat holding a bottle of champagne chilling in ice, two fluted crystal glasses and a fresh-cut rose from the garden. Hale had showered and shaved and now paced the expanse of his bedroom wearing a black silk robe.

He stopped cold when he noticed her enter the room. His eyes searched her face and then took in all of her. His mouth dropped open as his gaze started again at the top of her head and drifted slowly down to her toes.

Genevra allowed herself to revel in his reaction as he took in the freshly-shampooed hair she'd left down and the low-cut lace bodice and gossamer fabric of the pale-pink baby-doll nighty that barely covered her thighs. She wasn't sure he was breathing at first, but then she saw him swallow.

It took a long, long moment for him to find his voice, and when he spoke, his words came out in a rough, heart-melting whisper. "I would have endured the last twenty years of my life with far more grace if I had known I had this moment to look forward to."

Tears sprung to her eyes. "Hale," she choked. Strong arms engulfed her and she clung to him, unable to find the words to tell him all that he meant to her. Suddenly, she was off the floor and cradled in his arms, her choked sob turning into a choked laugh. Her hand flew from her mouth to his cheek where she caressed him with love and tenderness. This man. This man among men. She would do anything for him. Anything at all.

He grinned down at her. "Genevra, I've been so lost for so long. Hearing you laugh—feeling you in my arms—all the anger I've ever held is gone. It's all gone." He laid her head on his pillow and sat next to her. "I'm rejuvenated. I have hope and I'm excited. Life seems so good. There's so much to look forward to now that you are in it."

"Hale." She took his hand and entwined their fingers, pulling him down to her. "Trust me when I say I have never experienced love like this before."

Faces inches apart, they smiled like loons. "You'll marry me then?" he asked.

"Without hesitation."

He licked his lips, letting his gaze travel down to her plump and enticing cleavage. She watched as he bent his head slowly and kissed her right in the center of her chest. "You're being too easy," he said, moving his mouth to the right and placing kisses along the exposed skin of her breast.

"How so?"

He glanced up as she caressed his hair. "I've yet to give you an orgasm, and you've already agreed to marry me."

"Well," she sighed, "I figure if you can't deliver, your crazy shower in there will take care of me."

He laughed against her cleavage. "I refuse to be shown up by an inanimate object." His hands slid the tiny straps off her shoulders and down her arms. "I really like this nightgown. I'd like to see it again. So I'm going to carefully remove it and toss it over there."

Genevra lifted her arms from the straps and allowed him to roll the lace and chiffon down her torso, past her waist and over her hips. Hale pulled back onto his knees as he slid the lingerie from her legs, leaving her bare except for a tiny pale-pink thong. As he studied her body, she admired where his silk robe had fallen open.

He started at her ankles, sliding his hands up the outside of her legs while he extended his body at the end of the bed. His head came down at the juncture of her thighs, his lips landing right on the bull's-eye of that pink triangle.

Genevra sprang up and grabbed his shoulders. "Hale!"

"What!"

"I'm not…you're not…."

He squinted his eyes. "I'm not. You're not. What?"

"Just, please. Come here and kiss me." She tugged on his shoulders to move him up her body.

Not budging, Hale's face went from confusion to curiosity. "Genevra, hasn't anybody ever gone down on you?"

Her face blushed hot and red. "No," she groaned, covering her face with her hands and flopping back onto the pillows. Hale followed her there, covering her chest with his.

"Genevra." He laughed and then pursed his lips together to stop. "Okay. Just…. We'll take it slow. Because I really think you're going to enjoy it." He pulled a hand away from her face and snuck in a kiss on her lips.

Both of them burst out laughing.

"Oh Hale," she moaned, drying her eyes. "I'm sure I'm terribly inexperienced compared to what you're used to. Jake DuVal was nineteen when I got pregnant with Lolly, and then he was gone. So

I haven't really done much more than fantasize about sex when it comes right down to it."

Hale's mouth opened. And then closed. Then opened. Finally he said, "Heaven help me. I have so many burning questions I'm dying to ask. None of which are any of my business. Genevra!" He stopped abruptly. And then he lowered his voice to a whisper, "Genevra, Genevra, Genevra. None of it matters. Nothing except for you and me and right now." He started kissing the side of her mouth, moving by increments to her ear and jaw and down her throat as he spoke. "But there is...some very...important...information...I'm eager to know." His mouth found a nipple and his hand a full breast.

Genevra stroked his short hair while closing her eyes, allowing her body to relax into the sensations his teeth and tongue and his— she sucked in a deep breath—hands were creating. "What's that?" she asked as she arched her back.

"Every...single...one...of your fantasies." His mouth moved to her other breast. His hands became rougher and her body reacted in response. "You like this?" he demanded.

"Yes," she said. "I like this very much." She fairly hummed.

Suddenly his face appeared over hers. "Genevra. Have you ever fantasized about someone going down on you?" He kissed her lips even though he sought answers.

"Yes," she admitted. "It's just that faced with the reality of it, I got a little squeamish."

"Are you feeling squeamish now?" he asked as his erection stroked between her legs. When she didn't answer, he took her mouth in a soul-empowering kiss, his tongue diving in and claiming. The sounds the two of them made heightened the emotional energy, the pace of play.

"Genevra, I want to use my mouth on you. I long to do it. Let me be the one to show you that pleasure. Allow me to make you come undone."

He didn't wait for a response but slid his body and his kisses down the center of her torso until his breath, warm and soft, panted over the sensitive skin between her belly button and the edge of her thong. "You smell good," he said, his fingers running along the inside edge of the pink triangle. "I want to taste you, Genevra. I want to kiss you here." His hands stroked up her sides and back down again. "Tell me you want me to do it," he begged.

"Hale," she whispered.

"Say it. Tell me." He let his lips skim over the sensitized area the silk protected and she gasped. "You want this. I know you do. I owe it to you. Tell me, Genevra. Ask me to fulfill this fantasy."

She licked her lips. "Hale. Yes. I want it. If you…yes…yes… Hale."

She could feel him smile against her inner thigh. Felt him kiss her there. And then she might have heard him say he would make this good, but that was as things started to go woozy and become a little surreal.

Hale stroked both thumbs over the pink satin. His other fingers grasped the elastic at her hips and tugged it down her legs, quickly recovering his position. This time he stroked his thumbs over the dark curls covering her most feminine secrets and then let his lips press against the area gently at first and then with more intention. His tongue tentatively touched her clitoris, which brought Genevra's hips off the bed. She let out a shallow gasp.

"That's right, baby," he said over the spot causing all the distraction. "Just let yourself go." His hands slid down the inside of her thighs and underneath, pushing at her legs. His tongue licked its way up to her sensitive spot. Her legs tensed and a little 'Oh' slipped from her mouth.

He repeated the same stroke over and over until her body began to move with him, in sync. Then he spread her wider, applied a firmer stroke and a long 'Ahhh' was his reward. He grinned again. He didn't remember ever being giddy about this sort of thing, but damn if he wasn't feeling giddy about it now.

He pulled his hands back from under her thighs and used his thumbs to open her more fully. When her hands entangled in his hair she arched toward his mouth, and he thought, *You are so mine!*

He slowly worked in his middle finger and was rewarded with a strangled groan.

"God, I love this," he thought out loud and then started paying attention to exactly what Genevra reacted to and how he could give her more of it. Using two fingers and his mouth, he could feel her body tensing and her climax building. He stayed with what was working, increasing the pressure, increasing the momentum, and increasing his enthusiasm by slow increments until he heard a dirty word fall from her precious mouth.

That alone could have made him come, but he stayed with her body all the way to the crescendo and then sunk himself deep, deep inside.

❦

Brooks pulled up the short drive to his house, exited his truck, and hit his front walk before noticing a dark shadow at the top of his porch steps. He stopped short, head snapping to attention. His buddy Vance sat there nursing a beer.

"What alternate universe have I just stepped into? You? Alone? At two a.m.?"

Vance tossed him a beer from the small cooler by his side. "You don't know the half of it."

"Oh, I might know half of it," Brooks assured him, taking a seat on the landing with the cooler between them. "I had the pleasure of meeting Mrs. DuVal."

"That woman is smokin' hot."

"Smokin' hot and dating your dad."

"Does Lolly know?"

"No. But I saw his Maserati blow in as we headed out."

"They're telling her tomorrow."

"Oh. Good. How do you know?"

"We had the whole meet-and-greet over dinner tonight at our house. I told them I wasn't comfortable knowing about this while Lolly was kept in the dark."

"So you think this is serious?"

"Oh yeah. Which is why I'm bunking at your place tonight. I am not getting anywhere near all that. How was your night?"

"Pretty good," he said, popping the top and taking a cold sip. "All things considered."

"Yeah. What things are those?"

"Things like Lolly coming clean, as she put it, about why you *spanked* her this morning."

Vance's hands flew up as if he wanted to prove they weren't still on her ass. "I told you she deserved it. And what kind of woman tells the man she's dating that she kissed another guy?"

"The overly honest kind," Brooks muttered, taking another sip of beer. "Which I suppose is to her credit, but I could have lived happily not having to conjure up those images."

"Yeah, well, it only took about three minutes to pull her off of me."

"Fucking A. You are such an ass—"

Vance rocked back in hysterical laughter. "I'm kidding! Totally kidding! It was nothing. I egged her on and she was more pissed than anything else. It's not like she could get a punch in. She fought back the only way she could."

"Right. So I'm sure you'll understand why that tennis book of yours ended up in the dumpster behind The Tavern."

"What the hell?"

"Dude! You're spending time with Lolly so you can develop a friendship. Not goad her into kissing you. Or train her for a marathon. Or win a tennis tournament."

"I don't understand."

"Of course you don't. Look. Not everything is a fucking contest. Just ease up. On all of it. She's a girl," he said, drawing out the last word. "Try being nice for the sole purpose of being nice. Play tennis for the fun of it. No ulterior motives. Just enjoy her company."

"No ulterior motives? Fuck that. I practically invented ulterior motives."

"What was your ulterior motive for befriending me?"

Vance thought on it. "Survival, for one. Your mom's cooking for another."

Brooks laughed. "Well, I guess that's worked out well then."

"To ulterior motives," Vance said, holding his bottle up in a toast. "Speaking of which, why do I get the feeling this thing you've got for Lolly isn't new?"

Brooks shook his head. "It's not. Though I pushed it way, way aside during the whole Tansy thing."

"You dodged a bullet with that one, I keep telling you."

"Well, now I'm finally starting to agree with you." They clinked bottles across the cooler.

They sat in silence for a bit, and then Brooks had to ask, "Did you lose your little black book? I mean, I absolutely don't mind putting you up. I'm just surprised I was your first choice."

Vance rubbed his forehead before running his fingers through his hair, sweeping it out of his eyes. "Well, as much as I hate to say it, I think you're right."

Brooks laughed, relishing the words. "Imagine that. What was I right about...this time?"

Vance gifted him with a deadpan stare. "I actually don't like any of the girls in my...little black book."

"Is that so?" Brooks tried to hide his grin behind a sip of beer.

"Yes, asshole. And don't take this the wrong way, but ever since Lolly kissed me, all I can think about is kissing. Not kissing Lolly particularly—"

"Good fucking thing."

"But, *just* kissing. You know, PG-13 kind of stuff. So, I figure, okay, I'm trying to change my ways, maybe I'll shock one of my... ah, regulars, and start tonight out with a little conversation, a couple of laughs, and ease into a good make out session."

"Sounds very un-Vance like."

"Right? So I start thinking about who I want to make out with and for the life of me, I can't think of one I have any interest in talking to, much less swapping spit with."

"Now that's a problem."

"Don't I know it," Vance mumbled as he reached into the cooler, grabbed another beer, and popped the top. He took a sip and then a deep breath. "So," he started, "I'm pretty sure I could tolerate playing darts or pool with Lolly. You think we could take her out and give it a try?"

"Darts and pool? The three of us?"

Vance shrugged a shoulder. "Maybe she's got a friend who wouldn't mind participating in one of our so-called tutoring sessions. See if I can tolerate women in general without those ulterior motives at work."

"Don't see why not. And I gotta tell you, finding someone other than Lolly you want to kiss would make me sleep a whole lot easier."

Vance cracked a grin. "She's a damn good kisser."

"Don't I know it," Brooks sighed.

⟿⟾

Exhausted, Lolly tumbled into bed ready to fall into a deep sleep. The fact that her mother wasn't home yet brought up the married man scenario as she closed her eyes. Any fallout from that would drift over Lolly, making her less the town's sympathetic daughter and more the town's scandal-ridden offspring. She turned on her side, pulling the covers up and tucking them under her chin in an effort to feel more secure.

Secure. Lolly smiled to herself and snuggled deeper. That's exactly how she had felt while sitting on Brooks' lap, kissing him goodnight with those muscled arms wrapped tight around her. His hands had stroked over her with such possessive attention that she felt cherished, well cared for, and appreciated. Secure.

Nervous, crazy, passionate, and out of control—all those things too. All those exciting things, like lust. Oh, he did make her long for him. His body. His touch. She turned her face into her pillow and let out a little yelp thinking of the naughty, naughty things they'd done.

He'd wanted her since she turned eighteen!

She flopped over, kicked her feet free of the covers, and dragged a second pillow under her head.

'That's a conversation we are going to have at another time,' he'd told her.

'I just need to be sure it's what you really want,' he'd said, which she supposed was quite gallant. But when a girl stands up and takes her dress off, she's making a very bold declaration of what she really wants.

If you're going to fall for Vance, you may as well find out sooner rather than later.

Ah. Vance. As if dark, semi-brooding, and bossy were any match for radiant warmth, thoughtful tenderness and oh-so-sexy lips, hands, and body parts. Vance may be known as the Great Seducer, but Brooks seduced her emotionally as well as physically. When Brooks spoke, her soul held out its arms. He knew who she was and where she had been and more about what she wanted than even she recognized. And when *he* got a little bossy, her libido lit up.

She tucked her feet back under the covers, but threw them off the top half of her body.

Who has a naked woman in his arms and does not go for it?

Crap! Now she was wide awake.

He'd wanted her for five years, planned a very romantic evening, and left the condoms at home.

Who does that?

He was no prude. Didn't seem inclined to save himself for marriage. My God, her body hummed just thinking about what he'd done to her. He *liked* sex. He knew what he was doing. He'd given her an explosive orgasm that first night without even using his hands. Brooks Bennett was a master at the art of working a woman's body into a frenzy, yet he'd denied himself any sort of sexual gratification.

And that was what left her unsettled.

Why? Why? Why? she wondered, fingers twitching at her sides. She sat up and took a look at the clock, immediately starting to panic. *I've got to get up and play tennis. I need some sleep. I'll let this go for now and allow my mind to rest.*

So she took deep breaths trying to soothe herself to sleep. She felt her muscles uncurl and relax. She felt her body sink further into the mattress. She felt her mind go blank and felt herself…drift… away…almost…to sleep….

He's playing for keeps.

The thought appeared fully formed, causing her eyes to spring open.

Holy crap. Brooks Bennett wanted a wife. Not a summer fling.

And then Lolly's mind really started to tumble.

CHAPTER SIXTEEN

Tucked around the entrance to Genevra's kitchen, Hale sat at her tiny round table snuggled tight into a corner. He'd been in her home maybe ten times over the last three months, but today he sat and looked around with different eyes. It was nothing more than a modest cottage without air conditioning, granite countertops, or fancy appliances. But the kitchen was painted a sunny yellow and the pictures on the refrigerator and the colorful linens gave it a happy feel. It had seen a lot of action and probably offered a lot of comfort.

He wondered if she'd be willing to leave it.

Genevra came in and sat down at the table. "She's still asleep. From the looks of things, she had a restless night. I didn't have the heart to wake her."

Hale's hand came up of its own volition to stroke the cheek of the woman he loved. "Let her sleep. I'm not going anywhere."

She closed her eyes, turning her face into his hand and kissing his palm.

"So," he started, clapping both hands against his thighs, "once we're married, will you and Lolly move into my house? Or should Mother, Vance, and I plan to move in here?"

A tinkling of joy met his ears as Genevra laughed. "You all are welcome here. But now that I've been exposed to the multi-jet shower experience, I'm not sure I can live without it."

Hale growled as he grabbed her around her waist and wrestled her onto his lap. "You were so freaking hot in that shower," he said against her mouth before devouring her as he remembered their morning. "I swear to God, you're going to give me an early heart attack."

Genevra must have been remembering too because she wrapped her arms around his neck, straddled his legs and started to rub up against him. He pushed up the hem of her little Tommy Bahama skirt and gripped her ass in his hands, pulling her closer as his erection built. "Is this another fantasy, Genevra?" he said through his kisses. "Making it in the kitchen? 'Cause I'm ready, willing, and able to get this one checked off right now."

Her hands opened his belt, unbuttoned his linen shorts, and tugged at the zipper beneath. He thought about taking her on the kitchen table, but it was bound to bang against the wall and with Lolly upstairs, this was going to have to happen quickly and quietly. "Tell me," he whispered, even as he pushed off his shorts and boxer briefs without letting her move off his lap. "Tell me," he urged quietly as his fingers found her wet and ready.

"Yes," she whispered.

"Yes, what?" he asked, smiling and stroking her while she moved against him.

"Make love to me in the kitchen," she said, her eyes bleary.

"You don't want me to make love to you," he whispered, ripping her panties apart. "You want a quickie," he said, sliding his cock through the wet folds of her body. "You want to fuck," he teased, knowing she was too shy to say the word.

"Hale. For God's sake. Just do it."

He laughed into her neck and took her hips in his hands, lifting her and settling her on the tip of his erection. As she slid down onto him, he was transformed by the sensation her body provided. "Jesus Christ, how can this keep getting better?"

She started to move on him with a moan and a sigh. The sound was so poignant that he took his hands and brushed her hair back from her face. He cupped her head in his palms so he could watch her expression as she rode him in this cheerful little kitchen in the light of day. Her eyes were almost closed, dazed at best. She licked her lips often and continued with her small assurances in the way of sighs and moans that things were feeling really good down there. He kissed the corner of her mouth, her chin, and her cheek and egged her on to move as she liked. Her hips tilted a little then, and he couldn't help but smile as she took her own pleasure by increasing the friction where she wanted it. He moved his hands from her hair and captured her breasts through her tank top and barely-there bra, and when he dared to touch her more aggressively he was rewarded with a longer, louder moan.

"Yesss. I like it a bit…a bit rougher," she whispered.

Holy shit!

Hale about lost it right there. And even though it was probably a bad idea, he pulled up the hem of her tank top and whipped it over her head, tossing it on the floor. He pulled the lacy lingerie down under her breasts and allowed his hands to take on a no-nonsense attitude. And then he was the one moaning and sighing. Her soft, pale skin felt so good against his palms. Her beautiful full breasts were pliant in his hands. His fingers pressed into her flesh, playing with and molding her as he liked. He rubbed his thumbs forcibly over her taut nipples, and when she panted the word 'harder,' he pinched and plucked both nipples with increasing pressure.

He was moving underneath her now. He couldn't help it. Having Genevra get so turned on caused him to lose track of his breathing, and most of his thought processes started to shut down. He was desperate to lay her flat on her back and really go to work, but instead he moved his mouth to her breast, captured her hips with his hands, and held her down against him so he could grind up inside her. His thumbs met in the middle to cover her sweet spot as his mouth feasted on her flesh. Somewhere in his brain came the worry that he was going to leave a mark, so he dragged his mouth from her breast to her ear and told her in no uncertain terms that he was ready for her to come all over his cock.

And that set her off. Loudly.

He covered her mouth with his and reveled in the sensation of her internal muscles milking him into his own out-of-body climax.

And he wasn't any quieter.

"Jesus fucking Christ," he said through a tightly drawn breath as he came. "Don't move," he pleaded. "Don't move. Don't…. Holy Mother of God." His breath expelled, and then he groaned, spilling the last of what he had. His whole body shook in release.

Genevra caught his limp head in her hands. "Hale," she said against his cheek. "Oh Hale." His arms came around her and he crushed her to him.

"I'm sorry," he said as his body came down from the high. "I should…I should have had more restraint. My God! Did we really just do that? In your kitchen?"

They looked at each other with startled eyes. And then he whispered, "With your daughter asleep overhead?"

And the two of them burst into hysterical, albeit quiet laughter, covering their mouths and falling into one another.

Freshly showered just moments ago and here to introduce Lolly to her future stepfather, the two of them were now a mess. Sweaty. Sticky. Smeared. Clothes in tatters, literally. They laughed harder as they tumbled apart, realizing how ridiculous they looked and how insane their behavior was. "I had the restraint of Hercules for three months," Hale insisted. "And now," he said, holding his hands out to his sides, "nothing."

"Yes, but that restraint thing is so overrated." Genevra dangled her torn underwear at him.

Hale thrust a scolding finger in her direction. "I swear to God, if you tease me you will find yourself flat on your back. I have zero willpower around you. And apparently," he said as he felt his body start to respond again, "a lot of stamina. So don't get me started. He moved to the kitchen sink to clean himself up. Genevra joined him there, donning her tank top and combing fingers through her hair.

He took a fresh dish cloth and wet a corner and then carefully dotted under her eyes where her mascara had smudged. His thumb followed over the spot with a gentle stroke. After he surveyed her whole face, he finished with a quick kiss to her lips.

"I love you."

He said it so casually, with such little effort that he surprised himself. It caught him off guard. So much so that he grabbed Genevra's chin between his thumb and forefinger and stopped her movements by turning her face to his.

"I've probably said that to five people in my life. And it's never come out easily." He licked his lips, wanting to say more, but it was hard to get the words out around the lump in his throat.

Eyes the color of aquamarines brightened as she smiled up at him. "I understand," she said, "and you can just lean in to that, Hale. Because I am never, ever going to leave you."

Son of a bitch.

He released her chin so he could wipe the tears from his eyes. How could she know what was so deep inside of him, when he didn't even have a clue?

Just then a loud thump resounded over their heads along with a muffled curse. Then feet pounded across the floor above them and the shower sprang to life. A crash of cosmic proportions echoed around them from above. Hale and Genevra looked at each other and said, "She's up!"

Hale quickly put himself back together, allowing Genevra to drag a brush she pulled from her purse through his short locks. He relished the sensation of her fingers running across his brow as she fixed his hair just where she liked it. He went back to the tiny table tucked into the far corner of the kitchen and straightened the chairs. Finding her tattered panties lying on top of the table, he folded them into a tiny package and stuffed it in his shorts pocket. He sat down and gazed at his bride-to-be who primly touched up her makeup as she went commando underneath her short skirt. Her words 'I like it a little rougher' came back to him and his insides jolted with the knowledge that his pretty, rule-following accountant was turning into an out-of-control firecracker.

"I should have never kept you a secret from her," Genevra said, wringing her hands. Ah, the rule-follower was back.

"Mom! Are you here?" Lolly yelled from upstairs.

Hale raised his eyebrows. "Show time."

The staircase above them came alive with cascading footfalls and a giant thump at the end. Hale sank back into his chair, more curious than worried as Genevra went to greet her daughter.

"Lolly, Sweetsie, there's someone—"

"I am in such trouble!" Lolly announced as she blustered into the kitchen, passing her mother in a nonstop effort to reach the Keurig coffee maker. "Vance is probably already angry. I'm supposed to be on the court right now, but I've overslept. And I overslept because…."

Hale sat up straighter in appreciation of the unexpected phenomenon whirling though Genevra's kitchen. She was long and lean and pretty. Her dark hair was pulled into a high ponytail with a red ribbon tied in a bow with the tails hanging down the length of her hair. Her all-white tennis dress was sleek and fashionable, and her red Converse tennis shoes had him gaping at the whole picture.

"I couldn't get to sleep," she said, apparently finding her preferred K-Cup and inserting it into the machine. "At first I was up worrying about you and your mystery date—I swear he better not be married!"

"Well, Sweetsie, that's what we—"

"But Vance isn't just going to be angry that I've overslept. No." She went on flouncing about the kitchen, opening doors and drawers and setting a piece of bread into the toaster. All the while her back was kept toward Hale. "Vance is going to *kill* me because *Brooks* threw his book on strategies in the dumpster…."

Lolly fumed throughout the kitchen so that she never noticed him sitting there, and the attempts her mother made to interrupt her were completely futile. She was so alive and vibrant in her tirade that Hale decided to sit back and enjoy the show. In fact, he was wondering how he might inspire Genevra into a similar turmoil. The two looked quite a bit alike and he wouldn't mind seeing that heightened color on Genevra's cheeks or watching her spin herself into a frenzy. Then Lolly's tirade hit too close to home.

"Because Brooks was not at all happy when I told him I kissed Vance." Lolly grabbed up some peanut butter and a plate and pulled honey from a cabinet.

"You kissed Vance?" Genevra's eyes flew wide and landed on Hale.

"Yes, I kissed Vance! I am only human you know. After an entire week of his slick-tongued come-ons, I snapped." Her toast popped up and she began spreading the peanut butter and honey on it.

"What do you mean, snapped?"

"I threw myself at him and hopefully he's learned his lesson now." Lolly licked the knife clean of peanut butter and honey before she dropped it into the dishwasher. "He, of course, made me out to be the bad guy and now that Brooks knows I'm not sure how that's all going to work out."

Hale had to cover his mouth to keep from laughing.

Seeming to simmer down, Lolly said, "Actually, Brooks reminded me that I'm in charge of this Vance thing, so it really doesn't matter if I'm late because Vance is about to have his comeuppance." Lolly took a bite of her toast. However, it didn't take another moment for the twirl to wind itself back up.

"But, then Brooks—*Brooks*! That's why I was up all night! Thinking about Brooks! And what he did. I'm not even sure it was legal. And he thinks he's the good cop? It is a ruse, I tell you." She pointed at her mother. "The whole town thinks Brooks Bennett hung the moon and can do no wrong. Well, he's good, all right. Good at being bad. Very, very bad. I swear to God I have half a mind to have Vance lock him up." She turned and went about pouring her coffee into a to-go cup and Hale once again pressed his hand against his mouth. He loved this girl!

"Lolly. We have company…."

"And I can't have you making me crazy too, Momma. Don't you understand? The two of them are far more than I can handle. Your throwing me out of the house last night was just plain crazy. You have got to tell me who this man is you are dating, or I'll just explode." She stomped her foot in emphasis.

Genevra came and wrapped her daughter in a hug, whispering in her ear. "Sweetsie, I want you to meet Hale. Hale Evans." She turned her daughter around and he watched as Lolly went from shock to embarrassment to her natural default southern belle hospitality.

"Mr. Evans," she nodded.

Hale stood, taking her hand. "Lolly, I am so pleased to meet you."

"I'm sorry, I didn't see you sitting there."

"I understand perfectly. Your mind was elsewhere."

Lolly nodded, her eyes shifting as if trying to remember all she had said. She shook her head then. "So you're the one who's been dating my momma."

"I am," he smiled, reaching out for Genevra, who came into his arm and slid hers behind his back.

Lolly's gaze shifted from one to the other. "The two of you make quite an attractive couple," she said with no hint of approval. "So why the secrecy? Who are you?"

Hale's response was slow and measured. "I'm divorced. I have businesses all over the country, so I haven't spent a lot of time in town over the last many years. Your mother and I met when I was looking for investment opportunities closer to home.

"As for the secrecy," Hale went on, "that was simply to give the two of us time to get to know each other. Your mother suggested your uncles can be a little overbearing."

"So you're divorced. Not married."

"That's correct."

"But you're from Henderson? And your paths have never crossed until now?"

"I've kept a low profile since my divorce. And I'm usually out of town most of the week."

"Why don't we all sit down?" Genevra asked, and indicated the table.

Lolly looked at her watch. "I really am late for my tennis partner." She looked at Hale, then at her mother. "I should probably call him and cancel."

"No. That's not necessary," Hale insisted. "If you are free this evening, I'd love to take you both to dinner. That way we can get to know each other a little better and answer all your questions."

Lolly blushed. "Sorry…about the questions. It's just…."

"That's okay."

"Thanks," she said sincerely. Then she turned her attention to the more pressing matter. "Momma, may I borrow your car?"

"Can you drive a stick shift?" he interjected.

"Yes," Lolly said, hesitantly.

"Then take my car. You might enjoy driving it and it will certainly get you to your tennis date fast." He held out the keys he took from his pocket.

"What kind of car is it?" she asked, looking wary, but taking the keys.

"A Corvette."

"And you're letting me drive it?"

"I figure I owe you, keeping you in the dark and all."

Lolly smiled. Not a full-on grin, but Hale was happy to get what he could.

"Fun! And thanks," she said, turning quickly and picking up her coffee and equipment. "I'll definitely be at dinner," she said, looking at the two of them before she raced out of the kitchen.

Hale and Genevra held their breaths until they heard the screen door slam. Then they both exhaled loudly.

"Do you think that was a good idea? You do know what's going to happen when Vance sees her pull up in that car, don't you?"

"Yeah. He's going to have his hands full," Hale replied. "But better him than me," he said, shaking his head. "Lolly scares me."

Genevra laughed out loud.

CHAPTER SEVENTEEN

Lolly didn't have to wait to be educated by Vance. She stood on the top step of her momma's porch, looking out at the orange Corvette. She knew exactly who it belonged to.

Vance's dad.

There could only be one car like that in all of North Carolina, much less Henderson. And she'd already been in it.

It took her a moment to get it added up, but the total came to the whopping shocker that her momma was dating Vance's daddy. Which, was fairly obvious given that the man standing in her mother's kitchen right now was hot, she thought as she walked in a shell-shocked daze toward the vintage sports car. Hot and looked like Vance. Not to mention that he had the same last name. *Duh!*

He is freaking hot, she thought with a short, sputtered laugh. She maneuvered the driver's seat forward and hooked the seat belt over her hips. No wonder her mother wanted to *savor* it. Lolly stuck the key in the ignition and fired up the Vette.

She wasn't in the proper frame of mind to gun the sucker. Her whole world had slowed to about three miles an hour, so she had trouble doing more than that. She crept her way along toward the Club, all the while adjusting to the knowledge that Hale Evans was Vance's dad, that he was hot, and that he was dating her mother. Her mother, who didn't come home last night.

But he wasn't married. Simply divorced. And the two of them looked happy, she thought, trying hard to remember anything through the swirling confusion in her mind.

She found a parking spot close to the tennis courts, but sat for a long while staring out the windshield of the car. Something was tugging for attention at the back of her mind. Something pulling at her beyond the identity of the Mystery Date. Something else. Before she could put her finger on it, Vance was at her side, stooping down beside the car so he was at eye level, his arm resting across the open window.

"Hey," he said quietly. "You okay?"

She turned her head and looked at him. Yep. There was no doubt she'd just met his father. "This is your dad's car, isn't it?"

He nodded seriously.

"Are you aware that it also happens to be my mother's *boyfriend's* car?"

He cleared his throat. "I am."

"Are you now? Did you just find out? *Today?*"

Vance stood, opened the car door, and took her arm to help her out. "Lolly, I had dinner with the two of them last night."

"Oh," she said. Vance leaned in behind her to gather her tennis gear and coffee.

"Here." He handed her the to-go cup. "Your mom is smoking hot, by the way."

She cracked a small smile at that, touching her lips to the rim of the cup and feeling a little more grounded with Vance's unsurprising references. "I was thinking the same thing about your dad," she acknowledged.

They started walking toward the tennis courts.

A buzzing sounded from Vance's pocket. He pulled out his cell and read the text. He smirked and then handed it to Lolly. '*Possible powder keg heading your way. Please treat with kid gloves.*'

"Powder keg? I feel more like a zombie. Why would he say powder keg?" And then it hit her. The nagging at the back of her mind.

Hale Evans had just witnessed her tirade about all things heinous, including her volatile relationship with both Vance and Brooks. She stopped dead in her tracks and sucked in a breath like she was going underwater. Her whole body began to shake as she tried in vain to remember exactly what she'd said. Exactly what Mr. Evans had heard.

"Oh!" she gasped as she remembered claiming without conscience or remorse that she had thrown herself at his son and kissed him.

"Oh My God, oh My God, oh My God," she repeated before finding herself surrounded by strong arms that pulled her close.

"It's okay—shhh—it's okay," Vance soothed her, rubbing his hands up and down her back. "Whatever it is, it's okay."

She hid her face against his shoulder. "Easy for you to say," she moaned. "I have managed to make a complete spectacle of myself."

"A spectacle?" When she looked up, his grin was from ear to ear. "How does a girl in the twenty-first century manage to make a complete spectacle of herself?" He laughed.

"Trust me. I was worried about being late for you, so I didn't notice your father sitting at the kitchen table. Your dad is very quiet," she accused. "And I imagine I resembled something of a powder keg as I allowed all my…my…crap to spill out of my mouth and onto my mother."

"What?"

"Oh," she sighed, "I'm pretty sure I told her…well, them, about throwing myself at you and kissing you yesterday."

"Now that sounds like an interesting story," Duncan James interrupted from behind.

Lolly spun inside the circle of Vance's arms to find a none-too-pleased Duncan frowning at the two of them. Next to him, Annabelle Devine lifted her black designer shades from her eyes and tucked them up into her luxurious red curls. *She* had a grin on her face like she'd just opened an unexpected present.

"You two sure make a good-looking couple," she said in her full-blown southern belle accent.

Vance's arms dropped immediately. "Hey, y'all. Glad you're here," he said a bit too jovially. Lolly eyed him curiously as he reached his hand out to Duncan. Duncan took it, saying something about being a little early. Then he looked over at Lolly like he suspected she had his grandmother's silver hidden up her dress.

"Lolly," he acknowledged. Not, 'Hi, Lolly.' Not, 'Good to see you, Lolly.' Just, 'Lolly.' And a very disapproving 'Lolly' at that.

She searched Annabelle's face as the two men walked toward the courts. Annabelle smiled empathetically. "Sounds like you've had your hands full this summer."

"Oh." Lolly sighed long and hard. "That's becoming an understatement."

Annabelle might only be a year older, but she placed a kiss on Lolly's forehead as if she was her fairy godmother and could make all Lolly's troubles disappear. "Tell me all about it," she said as they started walking toward the women's locker room. "We'll let those two warm up without us. Give Duncan a chance to blow off steam."

And Lolly did indeed tell her everything.

She told her about her first date with Brooks and her second date with Brooks and Vance. And then backtracked to how she had stumbled into meeting Vance in the first place and how his magic hands had healed her feet. Then she gave an overview of her time spent running with Vance and how she ended up kissing him out of sheer exasperation. Next she explained how Brooks took the news of all that fairly well considering he only threw the book in the trash, not her physically. And how he still took her on the most romantic date of her life with the falling stars and then undid her with his... tongue she finished, blushing profusely.

"Oh and...." Lolly added as Annabelle repeatedly blinked her long lashes, digesting all she'd heard. "I just found out this minute that my mother is dating Vance's dad."

"Your mother is dating Mr. Evans! Wow! Oh. Wow! That's... that's...fantastic!"

"Yes. For my mother, I guess. She seems quite enamored. I mean, who wouldn't be? Right?"

"Right!" Annabelle laughed. "Oh my gosh. This is big news. What's everybody saying?"

"Nothing yet. I just found out myself."

"Hmm," she murmured, thinking. "I wonder why no one introduced them before? I mean, with your mom being widowed so young and what Vance's dad has been through...."

"You mean about his wife leaving him and Vance?" Lolly hadn't remembered that until just now. She tilted her head. "No wonder the two of them looked so happy. And they really are a gorgeous couple. I was standing there looking at the two of them and thought God, they look sexy. I mean, really sexy...like they'd just had...."

Lolly looked at Annabelle, startled.

"Okay. Time for us to play a little tennis," Annabelle coaxed. Lolly jumped at the chance.

Three sets later, Vance and Lolly emerged victorious, Duncan's mood had shifted back into his usually chipper self, and Lolly had left whatever stress she'd brought on the court way back in the second set tie-breaker. With the adrenaline from the win coursing through her system, she felt too good to worry about anything. Not only was she happy she'd held her own during the tennis match, but she'd pulled rank on Vance when he got cocky or tried to bully her during the game. Physical activity worked wonders for the mind. And her competitive spirit helped to tamp down everything that had been weighing heavily on her. When Annabelle suggested a celebratory drink to go along with their lunch, Lolly figured she deserved it.

They were meandering over to the umbrella-topped tables when she noticed Brooks heading toward them from the parking lot. "Perfect timing," she tried to call out, but was grabbed around her upper arm and pulled to an abrupt halt by Annabelle. When Duncan and Vance were out of earshot, Annabelle looked at Lolly and apologized.

"I'm sorry," she said. "I love you like a sister, but I will never have this opportunity again. I promise I will make it up to you, so please just go with it." She started walking forward before Lolly had a chance to object.

"Wait. What?"

"You have no idea what havoc Brooks and Vance wreaked on me last New Year's Eve during my first date with Duncan," she whispered as they headed toward the table. "It is payback time. Brooks!" she cooed, greeting him with a big hug and kiss. "What a surprise. What brings you to the Club this afternoon?"

Brooks came up short, shooting a glance at Lolly. He tried to move toward her but Annabelle stepped into his way time and time again. "I thought I'd join y'all for lunch," he finally said. "Figured it would be a good chance to catch up."

"Well," Annabelle sighed, turning away from him and strolling toward the table, "as long as you don't mind being a fifth wheel." She took hold of Lolly's arm, vigorously pulling her toward the table and the chair next to Vance. "Sit," she whispered in her ear as she pushed Lolly down. Annabelle took the chair next to Lolly's. "Come sit by me, Brooks. We have so much to chat about. Duncan, sweetheart, if you wouldn't mind walking over to the pool bar, Lolly and I are dying for a Mojito and it will be so much faster if you get them."

Duncan, who was sitting next to Vance, looked between Annabelle and the waiter who had just arrived to take their drink orders. Lolly noticed that one raised brow was all it took from Miss Devine to have her significant other doing her bidding without question or complaint. Wow, what would it be like to possess that kind of power?

"Thanks, sugar," she said as he moved off. Then Annabelle turned her full attention to Vance and Lolly.

"You two really make quite a couple. So good looking, the both of you. And your ability to partner each other so well in tennis—it's just a match made in heaven. Who would have thought it would take young Lolly DuVal to make Vance Evans fall in love."

Vance, who had been downing a tall glass of water, choked and spewed water down his chin.

Brooks tapped Annabelle gently on the arm to get her attention. Before Annabelle turned, she winked at Lolly.

"When I heard they were playing tennis together," Annabelle said to Brooks, "I thought how nice that there are no hard feelings between you and Vance."

"Annabelle—"

"I mean, after all, you were the one smart enough to invite her to the engagement party. And frankly, I thought the two of you made a rather nice couple. But now, after seeing them hugging in the parking lot this morning, with their dark heads together and their tanned and athletic bodies all cuddled up into one another, well, I guess it was meant to be."

"What the hell happened in the parking lot?" Brooks looked around Annabelle to Vance.

"Nothing!" Vance said, but his nervous laughter and playboy

smile indicated differently.

"Oh, Brooks! I didn't realize. I'm so sorry I brought it up," Annabelle said with a level of sincerity only found in Oscar-winning actresses.

"Are you?" Brooks eyed her suspiciously.

"Of course. Why would I want to create any animosity between you and Vance?"

"Why indeed?" he scoffed. "Lolly. What the hell is going on?"

Annabelle interceded, continuing to block Lolly from his view. "They really do make quite a stunning couple, don't you think?" With her mega-watt smile at full tilt, she nodded between Vance and Brooks.

"Duncan James!" Brooks hollered as he stood, turning to look behind him. Halfway back from the pool bar with a Mojito in each hand, Duncan stepped a bit quicker. Brooks reached behind Annabelle and held his hand out to Lolly.

"May I have a word with you?" he said quietly.

Annabelle started to object as Duncan arrived at the table. "What's going on? You're not leaving, are you?" Duncan asked.

"No. But get your woman under control by the time we get back," he said, pulling Lolly out of her seat to trot behind him.

"Be brave, Lolly," she heard Annabelle yell behind her.

"Brooks," she said, stumbling behind him as he dragged her into the clubhouse and down the long corridor. "Annabelle was just giving you a hard time." He looked in the window of a door or two as they passed and finally pulled her into the small gym outfitted with treadmills, ellipticals, and weight machines. They were alone. "Something about New Year's Eve."

"I know," Brooks said as he drew her into the corner of the room and then dragged her into his arms. "I know," he said against her lips. Then he gently bit her bottom lip and ran his tongue along the inside of it. The thrill of it jolted her body into awareness. She pressed up against his chest, wrapping her arms around his neck and angling her head so her tongue could wrestle with his. He deepened the kiss and then brought it to a conclusion just as her mind was starting to go blank.

Stepping back, he looked her over, taking assessment. "Are you okay?" he asked. "You look great, by the way," he threw in before going on. "Are we okay? After last night?"

Lolly felt her heart do a little flip. She nodded. "We're good." She smiled. "We're real good," she added, surprising herself with the words. She watched as no small amount of relief unwound his shoulders and torso.

"Good. 'Cause I didn't sleep much. And I wanted to…bring you flowers, but I didn't want to do it, you know, here. With the Keeper of the Debutantes and her social committee out there. Didn't want to…I don't know…draw too much attention."

Lolly could only nod her head up and down. He wanted to bring her flowers. After last night. Finally, she found her voice.

"I was up all night too."

"Really?" He stepped forward and wrapped his arms around her in a loose circle.

He was so broad and so tall that she had to look way up to see his face. She also had to stifle the urge to lick her lips as she surveyed the expanse of his chest. Why didn't she have her hands all over him last night when she had the chance?

"I freaked you out, didn't I? I got caught up in the night and you and—" he apologized, but when Lolly put her hands on his chest and started to rub, he stopped. "What?"

"I may have been a little freaked out," she admitted. "But after careful review, I'm sort of looking forward to the next time you want to freak me out."

"Fucking A," he whispered before kissing her hard. "I love when you talk dirty." He grinned. "We better go. We don't want Princess Annabelle to come looking for us."

"You know she was just kidding, right?" Lolly said as she followed him out the door and down the hall.

"Hmm. Why was Vance kissing you in the parking lot today? Or were you pissed off at him again? Seriously, I'm going to start trying to piss you off if that's the way you like to get retribution."

"No! There was no kissing." She grabbed his hand and dragged him to a stop so he would turn and look at her. "My mother is dating his father!"

"Oh. Yeah. How did you find out?"

"They told me. Why aren't you surprised?"

"As we were hightailing it away from the house last night, I saw a blue Maserati come down the street and pull into your driveway. There's only one guy in town who owns a car like that."

"Why didn't you tell me?"

"Lolly. Your mother begged me to get you out of there. It was her news to tell, not mine. I was just glad I could assure you he wasn't a married man."

"Okay, but that was big information you withheld from me. Information that could have helped me get to sleep a little quicker."

Brooks cocked an eyebrow. "Your mom dating Vance's dad was information that was going to help you sleep?"

"No. You're right. That has me freaked out too. Thus the parking lot incident this morning." They started walking back to the table hand in hand. "I was introduced to Hale Evans and did not connect him with Vance until he gave me his car keys and I wandered out to the Corvette. The Corvette Vance picked me up in for our second date. To put it mildly, I was still stunned and dazed when Vance found me sitting in his father's car in the parking lot. He was as sweet as he could be about it. Thus the hug." She turned to Brooks and eyed him seriously. "There's nothing going on between Vance and me."

Brooks eyed her back. "Don't kid yourself. There's plenty going on between Vance and you."

"Well," she sputtered. "Nothing you need to worry about."

"So you both keep telling me," he said under his breath. "Look. Vance wants you to come out and play pool with us one night. The kind of thing I've accused him of hating to do with women. He thought maybe you'd have a friend who wouldn't mind rounding out a foursome. He said he'd be on his best behavior."

Lolly's mouth opened and then closed. Finally she said, "I'm going to have to think about that."

Brooks pulled up straight and folded his arms over his chest, scrutinizing Lolly. "Either you want to keep Vance all to yourself, or you are concerned about throwing one of your friends to the big bad wolf."

"When you're right, you're right," she said, turning and walking toward the table.

"Well, which is it?"

Lolly just threw him an over-the-shoulder smirk.

Reaching the table, Brooks demanded, "Annabelle, move that pretty hide of yours one seat over. You think Vance is so good looking—you sit next to him."

"Payback's a bitch," she said, moving as directed.

"Your words, not mine," Brooks commented.

"Ah! Did you just call me a bitch?" Annabelle feigned insult.

"If the shoe fits—"

"All right!" Duncan intervened. "That's enough. Can we please order now? After being defeated by a cocky bastard and a girl fresh out of high school, I would like to console myself with a big cheeseburger. Who's with me?"

The waiter came over and took their orders. The food came and the conversation flowed. All seemed forgiven as the four friends who surrounded Lolly laughed, teased, and joked with each other. She sat there just a little envious. She missed Darcy and the rest of her friends. So many had moved away and came back only for holidays and brief visits. Henderson wasn't the same after college. People got jobs elsewhere and moved away.

Sweet Annabelle must have noticed her mood because she pulled Lolly into the conversation by asking about her tennis dress, which Lolly had designed and created, and then about the dress she'd worn to Darcy's engagement party, which Lolly had also designed and created. Annabelle pursed her lips saying, "You and I should have a chat. I may have an idea."

Lolly began to inquire but was interrupted.

"Dad!" Vance called and waved. Lolly and the rest of the table turned to see her mother and Vance's father walking toward their table, hands linked. While Lolly gaped, feeling shell-shocked all over again, the boys immediately stood in greeting. Vance began mooching chairs from other tables so the two could join them.

Her mother took the seat to Vance's right, and Mr. Evans sat next to her mother. Annabelle, being the perfect hostess in any awkward situation, opened the conversation beautifully. "We were all just saying how wonderful it is that the two of you have found each other."

Hale reached over and took her mother's hand, looking into her eyes before responding. "Annabelle, we appreciate the support. I'm afraid I've been keeping this pretty lady all to myself for a while now, and I guess it's time we made it known around here that we are… dating."

The table erupted into light applause.

"We thought we'd come up to see how Lolly was doing." Hale nodded in her direction and she gave him a nervous smile. She was terribly embarrassed about all that she'd divulged in his presence, but if he was willing to overlook it, so could she…. She hoped. Brooks reached for her hand under the table and gave it a squeeze. Her heart flipped again, and her thoughts started down a slippery slope of remembering the best parts of last night. But Hale's words drew her back.

"And we also hoped to invite all of you to join us on the Fourth of July, here at the Club. I'm going to reserve a table. It may be somewhat of a spectacle with the widow DuVal on my arm. And until I'm able to mend some neglected friendships, it would be a bit awkward for the two of us to be seated alone."

"We'd also like to invite Darcy and Lewis," Genevra added. "If they are planning to be back in town."

"They are," Brooks said.

"My parents are going to be thrilled with this news. I'll make sure the Devine table is located next to yours," Annabelle said. "More support. Though I think you'll be pleasantly surprised by the reaction Henderson will have to the two of you."

"It's Jeb, JB, and Jimmy he's worried about," Vance said quietly.

"Momma. Tell them ahead of time. They are bound to be happy for you," Lolly insisted.

Genevra, Vance, and Brooks all did the exact same thing. The three of them cast their eyes down and shook their heads in the negative.

Duncan asked the question Lolly wanted answered. "Why not?"

Everyone at the table looked to Brooks.

What the…? Lolly thought. *The Golden Boy of the 'hood is going to be the one to answer? About her uncles? About her own father?*

"Jake DuVal is a living legend around here," Brooks said. "Right or wrong…and excuse me if I'm talking out of turn, Mrs. DuVal, but from all I've heard as I've come of age, wrong seems more like it." Lolly's eyes went wide as her mother nodded her agreement. "The DuVal clan has enjoyed keeping the legend alive by taking care of their brother's wife and daughter, among other things. While Mrs. DuVal remains unmarried, she's helping to keep Jake's memory alive."

"They've been wonderful to us," Genevra said to the table at large as she rubbed Hale's hand. "They built my home. They've watched over Lolly. They stepped in whenever she needed a father figure for a dance or an event at school. I'm grateful for a lot of what they've done for me in their brother's name."

"For a lot of what they've done?" Lolly spoke the words back to her mother. "Sounds like there are things you haven't appreciated."

Hale stole a glance at Vance and Brooks. Brooks tapped Duncan on the shoulder and said, "How 'bout we get the ladies two more Mojitos at the bar?" Lolly noticed it only took Duncan a second to move after Hale, Vance, and Brooks started to stand.

"We'll be at the bar by the pool when you ladies are done," Hale said. He leaned down and kissed Genevra on the cheek and then followed the younger men away.

Lolly's heartbeat sped up so it pounded in her ears. She watched Brooks and Vance leave the table, her mouth gaping open. Then she looked at her mother and crossed her arms over her chest. "Why do I get the feeling that shit is about to hit the fan?"

CHAPTER EIGHTEEN

Annabelle started to rise, but Lolly flung her hand out to grip her arm. "You are not leaving me too," she insisted. "You are staying here and facing whatever I have to face. And then you are going to… to tell me how to keep my head from exploding!" Annabelle slowly took her seat and gripped Lolly's hand.

Across from them, Genevra clasped her hands on top of the table.

"Lolly. There is some information that may come out now that Hale and I are…dating. To be completely honest, I never had any intention of telling you any of this." She ducked her head as she said the words. "But what I have with Hale is serious enough—and you are old enough—to know the truth. I want you to hear it from me."

Lolly glanced around, noticing that previously occupied tables were now abandoned. They were essentially alone, and Lolly counted on Annabelle to send one of her stealthy, super-secret hand signals to the waitstaff so they were not interrupted.

"Momma," Lolly said, "I figured out I was conceived out of wedlock a long time ago. You had me when you were twenty, for God's sake. If that's what all this is about, well, whatever. You certainly weren't the first Henderson couple who had to get married."

"You're right," her mother conceded. "I wasn't the first Henderson bride who had to get married. But I am the first and only one whose groom got drunk enough to admit to his groomsmen that he didn't want to marry me."

Lolly's heart stopped. Dead. "What? He loved you. That's what everyone says. That's what they tell me all the time."

"Of course they do. What else would they say? That's what they wanted *me* to believe. Of course, when I found out the accident happened sixty miles in the opposite direction from the church where I stood waiting to take my vows, it became a little hard to cover up."

"What do you mean?" Lolly asked. "Sixty miles from the church where you…? He died on your wedding day?"

Genevra bit her lip and nodded. It was plain that she couldn't speak.

"Oh, Momma!" Lolly said. "I'm so sorry."

"Oh!" Genevra broke down a little. "Lolly, Sweetsie. I'm fine. Now. It's you who I'm worried about."

"Well, what's it got to do with…?" The dawning came slowly. Arriving in bits and pieces. "You were never married." Lolly watched her mother nod. "You and my father were never married. And…yet, everyone calls you Mrs. DuVal."

"Oh. My. God," Annabelle chimed in before clasping a hand over her mouth.

"It's all right, Annabelle. It is rather shocking what I allowed them to do to me." She looked at Lolly then. "Sweetsie, your uncles adore you. This changes nothing about your relationship with them, your aunts, or your cousins, many of whom will be shocked if they ever hear about this. Everyone simply followed your grandmother's orders, trying to make a good outcome out of a horrible situation."

"What orders?"

"To lie about the marriage. The accident. All of it."

"How did they pull that off?"

"When Jake took off, Momma DuVal made an announcement to the congregation that I was ill and that the wedding would have to be postponed. She sent everyone to the church hall for tea sandwiches and cake. Then she explained to me and my parents that Jake had a severe case of cold feet, but that given some time he would come around. She was going to speak to him. Under the circumstances she was going to see to it that he did his duty by me. And her, I suppose."

"How did you feel when you heard all that?"

"Oh, Sweetsie. It was so long ago. And now I look back on all of it with an adult perspective. Your dad was just a kid when this happened. He wasn't ready to get married and neither was I."

"Yes, but you were pregnant. He must have cared for you."

Genevra reached across the table and clasped Lolly's hand in both of hers. The gesture alone was enough to make Lolly's chest ache and her eyes well up with tears. "I was the end of a long line of girls your father...cared for. He was handsome and athletic and so bad." She shook her head. "He was the Vance Evans of his day."

"Momma!"

"I'm just trying to give you a little perspective. However, now you have a better understanding of why Jed and the uncles went a little crazy when Molly ran off with Vance for a weekend."

"I was right. My head really is going to explode!" Lolly lowered her voice. "Are you telling me that I am the result of a one-night stand?"

"Oh Sweetsie, it wasn't nearly as bad as all that. I said 'no' at least twice before...you know."

"You said 'no' on date one and date two? Or you said 'no' twice in five minutes before he then convinced you it was a good idea?"

Lolly was leveled with a we-will-not-be-discussing-this-further look.

"Oh My God," she said and then burst out laughing, tears spraying everywhere.

Four gorgeous heads from way down at the pool bar turned their way. Lolly covered her mouth but continued to laugh. And cry. "You were a slut!" she accused in a frantic whisper, wiping at her tears.

"I was not," her mother insisted, feigning insult. "And please, pot calling the kettle black. If Brooks hadn't walked in when Vance was rubbing your feet, where would you have allowed his hands to end up?"

"You told me that if someone like Vance wants to rub my feet, I should let him!"

"Because you're twenty-three and smart enough to use a condom."

Both women stopped abruptly, realizing that Annabelle Devine, Queen of All Things Proper, was sitting in on their very personal and very improper conversation. Lolly looked at Annabelle and started moving her fingers in a circle, indicating the shape of the table. "This probably goes without saying, but I'm saying it anyway. You are now in the Circle of Trust. Nothing you hear leaves this table, ever."

Annabelle pursed her lips and threw up her arms. "I wouldn't even know where to begin!"

Mother and daughter laughed at that.

"Okay," Lolly said, bringing the conversation back to her mother, "you were young and smitten with the bad boy in town back in the day when condoms were not handed out like candy in school. I get it. No judging. Still…my head is likely to explode."

"All right. So, basically, Jake could have gotten untold number of girls in trouble and Momma DuVal knew it. In fact, when my daddy went to her with the news that I was pregnant, he swears that she was practically giddy with joy."

"She was happy he finally got a girl pregnant?"

"Not at all. But at least I was from a good family, so she was relieved Jake had made his bed with someone she could tolerate. And, after raising four boys practically by herself because the Major was always deployed somewhere, I think she was excited about finally having a girl in the family. She had the wedding planned in two weeks and told everyone it was for the Major's benefit, so he could attend while on leave.

"Anyway, as irritated as everyone was with Jake for ditching me at the altar, of course when word came in that he'd been killed in a car accident, we were all devastated. No one more than Momma DuVal. She was inconsolable. When she gathered all of us and explained that the best way we could honor Jake was to pretend the marriage had happened privately that night in a family service, we all just went along with it. Somehow, she managed to hide the truth and got the minister to sign the marriage certificate. People were told Jake had been killed in a car accident on the way to our honeymoon in Hilton Head.

"Lolly, most of all, I believe Momma DuVal was thinking of you. You were her unborn grandchild, and she did not want you to be considered less in any way simply because your father got cold feet.

"I stayed with Nana and Gramps until you were a toddler, and then Momma DuVal had your uncles build us our own house. Your daddy's family are good people, Lolly, and they have loved me and treated me like I was truly married to Jake."

"Which was my point earlier. Tell them about Mr. Evans. They'll be happy for you."

"No. They won't, will they?" Annabelle said. "They've got a big secret that they don't want to get out. It would be embarrassing for all the DuVals and would change everything."

"Well, it's not like I'm going to tell anyone," Lolly insisted. "And why does Mr. Evans even know about this...and what about Vance and Brooks? Why wasn't this secret kept secret?" she demanded.

"Lolly, Vance and Brooks work for the police department. I'm sure there are records of what really happened. Back then, you could get your police chief to go along with a grieving family's deceit. Not anymore.

"But Hale's concern is that I'm applying for a passport. I've got to use my maiden name. My real name. Even if I go to Raleigh to handle everything, there's a chance that somebody who knows somebody will accidentally say something to somebody else, and then, before you know it, the rumors start flying. He didn't want you to be caught unaware."

"Why are you getting a passport?"

"Well, Hale...may want to take me to Europe."

"He wants to or he's planning to?"

After a brief stare down, her mother said, "Yes."

"Yes?"

Annabelle blurted out the question with great enthusiasm: "Are you two getting married?"

"Married?" Lolly scoffed at the same time her mother said, "Yes!"

"What?" Lolly cried. "What do you mean, yes? I finally get a name and a face two hours ago and you're already getting married? How long has this been going on?" she demanded. "No. Wait! Wait!" Lolly turned toward the pool bar and smacked her hand on the table until someone turned around. "Brooks Bennett, I need something to drink. Something strong to drink. Right freaking now!" She turned back to her mother then. "Are you at all aware that you are turning Vance Evans into my stepbrother?"

Both Annabelle and Genevra looked horrified, right before they burst into gales of laughter.

"Oh, Lolly," her mother soothed. "This is no big deal. If things work out with you and Vance, there is no problem."

"Work out with me and Vance?" Lolly shrieked. "Why does everyone think I'm dating Vance?"

"Maybe because you told me you kissed him yesterday," her mother suggested.

"Or because I found the two of you in a lovers' embrace this morning," Annabelle chimed. "And you do make a lovely couple. I was not kidding about that."

Lolly held her palm straight out and flashed it in the faces of both women. It was all she could do to protest. Words were finally lost to her. She collapsed back in her chair, her arms hanging limply toward the ground, every bit of energy drained out of her body.

An ice-cold Mojito in a tall, slim glass was set down at her side. She took a tired look at it and then slowly shifted her gaze up to Brooks, who towered beside her. In a quiet, unsteady voice she said, "I'm probably going to need two of those."

Brooks rubbed her back as he eyed Annabelle and her mother. "Coming right up," he said.

"And you may as well bring the rest of the Rat Pack with you. I want them sworn into the Circle of Trust before they leave the premises," she said.

Her mother got up and came around the table to sit in the chair next to her. She gathered Lolly's limp body into her arms. "Sweetsie, I'm so sorry. About all of this. I should have told you about Hale sooner. I should have told you about your father sooner. I just… wanted you to have your tidy little life for as long as you possibly could."

"I know," Lolly said into her mother's shoulder. "I know. And I'll be…fine. I will. I'm just having trouble remembering everything you've told me, much less digesting it."

"It's a lot," her mother agreed. "And truly, Hale and I came up to ask everyone to join us on the Fourth. Not to get into all of this here and now."

"So on the Fourth of July…?"

"We'll be announcing our engagement."

Lolly nodded. "Right. Okay," she said, moving out of her mother's arms and picking up the Mojito. "We'll just see how that works out."

CHAPTER NINETEEN

Monday mornings always found Brooks at his desk early. He liked keeping abreast of things, going over any incidents that happened while he was off duty. Plus, baseball camp started today, so he needed to be free and clear by early afternoon so he could head to the high school and throw his assistant coaching weight around.

He smiled at that. At Lolly giving him shit due to his lack of competitiveness.

That girl was something.

Something hot and sexy, and man, he had to use every ounce of his self control not to take full advantage of the state she'd wound herself into Saturday night. He lowered his head and grinned from ear to ear thinking about how their local dive bar, recently renamed The Situation, would never see the likes of that again.

Lolly had said she'd wanted to dance it out. Just blow off all those crazy DuVal family secrets and have a good time. And he was not about to deny her that. No, sir. He would have bet money he'd be holding her hair back from her face while she literally spilled her guts before the night was over, but she surprised him. She held her liquor like a champ. Especially since the bartender saw her coming from a mile away and made sure drinks number three, four, and five were as close to alcohol-free as he could manage.

Didn't hurt that she was sweating it out on the dance floor, and somebody was always shoving a bottle of water at her. These were good people. They were having fun and taking care of their own.

Vance slid onto Brooks' desktop like he always did whenever he made an appearance in the office.

"Hey!" Brooks said. "Didn't think I'd see you until I made it to the field. What's up?"

"Couple things. You didn't take advantage of Lolly Saturday night, did you?" he whispered. "I mean, I know that generally I'd be kicking your ass for not…you know, in a situation like that, but man, there were some extreme circumstances happening there."

Brooks eased back in his chair, pointing to himself. "Good cop, remember? I did not take advantage of the situation," he said, smiling his big, broad grin as he tossed a pen onto his desk.

"Riiight. I'm just askin' because she was on one hell of a roll. She wasn't wearing all that much to begin with, so when her clothes started coming off, I gotta admit, even I got nervous."

"Did you now?" Brooks slid him a glance over his deep grin. "That's not like you."

"No." He laughed. "It's not. Nor is it like you to pick her up, throw her over your shoulder, and head out the back door."

Brooks chomped his gum around his shit-eating grin. "She was getting a little handsy on the dance floor. Had to pull one of your bad cop moves."

"Right. And then I noticed your truck sat there. In the parking lot. For hours."

"Yeah. I had to spend some time talking her down."

The two men stared at each other.

"And did the talking sound a little like, 'Oh God! Right there! A little harder!'"

More like sweet Jesus, Lolly, where the hell did you learn to do that? "Something like that. And…ah, on a totally different subject, have any girls you've ever…been with asked about your, ah, handcuffs?"

"Only about ninety-five percent. Must be a cop thing. She want you to cuff her?" Vance grinned. "A very bad cop move, by the way."

"Let's just say there was some alluding to it."

"Christ! What? Like you're going to say 'no'? This makes her like the fucking perfect woman. You cannot tell me that picturing Lolly handcuffed to your bed is not your hottest fantasy."

"Regardless, I'm pretty sure it's against the law to use my department-issued cuffs on someone I'm not arresting."

"You are fucking with me, right? Okay, Boy Scout, time to cash in one of your stock dividends from Lewis' company and purchase yourself an extra pair. Actually, you don't want to use the real handcuffs. They'll hurt and leave a mark, and you'll freak out about that even if Lolly doesn't. So, I'll send you a link to a website that sells exactly what you two want."

"Vance, just order them. Send them to my house. And let's pretend this conversation never happened."

"Roger that. So how's she doing with all this shit? Not every day you find out your parents weren't married. Or that your mom is now planning to marry the town gay."

Brooks' head shot up. "The town what?"

"Apparently there have been rumors about my father's sexual orientation."

"On what planet?"

"Planet Henderson. According to the great Emelina, since he hasn't dated or taken up any of the offers he's had…."

"Offers?"

"Yeah. Wouldn't we give money to know who offered? Anyway, since his lady friends have been mostly out of town, the locals have concluded that he's gay. My grandmother thinks that's gone a long way to the town forgiving my…ah, promiscuous behavior. Everyone assumed I was making up for my dad, or trying to prove I wasn't like him."

Brooks stared at Vance, trying to digest what he'd just heard. "Your dad? Gay?"

"Right? So God knows what kind of shit is going to start flying once the local grapevine gets wind of the Hale and Genevra story. Lolly is bound to get hit by the crossfire. You and I are going to have to do what we can to, I don't know, protect her or something. Did you check on her yesterday?"

"Stopped by, but she and Annabelle had their heads together over some design project, and I didn't want to interrupt. She seemed excited about whatever they had brewing, so I just gave her the flowers I'd brought and told her I'd see her on the field today."

"Flowers? If you didn't take advantage of the situation, why did you have to bring her flowers?"

"Didn't have to. Wanted to."

Vance raised his eyebrows. "What the hell happened in that truck?"

"Vance, my friend," Brooks said, grinning even wider, "words cannot describe what happened in that truck."

"And you aren't even pissed I'm talking to you about it."

"Nope. I'm feeling very secure in my place with Lolly right now."

"A little too secure."

"Probably a little overconfident, yeah." He kept smiling, showing off his big white teeth. "And we are good to go Friday night. Lolly's got three of her friends from State coming up for darts and pool. Your opportunity to learn how to play nice with girls."

"Three? I asked for one! One to round out the foursome. Holy hell. If I hate playing pool with women anyway, why would she make me do it with three?"

Brooks laughed. "I sorta thought the same thing. She says she wanted to give you a choice. But I think what she really means is that there is safety in numbers. For her friends."

"I'm not taking any of them home," Vance insisted. "I promised I'd be on my best behavior."

"Yeah, but there is that kissing thing."

"Hmm," Vance thought, rubbing his chin. "There is that."

"So. What else you got?"

Vance stiffened. He slid two hands up and down his thighs and then looked at Brooks dead on and put out his hand. "Where's that ring? You better let me hold on to that."

"What the hell? I'd never give that ring to Lolly."

"It's not Lolly I'm worried about. Tansy's back."

"What?"

"Tansy Langford," Vance verified. "I saw her having brunch at the Club with her momma and daddy yesterday. I tried to steer clear, but she went out of her way to corner me. She was all sugar-this and sweetheart-that."

"That's Tansy."

"Yeah. I remember. I didn't like it then, and I sure don't like it now. Especially when she kept hammering me with questions about you. Very specific and pointed questions."

"Like what?" The grin was gone. Brooks took his gum out of his mouth and threw it in the trash.

"Like, are you still working here?" Vance ticked off his fingers. "What's your schedule this week? Are you still coaching? How did your house turn out? And the big one she tried to slide in like I wasn't paying attention: Are you seeing anyone?"

"What did you tell her?"

"I told her that of course you were still working here." He began to tick his fingers off again. "That I am not your keeper and have no idea about your schedule. That the baseball team couldn't have competed for State without you. That your house is a fucking mansion. Then I told her that you were dating the all-grown-up and totally hot Lolly DuVal. And then I added that I was insanely jealous, for embellishment."

"Embellishment?"

"Right. I ah…just threw that in at the end."

"Okay, well…." Brooks nodded his head over and over. "This is why you're going to be my campaign manager." He knocked Vance on the side of his shoulder. "Good work."

"Except that she laughed."

"Laughed? About Lolly?"

"Wasn't sure what she found so amusing. Totally pissed me off."

"Well, what the fuck do we care? I'm just glad I wasn't the one who ran into her."

"Oh, you're going to run into her."

"Doubt it. She's probably halfway back to whatever-big-fucking-city she flew in from. Good riddance."

"I'm glad to hear you say that because this wasn't just a family visit. She told me she's moving back. And from all those questions, it seems pretty clear she's moving back for you."

"Moving back? What the…? Fucking A."

"Yeah. So before she shows up here crying her eyes out, begging for your forgiveness, telling you she was a fool for ever leaving you, and then throwing herself at you to prove it, I want you to give me the goddamn ring."

Brooks closed his eyes and drew in a long, angry breath. He raised himself to his feet and got in Vance's face. "Tansy Langford turned her back on me and this town nine months ago." He ran a hand through his curls as he paced away and then back. "She… Jesus!" He kicked his chair and watch it slide into the water cooler. "This cannot be happening. Why the fuck would she leave if she was going to come back?"

"She left. She tried it someplace else. Realized Henderson is the greatest town on earth and came home. Can't blame her for that."

"Yes. Yes, I can. And I do. She left. She should have damn well stayed gone. Fuck!"

"You're with Lolly now."

"Well, there's the pisser, isn't it? I'm not exactly with Lolly, am I? I'm dating Lolly. Lolly's going back to school in a few weeks. Lolly is twenty-three!"

"And Tansy's a ball-busting bitch. I do not see a problem here."

"Really? Then why are you so intent on holding on to that fucking ring? You see the problem as clearly as I do."

"No. I see a man who might be faced with a choice. And if I've got that ring in my possession, at least I know you're going to have to talk to me before you make the wrong one."

Brooks slumped onto his desk next to Vance. He picked up his series-winning baseball and started working it with his hands like he was warming up for a pitch. "Fucking A." The two of them sat there in silence for a bit. "Tansy was everything I wanted a year ago. Beautiful, confident, wanted children. Liked the idea of being a mayor's wife someday. My age…ready to settle down. Or so I thought, until she headed out of town."

"Right. She was everything you wanted a year ago. But the question is, what do you want now?"

Brooks held up his hands and shook his head.

"Oh, for fuck's sake. You want Lolly. You wanted Lolly even before you wanted Tansy."

"Yes, I want Lolly! But I want Lolly to get her master's and race back to Henderson. I want Lolly to give up every opportunity outside of town and buy into my dream of raising a family here. I want her to want to be a mayor's wife and embrace all the shit that's bound to come with that. I want her to be all grown up. Now!

"But you know what? More than all that shit put together, what

I *don't* want is to spend any more time falling in love with her only to be kicked to the curb at the end of summer or watch her walk away from here like Tansy did. I *really, really* don't want that!"

"So you're scared."

"Yes, I'm scared! And I'm pissed. And why are you even arguing with me? You should be laughing your ass off. If I pick up with Tansy you have the perfect opportunity to swoop in and be Lolly's hero."

"And don't think I won't do it!"

"Of course you'd do it. And it would take her all of ten fucking seconds to forget about me."

"Oh My God. Have you forgotten who you are? You're the Boy Wonder who put Henderson baseball on the map. You're the rescuer of old folks and dogs. Everyone in this town loves you. How is it possible that you have no confidence where women are concerned?"

"Maybe because the last time I was confident I went out and bought a ring. And the next day I found out she'd left town. From her mother. Left without any discussion. Without telling me to my face. She just up and left."

"And other than the initial heartache and the obvious loss of one of your balls, it's worked out pretty damn well."

Brooks shot him a how-do-you-figure look.

"She did your ass a favor, can't you see that? It's practically divine intervention. If Tansy hadn't left, you'd never have this shot with Lolly. Tell me Saturday night wasn't one of the best fucking nights of your life. Would you really have wanted to miss that?"

Brooks felt an unbidden smile pull at the sides of his mouth. No freaking way would he have ever wanted to miss that. "No. I certainly wouldn't. Thank you. And putting it that way, I even feel a little bit less pissed off at Tansy."

"You ought to thank her. That's what you ought to do. She comes in here with some song and dance, you look her in the eye and tell her that her leaving was the best thing that ever happened to you."

"Yeah, well, I'd just as soon skip that entire conversation. This is probably all bullshit anyway."

"Well, I hope it is. I really do. I just thought you should know."

"I appreciate that."

"Okay. I'll see your ass this afternoon on the field. Remember, we're passing out Lolly's cock cradles today, too. Her shit better work. I don't want any of my boys getting their nuts cracked. The moms will be all up in my face."

"The moms love you."

"Yeah, I do have that working for me. Okay. So we're good here? If Tansy comes by, you're pulling a Lolly and kicking her to the curb?"

Brooks let out a chuckle. "Yeah. I guess I'm not ready to hand Lolly over to you yet."

"That's the spirit," Vance yelled as he headed out the door.

Brooks strolled over and retrieved his chair. Then he sat down at his desk and sighed heavily. He pulled his cell phone from his pocket and started texting.

⌇⌇⌇

"Darcy, didn't you say you received a text from Lolly yesterday?"

Typing frantically, Darcy responded with a distracted, "Uh-huh."

"What did she say again?"

"That…wait." Darcy hit a few more keys and stopped. Then hit a few more. "Okay." She nodded with satisfaction and then swiveled her chair around to speak to her fiancé.

"What are you working on?" Lewis asked, the phone in his hand clearly forgotten.

"The matchmaking website."

"Darcy, my algorithm is in the infancy stage. There's certainly no need for a website."

"Yes, but there will be a need eventually and I had some ideas I didn't want to forget. So, you had asked me something. Something about Lolly," she prompted.

"Oh right! Right." Lewis looked down at his cell phone and then back at his bride-to-be. He pushed his nerdy-boy glasses up his classic Roman nose. "You mentioned Lolly texted you yesterday. What was that about?"

"She told me I was wrong about nothing happening in Henderson. That so much was happening her head was spinning. But she wasn't going to elaborate over the phone and just wanted to make sure we'll be home for the Fourth of July. She says there will be a big announcement and we won't want to miss it."

"An announcement about what, exactly?"

"She didn't say. I believe she wants that to be a surprise."

Lewis looked up from his cell and blinked a couple times in her direction. He was thinking. And Lewis didn't think like most people. He thought and then speculated, followed the trail this way, then casted back and followed a different trail entirely. Darcy was used to it. She knew it could take a few minutes.

"Did she say anything about Brooks?"

"Yes!" Darcy's eyes took on her excitement. "I told you. She said that she and Brooks were getting on increasingly well."

He started blinking again. "Do you take that to mean that her feelings for Brooks are growing? Growing stronger than mere fondness?"

"I do."

"What were her exact words?"

"Lewis. Why are you asking about Lolly?"

He blinked twice. "No reason."

"Is Brooks fishing for information?"

Lewis sighed. "Yes, but you did not hear that from me. He wants my opinion and I'm trying to ferret one out."

"He wants your opinion on what?"

"Darcy," he said, putting his phone back in his pocket. "This is where everything gets a little sticky, isn't it? My being Brooks' best friend. Your being Brooks' sister. He's given me some personal information and asked for my opinion. If he wanted your opinion, he would have given you the information."

"Then why are you bothering me with this?"

"Because if I'm going to make an informed opinion, I need to know all that I can. And since I have you at my disposal, and you may have pertinent information that can help me properly calculate a strong argument or opinion, I would be remiss in not questioning you."

"Understood." She turned back to her computer and started typing.

"Understood? What's that mean?"

"It means that I'm not telling you a damn thing. You give my brother your opinion based on the piddly information you have at your disposal. If he wants a better informed opinion, tell him to call me."

Lewis stammered, "That's…quite reasonable, I suppose. Though Brooks is not going to think so."

"I'm counting on that."

—⁓—

Brooks grabbed up his phone the moment the ping sounded. For a smart man, Lewis sure took his time texting back.

'*Darcy and Lolly text often. If you need insider information, call your sister.*'

"Fucking A." He picked up his phone and pressed a button. It rang about a hundred times before she picked up.

"Why, if it isn't my long-lost brother. What a surprise."

"Darcy! Don't you remember how this game is played? I text Lewis. He asks you. You tell him. He texts me back."

"You mean the twenty-first-century version of the elementary school game Does She Like Me?"

"Yes. That one."

"It's been a while since I played. So yes, I had forgotten. Have you received any of the household feminine touches I picked out at your request?"

"Yes. Thank you. You were right. I was wrong. By the way, thank Lewis for the wine glasses and case of wine. Classes the entire place up. Don't know what I'd do without the two of you."

"Has Lolly been there to see it?"

"Ah. No. No, she hasn't been invited to the house yet. I wanted to get everything you sent placed correctly first. Which, you know, involved my having to invite Mom over to sort through all the crap and figure out where it was supposed to go."

"Brooks, I emailed you a very clear and detailed list of what was coming and where it should go. I even attached pictures so you could figure it all out easily."

"Right. Must have accidentally deleted that or something." He repeatedly tossed his baseball up in the air and caught it.

"Okay then. See you on the Fourth!"

"Darcy! Darcy, don't hang up!"

"Brooks. You are the worst big brother ever." She sighed.

"I know. I know I am and I'm sorry about that. It's just so… invasive…having you marrying Lewis."

Silence.

"Darcy? Darcy!" He looked at his phone. "Fucking A. She hung up! Hmm. Impressive," he admitted as he phoned her back. "Did not think she had it in her."

"Invasive?" she started in without preamble. "You mean like you covertly trying to find out what's discussed in private text messages between me and my best friend?"

"I wouldn't dream of invading your privacy if I didn't happen to be dating your best friend."

"And if I weren't marrying *your* best friend, you wouldn't have an avenue to invade."

"What the fuck are we talking about?"

"I don't know. Why don't you tell me what's going on with you and Lolly, and I'll do my best to forget you're my brother for a moment and see if I can help you out. For Lolly's sake."

"All right. Let's do this thing." Brooks bent over in his chair and put his head in his hand. "Lolly's great. She's awesome. She totally gets me. Better than anyone else. She's all I've ever wanted. She's also young, driven, talented, and competitive. She could go anywhere, do anything."

"And that's bad because you're stuck in Henderson."

"I'm not stuck in Henderson. I want to be in Henderson. Just because you and your super rich fiancé have fled the town doesn't mean there aren't plenty of people who still love it here."

"Defensive much?"

"Yes, I suppose I am." He took a breath and rubbed his head. "Look, this town has been very good to me and I'm grateful. I owe the town and the people here. I want to give back."

"That is all very commendable. But you don't owe anyone anything. You owe it to yourself to be happy. If Henderson makes you happy, then stay and be happy."

"What's making me very happy is that Lolly is in Henderson this summer. What's making me crazy is that I don't know if she's ever coming back."

"Ask her."

"I'm not going to just ask her. At least not yet, anyway. I'll wait 'til the end of the summer. And even then. She's still so young. I don't want to impose my will on her."

"Why the hell not?"

"I don't know. What do you mean? She needs to do what she needs to do."

"Hold on one second," Darcy said. "Lewis, sweetheart. Would you mind fixing me a bowl of ice cream? And heat up that hot fudge from last night? Then measure out a quarter cup and pour it on top? No hurry. Take your time. Thanks, babe."

"Ice cream? At nine o'clock in the morning?"

"Do you think he has any idea what time it is? He's working on about seven different projects at the same time. I just needed to get him out of the room so I can tell you to pull your head out of your ass."

"What the hell?"

"Brooks Bennett. You are the freaking Crowned Prince of central North Carolina. If you can't impose your will, then who can? How do you think I finally got Lewis to look at me as something other than your sister? I imposed my will. Heavily. To the point that he didn't know what hit him. I gave him no other choice but to fall in love with me."

"Really?"

"Suffice it to say that as my brother, you do not want to know the details. But it took serious scheming and planning on my part. I imposed my will and am happier for it. But the truth is I didn't have a choice. For me, it was Lewis. There was never anyone else."

"I'm crazy about her, Darce. I have been for a long time. I've just been waiting for her to grow up."

"Well, trust me. She's all done growing. If you don't start imposing your will, someone else might. And then where will you be?"

"Where indeed?"

"Besides, I'd say she's pretty crazy about you too. As much as I tried to talk her out of it," she teased.

"She told me as much Saturday night. It's just…something's come up that's got me thinking."

"Well, stop thinking and start imposing! Trust me. A girl likes to be imposed upon by the right guy."

"Is that right?"

Miraculously, Darcy's words took on the force of sunshine, clearing away the fog surrounding Vance's secret weapon. That damn novel. Imposing is exactly what the Scottish chieftain would do. Did. And now that he thought about it, imposing had been working out for him with Lolly ever since he'd imposed his truck up against her back. Apparently, he was Lolly's right guy.

"Okay then, I'll start imposing." He laughed. "And Darce, please keep this conversation confidential."

"Of course. And I know someday, when I need it, you'll do the same for me."

"Hmm. So your marrying my best friend might just work out for us after all."

"I'm counting on it. Laters, baby!"

"You did not just say that!"

"Oh yes, I did!"

CHAPTER TWENTY

A relative cold snap moved into Henderson at the start of baseball camp. The coaches and players enjoyed temperatures in the low eighties, and the weather also brought out more spectators than the usual helicopter parent or two. Moms gathered at the start of the day, and dads showed up in the afternoon. Lolly worked on her design projects all morning, but by one o'clock she couldn't stand the suspense any longer. She put on her running shoes and jogged over to the high school, wearing a tennis skirt and top in the team colors.

The tall, broad-shouldered pitcher caught her attention, and an unbidden smile surfaced as she watched Brooks on the mound. Protected by a portable cage, he lobbed pitches at the young batters. The sight dropped her back in time, and she headed to the grand stands, sitting in the exact seat she used to sit in when she and Darcy watched Brooks play ball.

Back then, Darcy's father had explained the game to both girls, especially from the pitcher's perspective. Early on, Lolly's focus had been all about the pitcher.

Today was no different, although her focus wasn't on the type or speed of the pitch, but rather on the sun glinting off the curls on top of the pitcher's head. And the broad grin that came whenever a batter connected with a ball and sent it flying. And the chiseled chin, the length of exposed neck, the muscled arms, and the large hands that massaged the baseballs before he threw them. He'd worn a red T-shirt, black athletic shorts, short socks, and athletic shoes. He went through the pitching motions in a casual, relaxed manner. There was no communication with the catcher, no consideration of the ability of the batter. His goal was to give the kids something to hit—out of the park, if possible.

Her heart melted at his obvious joy. She sighed deeply.

Movement caught her eye, and she smiled at Vance as he climbed the stands to sit beside her.

"Hey, Coach!"

"Hey, yourself," he said. "I've got good news. Your Junk Trunks are doing their job. We had some kid hit in the balls within the first thirty minutes. In fact, the whole place came to a standstill to see his reaction. He was a little in shock. Took a look down his pants and tapped himself a time or two before giving the thumbs up. Everybody cheered, reassured your gel packs were gonna work."

"That is good news. Sort of wish I had been here to see it. How many of your kids did you get to try them?"

"Christ, Lolly, you should have seen it. I took a couple of the older guys aside and explained about your prototype. I sort of put the fear of God in them because I don't want to be liable for anything. Then I showed them your squishy, golden, alien-jock-rocks and they couldn't wait to get their hands on them. Dropped their pants right in my office and applied them directly to the skin. The suction cup part worked great. Maybe too great. I thought I'd been transported to a Chippendales show the way these guys were wiggling and shaking their privates trying to get the things to drop off."

Lolly covered her mouth in horror.

"I get them to put their pants back on, and the next thing you know, I've got a line of kids wanting to try your cups."

"Oh, I would have loved to have been here for all that."

"No. No, you wouldn't. It got a little out of hand, but I have to say it started the day off with some team building I hadn't planned on. Right now most of the kids are wearing them. They all wanted to wear them directly against their body, but I figured we'd better have half of them wear them in their jocks, for comparison purposes. However, it wouldn't be a bad idea to design a jock to go with the cup since the shape is different enough. It was a tough fit in some cases."

Lolly looked at Vance as if he were a genius. "Oh My God!

Why didn't I think of that? Why didn't any of us think of that?" She jumped up and started down the stands. "Hopefully I can have a few to you tomorrow. More by the end of the week. Thanks, Vance. Great idea!" She stopped and turned. "Oh, tell Brooks I left to get started on this. Tell him to stop by if he gets a chance."

"Will do," Vance said, watching Brooks frown as Lolly ran off. He headed out to the mound to explain. No sense having his pitcher distracted.

Friday. Thank God, it's Friday.

After spending five days with sixty boys ages fourteen to eighteen, Vance had the overwhelming urge to write every coach, every teacher, and every adult who ever had a leading role in his life a letter of apology. He knew he hadn't been one of the lazy ones, but he was afraid he may have been one of the whiners. And probably one of the day dreamers. There was a good chance he had been found among the disrespectful. And he knew damn well he'd been right there leading the charge for all the complete idiots who thought they knew everything.

It was amazing how much you knew in your teens.

Right now, turning thirty, he didn't know which end was up. And while a cold beer sounded really good, spending time playing pool and having to be nice to the weaker sex, _clearly another apology letter to someone_, did not sound inviting.

Jesus! Now he _was_ whining.

He opened the door of The Situation and felt the tension and weariness drain from his body. Because right there in front of him was a fresh-faced Lolly DuVal looking as pretty as a bowl of strawberries. He licked his lips as his eyes locked onto her happy smile, a smile directed at him, with those red ripe lips just perfect for kissing.

Kissing. Jesus! Now he was daydreaming, and right into dangerous territory.

Still, it was hard not to notice that having her standing there waiting for him was a soothing balm for all his mental aches and pains. Brooks Bennett was one lucky son of a bitch.

"Miss DuVal," he smiled. "Sorry I'm late."

"You're fine," Lolly pacified. "And you look hot," she whispered, her eyebrows lifting twice.

"I always look hot. It's the other stuff we've got to worry about."

"You'll be fine," she comforted, taking his arm and walking him slowly off to the left, heading toward the pool room. "These girls are all here under the guise of meeting Brooks. Your joining the group will be a pleasant surprise. So, just…be you, but at half throttle."

Vance scoffed. "Like I do anything at half throttle."

"Which is why you need a tutor, isn't it?" she chided. "Now, Lisa is the redhead, and she knows everything there is to know about any sport anywhere. And when I say that, I mean she can probably tell you the names of the top Big Ten wrestlers."

"Who the fuck cares about Big Ten Wrestling?"

"Only their parents. But still, she'll be very easy to engage in conversation."

"I'll probably like Lisa."

Lolly laughed. "You probably will. Pam is the tall brunette. She's a lawyer and she's into music."

"Well, I'm interested in lawyers. And music."

"And the blonde is Holli. Don't let her airhead act fool you. She is a brilliant mathematician. Works for the military."

"I'm not interested in Holli. But I'll be nice."

"You haven't even met Holli."

"I don't do blondes."

"Well, tonight you aren't *doing* anybody. You're playing pool. You're playing nice. You are making three new *friends*," Lolly stressed. "You are going to be as nice, safe, and boring as you can possibly be."

"If I have to," he groaned and then smiled because he'd made Lolly laugh.

Lolly pulled him to a stop. "Vance, girls are so easy. Wait!" She held up her hand before he could ask her to tell him something he didn't know. "Let me restate that. What I mean to say is that usually, girls make small talk easy because we'll ask a lot of questions and you guys can talk about yourselves." They started walking again. "Since you aren't going to be falling back on any of your *lines* tonight and your goal here is to get to know these women personally, not in the biblical sense, then asking questions like where they live and what they do is just good social etiquette."

"I'm not a moron, Lolly. I just usually skip this part."

"Yeah, well, no skipping tonight. In fact, tonight we are going to drawww this part out," she teased. "But—now take this with a grain of salt and remember you are in half throttle—flirting is a part of the male-female experience. As long as it's fun. Light. Cute."

"Huh. And here I was doing so well with smooth and sexy," he teased back.

"Vance. We know you can pick up women. What we are here to find out is if you can tolerate them without the endgame dangling like a carrot."

"Endgame. As in end up in my bed."

"Exactly."

Vance took a deep breath. "Okay, but if they start throwing themselves at me I cannot be held responsible if light and cute turns into dark and dangerous. 'Cause women love dark and dangerous," he said as he left her side.

"And don't I know it," Lolly muttered.

⚬⚬⚬

Brooks winked at Lolly as she ushered Vance into the room. He had to laugh thinking about Lolly giving Vance directives. For Vance, winning over women was like taking candy from a baby. Any pep talk would have served Vance better had it been directed at her friends. No obnoxious giggling. No howling at inside jokes. No screaming when their favorite songs played on the jukebox.

Brooks shook his head as he racked up the pool balls. Lisa, Pam, and Holli were oozing a whole lot of young and innocent, reminding him of those Disney movies where the princess or mermaid or milkmaid broke into song every five minutes. He glanced up and watched as Lolly joined them at the bar. He motioned to the bartender to add their drinks to his tab.

Different shapes, different sizes, all ranging somewhere between cute and beautiful. It was a G-rated flick if he'd ever seen one. Nothing his XXX-rated buddy had any business trying to fit into. Good cop reared his head and started to think this was a very bad idea.

He held out his fist as Vance approached. "Coach," he greeted.

"Faithful assistant," Vance bumped him.

"Fucking A," Brooks laughed. "Now I'm not sorry I had to cut out early."

"That pitcher have my name on it?" he asked, nodding at the beer and mugs sitting on the windowsill behind Brooks.

"Help yourself."

Vance went over and poured himself a glass, topping off Brooks' mug while he was at it. "What are the ladies drinking?" he asked before taking a healthy gulp.

"I'd say we're about to find out." Brooks straightened and smiled a greeting at the four women heading straight for them. He took the lead.

"Pam, Lisa, Holli, I'd like you to meet a friend of mine, Vance Evans. Also a graduate of State. Vance, this is Pam, Lisa, and Holli, friends of Lolly's from Raleigh who are gracing Henderson with their presence tonight."

"Ladies," Vance smiled. "No need for a designated driver tonight?" he said, nodding at their margaritas.

"We're spending the night at Lolly's," Pam replied.

"And I know a cop or two who can make sure we get home safe!" Lolly grinned.

When Vance glanced over, Brooks knew exactly what he was thinking. *Girls drinking margaritas.* "Everybody like nachos?" Vance asked the group as a whole. "How 'bout I order some? Be right back."

"Good idea," Brooks agreed.

"Holli and I aren't much at pool," Lolly said as Vance headed to the bar. "But I think Lisa and Pam might give you a run for your money," she told Brooks.

"Is that right?" he said, addressing Lolly's ringers. "Which one of you is better?"

"I am," they both said at once.

Brooks' face broke out into a broad grin. "Well, now," he said, looking to Lolly. "I think I'm gonna like your friends. Pam, why don't you team up with me? Lisa, I'm going to saddle you with Vance. He's not much to look at, but he knows how to hold a pool cue."

The girls laughed. Lolly and Holli sat down and put their heads together at a table close by while Pam and Lisa stepped over to a rack to pick out their cues. When Vance returned and got the lay of the land, he shook hands with Lisa and said, "You drew the short straw, huh?"

"That's what they tell me," she replied, chalking her cue.

"Lolly says you follow Big Ten wrestling." He stepped aside indicating that she should go ahead and break.

"Oh, like you don't," she quipped, leaning over and lining up her shot.

Vance cracked up. "This just might turn out to be fun after all," he said to Brooks.

Three games and a heaping pile of nachos later, a third pitcher of margaritas was delivered as Vance and Brooks stood several feet away from the girls seated at the table.

"So either you're a great actor or you're actually enjoying yourself," Brooks teased.

"I've got to admit, Lolly must be working her magic because I'm having ten times the fun I thought I would. But I'm not gonna lie. I may not be considering which one I'm planning to undress, but I'm definitely picturing myself making out with them."

"Which ones?"

He held his beer out toward the table. "All four."

"Four? What four? Ah, no, no, no, you are *not* picturing yourself making out with Lolly."

"It's a fantasy, dude. And she's at the top of the list." As Brooks began to foam at the mouth, the music changed. "Ah and wouldn't you know it…." Vance bit his lower lip and gave his buddy a raise of his eyebrows. "Miss DuVal, I believe they are playing our song," he called out. "Would you care to dance?"

Lolly looked up, bright-eyed and a little stunned. She was definitely tongue-tied as Vance walked over, took her by the hand, pulled her out of her seat, and led her off to the dance floor. Right under Brooks' nose. "What the hell do you mean, they're playing your song?" he yelled as they passed.

"She's my best friend's girl—" Vance sang, with a unholy grin on his face. "She's my best friend's girl," he continued as he pulled Lolly out of the room and down the hall to the dance floor.

"She used to be mine," the lead singer of The Cars sang out, haunting Brooks down to the depths of his soul with every stinking note.

"Brooks!" Pam yelled, motioning him over to the table and pushing out the seat Lolly just vacated. He flopped down into it.

Holli pushed over the pitcher of margaritas and a fresh glass. "He's just messin' with ya."

"Trust us," Lisa nodded, picking up the pitcher and pouring him a glass. "She's worn that bracelet every day since we've known her. Never added a charm, even when we gave her one for her birthday. She's kept it exactly the same since the day you gave it to her."

"I gave it to her?"

The girls traded looks. "You are Darcy Bennett's brother, right?"

Brooks nodded lamely.

"Well, according to Lolly, you gave her a charm bracelet as a high school graduation present. Gave your sister one too."

Brooks' mouth dropped open. "I forgot," he said as he rubbed two hands through his curls. "The funny thing about that? When I bought that bracelet for Lolly, they wrapped it up real pretty. So my mom notices it sitting on my dresser. Tells me how delighted she is that I thought to buy my sister a gift. Truth was, I hadn't even thought about Darcy. Of course, then I had to go back to the store." He sighed. "I had completely forgotten about that."

"Well, Lolly never did. We can attest to that."

⌇⌇⌇

"I've got to give it to you," Lolly told Vance as they moved around the dance floor. "You can be charming when you want to be."

"I am my father's son."

"Well, you've done him proud tonight. The question is, are you having any fun?"

Vance smirked. "I think you know the answer to that. The real question is…are *all* your friends as funny as Lisa, or as beautiful as Pam or a little less blond than Holli?"

"What in the world is your problem with blondes?"

He shrugged a shoulder, grabbed her hand, and spun her under his arm. "They never seem to measure up to my expectations."

When Lolly scowled, he relented. "I have this vision in my head sometimes. It tends to pop up after I've taken some random woman to bed. A vision of a curly-haired, dewy-eyed blonde. Big smile shining bright." He shrugged again, taking both Lolly's hands in his. "It's just a head shot, a 3-D head shot, but there is emotion there. Or personality. Something."

"Who is it?"

"No one I know. Which is the problem. This vision sets a very high standard for all other blondes. I stopped trying to find one who'd live up to it."

Lolly squinted, tilted her head, and sighed. "You are one complex man, Vance Evans."

He laughed, pulling her into his arms and spinning the two of them around. "And don't I know it."

"My cousin Molly was blond."

"Your cousin Molly was a handful," he assured her. "And that happened a long time ago. Before the vision."

"She was engaged at the time."

"All I did was ask her is if she wanted to run away for the weekend. I cannot be held responsible for the fact that she said 'yes.'"

"When are you going to start using these powers of yours for good?"

"Lollypop, I've been a changed man for two whole weeks. And you've had a front row seat for all of it."

"You're kidding, right? Over the past two weeks you've tried to seduce me at least three times."

Lolly felt a wide, splayed hand surf its way around her waist, right before it yanked her hard against his chest.

A whoosh of air left her lungs. Vance's sculpted upper body emanated heat that synthesized with her own, causing a riveting, adrenaline-producing sensation to spread through her breasts and thread its way up her neck. Her chin was firmly clasped between his thumb and forefinger, forcing her gaze up to meet his eyes. Eyes that smoldered into a deep forest green with enough insidious emotion radiating from them to prevent her from drawing another breath. But she felt the rapid rise and fall of his chest as he slowly lowered his mouth to her cheek. Her eyelids fluttered shut as she felt his mouth slide to her ear and press against it.

"Foreplay," he growled. "Do not kid yourself, little one. If my intention was to seduce you, you'd know what the ceiling of my bedroom looks like. Brooks or no."

Holy God. She trembled.

Lolly's forehead dropped forward to Vance's chest when he released her chin.

His hands ran up and down her back. Eventually he cleared his throat. "Ah. Sorry," he said.

Lolly pressed a hand between them and pushed firmly against his chest, easing herself away from all of the warm, solid temptation. She muttered something about finding the ladies' room and turned without looking Vance in the eye.

She put one foot in front of the other and walked somewhat blindly toward a back hallway. Pushing into the bathroom, she headed into a stall while her body continued to swirl in its whirlpool of sensation. A whirlpool that could drag her under, she realized, hiding her face in her hands. It took about seven seconds for Vance to make that abundantly clear. And the worst part was he knew it. He'd known it all along.

She wasn't in charge of this relationship. Not a moment of it. Vance had, indeed, been on his best behavior over the past couple of weeks. She had been naive thinking his flirtatious behavior was the crux of his seduction skills. Thank God for Brooks. If it wasn't for him, there was no doubt she would have found herself the newest addition to a very long list of conquests.

She heard their happy chatter before they entered the bathroom and sucked in a long breath, expelling the air slowly as her friends called her name. She pinched her cheeks, fluffed her hair, and flushed the toilet before leaving the stall sporting a bright smile.

"So what do y'all think?" she asked, moving to a sink to wash her hands.

"We think you've been holding out on us," Lisa said. "If Brooks and Vance are representative of the men here in Henderson, we should have had an invitation long ago."

Lolly laughed. "They're a handful," she said, pulling a paper towel out of the dispenser. "I'll give you that."

"You are aware they're in love with you, right?" Pam said.

Lolly stopped short. "Who's in love with me?"

"Well, Brooks obviously," Pam said. "But the way Vance looks at you when he thinks no one sees? He's pining hard. It's a regular little love triangle."

"It really isn't," Lolly insisted, waving them off. "Trust me. Most of the time it feels like Vance and Brooks are the bromance and I'm the third wheel," she said, pulling lipstick out of her pocket and focusing on her reflection in the mirror.

"So why Brooks and not Vance?" Holli asked.

"Because there is history with Brooks," Lisa supplied. "She's been crazy about him since high school."

"Yeah, but Vance is hot," Holli insisted.

"Brooks is just as hot," Lisa countered.

"True. But Vance has this edge to him," Holli said thoughtfully. "Like he's all bottled up and his cork is about to pop."

"Well, there is *that*," Lisa laughed.

"Brooks was the one who asked her to Darcy's party," Pam said simply. "Vance is biding his time."

"Oh My God, will you all stop!" Lolly laughed.

Pam shrugged her shoulder. "Just saying. I think you're right."

"Right about what?"

"You've definitely got your hands full."

CHAPTER TWENTY-ONE

Thirty minutes later inside his truck, Lolly was desperately trying to get her hands full—full of Brooks' Polo shirt.

She was leaning her full weight against him as they tongue wrestled, frantically pulling the ends of his shirt out of the waistband of his jeans. Visions of getting it up over his head and getting her hands on his bare chest and shoulders were spurring her on. She wanted a firm grasp of all that brawn that turned her on and grounded her at the same time. She knew as soon as he wrapped those muscled arms around her she'd be secure. Able to think. Sort of.

Brooks broke the contact of their mouths, panting heavily. Helping her with his shirt, kissing her in between words as he spoke. "Please tell me this is the three margaritas talking and not that dance with Vance."

"Does it matter?" she said against his mouth. They both pulled his shirt over his head.

"Probably should," he said as he spun and laid her flat underneath him in the backseat of his truck's cab. He ran frantic kisses down her neck as he pushed the straps of her sundress down over her shoulders, exposing her naked breasts. "Jesus," he said before swallowing one whole.

Lolly's hands moved from his shoulders to the back of his head, pressing him to her. Her pelvis bucked against his lower body. "Hmm," she hummed, biting her lower lip, squeezing her eyes shut. "That feels really, really good."

He rocked against her, pelvis to pelvis, and groaned. He nipped at her breast and then sucked her nipple in deep.

"Ah!" Lolly cried, and raised her hips to meet his. "Please tell me you brought a condom."

Brooks moved over to the other breast, sucking it into his mouth and tonguing her nipple. "We don't need a condom," he said as he worked.

"We don't?" Lolly asked, panting as she stroked her hands over his shoulders, running them down the contours of his back and into the waistband of his jeans.

"Nope," he insisted as his mouth applied even more pressure.

"Why not—ah!"

"Because, Laura Leigh," he said, taking a break and smiling up at her, "we're just sayin' goodnight."

"But you have your shirt off," she said, ogling his chest. Then she looked down at herself. "And my childlike breasts are exposed," she laughed.

"Jesus Christ, Lolly. I already have issues with your age. Please, do not call anything about your anatomy childlike. Besides, as they say, anything more than a mouthful…." He went on to prove his point.

She groaned. "This hardly feels like saying goodnight."

"Because *this* goodnight kiss is neither nice," he kissed her mouth, "safe," he bent his neck and came at her from another direction, "or boring," he finished, sucking her tongue deep into his mouth.

"Mmm," she moaned, sliding her hand down around his hip and slipping it between them. She spread her legs as best she could and palmed his arousal through his jeans. "You just keep kissing me like this, and I'll take care of us both."

Brooks grunted against her lips. "Unzip my pants and *I'll* take care of us both."

Her eyes sprung to his. "Brooks Bennett, I never thought I'd hear you say those three little words."

"What three little words?"

"Unzip. My. Pants."

"Cute," he smirked. "Frankly, I can't believe I've said them myself. But trust me. I've got this," he said, lifting his hips while he worked her mouth.

It took two hands to undo the button on his fly, but after that it was easy to slide the zipper all the way down.

His mouth didn't leave hers, but his hands slid under her hips and pulled up her dress, bunching it around her waist. He left her panties where they were and did his best to pull his pants apart and shove them down a bit.

His rock-solid shaft, held tight against his body by his boxer briefs, scraped the front of her silk undies. Their bodies jolted at the same time.

He tilted his hips back and gave it another try, making them both moan. "Just like back in high school," he murmured, as he settled into a steady motion.

"I thought you didn't date in high school," she panted, closing her eyes and biting her lip.

"Right," he grunted. "Might have gotten lucky once or twice though. Back when we had to keep it PG-13."

"And we are keeping it PG-13 now, why?"

"Because," he stammered, starting to sweat. "Like I said. We're just saying goodnight."

Lolly opened her eyes to find Brooks staring down between them. Watching the action. She licked her lips and smiled. "Brooks?"

"Yeah?"

She kept quiet until he looked up. Then she gave him her best smile. "I really like the way you say goodnight."

❧

Hale Evans insisted Lolly borrow his orange Vette to follow Lisa, Pam, and Holli back to Raleigh on Saturday. She didn't argue.

But she did realize that was how Vance found out she was in Raleigh for a girls' night. And not just any night out, but a twenty-fifth birthday celebration for one of her sorority sisters. The first text from him rolled in at about nine o'clock.

'I don't like this.'

'Excuse me?'

'You. The Vette. Raleigh.'

'What's not to like?'

'Do not go to Spanky's.'

'Already there.'

'It's a meat market.'
'I think I can handle it.'
'Report in every fifteen minutes.'
'Is Brooks with you?'
'Brooks who?'
'Funny. Over and Out.'
'Fifteen minutes!'
She turned off her phone.

One hour later, Lisa's cell phone rang. It was Vance. Threatening to call her as well as Pam and Holli regularly if Lolly didn't turn her phone back on.

The girls retaliated by texting staged photos of Lolly carousing with the opposite sex.

"They are yanking your chain," Brooks said calmly as he sipped a beer and watched the ballgame.

Vance handed over his phone. "Yep. But as long as they keep sending pictures, I know she hasn't been slipped a roofie and is not being mauled by some predator."

Brooks used his thumb to flick through the images of Lolly and a bunch of harmless goofballs. When he handed the phone back, he cleared his throat and asked, "Exactly how bad do you have it for Lolly?"

Vance placed his phone on the coffee table and stared straight at the TV. He shrugged.

"Fucking A. I knew this was a bad idea."

"Yeah, well, it was my bad idea, so I'm dealing with it. Besides, it's working. I'm not out picking up women I find reprehensible, am I? I'm sitting here watching a ballgame with you on a Saturday night."

"Who's playing?"

"What the fuck do you mean, who's playing?" he said, pointing at the TV screen like Brooks was an idiot.

"Your head is in Raleigh. It's not watching this game with me." Brooks pulled another beer out of the ice bucket, popped the top, and handed it to Vance. "What the hell do you think is going to happen to her?"

"I don't know," Vance mumbled, taking the beer.

"No, really. Think about it," Brooks encouraged. "She's surrounded by friends. She knows you and I are as close as her phone. What could possibly happen?"

"I don't know!" Vance shouted, turning to Brooks. "I don't know what's going to happen to Lolly. Just like I didn't know the last time I saw my mother was going to be the *last time* I saw my mother. Or that the last time I saw Piper was going to be the last time I'd lay eyes on her. I don't know what the hell could happen to Lolly. But what I know for sure is that something damn well could."

"Okay, okay. Sorry," Brooks soothed. "I get it. You care for Lolly."

"Yes. And my caring for a female has proved to be a very dangerous thing. It tends to get them sucked into an alternate universe I can't access."

"Understood."

"Look, man. I know it's bullshit. Believe me. I *know*," Vance said, making a face and pointing to his head.

"It's not bullshit. It's your life. At least up until now."

"If something were to happen to Lolly," Vance said, rubbing his face in his hands, "I'd be done. Three strikes and I'd be out. Permanently."

"Thus, the panic."

"You'd be panicking too."

"I probably would."

They both went back to watching the game. Eventually Brooks said, "Is this gonna be a problem for us?"

"Nope."

"Cause if it's going to be a problem we might want to discuss—"

"Trust me. I've lived a long time without having the women I love put me first. I'll survive this."

That about broke Brooks' heart. "What's Duncan been able to find out about Piper?"

Vance looked at his beer a long time. Finally he said, "Duncan is going slow. Being discreet." He shrugged. "It's for the best."

Brooks disagreed, but let it drop. Both men turned their attention to the game.

CHAPTER TWENTY-TWO

"What do you mean you can't have dinner with me? Lolly, this is like the only seven minutes I have free all week."

"I'm so sorry," she said into her cell phone as her hands stayed busy at the sewing machine. "Annabelle's driving up from Raleigh to work with me and I couldn't tell her no simply because I have a dinner date."

"Why the hell not?"

"Because we are working on…something. Something big. And I can't tell you about it because I don't want to jinx anything."

"I need to see you."

"Brooks," she whispered, in case her mother was in the kitchen. "I could sneak out and see you during the hours you do have free. I could be at your house when you get home at midnight and stay right on through until you leave tomorrow morning at six."

"Don't tempt me."

"I'm trying to tempt you," she insisted. "That's the point."

"I get your point. I've done nothing but think about your point. Especially since you've been a no-show at camp and you're refusing to have dinner as promised."

"I haven't been to camp because I'm working on the jock straps for camp. Hopefully they'll be finished by tomorrow. I'm also working on my Fashion Week designs, which was the whole point of my being here this summer, remember? And now I'm working on this new project with Annabelle. Trying to fit all that in between the golf matches and tennis matches with…."

She could physically hear Brooks reigning in his temper. *Shit!* She fought for words to soothe him but came up empty. So empty she could do nothing but let the damning silence lengthen between them.

Finally Brooks said, "Lolly, I'm going to hang up now."

She managed to whisper, "Okay," before she heard him disconnect.

❦

Brooks had done his best to compartmentalize his frustration with one long-legged, soul-stirring, too-busy-for-him Lolly DuVal, but it spilled out into his job at the most infuriating moments.

Sure, Pansy the pit bull had now gotten loose five times. Still, barking at the Darleys was not the way he liked to handle things.

And yes, he'd been taking extra shifts to cover for two of the department's rookies for months now. But explaining to them at the top of his lungs—in front of a bunch of fellow officers—that a full-time job meant they couldn't go to the beach and get shit-faced every weekend wasn't his typical operating procedure.

Temper tantrums were for three-year-olds, not for veteran cops. And the pisser of it was it was his own damn fault.

He knew allowing Vance to get involved with Lolly was a bad idea. He knew it, and yet he had let Vance talk him into it anyway. And now the two of them shared hours on end together each week, and here he was suffering through day five of not having been allocated enough of Lolly's time.

Jesus! All this whining was making him want to kick his own ass.

He was tired. He needed to go home and get some sleep. And tomorrow, he thought as he headed for his truck, he'd start imposing his will like Darcy told him to. That's right. He'd roll it right up and over Vance Evan's back and then on up to Lolly's front door.

He tried to forgive himself for all the glaring missteps over the course of his day as he drove home. The lights shining through the front windows of his ranch-styled home caught him off guard until he remembered Lolly suggesting she sneak out to see him. He didn't know how she managed to get in the house, but suddenly he didn't feel so tired anymore. He was more than glad she hadn't listened to him when he'd told her not to come.

What the hell was he fighting her for anyway?

Oh, so very many things, his brain responded, but he tamped it all down until the only thought left was how good it was going to feel to wrap his arms around her and kiss her senseless.

His body flooded with adrenaline. "Lolly," he called as he closed and locked the front door behind him. He heard sounds in the kitchen and hoped she'd helped herself to some of Lewis' wine. His heart gave a little twist. He'd have liked to have been here when she first saw the place. Seen her reaction.

He turned and headed toward the kitchen only to be brought up short by the sight of the tall blonde standing there.

"Breaking and entering is a serious crime, and though I might not be able to make it stick, it sure would be entertaining to see your mug shot in the paper next week."

"It's not a B & E if I used my own key," Tansy said, holding up the shiny gold object Brooks had given her the day he settled on the house.

Brooks swallowed. Three inches of scrap metal dangling between a couple of manicured fingernails became his undoing. His jaw tightened and his breathing became heavy. His chest muscles clamped down on the emotion trying to crawl up into his throat, into his eyes.

Fucking A.

He turned around and slowly unlocked the door. He stood there a couple of moments before he pulled the door open and stepped aside, looking at the floor.

"Brooks, you have every right to be angry. I'm sorry for not talking to you before I left, but I—"

"We are not having this conversation."

"—had to go. If you had asked me to marry you—"

"We are not now, nor are we ever, having this conversation."

"—I would have said yes. But I would have always wondered."

"*Stop talking.*"

"I had to leave. I needed to make sure. I didn't want to have any regrets."

Brooks' head snapped up and he shouted, "And how did that work out for you, Tans?"

"What?"

"You feel good? Right now? You feel…regret-free?"

"I…I." Her eyes welled up with tears.

"You do not get to cry! You didn't have the guts to tell me 'no,' so you didn't say anything."

"I didn't want to say 'no.' I just wasn't ready to say 'yes.' I'd always wanted to live in a big city, and if I stayed in Henderson, I would have regretted not taking the opportunity to live somewhere else when I had the chance."

"And how hard would it have been to spit those three sentences out before you packed your bags? What the hell did you think I would do? Handcuff you to the flag pole in the center of town and not let you leave? Jesus, Tansy, I was in love with you. If you needed time, I would have given you time."

"You would have talked me into staying."

"I sure would have tried."

"And then everyone would have talked me into staying."

"It was still your decision."

"I took the easy way out. I admit it. It was hard enough thinking about disappointing you, but I knew I didn't have the resolve to face down the Brooks Bennett Fan Club, too."

Her words stemmed the flow of anger as he considered them. He'd never quite seen it that way. And for one long, uncomfortable moment, he stood in her shoes. Then he gently shut the door.

"Okay," he said.

"Okay?"

"I get it. Sort of," he admitted.

"Brooks," she said through a sigh of relief, closing her eyes. "Thank you. Thank you for understanding."

He held out his palm. "If you don't mind, I'll take that key."

"Oh." Tansy dropped the key into his hand. "I know it's late, but I was hoping we could sort this out a little further. Maybe tomorrow we could…."

"Not happening." He opened the door.

"Brooks, we have a history. Surely nine months apart didn't wipe it all out."

"No, not nine months, Tansy. That happened somewhere within the first twenty-four hours."

CHAPTER TWENTY-THREE

Whack!

"I offered to meet him at his house at midnight but he refused. He really doesn't want me to see his house."

Whack!

"That's because he knows you'd end up flat on your back in his bedroom before he finished giving you the tour."

Whack!

"And what's wrong with that?" She stopped abruptly and turned. "Is this one of your bad cop moves?"

"How could *not* taking a girl to bed be a bad cop move?" Vance wondered aloud, spreading his arms wide and looking her up and down. "Although," he considered, "it's clearly making you crazy for Brooks. So, if I ever actually do meet someone I'm interested in, I am totally putting it in my arsenal."

She rolled her eyes and addressed the ball with a big sigh. "I'm telling you, Vance, I have not been sending mixed signals."

Vance had to laugh at that. "No, I'm sure you're not. If there is one thing I'm learning about you, Miss DuVal, it's you don't pull a lot of punches."

Whack!

"What's that supposed to mean?" Lolly turned to Vance and watched him tee up another ball.

"It means you're pretty good at speaking your mind. And telling the truth about things when you probably should have kept your mouth shut. You are getting me into a whole lot of trouble."

"Honesty is the best policy." That little saying floated in the air for about three seconds before Lolly broke out into hysterical laughter. "Oh My God. A fine standard to live by for someone who just found out she's been living a lie."

"Lolly," Vance chastised, stepping over his bucket of balls and moving into her space. "You aren't responsible for the insanity imposed by your relatives." He took hold of the end of her ponytail and tugged it down. Her face turned up toward his. "You are absolutely perfect. Stay above all that. As crazy as it sounds, none of what went down twenty-four years ago has anything to do with you. I'm here to make sure you don't own any of it. Ever."

Lolly stared up into Vance's handsome face and let his words grant her absolution. "Thank you," she whispered.

"You're welcome," he said, right before he kissed her.

It was supposed to be a brotherly kiss. A friendly kiss to offer her confidence. Lolly knew without a doubt that was what Vance had intended. But his lips lingered a little too long, allowing her to feel and acknowledge their softness. And the kiss was a little too tender, causing heat to stir.

She stepped back and wiped the back of her hand across her lips. "Sorry," she said, looking at the back of her hand as if checking that the kiss did come off. "That was just a little," she murmured, raising her head and looking into Vance's eyes, "felt a little…."

"Too good," he acknowledged.

She nodded.

"I so need a girlfriend," Vance groaned. "Lolly, I didn't mean…."

"I know. I know you didn't." Her breathing was heavy. She couldn't drag her eyes away from Vance. "This is why, isn't it? This is why Brooks won't take me to…invite me to his house."

"Probably."

"Because he doesn't trust the two of us."

"Probably more to it than that."

"Because he doesn't trust that I've chosen him. Over you." Lolly blinked a couple of times. "And why should he? I broke a date with him last night, but I'm unwilling to forfeit a match."

"He knows you're competitive to a fault. He's not going to hold that against you."

Lolly rolled her eyes. "Being competitive is not a fault," she insisted.

"You'll get no argument from me," Vance agreed.

"So what is the holdup? I swear to God if he'd just…do the deed, all this sexual tension would dissipate."

"Well, there's the short answer."

"What's the long answer?"

Vance rubbed the back of his neck, hesitating.

"How long can it be?"

"Lolly, have you not noticed that Brooks is *loyal* to a fault? I don't deserve it, but he and I bonded in the trenches a long time ago, and in Brooks' world that means he's not giving up on me. Ever."

"Bonded in the trenches? Is that the hazing thing Brooks told me about?"

"Exactly. What did he tell you?"

"He said you kept telling him that it was nothing. He said he would have quit the team if you hadn't been through worse."

"He said that?"

"Yeah. You pulled him through."

"Well, did he tell you what happened the following year? When we were sophomores?"

Lolly shook her head.

Vance rubbed his chin and muttered, "Of course he didn't." He took a deep breath and said, "The truth is that a year later when ten freshmen joined the team, I was all ready to turn the tables on those guys and continue the tradition. I mean, it was my right. Right? I'd lived through it, and now it was their turn. In fact," he laughed, "I had been harboring a slew of goldfish all summer, feeding them three times a day so they would be huge when the time came for their demise.

"Brooks took one look at the goldfish and literally knocked some sense into me. He got in my face as I lay flat on the ground and asked what the hell kind of team building did I think continuing the hazing was going to do.

"And he was right. I hated those upperclassmen with a passion, and here I was ready to make ten new *teammates* hate me like that. It was stupid, but I saw the light quickly. When Brooks pulled me off the ground, the two of us got into the faces of the juniors and seniors and ended the hazing. Right then. Forever."

"Oh My God," Lolly shrieked. "Is there no part of this town that the two of you haven't single-handedly changed for the better?"

Vance laughed. "Well, if there is, we plan to take care of it when Brooks is mayor."

"Why do you two love this town so much? I mean, sure it's home and I like the people, but nothing ever happens here!"

"Anything you want can happen here! Don't you see? It's fertile ground. Plenty of room for new homes and new businesses. Plenty of room to work and to play. Granted, we are removed from a big city, but we don't have many of those big-city problems either. The weather is perfect and the lake is beautiful. There are parks and recreation areas as far as you can see. It's paradise, and all we need is a little publicity to put Henderson on the map. And that's our plan."

"So you and Brooks are in a committed relationship and have a long-term plan," Lolly quipped, but held up a hand when Vance started to object. "No seriously. I get it. I do. In fact, I'm doing my best to jump on board."

"Well, my point in all this is that Brooks is loyal. His close personal relationships are extremely important to him. It makes him cautious. The last thing he wants to do is mess things up for any of us."

"Mess things up?"

"Well, what if you and Brooks become intimate? And for whatever reason, things don't work out between you two."

"Uh-huh."

"And you and I continue to play tennis together. Continue to play golf together. Continue to kiss every now and then. One thing leads to another, and—follow me here—the two of us, somehow, end up together."

"Hmm."

"Brooks is still going to be my friend. He's going to have to sit across from the two of us and pretend to be okay about it. He would hate that. I would hate that. You would hate that."

"I don't know. I might not hate that." Then she burst out laughing.

"You are bad!" Vance accused.

"And it's only going to get worse," Lolly assured him. "Please, do us both a favor and go get laid. For God's sake, it's like you've taken a vow of celibacy."

"That is a dirty word. Now take it back."

"I'm serious." She glanced at her watch. "Come on, we're on the tee in five minutes."

"Lolly." He grabbed her shoulder as she began to gather her clubs. "In all seriousness. Brooks wants you. Don't doubt that for a minute. He's the good cop, remember. He's just trying to protect all of us. He's just waiting for you to be sure."

"Be sure about what, exactly?"

"That he's the love of your life."

CHAPTER TWENTY-FOUR

The love of my life?

Lolly repeated the phrase over and over as she pulled the finely-woven pink canvas through her sewing machine. She'd come up with the idea during the golf match the other night, which probably saved their victory. Stupid Vance had distracted her with the love-of-my-life stuff right before teeing off, and she couldn't concentrate on anything until she'd devised a plan to seduce Brooks.

Really. Enough was enough. Wasn't being the love-of-her-summer good enough for now?

The sewing machine stopped.

Who was she kidding?

She'd figured it out weeks ago, she realized as she resumed sewing. She figured out that Brooks was playing for keeps and that had scared the bejesus out of her. For all of fifteen minutes. Then she'd fallen into a deep, restful sleep. And when she laid eyes on Brooks the next day, her body responded mightily to the idea.

Let's face it. Brooks Bennett became her knight in shining armor the day he fastened that bracelet around her wrist five years ago. And when he pulled her into his arms for that slow dance at Darcy's party, well, she started falling hard. And while her grip had started to loosen on the dream of moving to New York City—thanks to Annabelle Devine another dream had started taking its place. One that frankly made a lot more sense, considering Annabelle's contacts. The fact that it also gave her a way to buy into Brooks and Vance's dream of Henderson was just the icing on the cake. Who said Henderson wasn't the next textile capital of the world? She and Annabelle were planning to put it on the map. The only person who wasn't aware of it yet was the future mayor.

Brooks hadn't exactly been avoiding her calls over the last several days, but he wasn't knocking down the door to see her either. With his working mornings and nights so he could be on the baseball field during camp hours, he had zero free time. Still she'd be more worried if the whole Sweaty Balls Debacle hadn't erupted with the heat wave that crashed into this week's baseball camp.

A frantic, albeit humor-ridden, call from Brooks had Lolly on the phone rallying the males from her design team at State to come to Henderson and take stock of the situation. While the cups worn up against the skin managed beautifully in eighty-two degree heat, they produced a rash of untold proportions when the thermometer hit ninety. Brooks and Vance's description of the locker room fallout went on for at least two beers that night. Describing how boys of all body types and sizes—naked from the waist down—had laid themselves out spread eagle trying to cool their appendages and soothe the pimpled rashes.

The thirty minutes she and Brooks stole before he headed back to work made it all worthwhile.

And tonight he was working the desk by himself until eleven o'clock. At least that's what Vance had told her. She hoped he was right because what she was planning to do was actually illegal. Which was sort of the point. She just wanted to make sure it was the right cop handcuffing her.

⁓⁓⁓

Brooks sat back in the desk chair with his arms crossed over his chest and his eyes closed. He wasn't asleep, he told himself, he was just resting his eyes. A half hour to go and thankfully things were quiet. It had been a long, eventful week and though he truly loved every minute of being a coach—the sun, the kids, and the extra hours of being in charge had taken its toll.

He noticed as a flash of light crossed over his closed lids and figured it was the headlights from a car pulling into the lot. He opened one eye and watched as the black, Smokey-and-the-Bandit

Trans Am parked across from the double swinging doors.

His own truck blocked the view of the driver's door, but he kept watch just the same, wondering what Vance was doing here at this hour and why the hell he was driving that car. But surprise, surprise! Vance did not rear his ugly head. No, thanks to the well-lit parking lot, what he saw was a lot of long, lean, exposed leg walking his way. His gum dropped out of his mouth as he sat up straight and took in the sight.

Bubblegum pink pumps. Dainty ankles. Long calves. Knobby little knees. Firm, sleek thighs. And just a tad further up his heart stopped at the brief flash of tender, stroke-me-right-here inner thigh teasing him as she walked. He licked his lips and ordered his eyes to move up the hemline of a hot-pink, double-breasted trench coat, all buttoned up and cinched tight with a matching belt. Above that, one more button and then the coat was left undone, exposing an enticing V of flesh leading to a long neck, a dimpled chin, and pale pink lip gloss.

His eyes darted between the flashes of stroke-me thigh and kiss-me-silly lips. In fact, he didn't realize he was standing, hands flat on his desk, until the distraction of the flashing thighs stopped and he was able to lift his gaze to sparkling sapphire eyes and an innocent dark brown ponytail all tied up neatly with a narrow pink bow.

"I love pink," he said as if his left brain had shut down. Was he drooling? He felt like he was drooling. He wiped at his mouth with his hand, all the while wondering what she had on underneath that trench coat. "I mean…the coat. I love the coat. Although…" he said, sitting down again very slowly as she came around his desk and propped a hip against the side, "it's a little hot for a coat. Did you make this?" His eyes flashed up toward hers. "I really love your sewing machine."

Lolly gave him a broad smile as she stood up straight on her three-inch heels. She started slowly untying the belt.

"Laura Leigh." Brooks licked his lips, watching her fingers closely. "Just so you know, we are being recorded."

She stopped abruptly and glanced around. He pointed up. Little half globes graced the ceiling in various spots. She wiggled her fingers at them to say hello. "What are the chances this video will ever be reviewed?"

Brooks reached out and stroked one fingertip up the outside of her left thigh. "I wish I knew."

"It's not recording sound, is it?"

He shook his head back and forth as he scooted his chair closer and began to drag two fingertips up the outside of each of her thighs.

"That feels good," she said, smiling down into the curls on the top of his head. When he kept it up, she added, "You seem intensely focused."

"Just trying to puzzle this out," he said to her shoes. His fingers took hold of the sides of her hem as he raised his head. "I'm trying to figure out what you had in mind." He smiled.

She stroked her fingers through his hair and then down one side of his face. "I thought I'd come in here and try to get myself arrested."

"By flashing a police officer?"

"For starters."

He turned his head and captured her lingering fingers with his teeth. He eyed her for a moment before circling her wrist with his right hand and spinning her into his lap. His arms came around her waist and pulled her back tight against his chest. He leaned back so that her feet came off the floor and her body slid to his left side and settled in.

He whispered in her ear. "You leave me no choice but to do a little interrogating." Then he licked the skin beneath her ear, down to the hollow little hot spot above her shoulder. He scraped his teeth on the tender flesh there. "What's underneath the coat?"

"A little bit of this," she sighed, closing her eyes. "Not so much of that."

His hand slid up her outer thigh and felt unimpeded flesh all the way to her hip. "That's not much of an answer," he said, his lips brushing over hers. "I'm afraid I'm going to have to apply a little pressure to get you to talk." His tongue traced her bottom lip and then tucked itself in at the edge of her mouth, urging her to open for him. She capitulated immediately, waving off any protest with a soft moan.

Brooks took his time with the kiss. He wanted to be thorough. He wanted to ease all her secrets from her lips before she knew what was happening.

"Where did you get the Trans Am?" His fingers stroked her hip. His tongue stroked the inside of her bottom lip.

"The what?" Her tongue snuck into his mouth and he mumbled a 'never mind' as he let her take the lead.

The phone on his desk rang. He looked at his watch as he eased his mouth off Lolly's. He looked into her eyes and promised, "Fifteen minutes. Unless this is a life-threatening emergency, we are out of here in fifteen minutes."

"Henderson police," he answered. The fog in his brain dissipated as he focused in on the Spanish accent. "Mrs. Flores? This is Brooks." His eyes shot to Lolly's. "DuVal? All three of them?" Lolly rose off his lap and started tying the belt of her coat. "Where are they now? Okay. And where is your son? And how 'bout Vance?" He nodded his head three times. "Okay, I'm on my way. Just…you know…open another bottle and play the gracious hostess. Ten minutes tops," he said before hanging up the phone.

He immediately picked it up again and called 911. "Gail, it's Brooks at the office. There's a disturbance out at the Evans' place. Probably nothing serious but if you can get the word out to Vance and have him head home, I'd appreciate it. I'm on my way and I'm forwarding calls from the office to you." He hung up the phone.

"Evans' place?" Lolly asked. "You said Flores."

"Vance's grandmother, Emelina Flores," he said, steering her to the front doors and hitting the lights and setting the alarm as they headed out. He turned and locked up, saying, "Haven't you met her yet?"

She shook her head. "You said DuVal. What's happening?"

"Hopefully a whole lot of nothing," he muttered. "We'll take the squad car just in case I have to act in an official capacity."

Once they were on their way, sirens blaring, he told Lolly what he knew. "So it seems your uncles have managed to get themselves liquored up and ridden horses out to the Evans'."

"Horses? Why are they on horses?"

"I have no idea," Brooks said, taking a corner as gently as he could without losing too much speed. "Emelina is the only one home, and it seems they've invited themselves in and have found Mr.

Evans' wine cellar."

"Oh, God. I really thought everyone was over-reacting. My uncles are nice guys. They love my mother. They love me!"

Brooks reached around all the police equipment between them and patted Lolly on the leg. "I'm pretty sure this is just a pissing contest. Still, I'm not happy they've upset the Big Em."

"The Big Em?'

"Vance's grandmother," he said smiling. "Our pet name."

They pulled up the long front drive, which ended in a circle in front of the house. Sure enough, there were three saddled horses nibbling grass in the center of the drive. Completely untethered but uninterested in running off, from the looks of it.

"They're probably from the stable where my cousin rides. I can't say I've ever seen any of my uncles on a horse," Lolly said, exiting the car and pulling her trench coat down as far as she could. As Brooks rang the doorbell, Lolly pulled off the pink heels to carry them in her hand. It was then that Brooks looked her up and down.

"You're going to have some explaining to do in that outfit," he said, grinning.

"I'm sort of hoping for enough action that nobody pays attention to what I have on."

"You could wait in the car," he suggested.

She scoffed at him, "And miss this? Not a chance."

Emelina Flores opened the door wide with a flourish. She said rather loudly, "Ah, Brooks! What a pleasant surprise. You'll come in, won't you?"

"Don't mind if I do," he said as he winked at Big Em.

"They are in the kitchen," she whispered. "I haven't been able to get ahold of Hale or Vance. But now that you're here, I'd prefer we get them out before either of them come home."

"Why don't you ladies stay here? Give me a minute to size up the situation. Oh, this is Lolly by the way. Lolly DuVal," he pronounced the last name to ensure the Big Em could figure out who she was standing next to. He heard Emelina's surprise as he wandered toward the kitchen.

Brooks really wished he wasn't on duty. One look at the situation had him close to howling with laughter. Since it wasn't Halloween, he wasn't exactly sure what he was seeing, but he choked all that back and proceeded cautiously, following protocol as best he could since he was entering the scene wearing his police uniform.

He took another step and stopped. *Fuck this good cop shit,* he thought. This was too good to pass up. Besides, he had information he probably shouldn't, but there it was. He'd use it to his advantage.

"What the hell kind of a lame-ass rodeo is this?" he said, walking into the kitchen where Jeb, JB, and Big Jim DuVal were sprawled about with a dozen wine bottles scattered between them. There were cowboy hats, bandanas, and fruity Texas shirts everywhere he looked. Big Jim had on chaps, for Christ's sake. Jeb's belt buckle was as big as his head. JB's loafers looked ridiculous with the rest of his get-up, but they were the only things that resembled what the DuVal brothers usually wore.

"Hey!" they all hollered at him at once.

"If it isn't the great Brooks Bennett! Come on in here and have yourself some of the finest wine we've found in all of North Carolina," Big Jim offered as he got up to pour Brooks a glass.

"I didn't know cowboys took much stock in wine."

"Well, this ain't exactly a rodeo," Jeb confessed. "It's more like a hootenanny."

"Right. And what are we hooting about?" Brooks asked as he took his first sip. "Didn't realize y'all were so friendly with the Evans family."

"Well, now," JB said, "our sweet Genevra has informed us that the Evans clan and the DuVal clan are likely going to be joining forces, if you will," he said, swaying right off the countertop he'd propped his elbows on. He caught himself and continued without missing a beat. "Being as we are the bride's family, it's our duty to extend a greeting to the groom's family. So we formed a posse, mounted up, and rode ourselves over here." He indicated with his arm. "Took us a little longer than expected with all that whiskey-for-my-men and beer-for-my-horses bullshit Jim insisted on. We had to stop at The Situation to gird our loins, so to speak." JB leaned in toward Brooks and said, "There are some delicate family matters that need discussing, you understand. We just wanted to reach an understanding as soon as possible."

"Understood," Brooks acknowledged, preparing to clear the room and get Lolly's uncles home to bed. But his plans were thwarted with one big cheer.

"Lolly!" JB, Jim, and Jeb shouted in unison, holding up their glasses in a toast. Brooks turned as Emelina and Lolly entered the kitchen hand in hand. "Come here and give us a hug, darlin'," Jeb suggested. They were too inebriated to either notice or comment on Lolly's hot-pink trench coat, which she tugged down with both hands as she made the rounds.

"Are y'all all right?" she asked, giving each man a big hug in turn. Brooks watched with great appreciation as she reached one arm around her uncles' necks and went up on her toes. Her sweet little ass and high-cut lace underpants were on full display no matter that she kept one hand on the hem. "Why are y'all here?"

"A friendly how-the-hell-are-you and welcome-to-the-DuVals meet and greet," Jeb said. "It's the…you know…right thing to do in this situation, darlin'. Your momma. Well, she's got a special place in our hearts and we just want to make sure she's happy."

"That's very sweet, Uncle Jeb. I think she's going to be very happy." Lolly's voice rose to encompass the entire room. "Especially now that all of her favorite brothers-in-law are standing behind her one hundred percent. She told me you would, you know. Momma said that she didn't want to tell y'all until she was absolutely sure about Hale Evans. But now that she is, she wanted you to be the first to know just how much she loves him, because you have been so good to me all these years. Some people might think I drew the short straw having my daddy pass away before I got to know him. But in truth, I haven't known one day of sorrow because I have three uncles giving me more love than one daddy ever could."

"We do love you, Lollypop. And we will stand one hundred percent behind your mother and her choice to…remarry." Jeb looking pointedly at his two brothers as he said, "She's been a loyal DuVal for a long, long time, and…" he continued, looking back at Lolly, "the two of you can always count on us."

"Gentlemen, forgive me my manners," Emelina said, holding a beautiful tray of grapes, meats, and cheeses. "Where I grew up we always enjoyed a little Spanish cheese with our wine. May I?"

she asked as she set the platter down on the kitchen table, quickly clearing away empty bottles.

"You're a beautiful woman, Miss Emelina," Big Jim gushed as he pulled up his jeans on the way over to the table. "We're not going to be able to let the Major near you at the weddin'."

Lolly's three uncles broke into gales of laughter, each digging into the platter as Lolly helped Emelina clear away bottles and deliver small plates and napkins to the men. Brooks had joined right in with the uncles like he was one of them. They had their heads together laughing about Mamma DuVal's keeping the Major on a short leash.

The women worked quickly and efficiently. Once the place looked like a respectable party they each poured themselves a glass of wine. Emelina drew out another large wedge of cheese, surrounding it with crackers. She and Lolly pulled a couple of tall stools up to the kitchen island, fixing themselves a midnight snack while they reintroduced themselves.

"You are playing tennis and golf with Vance," Emelina said.

"That's right," Lolly agreed.

"Yet you are trying to seduce the big one over there." Emelina indicated Brooks at the kitchen table.

Lolly laughed, blushing profusely. "Correct again," she said, covering her mouth so she wouldn't spew cracker all over the counter.

Emelina looked over Lolly's pink trench coat and said, "I think Vance would have been much easier than all this."

Unfortunately, Lolly had just taken a sip of wine and it did spew all over the countertop. She choked and she laughed and she cleaned up the mess, all the while agreeing with Vance's grandmother: Vance would have indeed been easier to seduce.

As if conjured up by the mention of his name, the French doors at the back of the kitchen opened and in stepped Vance, sporting his best WTF look.

All three uncles turned their heads, their drunken gazes landing on Vance. Silence echoed around the kitchen. Finally JB slurred, "Isn't he a little young for Genevra?"

Emelina raced over and wrapped her hands around Vance's shoulders. "Gentlemen DuVal. This one is my grandson. Not Genevra's intended, I assure you."

"Well, okay then," JB said, beckoning Vance over with his arm. "Come on in, boy. Pull up a chair!"

Scanning the crowd, Vance eventually shrugged his shoulders and said, "I'm down with that." He moved across the kitchen, opened a cabinet, and selected a wine glass. Then he surveyed the open bottles at the table and disappeared. When he came back, he had two bottles tightly gripped in each hand.

That's when Hale and Genevra stepped through the same doors. Their eyes shifted over the scene, unsure about what they'd just walked into.

Uncle Jeb stood slowly, holding up his wine glass as he did. "Forgive our imposition. My brothers and I wanted to stop by and congratulate Mr. Evans on his good fortune. And Genevra, we'd like you to know that we are one hundred percent behind you. Now and always."

Lolly's mother blinked several times, obviously holding her breath. "Well," she said as she let the breath out.

Hale looked over at Vance, who stood in mid-stride with four bottles of wine hanging from his hands. He pointed to the wine. "That better be the good stuff!" he quipped, offering up a big smile and moving forward to shake Jeb's hand.

The room erupted with greetings and merriment, and Lolly and her mother looked at each other from across the room in dazed amazement. Lolly shrugged as she brought her wine glass to her lips, watching her mother be engulfed by each of the men in turn.

At one in the morning, Emelina snuck away from the party, missing three completely different, but highly-entertaining, versions of how the horses got into the act. At three o'clock, Brooks had the foresight to call the on-duty police officers and tuck Lolly's uncles into two cruisers for a ride home. The horses were nowhere to be seen, so he asked his fellow officers to be on the lookout for three fully-saddled horses as well.

By the time Brooks got back inside, the kitchen was being wiped down and looked no worse for the wear. Genevra and Hale thanked him for his help in handling the situation and told him breakfast would be served on the pool deck at ten o'clock if he cared to join them. Then they walked down the hall hand in hand. Brooks watched as Genevra dropped her head on Hale's shoulder.

He turned as Vance came through the French doors with a T-shirt in his hand. He handed it to Lolly and reiterated what Hale had just said, word for word, about the guest room and where she could find anything she needed. Vance grinned at her then and said, "You owe me big."

"Why is that?" Lolly yawned.

"Because I've got a hole in my tongue from biting it every time I started to ask if you wanted me to take your coat."

"Such a gentleman." She yawned again. "I've got to go to bed."

Vance slapped Brooks on his back. "The Big Em has the pull-out couch sheeted up for you. I'll leave the door unlocked."

"Thanks, man," Brooks said as Vance left the kitchen.

Brooks sat on a tall stool and pulled a tired Lolly to him, tucking her in between his legs. "Hey," he said quietly, tilting her chin up so he could see her eyes. "I might have to see about getting you on the payroll."

Lolly looked up, bewildered.

"Terrorist negotiations. You're like a secret weapon."

She rolled her eyes.

"Laura Leigh, you changed everything. You disarmed your uncles and changed their minds. Instead of an intensely awkward, no-win situation for anybody, you managed to create a bond between two families. Your two families. Your uncles ended up having the time of their lives tonight. And with them firmly behind your mother marrying Hale, well, Henderson will roll out the red carpet. You did that."

"They love me. And they love Momma. I just reminded them of that."

Brooks took his big hands and placed them on either side of her face. "I hated having to share you and your trench coat. But your being in the right place at the right time made all the difference."

She laughed and pulled away. "Not exactly the night I had in mind."

Brooks hopped off the stool and dragged her back into his arms. "I want a do-over. Another chance with the trench coat. Another chance to slap some cuffs on you."

Lolly tucked the bangs that had long ago fallen out of her ponytail back behind her ear. "If that call hadn't come in and none of this had happened—if your shift had ended as planned—where would we have ended up?"

"In my house," he said against her lips. "In my bed. No doubt about it."

Lolly pushed him away and started strolling off toward the guest bedroom. "All right then. Because you might want to take note that I'm actually spending the night at Vance's house."

"Duly noted," he said, watching her walk up the staircase.

"And wearing his T-shirt," she said as she swung it around and stepped out of sight.

Brooks smiled at her, at himself, and at the situation. Then he turned out the kitchen lights, closed the French doors behind him, crossed over to the pool house, and quietly stepped inside Vance's bachelor pad. Vance appeared in the darkness at the door to his bedroom.

"She meet you at the office dressed like that?"

"Yes, she did," Brooks said, pulling his shirt over his head.

"I'm sorry, man."

"Don't be," Brooks said, sitting down on the couch and kicking off his shoes. "I mean, don't get me wrong. She totally called my bluff. There was no way I was turning that down. But as the evening wore on and my hopes and expectations had to...shift gears, as they say, I started to realize what a lucky SOB I am."

"Lucky?"

"Damn lucky."

"How do you figure?"

"Because now I get to see just what the hell she's going to come up with next."

CHAPTER TWENTY-FIVE

On July third, Annabelle sat outside the Henderson Country Club wearing a crisp, cool sundress in her signature white. The temperature was heading from warm to hot, so she hailed one of the waitstaff to help her maneuver a table and three chairs into the shade and then ordered a pitcher of Mojitos to celebrate the start of the long weekend.

The final match of the mixed-doubles tennis tournament was beginning at eleven o'clock, and she'd finagled a prime spot to watch it, high above court one on the Club's terrace. Now having a vested interest in Lolly DuVal beyond friendship, she was here to support her new business partner.

"Thank God, it's almost over," Brooks said, collapsing into the seat next to Annabelle. "Lolly and Vance are ridiculously competitive."

"This from an ex-baseball champ," Annabelle smirked.

"Exactly. Between their golf and tennis and whatever top-secret shenanigans you and Lolly have gotten yourselves into, she has zero time for me. I hardly remember what she looks like," he said, before waving off a Mojito and asking a waiter for a glass of water and an ice-cold beer. "Where's your better half?"

"Duncan's on his way. He needed to wrap up some work this morning. But we're both staying for five long days," she drawled out with a grateful sigh. "My sisters are coming home for the Fourth, so my parents will have a full house."

"Mine too. Lewis and Darcy get in this afternoon. And Lewis' parents are driving in and staying with Mom and Dad as well. It'll be good having everybody back in town."

A murmur of unrest rose from the court below, drawing their attention to Lolly and Vance. The two of them looked to be in a heated debate at the far end of the court. Vance was pointing his finger at Lolly and then flailing it around. Lolly stepped right up in Vance's face, apparently telling him a thing or two before spinning about and stalking off. Annabelle heard Brooks' breath hitch as Vance reached out and grabbed Lolly, pulling her around to face him and bringing her tight against his body.

"What the...?" Brooks said as the two of them watched Vance stroke Lolly's arm, soothing her into a less-agitated state. Finally, they saw her nod at Vance, relax, and release herself from his grip. When she turned to walk away, Vance swatted her on the ass with his racket.

Annabelle bit her lip, glancing at Brooks for his reaction. She noticed he didn't take his eyes off the court. "So, how much time have they been spending together?" she asked.

"Way, way too much," Brooks growled.

"Well, they're just tense," Annabelle reasoned. "They've worked hard to win this and they're probably just...you know, nervous and taking it out on each other."

"Yeah, well, unfortunately I know just what tactics Lolly resorts to when frustrated with Vance."

"What do you mean?"

"When Vance makes her crazy, she kisses him."

"Kisses him?"

"Yes, kisses him. That sound a little strange to you? Because it sure sounds like bullshit to me."

Annabelle waggled her head, unwilling to throw her new business partner under the bus but unable to disagree. "Well, you don't think she does that a lot, do you?"

The way Brooks rubbed his hands together and the way his jaw got all tense didn't bode well. "As far as I know, it's only happened once."

"Oh, well, once," she grinned. "Even *I've* kissed Vance Evans once. Let's order lunch, shall we?" Annabelle suggested, waving over a waiter with some menus.

Lunch came. The match started. The first set went easily to Vance and Lolly. Mr. Evans and Genevra came up from where they were watching to say hello between sets. Duncan arrived in the middle of the second set, just as Vance lost his serve.

"Uh-oh," Duncan said, sitting down. "That's not good."

"They're doing well," Annabelle assured him. "Won the first set 6-3. It's fine."

But it wasn't fine, Annabelle started to realize. It wasn't fine at all. Lolly and Vance continued to play well, but their opponents started playing out of their minds. Out of reach shots careened by Lolly. Drop shots landed dead on the line for the other team and just out for Vance. The two of them weren't talking for several games, and then they appeared to start sniping at each other between points. They lost the second set 4-6.

The couples took a water break when they changed sides after Vance and Lolly lost another game. Vance stood close to Lolly's side, barking in her ear until she finally nailed him with her elbow. He grabbed her arm, pulled her close, and put his face right up in hers. They stood like that, arguing, until their opponents had been standing on the court ready to play for a full minute. Finally, Vance released Lolly and they moved to their side.

Brooks cleared his throat, leaned forward, and put his forearms on his thighs, rubbing his hands together. Quietly he asked Duncan, "Any luck finding this Piper Beaumont? Because, in case you are fucking blind, Vance has fallen for my girl and distracting him from her right now would be a really good idea."

Duncan shot Brooks a horrified look. "What do you mean, he's fallen for Lolly?" There was no missing the panic in Duncan's voice.

"He admitted as much a couple weeks ago. Said he could handle it. Told me it wasn't going to be a problem." Brooks glanced down at the court as Lolly won her serve. Watching as Vance celebrated by pulling her ponytail. "But from where I sit at the moment it looks like one giant nightmare."

"Oh, shit," Duncan cursed.

That caused Brooks' head to swing toward Duncan. "What?" he demanded.

Duncan assumed the same position Brooks was in so their heads were close together. Annabelle had to strain to hear their conversation.

"He called off the search for Piper."

"What are you talking about?"

"When I called and told him I'd found her right where he told me to look, he told me to drop it. Said he didn't want to go down that path anymore. I told him I could easily arrange an introduction and why not just see where it would lead? He shot me down. Wasn't interested."

"He told me you were taking your time finding her. Being discreet."

"Didn't take me any time. She's a friend of a friend. He could have met her weeks ago."

Below them, Lolly and Vance broke their opponents' serve and celebrated with a high five.

Brooks leaned back in his chair, blowing out a long breath. He crossed his arms over his chest and shook his head. "Okay. So… obviously…he's, what? Attached to Lolly," he answered his own question with an air of finality. Then he started to rub his hands through his hair, speaking slowly as if trying to unravel a mystery. "Which isn't surprising because she's the first woman who's treated him like a human being in years. He's latched on to her because she's made him use his verbal and physical skills to do something other than give her an orgasm. They talk about books. They engage in sports. They joke, they laugh, they argue, and they piss each other off. Of course he's going to fall for her. She's pulled him out of his five-year abyss of feeling nothing but momentary sexual release."

The three of them sat in silence, watching as Vance won his serve. Then all three heads jolted at once when Lolly smacked him on the butt.

Annabelle wanted to bang her head on the table because the more points Vance and Lolly accumulated, the more intimate their touches became. The wider their smiles. The more flirtatious their actions. And as much as she heard Brooks trying to reason it all out, he was now standing with his arms crossed over his chest, rubbing his face whenever the interaction below got too uncomfortable to watch. One look over at Duncan told her this was bad.

Finally…finally the match came to an end. Lolly and Vance threw up their arms in victory as their opponents' last shot bounced just outside the back line. They embraced and walked up to the net to shake hands with the other couple. Once the sportsmanship had been handled, Vance picked Lolly up, twirled her around, and kissed her hard on the lips. The kiss lasted just that much too long.

Annabelle sat defeated, unable to offer any sort of pretense as the three of them silently watched Vance and Lolly head into the clubhouse together.

Brooks could feel the weight of Duncan's concern. But the complete and utter numbness he was experiencing prevented him from pulling his gaze from the ground. He was numb. And hurt.

Numb and hurt and pissed off and…numb.

He held a palm up toward Duncan and Annabelle and turned to walk away. He heard Duncan murmur something and then the sound of his footsteps coming from behind. He appreciated his friend's dedication, but he didn't want to discuss it. He really didn't.

"Hey," Duncan said quietly as he maneuvered alongside him— slow, steady steps heading to the parking lot. And then to God knows where.

"Hey," Duncan said again, and Brooks sucked in a breath and did what he had to do. He turned and faced his buddy. It cost him about everything he had left.

"You know. That was just a— "

"A what?" Brooks asked. "That was just a—what?"

Duncan met his eyes and Brooks watched all the life drain out of them. Just like his own. "Yeah. I think we both know what that was," Brooks acknowledged and started walking again.

"Look, man," Duncan said, coming after him. "I'm sure it wasn't exactly what it looked like. I'm sure it was the heat of the moment. Competition and tension and neither of them meant it."

Brooks' hands flew up in the air as he spun on Duncan. "I'm not an idiot! I mean, I'm not a complete idiot. After knocking my head against the wall a few times even I can read what they could not have spelled out any clearer. And yeah! It sucks. And it must really suck for you as you are caught in the middle of this shit. But—" Brooks turned around, looking for a solution to materialize out of thin air. Finally he slapped his hands down against his sides. "I can't help you with this," he said, shaking his head.

"You don't have to help me," Duncan said, following after Brooks. "I told you I had your back on this. If we need to roll Vance, we roll Vance. If you need to kidnap Lolly and shake some sense into her, then I'll run interference. I'm your wingman. You tell me what you want and I'll make it happen."

"Tell you what I want?" Brooks shouted, stopping and turning so fast that Duncan ran into him. "What I want is for Lolly to have taken her head out of the game for one split second, long enough to find me in the crowd and throw me a goddamn bone like I mean something in her life." He pushed at Duncan's chest as he moved forward, picking up steam. "I want you and Annabelle to move your asses to Henderson so you can help me run interference on this kind of shit with Vance regularly." He resorted to poking Duncan in his chest while saying, "And I want Lewis to figure out that his business is now stable enough and he's now rich enough to move his multi-million dollar company *back* to Henderson so he can attract bright and energetic young people here by creating a whole lot of new jobs.

"What I want is to be surrounded by my friends. What I want is for all of us to be happy. And if you can find a way to make that happen, then you are a miracle worker. Because after what we just witnessed, it is painfully obvious that the best thing that ever happened to me is also the best thing that's ever happened to Vance. He's in love with my girl. My girl! And she's…she's Lolly. And there isn't anything you or I or a thundering herd of archangels can do to change any of that."

Brooks turned and headed to his truck, leaving Duncan to call after him. "You can't just walk away."

"Watch me!" Brooks shouted back and then picked up his pace. He was gonna walk away, go throw back a few shots, and eventually get himself to work right on time—like his heart hadn't just been pitched, tipped, and slammed against the cage, shattering into tiny glass fragments left for someone else to stomp into the dirt. He was walking away.

"You gotta fight for her," Duncan called.

Ha! He almost laughed. He'd been fighting his whole life. Fighting to do the right thing. Fighting to be the stand-up guy.

Fighting to keep friendships thriving. Yeah, he'd fought the good fight and look where it got him. Sick and tired. Sick of being the Hero of Henderson and tired of excusing Vance because his mother left him.

Yeah—he was done with that.

And good for Vance, he thought as he opened his truck's door. *Ended up landing himself a great girl. And like Annabelle had said, they sure look good together.*

Well, fuck that. Fuck all of that. He was now an island.

There was a loud banging on his passenger window as he started the truck. He turned his head to shout at Duncan, but his words caught in his throat. "What the hell?" he muttered as his ex, Tansy Langford, opened the door and slid inside.

"I need a ride," she told him.

Like hell.

He didn't fasten his seat belt, didn't bother to look at who was calling his cell—he just threw his truck into reverse, backed out of the spot, and then hit the gas, throwing it into first and laying rubber on his way out of the parking lot. He managed to get up some pretty good speed heading down the long driveway of the Club.

"Wow!" Tansy said after falling forward and slamming back into her seat as he hit the brakes at the end of the drive. "Is there a fire somewhere?" she asked.

Brooks turned his head and shot her a long, hard stare. Finally he said, "You're smart enough to know what's going to happen here, right?'

"I am."

Brooks simply nodded and turned his truck west, toward home.

CHAPTER TWENTY-SIX

Vance and Lolly had played a couple of tough matches to get to the finals, but nothing like that one. Which made the win all the sweeter.

They stood at the water fountain going over their game, analyzing the second set for several minutes. Then they shared in the exhilaration of winning all over again by reliving their comeback in the third set, point by point.

Genevra and Hale showed up to congratulate the newly-crowned mixed doubles champions, offering to buy drinks and lunch up in the mixed grill to celebrate. Vance accepted readily, as Lolly checked her watch and looked around.

"Where's Brooks?" she asked.

"Brooks?" her mother questioned, shooting a look at Hale.

"He usually meets us here after a match."

"Are you …? Aren't you two …?"

"I think what your mother is trying to say is. What the hell is going on?" Hale snapped. "By the middle of that third set, we'd become convinced that you two are now an item."

"What?" Lolly said, looking horrified. She pulled out her cell and dialed. "That's ridiculous," she said, putting the phone to her ear. She waved her other hand between herself and Vance. "That's just the way we roll."

"That's the way you roll?" Hale repeated, his brows lifting, his eyes zeroing in on his son. When Vance only returned his father's steady stare, Hale placed a hand on his son's shoulder and moved him away from the women. "You want to tell me what's going on here?" His low voice was almost a whisper. "Because I'm not quite as young and naive as lovely little Lolly. And neither are you," he said pointedly.

"Nothing," Vance said, dragging a hand through his hair. "Nothing is going on. Unfortunately. She's mad for Brooks and I'm…I'm just an experiment in socialization."

"Come again?"

Vance let out a long exhale of breath. "She's helping me refine my taste and appreciation for women."

A single burst of laughter exploded from Hale. "And how's that working out for you?"

"Obviously, it's boomeranged, Dr. Phil," Vance scowled, exasperated that his father would find it all so amusing. "Because now we're *friends*. Which boils down to her being the woman in my life in all things—except the bedroom."

"You're in love with her."

"It sure feels that way."

"And Brooks loves her too?"

Vance barked a harsh laugh. "For a whole lot of years now. I can't mess with that."

"But you are. You know that, right? You're definitely messing with that."

Vance simply stared at his father. *Yeah, he'd been messing with that.*

"Listen, son. Even *I* can see Lolly is about ten sticks of dynamite tied together in one pretty red bow. And right now you are waving around a BIC lighter while Brooks is striking a pack of matches."

"Your point?"

"This thing is about to explode."

The two men looked over at the women. Lolly redialing and Genevra laying a hand on her cheek, trying to get her attention.

Hale turned back to his son, releasing a deep breath. He spoke quietly. "You know about risk and reward. What's the risk in lighting this thing up? Telling her how you feel?"

Vance tilted his head in her direction. "She's in love with the good cop."

"Didn't see a lot of evidence of that during the tennis match."

"The heat of the moment. Like you said. Dynamite."

"Maybe. But it's time you two had a serious conversation. When the Hero of Henderson doesn't show up to congratulate his best friend and his girl, there's a problem. He might be the good cop, but he's also human."

"Yeah," Vance moaned. "I am so getting my ass kicked over this one."

Hale chuckled while patting his son on the back. "Let me see if I can extract Genevra from the situation. But do yourself a favor and be honest. With Lolly, with Brooks, but most of all, with yourself. If Lolly's the love of your life, by all means fight for her. But if you love her because of her friendship, because of what she's added to your life, then tell her that. Appreciate that. And then honor what she has with Brooks by keeping your hands to yourself."

Vance smirked, glancing down and then back up at his father. "Would it have killed you to have had this conversation back when I was sixteen?"

Hale tapped his son gently on his cheek. "My bad," he said with a wink and a smile. Then he left to drag Genevra off, mouthing a 'good luck' before leaving him alone with Lolly.

"He's not answering his phone," Lolly told him as he approached.

The desperation in her eyes opened a hole in Vance's gut with pain so sudden and real it caused him to suck in a harsh breath and pull up short. Emotion spilled from his five-year-old, ironclad, blissful state of denial. And it burned.

He'd actually been harboring hope. *Jesus.*

In an effort to leverage himself against the torment, Vance straightened his shoulders, tucked his hands in the pockets of his tennis shorts, and took a long, deep breath.

His gaze softened as he took in the complete picture of the girl he'd been crazy about for the past eight weeks. Ever since she'd hobbled into his training room with her pretty brown ponytail and her smoking hot sundress. Ever since he'd picked her trim body up and sat her on that table, massaged her feet, and tried to seduce her into going out with him.

The sharp jab of disappointment he had felt when Brooks barged in that day and claimed her as his own was a minor blister compared to the wound that was starting to ooze and fester around the area of his heart.

His throat clamped down on the swell of emotion threatening to rise up and swamp him. Oh, he loved Lolly. There was no denying that. Spending time with her had changed him. Just as they'd planned. So here he stood: a new man. Celibate. Appreciative. Enthralled. Hoping against hope that she wasn't the love of his life, since she was already the love of Brooks'.

He'd intended to tell her it was going to be all right. That Brooks would understand. That he'd forgive their public display of... whatever on the tennis court. He intended to release whatever claim he might have on Lolly—but then he stopped. And an internal war started to rage.

"Has Brooks told you why?" he asked. "Why he's been... *interested* in you for so long?"

Lolly lowered her phone, her expression uncertain. "He said something about low-riding jeans when I was eighteen."

"And you believed that? I mean, considering this is Brooks we're talking about, doesn't that sound a little...shallow? A little more like something I'd say?"

"You're confusing who you are with your...your act. The real you is complex and complicated. Driven, disciplined, and self-aware. It's going to take a lot more than a pair of low-riding jeans for you to fall in love."

"You sure about that? I'm pretty sure all it took for me to fall in love with you was your short little sundress."

"You're not in love with me. You just want to take me to bed."

"That too."

Lolly smiled then, gifting him with warmth and affection in that one simple gesture.

The time had come to end this one way or another. Vance pointed in the direction of a pair of comfortable chairs. As they sat, he took her hand, and after a few deep breaths he spoke to her fingers.

"If there were no Brooks, would there be an us?"

"If there were no Brooks, there probably would have been a very hot *week* of us." When he scoffed, she relented. "Okay, maybe a wild, crazy month of us...or even a long, steamy summer of us. Because I was looking for the opposite of milquetoast and you certainly…are that."

He smiled and squeezed her hand, still unable to look at her.

"But it would have burned out. You'd have stuck me into the Old Vance style of romance. One shot at the bar and then off to your truck."

"I never…okay, rarely ever, do it in my truck anymore."

"And I would have gone along with it because a summer fling was all I thought I wanted. Then I'd go back to school and you'd… you'd be off doing shots with someone else."

"You sure about that? I was hellbent on settling down before you walked into my training room."

She turned her head and looked over at him, so he dragged his gaze up to meet hers.

"But there *is* a Brooks," she said softly.

God, he hoped she didn't notice the moisture accumulating in his eyes.

"I'm not choosing Brooks over you."

A bitter laugh erupted. "Of course you're not," he quipped, rubbing his eyes.

"Brooks chose me. He asked me to be your friend. He's put up with a lot from the two of us. He's hung in there, waiting it out. Making sure I'm okay, making sure you're okay. At the same time he's making sure Darcy's okay, and Lewis and Duncan and Annabelle are okay. Not to mention his parents, *our* parents, your baseball team, and the whole darn town. He's that big. Cares that much. Why he chose me?" She shrugged. "All I know is that I've fallen into our all-encompassing Hero of Henderson more and more each day.

"You're one of my best friends, Vance. Brooks is my strength, my security, my past, and hopefully my future. He's too much for me not to love. And if I've blown this because I'm…flighty, competitive, and flirtatious and fickle when I'm around you…" she said, giving his arm a punch, "then I'm exactly what he's been saying all along: too young."

"You're not too young. You're perfect."

"I hope I'm perfect for Brooks. I know I'm a good teammate for you. That's not going to change."

"It's going to change. It's gotta change," Vance said, feeling sorry for himself. "At least until the dust settles." He felt his phone vibrate against his thigh. He pulled it out, read the text twice, and then cursed.

"What?"

"Okay," he said, his head snapping up. "You! Hit the showers. Get yourself all prettied up so Brooks can't resist you when you apologize for having your hands all over me."

"Having *my* hands all over—"

"I'm gonna go find the guy and knock some sense into him. Go!" he ordered before she could question him further.

"Fine. All right," Lolly said, collecting her things. "I'm going. Yeesh."

Vance waited until Lolly was shut up tight inside the women's locker room before he called Duncan and made a mad dash for the door.

"I sure hope you're bullshittin' me," he said when Duncan picked up. "Because if he left with Tansy, we could have a real problem on our hands."

"You had a real problem on your hands before Tansy leapt into the truck. What the hell is going on with you and Lolly anyway?"

Vance bounded up the steps as Duncan was racing down them. They both stopped dead, eyeing one another and cutting off their cells. Duncan looked as angry as Vance had ever seen him.

"I'm going to fix this," he promised.

"How? How the hell are you going to fix this?"

"Dude. I may not be much of one, but I *am* a cop." Vance pushed a few key buttons on his cell. "Got any idea where he was heading?"

"He turned west out of the drive."

Vance nodded and then started issuing orders. "Rookie One. I need you and Rookie Two to find Brooks Bennett and drag his ass to the Henderson Country Club. You're looking for his truck. Check his home first and then the lake. If that doesn't turn him up, scout the town. When you find him, interrupt whatever the hell is going on, and I mean *whatever* is going on, and tell him you have a situation only he can handle. He won't come willingly if you tell him I sent you or if he knows where you're taking him. Lie through your teeth or cuff him if you have to, but get him here."

When Rookie One started to talk back, Vance talked right over him. "I'm taking full responsibility. Just find him and get him here fast. Oh, and if there is a woman with him named Tansy Langford, put her in a separate car and take her ass home. Got it? Consider these orders. *My* orders. And you don't want to be messing with me right now." He disconnected the call.

"Brooks isn't going to like this," Duncan cautioned.

"Yeah, well," Vance sighed. "Nobody ever likes being saved from themselves. Especially the Hometown Hero. Come on," Vance said, resigned to whatever fate was about to go down. "Let's get ourselves a shot and a beer."

"A beer?" Duncan sputtered. "Don't you think you should be a little worried about blocking his right hook?"

"I've never once fought anybody while sober," Vance said, stomping toward the bar. "And I sure as hell see no good reason to start now."

CHAPTER TWENTY-SEVEN

The higher part of Brooks' brain, the part that was actually thinking calmly while the rest of his mind waged war on Vance, Lolly, and himself, realized that having Tansy Langford in his truck right now signified the most egregious poor choice Brooks had made over the last eight weeks.

And that was saying something, because the list was long and mighty.

But as his phone buzzed for the fifth time, he reached into the center console and turned the damn thing off. He sure as hell wasn't having any kind of conversation in front of Tansy. Tansy, who sat basking in his anger, a prime and willing colluder for making a bad situation worse.

And wasn't he considering doing just that?

Payback is a bitch, he thought. Throwing Tansy into the mix was sure to ignite some kind of explosion. As if that little love-fest on the tennis court hadn't already taken care of that. He was here, wasn't he? In his truck with his ex-girlfriend. Running away from the scene.

Fucking A.

And the one thing he desperately wanted to do—punch his fist into the dashboard—wasn't something he wanted a witness for either. Yeah, having Tansy here was a really, really bad idea.

"So," she said, her voice scraping over his raw nerves, "is it safe to assume this marks the conclusion of your adventures in babysitting Lolly DuVal?"

Brooks almost let out a laugh. *Clearly, I dropped the ball on babysitting.*

"You're smart enough to know she's your rebound, right?"

"And you're smart enough to know that one more word is going to get your ass thrown out of this truck, right?"

"Sorry. I just...."

"Just what? Want me back? Like this?" he shouted. "Are you insane?"

"No. I'm not insane. But I am here for you, Brooks. And yes, I do want you back. As soon as you get over this ridiculous infatuation."

"Ha," he laughed humorlessly. "I wish it were a damned infatuation," he said. "I really do. But I hate to break it to you, Tans. Lolly wreaked havoc on my heart long before I met you."

"What are you talking about? She's a child."

"Yeah, well that *child* helped me through one of the worst nights of my life back when I was just a kid myself. And I never forgot it. Not likely to now."

"So, what? You're going to forgive her an affair with your best friend behind your back?"

"If they're having an affair, it clearly isn't happening *behind* my back."

"They are *in love* with each other. Anybody watching that match could see it."

"It's complicated."

"Oh My God! It's not that complicated."

"What do you know about it, huh? You never once tried to get to know Vance. And you sure as hell don't know a thing about Lolly. You've been off living in some...city."

"And you're angry about that. I get it."

"I'm not angry about that, Tansy. That may be the *one* thing I am not angry about right now."

"You sure about that? Because it sounds like you're making excuses for everybody involved but me."

Brooks let out a long breath as he pulled over to the side of the road, hearing the rough tumble of loose gravel underneath his tires as he came to a stop. He put the truck in park, put both hands on the steering wheel, and stared at it, thinking. Hard.

He wasn't making excuses. Things with Lolly and Vance were

complicated. No one understood that better than he did. Yet he'd allowed their little love affair on the tennis court to get the better of him.

Because he'd shown up vulnerable.

Because he hadn't been allocated enough of her time.

Which was his own damn fault, because all along he'd been holding Lolly off with one hand and egging her on with the other. Trying to protect himself.

From?

Falling in love with Lolly.

In case you hadn't noticed, asshole, that ship has sailed.

From losing Lolly.

Brooks turned his head and looked over at Tansy.

Running away with your ex-girlfriend is a surefire way to take care of that.

He might not have all the answers at the moment, but he was damn certain of one thing. He'd rather be stuck in a love triangle with Vance and Lolly than sitting here with Tansy or any other girl.

He threw the truck in drive and made a U-turn.

"Where are we going?" Tansy asked.

"Back."

"Back? Why?"

"Because it's time."

"Time for what?"

"Time to start throwing my weight around. Time to start imposing my will. Time for me to lay down the title Hero of Henderson and become Chieftain instead."

"Chieftain? I thought you wanted to be mayor."

"Yeah. No. Chieftain."

Tansy let out a big sigh. "I guess this means you're going back to Lolly."

"I love her," Brooks said without apology. "I don't want to hurt you, Tans, but the truth is I love her and I'm going to fight for her. You may as well pack up and head back to your big city because I aim to make her the Chieftain's wife."

A long, sad silence emanated from the passenger side. Then, with a sigh of finality, Tansy offered, "Well, as long as the two of you plan to adopt Vance, I'm sure you'll be very happy."

Brooks started laughing. "God, that's the truth."

Tansy nodded and began laughing with him.

Once Brooks pulled back into the same parking spot he'd recently vacated, he hopped out of the cab, sent Tansy off with a quick hug and headed to the front doors of the Club. He turned on his cell and scrolled through the missed calls, voice mails, and one text message from Duncan.

'Annabelle and I are turning this thing around. Trust us.'

Good. *Finally*, he thought as he picked up his pace. The Chieftain had backup.

About damn time.

He hit the foyer, bounced up the stairs and didn't have to venture any farther to know where to find his clan. Because although the volume might not have been loud, the air filtering out of the mixed grill was so loaded with tension it would have stopped anybody in their tracks. Brooks pulled up short underneath the frame of the double doors and blinked.

Annabelle Devine—beautiful, sweet Keeper of the Debutantes and Miss Manners in all things—was right up in Vance's face chewing him a new one.

Words like 'shameful,' 'lowdown,' and 'vile' were raining down on Vance, punctuated with finger pokes to the chest as she launched phrases like 'public display,' 'rules of civility,' and 'bonds of friendship' at him.

Clearly Duncan's precious southern belle was this Chieftain's military leader. She was doing such a thorough job of evisceration that Brooks was half tempted to jump in and stop it.

He looked around for Duncan and found him standing in the background gnawing on a knuckle, his expression a mix of mirth and horror. When he caught Duncan's eye he mouthed, 'Where's Lolly?'

Duncan mouthed back, 'Locker room.'

Brooks headed directly there, ready to start imposing his will.

After five minutes of waiting for her to emerge, he imposed his fist on the door and shouted for Lolly.

No answer.

He knocked again.

This time the locker room attendant, a stout, frowning, and territorial woman named Lulu opened the door and looked him up and down.

His heart sank. *Lulu. It had to be Lulu.*

"I'm looking for Lolly DuVal," he said, offering up his best Golden Boy grin.

"Mmhmm," she huffed, crossing her arms and looking him up and down.

Okay. That's not good.

"She was here. Fixin' herself up all pretty. Until her phone started beeping and shaking and sputtering like the world was coming to an end."

Uh-oh.

"Sat there a good ten minutes reading text after text."

Brooks took his phone out of his pocket and started dialing.

"Then she just sat there staring into space. Like she'd been *blindsided.*"

At the same time Brooks rang Lolly, he could hear a phone ringing from inside the locker room. Lolly's ring.

"Excuse me a minute," Lulu said.

Lolly didn't pick up. But when the door to the locker room reopened, there was Lulu holding Lolly's phone.

His hand dropped as he disconnected the call.

"I guess she had enough…of all the shaking and beeping."

"Where is she?"

"Sounded like a friend was picking her up."

"Can I see that?" Brooks was more than a little surprised Lulu handed it over. He pushed the *Recent* button and looked at the calls. "Darcy," he whispered.

"Thank you," he said honestly as he handed her back the phone.

"That's it? You aren't going to snoop through all those text messages to see what kind of trouble you're in?"

"Lulu, I know as well as you do what kind of trouble I'm in. Thanks for your help," he said as he turned and put his phone to his ear.

He was walking out the side door to the parking lot when Darcy answered her phone.

"Tansy Langford?" came the harsh whisper. "You are *dumping* my best friend for that bitch who snuck out of town?"

"Of course not! Where are you? Where's Lolly?"

"Like I'm gonna tell you."

"Darcy. I swear to God…." He seethed. He caught himself. "Okay, okay," he said as he stopped beside his truck and started thinking. He checked his watch, realizing it wasn't long until he had to suit up for work.

"Darcy, listen to me. Whatever gossip is flying around about Tansy is completely false."

"So you didn't burn rubber all the way down Club Drive with Tansy Langford sitting on your lap while fifty people looked on?"

Fucking A.

"She wasn't sitting on my—" He stopped himself and took a deep breath. "Darcy. I love Lolly. You *know* I love Lolly. And, I probably—no, I *definitely*—should have taken your advice sooner and started imposing my will. But I assure you, I plan to make up for lost time just as soon as I get off work tonight. So do me a favor and don't let her out of your sight. I get off at midnight. If you can find it in your heart to throw me a bone and text me where you two are then, I'd be eternally grateful." *But I certainly won't be holding my breath.*

"Roger that, Rambo."

"Not Rambo. Chief," he said as he hung up.

CHAPTER TWENTY-EIGHT

Brooks hit the office at the end of his patrol feeling uneasy. It was getting close to midnight and Henderson was just a little too quiet. The third of July held just as much potential for disaster as the Fourth, with amateur fireworks and parties for every age group scattered around town and at the lake. He'd driven by all the hot spots and found the gatherings small, safe, and sane. That did not bode well. He was missing something.

But he wasn't missing Vance apparently. Vance was there, sitting in Brooks' chair.

"Fuck off," Vance said as Brooks approached. "Annabelle already laid into me."

Brooks held up his hands but couldn't keep the grin off his face. "You'd have gotten off easier with me. I'd have hit you once and it would've been over."

"No doubt," Vance growled. "Right now my ego, my manhood, *and* my pride are lying in an ICU trying to recover."

Brooks laughed at that, plopping himself up on his desk facing his buddy. "Well, you sort of deserved it."

"I sort of did," Vance agreed. "I'm sorry, man. Won't happen again."

Brooks gave him a short nod. "And just to make sure, I'm giving you a week to arrange a meeting with Piper Beaumont." When Vance looked up sharply, Brooks went on. "I know Duncan found her and the idea of meeting her again made your balls drop off, but you need to grow a new pair, and fast. Because if you don't make contact in the next ten days, I will."

"You will what?"

"Contact her. Cuff her. Throw her in the back of my truck and dump her on your damn doorstep. You need a woman, my friend. A woman of your own."

"Don't I know it."

"Okay then. Damn glad that's settled. One down, one to go."

"You haven't seen Lolly yet?"

Brooks shook his head as the precinct door opened behind him. Both men turned to watch Lewis Kampmueller walk in, staring down at his cell phone. Duncan shouted a greeting as he came in behind Lewis. "Thought we'd stop in and see if you two were up for a beer after you get off work."

"Sounds good to me," Vance said.

Lewis continued to stare down at his cell.

"How's everything over at the Devine household?" Brooks asked Duncan.

"Lotta gorgeous women in one house right now," Duncan supplied. "Grace and Tess arrived early this evening. Grace's spy guy is here too. That dude scares me."

"And you're sleeping under the same roof."

"Worse. I'm bunking with him. Dude probably sleeps with a freaking gun under his pillow."

"Don't be ridiculous. I'm sure it's just a knife," Vance offered.

"Yeah. It's Mr. Devine who sleeps with the gun under his pillow," Brooks teased. "I wouldn't be wandering the halls trying to stumble into Annabelle's room."

"I hear that."

Duncan's phone dinged. He pulled it out of his pocket and read the text message.

"Hey. Ah—guys," Lewis said, nose still in his phone. "It looks like we've got a situation at The Situation."

Duncan smiled as he texted. "I think Lewis is right."

"What's going on?" Brooks asked.

"Annabelle just asked if it would *embarrass* me if she entered a *wet T-shirt contest*. For *charity*," Duncan explained.

Vance's chair legs snapped to the floor. "A what? For what?"

"Not happening. That sort of thing doesn't go down in Henderson," Brooks said.

Duncan lifted a brow. "You sure about that? I don't think it's illegal. Big night. Lots of young people back in town. And those girls seemed to be ready for a wild night from what I gathered."

"What girls?"

"Our girls."

"Lolly?"

"And apparently Darcy," Lewis added, finally taking his nose out of his phone.

"I don't believe this," Brooks said, incredulous. "What the hell did you tell Annabelle?"

"I told her she'd better win!" Duncan grinned.

When all three of his buddies looked at him like he had handed in his man card, he added, "I'm not about to tell Annabelle Devine what she can or can't do. And I'll tell you what. If you know what's good for you, you will follow my lead. At least my girl gave me a heads up."

"Fucking A."

Vance turned a smug smile toward Brooks. "Feeling like a lucky son of a bitch now? You wanted to see what Lolly was going to do next. Well, now you know."

"This is bullshit," Brooks said. "No way in hell is Annabelle Devine going to be caught dead in a wet T-shirt contest. It's not part of the Miss Manners guide book. One picture of her shows up on the Internet and her reputation as Keeper of the Debutantes is finished."

Brooks shot up and started reaching for the desk phone. "Photos! Every fucking asshole has a camera on his cell." He dialed 411 and waited until he was connected to The Situation. He hit the speaker button.

"Ed! This is Officer Bennett. What the hell am I hearing about a wet T-shirt contest?"

"Not a bar-sponsored event. Phi Delts from State are raising money for Children's Hospital."

This had Brooks standing up straight and throwing another 'fucking A' around. It couldn't have hit closer to home. Not just his old fraternity, but Vance and Duncan's as well, for Christ's sake. How was he going to stop something he was semi-connected to?

"Why? Is it illegal?" the owner of the bar asked.

"Definitely unconventional, even for a fraternity."

"They've been charging a twenty-dollar cover charge and the place is packed. If the girls volunteer to participate, they get in free."

"This is not the kind of thing we want Henderson known for; you got me?"

"I hear you. I'm not crazy about it, but they assured me it would be old school. Shirts are wet, but they stay on. I told them no nudity. I don't want to be run out of town tomorrow by a bunch of angry fathers."

"When is this debacle starting?" Brooks asked as he checked his watch.

"Like I said. It's not a bar-sponsored event. I'm not running it."

"Okay, Ed. This is what we're going to do. You set up four chairs front and center. Then tell the brilliant assholes in charge of this fucking nightmare that off-duty police will be sitting there making sure this *stays* old school. We aren't going to stop it, but we'll be there to make sure things don't get out of hand. And Ed. No pictures. Spread the word. Anybody takes a picture and their equipment will be confiscated." He cut off the call saying, "And that will be the least of their worries. Okay," Brooks said, rubbing his hand through his hair.

"So? If you can't beat them, join them?" Duncan questioned.

"The cop in me wants to put my father, Lolly's mother, and Harry Devine in those seats. But the Phi Delt in me is screaming, 'Where's the fun in that?' Lewis, is this for real or are we being set up?"

Lewis shook his head. "I've got this algorithm I'm working on. To be honest, they could have been discussing it over dinner and I wouldn't have noticed."

"Right. Well, you do realize I have no intention of allowing my sister to participate in a wet T-shirt contest while I'm standing there, right?"

Lewis looked at him for a moment as if he was trying to figure out who Brooks was talking about.

"Darcy! My sister!"

"Oh! Right, right," said Lewis. "Probably why her text said not to mention it."

Brooks' smile broke broad and wide. "Yeah. You and Darcy getting married is going to work out just fine for me after all."

⌬

The Situation looked to be in desperate need of a little law enforcement. The cars from the parking lot overflowed into the street. The partying from inside the bar had overflowed into the parking lot. As Brooks pulled the cruiser up, he turned on the siren and lights briefly, hoping to scatter underage drinkers before he had a chance to recognize any of them.

"Start carding people immediately. Let's get these numbers under code," he said as he came up on Vance, who had parked his truck in the back alley. "We're off duty in five minutes but nobody needs to know that."

"You're fucking with me, right? We aren't really going to let this happen?"

"Oh, it's going to happen. It's just not happening with Lolly or Darcy in the mix, that's for damn sure."

"Thank God. For a minute there I thought you'd gone soft in the head like Duncan."

"He's screwing with us. No way is Annabelle shaking it loose in a wet T-shirt in this time zone or any other."

"Yeah, but she stirred this whole thing up."

"Lolly needs no help stirring things up. And what better way for her to get back at me for running off with Tansy? Face it. Annabelle sent the text to get us here. She's on our side."

Brooks and Vance worked their way up the stairs and into the bar. A rickety table sat just inside the door where three pretty boys stood collecting money. Brooks put down a twenty along with his badge. That had two dark heads and a sandy blond one snapping to attention. "Make all the money you can tonight because this is *never* happening in my town again. We clear?"

"Yes, sir!" they agreed in unison.

Vance slapped his twenty down and pointed to Brooks. "He's the good cop. The bad cop is gonna tell you that if one picture or video is taken tonight, the three of you Einsteins are going to jail."

"How can we stop that?"

"I just said you were Einsteins, didn't I? Figure it out!"

Usually full of locals, tonight every college kid between there and Chapel Hill had gathered, sporting their best preppy attire. It looked more like a sorority sock hop instead of a local dive bar. There was a DJ playing the latest in country and rock, and a line dance starting up with a lot of girls and a healthy dose of guys. A quick survey of faces and demeanors let Brooks know that there weren't a lot of terribly inebriated people…yet. Everyone was just plain having fun.

Well, damn if he didn't want to jump in and join them.

"They're here," Lewis said, handing beers to both Vance and Brooks. "They were on the dance floor when we arrived. Then an announcement was made for all the contestants to meet in the back room. Off they went."

"Goddammit. I thought they were bluffing."

"Nobody's wet yet," Vance growled, stomping off through the crowd.

Lewis slapped a hand against Brooks' chest, stopping him from following. "Lolly's not back there." He tilted his head in the opposite direction. "That guy she broke up with before coming home? He's a Phi Delt and he's here. According to Darcy, his name is Davis Williams and Lolly's been dodging him all night. But he got in her face when she was coming off the dance floor and convinced her to follow him in that direction."

Brooks took a look. There was a hell of a lot of crowded real estate in that direction. And it narrowed into a hallway, which led to another room with pool tables and dart boards. Beyond that was another, smaller bar area and an emergency exit door. An alarm may sound if it was opened, but on a night like tonight, nobody would hear it or care if they did.

"Thanks, buddy," Brooks said rather distractedly, his eyes searching the crowd for Lolly's dark ponytail. "I'm going to leave it up to you to take care of Darcy. Text me if Lolly shows up."

"Will do," Lewis said as Brooks moved back through the front door and surveyed the parking lot. He didn't think Lolly would leave with Davis Williams. After all, she'd kicked him to the curb. But it was heading toward midnight and she'd probably had a few drinks. Brooks' gut twisted, remembering the end of their first date and the moment he realized how vulnerable she was.

He took a deep breath, trying to clear his head as he jogged along the front of the building toward the emergency exit. It was relatively quiet as he turned the corner with no one coming or going. He tried to pull the door open, expecting to find it locked, but it came easily. Brooks shook his head and shot inside.

The back room was crowded and loud with music piped in from the main bar. Although he'd turned a few heads by coming in the emergency exit, everyone went back to their conversations and drinks quickly. The lighting was dimmer back here, and everywhere he looked his mind conjured up a dark ponytail.

Jesus.

Lolly was somewhere between him and the front door, and he did his best not to shove people out of his way in his impatience to find her. He checked the dark corners before moving into the game room. Here the crowd grew, but the light was better. He scouted the four pool tables lined up to the right, all of them utilized, but then his internal radar kicked in and pulled his gaze toward the front of the room where it zeroed in on Lolly.

She stood there in that sexy white eyelet dress with her back to the wall, her hair loose and hanging forward as she looked down at her red cowboy boots. Separated by inches, some guy in a pair of pink Bermuda shorts with a lime-green belt and a white button down was pouring his heart out, complete with hand gestures that included a lot of hair pulling.

The poor bastard.

Brooks knew exactly how the guy felt, because for the last dozen hours he'd been tearing out his own hair over Lolly DuVal.

He slowed his pace and stood away from the scene. If pink-shorts made a move and laid a hand on her, Brooks would be on him in a second. Unless there was a need to intervene, Brooks figured he'd just as soon let them hash it out once and for all.

~✦~

Lolly stared at her boots as she listened to Davis. She was sorry she'd let herself get drawn into this situation. Davis was a nice guy, a really nice guy, and he was doing his best to convince her that they deserved another chance. But Lolly knew that ship had sailed, regardless of Brooks, and she was struggling for the words that would make that clear without further damaging Davis' pride.

"Look, Lolly. This guy you're dating is too old for you."

That had her head snapping up. "How do you know who I'm dating?"

"Word spreads. Plus he's an alum. He's also a player and he's just using you."

Lolly squinted at Davis. *Brooks, a player? Hardly.* "I'm not sure your information is all that correct. Regardless...." Her phone vibrated in her pocket. She pulled it out and read the text.

'Tell Pinks to take two steps back.
Fond memories of that dress by the way.
Send me a ! if you need intervention.'

Lolly smiled. "He wants you to take two steps back," she told Davis.

"He's here?"

"Apparently. You want me to wave him over so you can call him a player to his face?"

Maybe Davis didn't believe her because instead of two steps back, he stepped in and put his right hand on the wall next to her head.

What the hell? He's choosing now *to throw nice, safe, and boring to the wind?*

"Only a player would allow his girlfriend to sign up for a wet T-shirt contest."

"Not sure he knew about that," she said, putting her hands up to press Davis' chest back from hers. "But hey, you can ask him," she said as a large hand landed on Davis' shoulder.

Davis threw up his hands and turned toward the intruder. Lolly couldn't see his face when he recognized Brooks, but she knew something had changed because all of a sudden Davis was glad-handing Brooks like he was the super-star alum that he was. And then he turned to introduce the two of them.

"Lolly. Do you know Brooks Bennett?"

"You're kidding, right?" Lolly scoffed.

"Oh. Well, I guess everyone from around here knows Brooks. Say, Brooks, Lolly and I were just talking about a friend of yours. Vance Evans."

"Vance?" Lolly scowled.

"I know the two of you are close, but you know better than anybody that he's a notorious player. Lolly shouldn't be dating him, should she? Help me talk some sense into her."

While Brooks folded his arms across his chest, Lolly clenched her jaw. "Why the hell does everyone think I'm dating Vance Evans?"

"Maybe because you've been seen sucking face with him at the tennis courts," Davis said. "I mean, really, Lolly. Vance?"

"Wow!" Brooks said, rocking his body forward and back, his eyebrows shooting to his hairline. "I don't think I could have said that better myself."

"Vance Evans is not for you," Davis insisted.

"Again." Brooks pointed to his chest. "I'm in complete agreement."

With that Lolly watched the two of them do some sort of ridiculous fist bump, handshake thing that had them bonding for life. She eyed Brooks. "You realize this is absurd, don't you?" Then she looked at Davis. "Davis, Vance is a friend of mine. And yes, he's a player. But your information is not correct."

"You haven't been seen kissing him?"

Brooks spouted a loud ,"Ha!" Lolly shot him a look she hoped would quell his enthusiasm. No such luck. "He's got you there," Brooks said.

"Regardless of the kissing," she said, dragging her eyes from Brooks back to Davis, "I'm not dating Vance. The truth is, I'm dating Brooks." She indicated him with her hand.

Davis' mouth dropped open and he looked back at Brooks.

"Sorry, man. It's true." Brooks slapped Davis on the back. "She thinks you're a nice guy and the fact that you don't want her dating Vance makes you a hero in my book. Problem is, you're a little too nice, if you know what I mean. A little too safe. And maybe a little too, what was the word you told Vance? Oh, boring. You're a little boring."

"Brooks!" Lolly gasped, appalled.

"Lolly, you're not doing the man any favors by not telling him the truth." He turned to Davis, who was clearly stunned. "It's hard to hear, but I'm telling you, this kind of information is invaluable when dealing with the opposite sex. That move you just pulled. Trapping Lolly up against the wall. Beautiful! Am I right, Lollypop?"

Lolly stared at Brooks, wondering what the hell he wanted her to say.

"Tell him the truth. If I hadn't been standing right here watching, that move would have gotten your attention."

She nodded, wide-eyed. The move had definitely gotten her attention.

"See what I mean?" Brooks turned Davis away from Lolly and pointed out all the other women in the room. "Now you know pretty much all you need to know to get any girl you want. Channel your inner Vance Evans and see what happens." Then Brooks reached around him and clasped Lolly's wrist. "But this one," he said, pulling her to his side, "this one is mine."

The way he said the word *mine* had Lolly's heart doing a back flip in layout position. He might have been all good ol' boy up to that point, but he was no-nonsense about laying claim to her. Finally!

Then…then he pulled her up against his chest, wrapped his arms around her back, and kissed her like he meant it.

"You're not planning on entering that damn contest are you?" he asked against her mouth.

"Not if you've got a better offer."

His Caribbean-blue eyes twinkled over his trademark grin. "How 'bout a much overdue tour of my house?"

"I literally thought you'd never ask," she said as he steered her toward the rear door.

CHAPTER TWENTY-NINE

Brooks bit back his grin as best he could while glancing around for any witnesses as he twisted Lolly off his body and hustled her into the back of the cruiser. He wished he could have indulged her, he really did. But making out against the side of a police car was a general no-no.

"Whatcha been drinking, Laura Leigh?" he asked as he buckled her into the back seat.

Two hands smoothed dark hair away from her face, pulling it high in back like she was going to tie it into a ponytail. Her sapphire eyes glistened and her pink lips parted into a brilliant smile, showing off white teeth when she said, "A little bit of this. A little bit of that." When he ducked in to kiss her cheek, she grabbed his shirt and pulled his mouth back to hers. "Wasn't really feeling it until I started kissing you. Obviously, you're very intoxicating."

"Back atcha." He smiled, giving her a quick peck on the lips as he rechecked the tightness of her seat belt and then shut her inside.

No one has me jumping through more hoops, he thought as he came around the car and situated himself behind the steering wheel. He adjusted the review mirror so he could see her reaction as he asked his questions. He pulled out of the parking lot and into traffic, making a U-turn and heading back to the station.

"So. The wet T-shirt contest. That your idea, Lollypop?"

"Darcy's. She's brill-iant!" Lolly claimed, throwing her arms wide in exclamation.

"Brilliant, huh?" Brooks looked into his rearview mirror.

"Annabelle think it was a brilliant idea too?"

Lolly used her hand to wave that idea off. "Annabelle! Pffft! She was all, 'It's all fun and games until someone gets hurt,'" Lolly imitated in a high voice. "Annabelle can be a lot of fun. But a wet T-shirt contest is not her style. Besides, she has a boyfriend who took her to bed the first week they dated, so pfft! She has *no* idea what I've been up against. Oh! You know who did think it was a great idea?"

"I truly cannot imagine," Brooks said, turning off the main drag and heading into the station's parking lot.

"That guy! That magic guy. What's his name? Harry! Harry the Bartender! The one who waited on us that night that you and Vance asked me to have a three-way."

"Lolly!" Brooks shouted as he pulled into his parking space. "We did not ask you to have a three-way," he growled into the rearview mirror.

Lolly didn't even try to hide her laughter. "Oh My God, you should see your face. And I know you didn't ask me to take part in a three-way, but if you had I would've gotten laid by now."

"Fucking A," he whispered, throwing the car into park. He turned off the ignition, sprung himself from his shoulder strap, and exited the vehicle. He pulled Lolly's door open and reached in to unfasten her seatbelt. "Where did you run into Harry, and what the hell did that guy serve you?"

"He was tending bar at the Club." Lolly put her arms around Brooks' neck, so he scooted his hands under her tight little ass and maneuvered her from the car. "Annabelle asked Darcy and me to meet her there. She wanted me to meet *Tansy Langford,* so Tansy could set the record straight about what happened with you two this afternoon."

"You started drinking this afternoon? With Tansy Langford?"

Lolly straightened up and leaned against the police cruiser. "The wet T-shirt contest makes a little more sense now, doesn't it?"

Brooks saw it in her eyes. He'd hurt her. "I'm sorry about running off with Tansy," he said circling his arms loosely around her waist. "It won't *ever* happen again. Now tell me. What did Harry serve you?"

"His famous tequila shots, of course," she said swaying forward.

"Of course," Brooks nodded. "Lolly, I think you're drunk."

"A little," she agreed, dropping her forehead to his chest. "Your father served a couple bottles of wine at dinner. It was *good* wine. And then when it looked like we were going to have to go through with the wet T-shirt thing, Darcy and I slammed two more shots. I think that's what I'm feeling now."

Brooks would have been hard-pressed to put into words what he was feeling now. He touched a finger beneath her chin to get her to look up at him. "Lolly. Are you sleeping this off in my bed or yours?"

Lolly looked at her watch. "You know, I can probably make it back to the bar in time for that contest."

"Like hell."

Brooks pulled her off the car and led the way to his truck. "Why in the world would *Darcy* participate in the contest?"

"Oh! That! You know. She's my best friend, so we were going to do it together." She stopped abruptly and pulled him back, giving him her best I'm-in-love-with-life and I-have-a-little-secret smile. "I'm in the wedding, you know."

Brooks smiled. "I did not know that," he said, genuinely happy.

"I am. Darcy asked me tonight at dinner." Then Lolly waved that off and started walking again. "Mostly I think Darcy wanted to test Lewis. See if he'd even notice she was walking around a bar in a wet T-shirt."

"Lewis," Brooks grumbled. "Darcy is going to ride roughshod over him."

"He is crazy geeky."

"He's also crazy rich."

"And you're crazy cute," she said, pushing firm breasts up against him after he opened her door. He caught her hand and pulled it free just as she was going for his crotch.

"Laura Leigh," he warned.

"Remember what we did in your truck the night I found out I was completely illegitimate?"

"Fondly," he said. "Which is why, if you want to get the Brooks Bennett house tour, you're going to need to keep your hands to yourself."

"Maybe you should cuff me?" she said, holding up both her fists.

"Be careful what you wish for," he said, pulling a pair of cuffs from the inside pocket of the truck's door. He dangled them in front of her.

Her eyes went wide. "They're red!"

"To match those bad-girl boots you've got on." He slapped one on her right wrist.

"Oh."

"In you go."

Lolly obeyed, stepping up into the cab looking mesmerized by the cuff dangling off her wrist. Brooks pulled the shoulder strap down and reached over to secure it across her lap. Then he took the dangling end of the handcuff and clipped it around the handle attached to the ceiling.

"Oh."

"Yeah," he said, laying a kiss on her. "Oh." He closed the door and thought he probably shouldn't be enjoying locking her up this much.

"When I mentioned handcuffs, this wasn't exactly what I had in mind," Lolly huffed, testing their sturdiness as they drove toward his house.

Brooks couldn't help but make a sardonic sound.

"What?" she insisted.

"Trust me," he said, glancing over. "I know exactly what you had in mind. That night of your so-called illegitimacy, you spelled it out for me in no uncertain terms. And when I say no uncertain terms, I mean you painted a very…colorful and elaborately detailed picture."

"Ah! I did not!"

"Well, that's how I remember it," he smirked. A few moments later he asked with all seriousness, "Are they hurting you?"

Lolly looked up and twisted her captured wrist. "No. But my fingers are starting to tingle from my hand being raised over my head."

"We're almost there."

"I'm not complaining. I'm just giving you a very colorful and elaborately detailed picture," she said primly.

"I expect nothing less," he said with a smile, pulling into his driveway.

❧❧❧

Lolly was a little giddy entering Brooks' home. After all, up until now it had been forbidden territory. The cuffs were off and she stood in the center of the great room with Brooks at her back.

She tucked her hair behind her ears, taking in the gleaming blond hardwood floors, the whitewashed brick fireplace and walls, and the surprising splash of color in the orange chenille couch and chairs complete with handsome throw pillows. The feel was comfortable and modern, not sparse, but uncluttered and neat.

Beyond the sitting area was the kitchen, shiny white and sparkling stainless steel. Fruit spilled over a beautiful green glass bowl that sat on the granite countertop. There were even window treatments on the windows. Masculine but customized. It was so far beyond what Lolly had expected that she was struck speechless.

And then an agonizing thought slithered into her awareness, all the more constricting her efforts to speak. Tansy Langford. Brooks' ex. For all Lolly knew, he'd gutted and rebuilt this house for her. Was this supposed to be Tansy's house? Did she design and furnish it? Is that why it had taken Brooks so long to bring her here?

She heard Brooks move behind her. Probably tossing his keys into a dish somewhere. He cleared his throat, and she realized that she was standing perfectly still, unable to move. There was a ringing in her ears, and she knew the alcohol she'd consumed was probably responsible for the wave of emotion expressing itself in tears. She really didn't want him to see that, didn't want to have to explain it, so she moved toward the kitchen, away from him.

"Laura Leigh, in all the years I've known you, you have never once been at a loss for words."

She nodded her head. It was all she could give him at the moment. Her anxiety escalated as she felt him come up behind her.

"Talk to me," he said, his broad hands cupping her shoulders as he placed a kiss on the back of her head. "I'm dying here. I cleaned it all up. Even have a little champagne in the refrigerator. Although maybe a cup of coffee would be a better choice at the moment."

She swallowed and prayed her voice wouldn't give her away. "It's...it's...."

"What the—?" Brooks spun her around. His face held a mixture of shock and incomprehension as he searched her eyes, then her limbs and her body, checking to see what could possibly be so wrong.

She tapped her chest, indicating the pain was inside. That the struggle was internal. When he wrapped her up in his arms, the dam broke. Pent-up tears and emotion flowed out of her onto his chest. She tried to push away, to turn away from him, but he held on. "Sweet Jesus," he said, clutching her to him. "Whatever it is, I'll make it all right. I promise."

When she still couldn't get any words out, he picked her up and carried her to the couch, sitting down with her folded into his lap. She sank into him then, relaxing in the security of his arms. She realized she'd never felt more secure than when she was in Brooks' arms. Lately, his arms weren't around her nearly enough, leaving her feeling exposed and vulnerable. So she burrowed into his chest, getting as close to him as she could. She closed her eyes, relishing this opportunity, which seemed to do a lot for stemming the flow of her tears.

"You have got to talk to me, honey. Was it the handcuffs?" He found her right wrist and inspected it, running his fingers over and under, feeling for any problems. She shook her head and reached her arms around his neck.

"That's not it," she croaked.

"Then the house?"

She nodded into his neck.

"What about the house?"

She breathed deep and let out a long sigh. "I…I don't want to tell you. It's petty jealousy that is terribly unbecoming," she sniffed.

"You're jealous of this house?" he questioned, astonished.

"Not the house. Tansy Langford. And whatever she had to do with this house." There. She'd said it. And the whole thing felt so uncomfortable that she had the compulsion to extract herself from the very arms that soothed her. She started to move off his lap, wanting to be out of his sight. Wanting to go home, get in her bed, and hide under the covers. And the more Brooks tried to hold on to her, the more desperate she became to leave. To reverse time. To go back to the beginning of the summer. To say 'no' to the best first date she'd ever had.

"Lolly, stop! Tansy had nothing to do with this house. Nothing whatsoever."

"I don't believe you," she said as she continued to scramble to get off of his lap. To untangle herself from his arms. "The house is too perfect." She stumbled off of him, catching herself just before falling into the large, glass-topped coffee table.

Brooks stood and made a move for her, but she spun and put her hands out in front of her. He immediately stopped, palms out.

"Lolly, I want you to call Darcy." The more sane part of her mind noticed that Brooks spoke in a manner he might use when trying to talk someone off the ledge of a very tall building. He slowly pulled his cell phone out of his pocket and held it out to her. "Confirm with her that she is the one who helped me decorate the house. The architect I used is David Gaudreau. It's too late to call him tonight, but he'll confirm that he and I came up with the plan we used to renovate this place. He's never met Tansy. Never once heard me mention her name."

She knew he spoke the truth. Brooks Bennett was nothing if not honest. And she of all people knew he was so much more. "I'm scared." The words came out of her mouth before she knew they'd entered her head.

"Scared?" he repeated, the cell phone still halfway between them.

"I've never been jealous before."

"I'm not following."

"I know. I know," she said, moving in a circle, hand on her forehead. "I just—I walked in here and…and it's so beautifully done. So perfectly put together. I was expecting more of a man cave. You being all single and into sports. So at first I was just in shock. And then it popped into my head about Tansy, and I figured she was in on this. All of it. That you built it for her. That you did this together. And this sick wave of jealousy crashed over me to the point that I couldn't breathe." Her breath hitched, and she was afraid she was going to cry again. "I've never experienced anything like that."

"Okay. First of all," Brooks said, being very patient and careful with his words, "I will never lie to you. So when I tell you that Tansy happened to be the girl I was dating on the day I settled on this house, and that is the complete extent of her involvement, you need to believe me."

"I do. I believe you. But just the thought of it made me crazy. Obviously," she said, indicating the state of her being. "Because it made me aware of how much you mean to me. How much I've come to depend on you. How secure I feel having you in my life. How completely...." Her breath hitched again. "How completely devastated I would be if you wanted somebody else."

"This is music to my ears."

"Well it's making me a stark, raving lunatic, and I don't like being out of control."

"Lolly. If you had any idea—any idea at all—how long I've been in love with you, there would be no way.... Oh, shit. Oh, sweetheart. It's okay. Please don't cry."

But she couldn't help herself. The rest of her emotional dam burst forth with a combination of fear and relief. Joy and anguish. It had her doubled over until she felt herself pulled up against the solid wall of his chest. She wrapped her arms around him and clung tightly.

The words 'how long I've been in love with you' rang true so deep in her soul she hadn't understood what had been happening until now. Brooks had been filling the needy places in her for as long as she could remember. In middle school, he was her sports hero, her protector, and even her disciplinarian. Later, he became her coach, her teacher, and her confidant. She never longed for her missing father after she met Darcy Bennett. Because Brooks had filled so many of the missing parts, throughout her whole life. And this summer, he'd finally become her suitor, her inspiration, and the outlet for her wildest dreams.

Yes, he was the one who spoke the words 'how long I've been in love with you,' but those were her words. Her thoughts. Her feelings. And that was the reason why she'd eventually slept so well that night after realizing he was playing for keeps.

Because she loved him. And had for a long, long time.

CHAPTER THIRTY

Brooks didn't have a lot of experience with weeping women. And he sure hadn't ever sent one into a crying jag by confessing his love. How was this such a shock to Lolly? he wondered. How could she not know how he felt? And why was she crying, for God's sake? For a woman who was willing to stick her tongue down his throat in public earlier, you'd think a confession of love would have borne a different reaction.

It was the strength of her arms around him that convinced him this wasn't necessarily a bad turn of events. She was wrapped around him something fierce, sobbing into his chest. It wasn't gale-force sobbing though. Just shaking shoulders, lots of tears, and breathy intakes and sighs. Brooks had to agree with the majority of his sex—he was never going to understand women.

"Lolly," he whispered, using both hands to try to tilt her face up to his. She was having none of it. So he scooted them over to the couch and gently pulled her arms from around him, lowering her onto the cushions. He sat next to her and pulled her down so her head rested in his lap. She curled her feet up and tucked her hands against her chest, pulling in deeper and deeper breaths. Brooks ran his hand along her hair, along her shoulder and her back, over and over until he thought she'd fallen asleep.

He laid his head back and closed his eyes, his thoughts drifting back to the very first time he recognized Lolly as something extraordinarily special.

He'd thought he was doing a pretty good acting job that night.

The night they won the State Championship. The victory party was at his parents'. Half the town showed up to celebrate. Everyone was exhilarated over the first State Championship ever won at Henderson High. It was a banner night for the team, the school, and the town.

Brooks knew he ought to feel like the rest of them, but he couldn't get out of his own damn way. Frankly, he'd expected people to acknowledge what had almost happened. It's not like anyone watching didn't realize Brooks had a perfect game going.

But no one said a word.

His father didn't take him aside and commiserate with him. His mom didn't shoot him one of her I'm-so-sorry smiles. Or hug him, knowing that inside he was torn in half. Happy he'd pitched the winning game, but frustrated and angry that for the second time in his high school career a perfect game had slipped from his fingers.

He'd wanted it bad. And it had been *right there*. The crowning glory of his storied high school career. He could see the headline in the paper.

Perfect Game. Perfect Season.

And now he just felt like an ass. He was part of a perfect season. A big part. And everybody acknowledged that. He'd been slapped on the back so many times he was sore. But it did nothing to soothe his bitter disappointment. He should have had that game. He was thirty seconds from a perfect game when the shortstop took a split second too long to throw the ball to first and the umpire called the runner safe. It was a routine play. He'd thrown a great pitch. The batter, known for relentlessly knocking it out of the park, couldn't do a thing with it. Yet fucking Dale Sixby couldn't get the job done.

The fact that the next batter immediately hit a pop fly to end the game and win them the championship pushed Brooks' lost perfection out of everyone's mind as the celebration erupted.

And there he was, numb. Completely disconnected from the joy surrounding him. And he *hated* that. He was a team player. He never worried about his own glory. Being written up in the paper every week brought more pain than pleasure, and he would have preferred it if the town's focus was on somebody else. But this game, he wanted. This opportunity that never comes around had arrived for him twice in one season, and he could not get it done. He was sick about it.

And felt even sicker now that it was ruining what should be one of the best nights of his life.

Lolly stirred, her movement drawing him out of his memory. He looked down to find her on her back, staring up at him.

"You've been taking care of me all my life," she whispered.

He ran his fingers back from her forehead through her hair. "Not all your life."

"As far back as I can remember."

He tilted his head. "Maybe."

Her eyes filled with tears again.

"Does that make you upset?" Brooks asked.

She shook her head and tried to get out the word, 'Happy.'

"Me too," he whispered.

"I just realized," she said on a hiccup. "Realized that all those times you showed up out of the blue, it wasn't out of the blue at all." She caught her breath, wiping a loose tear away from her cheek. "The coaching, the gifts. Following Darcy and me around on the nights we were up to no good. The night I got my award, you had to drive in from Raleigh to be there. My mom couldn't be there, but you were there. Your whole family was there."

"Everybody deserves a cheering section."

"You were…." Her breath hitched and the tears started to come back. "You were taking care of me because I didn't have a dad."

"No," Brooks said. "Not because of that. It had nothing to do with that. And it had nothing to do with your twenty-first birthday or your eighteenth birthday. I don't really know how old you were. All I know is it was the night of the State Championship. The victory party was at our house. Everybody was celebrating the win."

Lolly sucked in a breath.

"You remember."

"I remember," she said, releasing a shuddering breath.

Brooks closed his eyes for a moment. "You were the only one who acknowledged I had been thirty seconds from a perfect game. For the second time that season. In fact, you said chances like that don't come around often—that it was okay to be mad. Which was exactly, *exactly* what I was thinking."

"But you couldn't let it show."

272 LIZ KELLY

"No."

"Because it's all about the team."

"Right. But you saw it. You alone understood my pain."

"I wanted you to pitch a perfect game. Everyone else wanted the team to win the championship."

"How did you even know what a perfect game was?"

"You were a pitcher."

"So?"

"Well, I wasn't at the games to watch the first baseman! And then I started paying attention to the pitchers on TV. I just listened to what the announcers were saying. I knew perfect games were rare, so I knew it would be a big deal if you threw one."

"It would, indeed."

"Still gets to you, huh?"

"Like it was yesterday," he sighed, resting his head on the back of the couch, looking toward the ceiling as he spoke. "Lolly, you have no idea what a gift you gave me that night. I was desperate for someone to acknowledge my pain. To give me the freedom to be upset in spite of the win. Once you did that…it was like…*poof!* The anger and disappointment vanished. I was able to enjoy the rest of the party and feel like a part of the team again." He rolled his head and looked down at the grown-up version of the kid who had saved one of his best nights. "I just needed to be seen. You saw me."

Lolly wiped away a few more tears.

"So now I'm aware and intrigued by this little kid. Who just happens to be a twelve-year-old *girl*. A very pretty *girl*, who always had a bow in her hair."

"My mother," Lolly insisted.

"I paid a little more attention to who you were, what you were doing, and the things you said. And as your competitive nature exerted itself, I saw we had that in common. I figured someone better get you into sports. You were so different from Darcy in so many ways, and I guess I really liked that," he laughed. "I wanted to encourage that."

"Oh My God. I do not understand what you have against your sister."

"She's my sister! A spoiled pain in my ass," he insisted. "But she did bring you around."

"If it weren't for Darcy, you would have never noticed me."

"Oh, I would have noticed. You were nowhere close to eighteen when I realized I needed to distance myself."

"I had no idea."

"And thank God for that. If you'd started throwing yourself at me then the way you've done this summer, I'd have been tossed into jail."

"Hmm. So you'd think, after all this time, you'd be eager to get your hands on me."

"Laura Leigh, I think I've demonstrated just how eager I am to get my hands on you."

"You're afraid to take me to bed."

He let out a long breath and said, "You have no idea."

"Brooks."

"Lolly. Sweetheart. Aren't you careful with the things most precious to you? There is nothing my body wants more than to make love to you. But I'm old enough to know that it will change everything. And it can't be undone. So after all these years, can you blame me for being a little cautious?"

When she twisted her mouth into a grimace, he laughed.

"I see that you do."

"It's not that," she sighed.

"Then what is it?"

"It's that I've been crying uncontrollably, so my sinuses are clogged, my make-up is gone, and my hair is probably a rat's nest. And now my head is starting to pound because I was clearly over-served, and I'm guessing it's close to 3:00 in the morning." She sighed deeply. "This isn't going to happen tonight, is it?"

Brooks gave her a sad smile as he shook his head 'no.'

"I didn't think so," she said, turning to her side and curling her hands under her face.

Brooks resumed the stroking of her hair. "But Laura Leigh, I've got Tylenol for your head, a shower for your face and hair, and as soon as those fireworks are finished at the Club tomorrow night, I am bringing you back here to light off a few fireworks of our own."

"Promises, promises," she sighed. And then a tired 'I love you,

Brooks' eased out so quietly he almost missed it.

Almost.

His heart ate it up and thumped hard with the energy it instilled. He laid his head back against the couch and smiled, grateful for the new treasure she'd bestowed on him.

CHAPTER THIRTY-ONE

The Fourth of July festivities started early at the Henderson Country Club. Every member of the staff was on duty, and the grounds were packed with activities for all ages. A Moon Bounce, pony rides, horseshoes, croquet, golf, tennis, and putting contests went on around each other in controlled chaos. The day was hot and sunny so the pool was packed with young families while the teens and twenty-somethings converged on the makeshift beach volleyball setup, complete with sand.

Genevra and Hale walked hand in hand around the scene. They'd arrived earlier than the said meeting time for their guests. "This is it," Hale said. "Here we are. In public. Holding hands. So far, so good."

Genevra squeezed his hand. "After the DuVal clan has bent over backwards to assure me how happy they are that I'm finally moving on—"

Hale barked a disbelieving laugh.

"—I think our biggest hurdle is behind us. Oh, come on now. The Major and Momma DuVal have been nothing but gracious."

"After we assured them we would carry on their charade as best we could."

"Can you blame them? No good can come from any of that nonsense surfacing, especially for Lolly."

"Which is why I've agreed to all their demands and am knowingly allowing my son to risk his reputation as an officer of the law by destroying any evidence."

"He really isn't much of a cop, is he?" Genevra laughed.

"I guess not," Hale smiled. "It was his idea, after all. Besides, it sounds to me like he's planning to follow in my footsteps."

"Is that right?"

Hale nodded, beaming proudly as they walked. "He's already got a foothold. He's part owner of a shoe store in town and the Gyro Garden. Businesses like yours that were doing well on their own, but have greater potential for profitability in the long run."

"So he's a chip off the old block," she said.

"I'd like to think so. Though his mind is far more like today's technology. His sees things I miss. His brain calculates faster than mine ever could. He sees potential in businesses I overlook. He's born to this."

"Why aren't you in business together?"

"We should be! I'd always hoped he'd be interested in my work, but when he told me he was joining the Henderson Police Force, I figured he had a calling in a different direction. So I didn't press. I've just found out about his investments recently. As a matter of fact, it was when I told him about your accounting firm. He told me he had grand plans for the economic growth of Henderson. He's even planning to push Brooks into running for mayor."

"I heard Brooks has an interest in the job."

"Vance is going to be his campaign manager. He already hit me up for a big donation. He wants Brooks in office so they can work together to put Henderson on the map. You know that list of the ten best places to live in America? Vance and Brooks want Henderson on that list. That's their dream."

"Why? I mean, I love it. Of course, I love it. It's just surprising that they're so pro-Henderson. Their generation seems to want to leave and never come back."

"Is that Lolly's plan?"

"It was at the beginning of the summer."

"I bet Brooks has something to say about that."

"She didn't come home last night."

Hale stopped and turned to look at Genevra. "How would you know?" he smiled. "You haven't spent the night at your place in a month."

She ducked her head and sighed. "It's true. My mothering skills have deteriorated completely. It's like I'm the teenager when I walk into the house. I never know if I'm going to be confronted with my moral lacking."

Hale abruptly pulled her to him, bumping her chest to his. He took hold of her chin with one hand and circled her back with his other. "I find your moral lacking *very* satisfying," he said, running his lips over hers before he deepened the kiss. She felt both hands on her back and then his tongue searching its way into her mouth. She opened for him, unable to deny him, ever. Her hands reached around his back as they kissed like greedy teenagers.

"Genevra? Genevra DuVal?" The high-pitched voice interrupted their public display. "Are you standing here kissing Hale Evans?" asked Shiny Davis, waddling her low bulk toward the two of them. "Whatever does this mean?" she inquired, wide-eyed and starstruck.

Genevra turned and greeted one of Henderson's greatest gossips with a bright smile. "Mrs. Davis, have you ever been properly introduced to Hale Evans?"

"I haven't laid eyes on you for a good twenty years," she said, shaking Hale's hand. "If it wasn't for your delightful mother and that handsome son of yours getting into so much trouble, I'd have thought you'd packed up and left town."

"Only for my work," he assured her. "But now that Genevra has agreed to marry me, I'm sure we'll be seeing a lot more of each other, Mrs. Davis."

"Marry? You two are getting married?" Shiny looked like she was about to pop. "Why, this is wonderful," she said graciously. "I'm so happy for both of you. Have you told the Major and Emma yet?"

"They've told us and we couldn't be happier," the Major interrupted from behind.

"Shiny Davis, you of all people know how much Genevra means to us. We are thrilled that she and Hale are getting married," Momma DuVal said in support. "We couldn't be more tickled to be claiming the entire Evans family as kin."

Shiny looked from the Major to Emma and back again, her mouth hanging open in wild delight. "Well, isn't this just the biggest bit of news. Bigger than that wet T-shirt contest ol' Fancy Adams called to tell me about this morning."

"A wet T-shirt contest?" the Major and Hale said at the same time.

"At The Situation. Last night. Lots of local girls gone wild. Of course, I wouldn't name any names. You know I'm not like that."

"Being as the Major and Momma DuVal have several granddaughters, including my Lolly, I think I speak for all of us when I say we appreciate your doing your part to protect our local girls," Genevra said. "Wouldn't want any reputations tarnished on your watch. Maybe you can suggest that to Mrs. Adams when you tell her about our wedding."

"Anything for our newest bride-to-be," Shiny gushed. "I'll just run right over to the Adams table and tell Ol' Fancy to keep her big trap shut. Y'all have a happy Fourth now," she called as she waddled off.

Momma DuVal leaned in as she watched Shiny go. "Don't tell me Lolly was involved in this T-shirt thing."

"I haven't the slightest idea," Genevra said. "But there's a good chance one or more of your eight granddaughters was at that bar last night. I'm just trying to head off disaster."

"Oh Lordy. You know how our Molly likes to party," Momma DuVal said. "Let's hope the news of your impending marriage gives the gossips something better to talk about. Come on, let's get you two mingling."

For the next two hours, the Major and Emma DuVal reintroduced Hale to the old guard of Henderson, extolling his praises and coming darn close to claiming they'd handpicked him for their favorite daughter-in-law's future husband.

❧

A member of the Country Club staff escorted Brooks and one hurtin' cowgirl to the Evans' table. "I keep telling you, Lolly, a little hair of the dog and you'll be feelin' more yourself," Brooks assured her. "Jesus!" he said, pulling up short at the outrageous sight strewn across the large round table before him.

Never before had he witnessed such obvious pain. The always impeccably dressed Duncan had left his navy Izod unbuttoned, the collar stretched and pulled to one side. He was sweating profusely from the sheer force of will it took for him to be upright. Lewis, similarly outfitted, was sprawled out with his head dangling off the back of his chair and his mouth wide open, as if he'd passed out. Miss Manners Annabelle, looking like she'd run her fingers through her hair one too many times, sat with her elbows on the table and her forehead in her hands. Darcy looked fresh from the shower in a pretty patriotic-blue sundress but sat perfectly still, as if moving her head in any direction might make it fall off. To top it off, the Men in Black had nothing on the dark shades every one of them was sporting. Just like Lolly's.

"Rough night?" Brooks addressed the table at large, never feeling so happy to have missed out on all that fun.

Various moans and groans met his greeting. Lewis' head drifted to one side. Lolly flopped into the closest chair and laid her head on top of her arms.

"I'm not sure y'all are the picture of reinforcements Mr. Evans and Mrs. DuVal had in mind. Somebody want to tell me why I'm sitting with a bunch of refugees from Camp Tie-One-On?"

Annabelle tried to wet her lips with her tongue. When that didn't work, she took a sip of water from the glass in front of her. "We decided to stay and watch the wet T-shirt contest. The atmosphere was…well…'festive' is putting it mildly."

"Big shot Lewis bought a bottle of this new brand of tequila. Avione. So smooth it slid right down. We all thought it was a great idea at the time," Duncan said. "I swear to God I do not remember one minute of that contest."

"It's like a sick joke," Lewis said, pulling his head upright. "Might have been the best night of my life and I've got limited recollection."

"Lewis was the official judge," Darcy muttered. "After three shots, he donated ten thousand dollars, so they made him Contest King. I'm pretty sure it was supposed to be an honorary position. But he took over the DJ's microphone and decided to interview all the girls like it was a Miss America Pageant. That's when Annabelle and I hit the bottle."

"Wow, Lewis!" Brooks stifled a grin. "How'd that go over, buddy?"

"I'm certain it added a touch of academic sophistication."

"Which every good wet T-shirt contest needs," Duncan added.

Brooks looked up and started laughing because right on cue—but out of nowhere—appeared Harry the Bartender with a silver tray full of his infamous tequila shooters. "Harry!" Brooks greeted. "I hope you've got the power to revive this motley crew."

"Have I ever let you down?" Harry flaunted his infectious smile as he gently placed the shots, lime wedges, and salt shakers in front of each person. "This is guaranteed to make you feel better," he told the ones trying not to gag at the sight. "Trust me."

"I've been telling Lolly that a little hair of the dog might be the cure. Come on, y'all. You can't feel worse than you already do. Pick it up. We'll do this together," Brooks said.

Harry stood by the table with the silver tray in both hands, coaxing his charges. "It's team building. Puts hair on your chest. Takes the edge off. Whatever floats your boat. And if it doesn't make you feel better, the shots are on me."

"To Harry!" Brooks urged them on by toasting Harry with his glass.

"To Harry," the group grumbled, following suit.

It wasn't pretty, but when the job was done and everyone's shuddering subsided, Brooks looked at Harry and asked him to bring each of them an ice-cold beer. Then he sat down next to Lolly and rubbed her back.

Vance arrived, fresh-faced and full of energy. "Well, what do we have here?" Vance grinned, pulling out the chair next to Brooks for his grandmother, Emelina. "Don't tell me y'all closed The Situation down. Aren't we getting a little old for that?"

"Old," Duncan echoed. "Way, way too old," he agreed.

Miraculously, the group seemed to be moving a little easier as they filled Vance and the Big Em in on how Lewis had earned the prestigious honor of being named Contest King.

"Lewis, you old dog, you!" Vance teased. "Since when have you been interested in anything going on south of a woman's brain?"

"I was completely interested in the size of their…brains last night. Obviously, since I asked compelling questions."

"Right. Like if you were a flavored vodka, which flavor would you be?" Darcy rolled her eyes.

"Please tell me that was *not* one of the questions," Lewis groaned.

"That was the *one* question you asked them *all*," Darcy said. "And I'm still irritated with the way you were so enamored with Darla Weaver's cantaloupe-sized breasts that you could not comprehend the word blueberry when she answered the question."

Duncan came to Lewis' defense. "Let me assure you that none of the men present could reconcile blueberries with those cantaloupes. Lewis, you were not alone."

Harry arrived and began placing pints of ice-cold beer in front of everyone. He even had Big Em's preferred Long Island Iced Tea.

"I was alone when I woke up this morning," Lewis grumbled.

"Good thing," Brooks sneered under his breath.

"Oh My God," Lolly snapped. "They are engaged. You are such a prude."

Mirth floated across the table. Most everyone reached for their beer to cover it.

"She's my sister," Brooks countered. "And they are staying under my parents' roof. I'm not a prude. I'm a proponent of propriety."

Lolly spelled, "P…R…U…D…E. Prude."

"Like hell," Brooks mumbled, taking a sip of his beer.

Lolly turned to the rest of the table. "I finally spent the night at Brooks' home last night. And I'm *still* a virgin!" she said, causing all four men to spew beer across the table.

"Sweetsie, that's certainly refreshing news," her mother said as she kissed Lolly's cheek. All the men immediately stood to greet Genevra and Hale, who had managed to extract themselves from the DuVals at just the right time to hear Lolly's pronouncement. The two of them circled around the table, greeting everyone individually.

The engaging grin Brooks offered Mrs. DuVal as she thanked him for taking such good care of her daughter shifted to a reserved look of surrender when Hale shook his hand, apologizing for their timing. But the look Brooks leveled on Lolly when he sat back down ricocheted between utter disbelief and an angry glower. He leaned close to her ear and whispered, "You are not serious about that virgin thing, are you?"

"As far as you're concerned I am."

"That's not exactly answering my question."

"Does it make a difference?"

"Of course."

Wide-eyed and outraged, Lolly turned her whole body toward Brooks. "How exactly would it make a difference?"

Brooks leaned in, closing the distance between their faces. "Because tonight wouldn't just be our first time. It would be your first time."

"And you'd what? Handle things differently?"

"Probably."

"Hmm," she said, letting her gaze wander all over his face. "You really are perfect, you know." She leaned in and kissed him.

Brooks kept his eyes closed and whispered over her mouth. "They don't call me the Golden Boy for nothin'," he said before giving her another quick kiss.

Their table was invited to line up for the buffet, but Brooks held Lolly in place as the others rose, eyeing her speculatively.

"No special consideration will be necessary," she finally said. "So you can relax."

"You're kidding, right? Now I have to worry about surpassing whatever phantom lovers have come before me."

Lolly popped a loud laugh. She put her arms around Brooks' neck and snuggled onto his lap. "You surpassed even my wildest dreams on our very first date," she told him as she kissed his cheek.

Brooks turned his head and slid his lips under hers. He let himself ignite while they were alone in the crowd. With Lolly on his lap, his tongue in her mouth, and his body hardening, it was as delicious a torture as he could imagine. The sun wasn't close to setting, but that was okay because tonight was the night he was going to finally make this pretty young thing his.

"I love you," she said.

"I love you back," he responded.

"What do you think of this dress?" she asked.

"I told you earlier it's fun and sexy, just like you."

"You said that? When?"

"When you first came downstairs, back at your house. Don't you remember?"

"I was still feeling off," she said. "You said the dress was fun and sexy?"

"My exact words."

"Oh." She smiled, hopping off his lap.

She twirled around, showing off the red raw silk halter dress tied with a big blue satin bow at the back of her neck. The bow's tails hung down Lolly's bare back in a sexy dare that tempted him to tug one to see what would happen. A dare he was *so* taking, in just a few short hours. The front of her dress fit like a glove from the waist up. In fact, at the moment, he could see her nipples were as erect as his Johnson. He really did love this dress. He glanced down at the short, full skirt and wondered at the little bit of blue netting showing at the hem.

"Very patriotic. Very sexy," he said, standing up and grabbing her hand.

"Did you notice Annabelle's dress? Or Darcy's? Or my mother's?"

"Should I have?" Her big grin along with her head nodding up and down told him he'd missed something, so he turned and looked toward the buffet line.

He saw Annabelle in her traditional white. It was a strapless dress. Simple and beautiful with a big red sash tied into a large bow at the back of her waist. Definitely eye-catching. It stood out in the crowd. But then again, Annabelle always did.

He looked for his sister, Darcy, and found her smiling up into Lewis' face like she was crazy in love with the guy. He still didn't get those two, but if she was happy, he was happy for her, he supposed. His eyes scanned her dress as she moved through the food line. He didn't know much about fashion, but Darcy's dress looked like a throwback to the fifties. And it suited her personality beautifully. It was fresh and fun. Easy. Royal-blue with red trim and a wide white band of ribbon circling the hem.

"You girls certainly got the day's color scheme right," he said. "What? Did y'all go shopping together? The dresses are different, but similar, if that makes any sense. And, I have to say, now that I'm looking around, they're all very dramatic compared to what the other women are wearing."

"Dramatic?"

Brooks looked back at Lolly. "More exciting? I'm not up on

fashion so maybe I'm not using the right word. They stand out in the crowd."

"Good. We're probably a little over-dressed, but we're hoping to be noticed."

"And your mother," he said, his eyes locking on the very happy future Mrs. Hale Evans as she chatted with a crowd that had surrounded her. "Well, she looks like a bride today, doesn't she?"

Lolly nodded her agreement. Brooks' gaze drifted back toward her mother. "White lace dress. Off the shoulders. Shows off her figure but in a Jackie O way."

Lolly smacked his arm. "Jackie O? And you said you didn't know fashion. That's exactly what I was going for."

"Lolly." It came out on a breath, Brooks' eyes opening both physically and metaphorically. "You did this? Those? They're *your* dresses? *Your* designs?"

She nodded brightly.

"Lolly," he said again in awe, looking down at her dress and then looking back toward the others.

He was so proud. His chest puffed up and he smiled. Just as he turned to tell her how brilliant she was, he had a moment of clarity, felt his stomach clench and a shooting pain spike through his heart.

"What?" Lolly asked.

"Ah, nothin'. Nothin'. They're brilliant. You're brilliant. No wonder you've been so busy."

"Brooks, what's wrong?"

He looked over her head and ran his fingers through his hair, sighing deeply. "Lolly. I'm kidding myself, aren't I? You're too good to come back to Henderson after you get your master's. You'll need to go…where? Paris? New York?"

"Well, I was thinking…I mean, Annabelle suggested—"

"Laura Leigh, I love you. But I'm not going to be responsible for holding you back. You go where you go and I'll…I'll," he put a hand on his waist and spread his other out in jerky motions.

Lolly's face turned accusing. "You'll what? Hook back up with that old, decrepit Tansy Langford? Brooks Bennett, either you love me or you don't!"

"I love you," he soothed, rubbing his hands down her arms. "I do. I was going to say I will follow you. To New York or Paris, I will go where you need to be."

Lolly took a step back and poked him in the chest. "Well, now you're just being ridiculous. What about this town? What about your dream of being mayor? You're like the king around here. You'd never be happy leaving all this behind."

"I'm not going to be happy without you, Lolly. Not after getting to this point. After all these years? I don't know much, but I sure know that. I'm ready to settle down, but I'm willing to wait until you are too."

"You'd wait for me?" she asked, amazed.

"What else can I do?"

"I think you're really gonna like what I have to tell you."

"I hope so," he said. He really did because he *hated* the idea of New York or Paris.

"Annabelle says there's a severe lack of dress shop options for debutantes. Every season the girls have to go to the same old dress shops or bridal salons that are owned by the same old—and getting older—merchants. She wants me to design deb dresses and other party dresses. Since she has such a corner on that market, she'll send the business to me."

"So you'd open a shop in Raleigh?"

"No. I'd open a workshop here in Henderson," she smiled. "We'd transport sample dresses to Raleigh for shows. Or anywhere for that matter. We could carry them right onto the college campuses I suppose. Annabelle said she'd take care of all that. All I have to worry about is designing gowns that will wow the younger crowd and their mothers."

"Why their mothers?"

"Their mothers pay for the dresses."

"Oh. Right."

"Which is *why* I asked you about the dresses we are wearing. Today we are hoping to drum up interest in the *House of DuVal*."

"'House of DuVal.' I like the way that sounds." Oh God, he did. He really did. He liked the way all of it sounded. "Lolly, not only are your dresses brilliant, the business plan is brilliant. With the Keeper of the Debutantes involved you'll get the exposure every new business craves. With no storefront your overhead will be lower. Henderson is cheap, especially if you're just looking for space for a workroom. And it's good for our citizens. Eventually you'll need labor and be starting a whole new business for the town. As the future mayor, I gotta say I love this idea."

"I thought you would!"

The rest of their crowd was starting to return to the table, their dinner plates loaded with corn on the cob and barbecue. "Vance!" Brooks shouted. "You're the economic development guy. You're going to love what Lolly and Annabelle have planned."

"Wait." Lolly grabbed his arm and his attention. "Suddenly I'm starving. Let's go get some food and we can tell everyone over dinner."

"Good idea," Brooks said leaning down to peck her on the lips. "And aren't you just full of 'em?"

CHAPTER THIRTY-TWO

"Oh My God. Can you believe all that?" Lolly exclaimed. She'd been giggling uncontrollably during the fireworks display, unable to contain her elation. Now that they were alone in his truck, stuck in the parking lot, she couldn't wait to discuss all of it with Brooks.

"How many deals went down tonight?" He stared at her in just as much disbelief.

"I don't know. I don't know," she said in rapid-fire. "When Mr. Evans asked to see our business plan for the House of DuVal, I thought I'd hit the jackpot."

"You *did* hit the jackpot."

"And when Vance chimed in saying he'd like first dibs, well, I didn't know what to say. Who knew Vance was interested in investing in small businesses?"

"Just like his dad."

"Just like his dad! So when his dad agreed to let Vance make an offer first, I figured, okay, well, having two interested investors was better than none for sure. I just didn't know how I felt about Vance being heavily involved. But then his dad's seemingly off-hand comment about the two of them going into business together…."

"And the next thing you know, Duncan's in the middle of it, designing a deal between the two of them." Brooks shook his head in complete awe. "I couldn't be happier for Vance. Or for what all this means to Henderson. But, Lolly, you have to know that none of that matters as much to me as your having a plan that will bring you home."

"To you!"

Lolly gave a startled shriek as Brooks grabbed her up and dragged her across his body. His mouth was on her before she'd settled on his lap with his thumbs pressing the hinges of her jaw, forcing her to open for him. His tongue initiated a no-holds-barred mating dance, causing Lolly's excitement to boomerang into hot, greedy lust—her fingers gripping handfuls of his curls while she moaned against his mouth.

Brooks moaned back, sliding his palm along the raw silk covering her torso and claiming her breast in hot demand. Lolly felt her internal core wind tight and felt Brooks grow hard beneath her, his erection pressing against her thigh. His mouth devoured, as if he'd become desperate for what he'd been denying himself. So it was a shock when Brooks broke the connection, knocking his head back against the headrest, breathing heavily.

"I shouldn't have done that," he said, panting. "I'm so—" He sucked in air between his teeth as if in pain. "Hard. I'm not going to be able to drive."

"You want me to help you with that?" Panting just as hard as he was, she really wanted to help him with that.

"No! God, no. I mean, yes," he clarified, pulling her in for a quick kiss. "But not here." He turned his head to check the long line of traffic jammed up on Country Club Drive. "I wonder how much shit I'd catch if I put it in four-wheel drive and tore off across the tenth fairway."

"I think you might like my idea better," she said, coaxing his mouth back to hers, seducing him right back to where they'd been. When Brooks wrapped both arms tight around her waist and pressed her down while canting himself up, they both moaned and then smiled against each other's lips.

"Let's try this," Lolly whispered while ever so slowly sliding out of his lap.

"Lolly," she heard Brooks say as she twisted around. The palm of her hand stroked the swollen length bulging his khaki shorts. "Lolly. You don't have to....I can wait." But she noticed he slid down in the seat, easing her work of unbuckling his belt and releasing the button. She pulled up his shirt and pressed her lips to a spot of bare skin just above his zipper.

"Jesus," he said, sucking in his abdomen, making it easy for her to pull down the zipper. As the soft, black fabric of his boxer briefs was exposed, she wondered if Brooks had his eyes closed or if he was watching. She stroked him over the fabric once more before tugging the band of his boxers over the top half of his erection. She'd felt it in her hand before, felt it pressed against various body parts, but she'd never laid eyes on it until now. It was thick and proud, and as she exposed him further, it became apparent that Brooks Bennett's most masculine appendage was completely in proportion with the rest of his very large body.

Her mind went straight into the gutter thinking about the dirty things he might do to her once they finally got into bed, which wound her core even tighter. Unsure about technique or exactly how to pleasure Brooks with her mouth, she was eager to try—eager to give him a little of what he'd given her. So she pushed herself up, positioned her mouth over the head of his penis, puckered her lips, and went down on him slowly.

From the sharp sound he made and the way his stomach muscles tightened, she worried she was killing him, though from pain or pleasure she wasn't sure. When he arched himself further into her mouth, she concluded he was probably okay with what she was doing. And that thought made her laugh, causing her to hum against him. He let out an appreciative groan. She attempted to use her tongue on one side and the roof of her mouth on the other to create suction as she pulled her head back up slowly. Another loud groan met her ears as she started down again, breathing through her nose so she could keep the suction tight. His hips tilted to press further into her mouth, and then retreated to draw himself out as her head came up.

"Laura Leigh," he said as her mouth continued to work on him. "I'm struggling here." His hips pushed back up. "You're making this feel too damn good." That made her smile, releasing the suction. She took that opportunity to sneak her fingers into his bunched-up boxers and scrape her fingernails lightly over his balls. She moistened her mouth, closed her lips over his shaft, and renewed her efforts.

"Too good," he hissed when she got the suction strong again. His hips were moving faster now, so she followed his lead. Her fingers felt his testicles start to tighten. "If you don't want me to come in your mouth, I'm tellin' ya, you'd better stop now."

Something about him using the word "come" made the tightness between her thighs twist up another notch. She kept her mouth on him, kept their rhythm going. Then she felt his hands in her hair, gripping her head and holding her still as he took control, moving in and then retreating from her mouth. She held herself steady, allowing him to use her.

"Laura Lei…" he begged. "Just…a little…more…a lit—oh, Christ! Oh, fuck!" He shoved his cock to the back of her throat and held it there, straining as he began to pulse. "Fucking A," he moaned, and she did her best to swallow him down, relishing that his entire body was steeped in a shuddering climax.

When his hands relaxed and his breathing decreased, his fingers started moving through her hair. Lolly lifted her head from Brooks' lap and struggled to sit up, finding every muscle had gone stiff. She wiped a hand across her mouth just before Brooks pulled her onto his lap, kissing her thoroughly. His hands moved over her now as if she were a precious and fragile object, touching her everywhere, gently and with reverence.

"Lolly," he whispered against her lips. He was breathing heavily. Talking around his breaths. "I have never lost control like that before. You do that to me. I knew you would. Now maybe you understand. I just don't trust myself."

"Isn't that the point?" she said, smiling and kissing him back. "To lose control?"

"My language. The way I held your head."

"Frankly, I liked it. Both of those. If that's you losing control, knock yourself out."

"But…" he said, breathing deep a few times. Finally, he squeezed his eyes shut and ran a hand over his face. "Okay. Good. But you'll let me know. When I cross a line, you'll let me know."

"Absolutely," she teased.

He eyed her seriously. She was sure he was about to say something else, but then he bit his lips and nodded. "Okay." He reached past her and turned the key in the ignition. She slid off his lap and buckled her seat belt.

"So you're okay to drive now," she said, smiling into the dark.

"I'm okay to drive," he agreed. "But I sure as hell am not in any shape to do much else."

⚮⚮⚮

Brooks knew his silence was creating tension between them during the drive home. But he was at a crossroads the likes of which he'd never thought he'd have to face. Not in a million years did he think he'd ever have to worry about losing control while making love to a woman. But when his hands had clamped down on Lolly's head and he'd taken over that blow job she was so willingly treating him to, he knew his mind had snapped.

He loved her with all his heart and soul, but when it came to his body? Whoa. His body wanted to *own* her.

That night under the stars when he'd freaked her out? It'd freaked him out too, and that was just the beginning. Since then, his fantasies hung on the edge of the dark side, and he was now more convinced that being intimate with Lolly was an aphrodisiac so intense that at some point his body would go into auto-drive and do as he'd just done. Take control and use her for his own pleasure, exactly as he wanted.

"Brooks?"

"Laura Leigh."

"You okay?"

"No."

He noticed she let the silence lengthen. Let him stew. She didn't continue to ask questions. She knew he'd talk when he was ready to talk. Damn! The woman was perfect in every possible way. She continued to understand him like no one else. Here he was being an ass and she allowed him that privilege.

Well, he wasn't letting her go, that's for damn sure. He was going to be the selfish bastard for once, and he was going to keep her. He was going to suck this up and spell it out. Trust that she'd know how to handle him just like she always did. And if she ran scared, well, he'd just run after her.

He pulled into his driveway, slowed to a stop, put the truck in park, and turned off the ignition. He was prepared to grab her hand if she started to leave the cab, but of course, she sat there and waited for him to speak. She always read him right.

When he continued to sit there, she finally said, "Just don't tell me you've changed your mind about taking me to bed."

He laughed then, and it felt good to break the tension. He turned to her with a genuine smile and shook his head. "Oh, I'm taking you to bed. That's a done deal. In fact, if you start begging me to take you home instead, I'm not gonna do it. So you may as well resign yourself to helping me work this out. To come to some kind of understanding."

"Okay. Can we talk about this inside? Maybe open that bottle of champagne?"

"Probably a good idea," he agreed.

He followed her inside, feeling better already. Just her voice, her manner soothed him. She was the fucking horse whisperer when it came to him. He downed a glass of champagne and poured himself another before following her over to the couch.

He tried to sit, but he was too anxious. So he stood and started pacing. He thought she might be laughing at him a little and that was okay. He wished he could find it a laughing matter. *Jesus*, he needed to lighten up.

"How 'bout I take a crack at it," she offered.

He shot her his best oh-really look. "You think you know what I'm about to say."

"I do," she said, pulling her bare feet up and tucking them under her pretty red dress. Her dark hair hung in front of her shoulders as she hugged her knees. "Because you said it thirty minutes ago, and you haven't said anything since. You're afraid of being too aggressive with me."

That was it. Exactly. And she knew it too, because whatever look he had plastered over his dumb ass face apparently confirmed it.

"I thought so," she said. "But here's the thing. And I want you to hear me when I say this, because that limb you're afraid to step out on right now?" He nodded for her to go on. "I'm way, *way* out on it."

She took a deep breath. Looked away and then looked back. "I like the idea of your manhandling me. I like the idea of your being aggressive. The way you were with me that night under the stars was shocking, but I haven't been able to think about anything else since. I liked it. I liked how you were with me in the truck just now. The language you used just made it that much hotter." She began to uncurl her legs and move off the couch. "I like being the one who makes you lose control. I'm not afraid that you'll hurt me. And I promise to tell you if you do." She stood and came toward him slowly, stopping right in front of him. "We're both athletic. We both enjoy physical activity. Our sex life is bound to reflect that. I haven't had that much experience, but I never had anyone bring me to orgasm during a goodnight kiss either. You made that happen for me, Brooks. That's what you do to me."

He wished he'd had the recorder on his phone going. He really did. Because after she said she liked the idea of being manhandled by him, his brain shut down and his dick took over. And from the strain against his pants, he figured his dick heard every word coming out of her talented little mouth and was poised and ready at the starting line of a long sex marathon.

"Laura Leigh," he said, holding his hand out to indicate the hallway. "Would you like me to show you the rest of the house?"

Her smile grew slow and full as she tucked her hair behind her ears. She turned, picked up the little overnight bag she'd brought in from the truck, and followed him down the hall.

"This is guest room number one," he said, flipping the light on as she stuck her head inside the door. "There's a bathroom that adjoins this bedroom to another farther down the hall."

He followed after her until she stopped at the threshold of his room. He stood behind her and tried to see it through her eyes. On top of his four-poster bed, the new comforter, shams, and throw pillows transformed the space from utilitarian to inviting. He sure was happy it looked inviting now.

Lolly stepped inside and walked toward the master bathroom. He followed her in, watching her survey the green stone tiles, the Jacuzzi tub, and the separate shower stall with the rain water fixture. She put her bag down and walked to the green granite countertop housing two sinks. She ran her hand over it and then noticed a separate room with an opened door and the toilet just beyond. "Wow."

"That's what gets the wow? I thought the Jacuzzi might get the wow."

"The wow is for the bathroom in its entirety," she clarified. "After seeing your beautiful home and the Evans' place, I now realize how long my mother and I have lived in squalor."

"Your mother's home is charming."

"Yes, but new is new," she said, spinning around. "And I think I like new."

"I'm glad you like new. New is all I have to offer."

She put her hands on his chest and reached up on her tiptoes to kiss his lips. "You have charming to offer as well," she assured him. "Now would you mind if I took a moment to put your beautiful bathroom to good use?"

"Not at all. Just don't take off your dress. I've been dying to untie you all night."

She grinned brightly. "You like the bow?"

"I like the bow," he said, backing out of the bathroom. "Very sexy bow."

Brooks closed the door to give her privacy and then continued to stare at it. What now? He looked around his room and saw the group of candles Darcy had sent with all the other foo-foo crap. His sister was a genius, he thought for the first time ever. He raced out of his room to gather the champagne bottle, their glasses, and the long lighter he used for the fireplace. He set the bottle and glasses on his bedside table and lit the candles before rolling down the shades. He turned off the lamp and smiled at the lighting. Fucking A. Darcy was brilliant.

He undressed inside his walk-in closet, rolling his clothes in a ball and depositing them in the built-in hamper. Then he stepped into a pair of athletic shorts. His hard-on tented his shorts, making him look ridiculous. He figured a quick shower was not uncalled for, so he headed into the bathroom across the hall and doused himself with tepid water as he soaped up and shampooed his hair.

Lolly was waiting for him when he returned, standing on the other side of the bed and drinking her champagne. She'd pulled down the comforter and laid it on the bench at the end of his bed. The sheets were turned down invitingly.

He forced himself to speak around the lump in his throat. "If you had any idea how many times I've pictured you standing right there...."

"If you had any idea how many times I've pictured you with your shirt off," she countered.

He laughed, his tension easing. "How 'bout that dress? You ready for me to untie you?"

She turned, offering her back, holding her champagne and hair to the side.

God, what a picture that made.

Brooks moved in close and slid the wide satin ribbon between his fingers. One good tug and the bow unfolded. He leaned over and kissed her neck as his hands worked the rest of the ribbon loose. The bodice fell forward. Lolly ducked her head and shimmied the dress down her legs. He stepped back as she turned around.

The candle light gave him the view he didn't have that night under the stars. "Sweet Jesus," he said, taking her in. He didn't know what he'd expected, but red lacy boy shorts was not it. Those long, tan legs were bared to his gaze. Her small hips, flat tummy and perky white breasts had his shorts tenting fast.

"You are beautiful," he said, dragging his eyes up to hers. "You gonna finish that champagne?"

She drank what was left in two dainty sips. He held out his hand for the glass, took it, and placed it on the bookshelf beside him. Then he stepped behind Lolly and ran his fingers through her hair, gathering it and pushing it over one shoulder.

He leaned in to kiss her neck, his hands caressing her shoulders and sliding down her arms. He threaded his words between long, slow kisses. "For five years I have ached for you. To touch you like this." His hands moved under her arms, skirting down her sides and then over her stomach. "Five years is a very long time," he said against her ear, letting his chest press against the soft skin of her back. "No wonder I can't control myself."

His hands separated. One moving north, the other south. One roamed over her breasts and the other dipped into red lace, easing his fingers through damp curls. His middle finger found her slick and slippery and so damn ready—the heady scent jacked him up harder. When Lolly jolted as he touched her hot spot, he gripped her tighter and stroked it again.

He kissed her neck with his teeth, using both hands to push the boy shorts down past her ankles. He tossed them to the corner, planning for Lolly never to find them. He dropped his shorts and skated his hands up the curves of her legs, all the way to her tight little ass. He gripped both sides firmly, molding her with his hands. Fitting himself along the seam, he bent his knees and slid between her legs, along the hot, damp pool inside those feminine folds.

Lolly responded, her pelvis canting backward and moving against his shaft.

"God, I want you, Laura Leigh," he whispered against her ear. "Just like this." He slid himself through her wet heat again. "Stay right here. I'm going to get the condoms."

She grabbed on to his hand before he moved. "Unless you need to protect me from something other than pregnancy, I've got us covered."

"You what?"

"I went to the doctor and got an IUD. 99.9 percent effective. I wanted to be prepared. For anything."

"Well, aren't you the little Girl Scout?" he said, twirling her around and kissing her soundly.

"All checked out for any of those unmentionable diseases as well. How 'bout you, Mr. Experience?"

"Lolly, if you're sure about the birth control then we can forgo the condoms," he said, backing her around to the side of his bed. "Not that I'd have any problem knocking you up so I could drag your pretty little fanny to the altar. But beyond that, your health is safe in my hands."

"It's not your hands I'm worried about," she said as he spun her back around, sliding both palms up her back and over her shoulders.

"Your health is safe from all my appendages then," he said, pressing her upper body down to the bed. He splayed his hand possessively over the small of her back.

The perfection of her long legs further aroused him. With her feet on the floor, even as he nudged her legs wider, her sweet curvy backside stayed higher than his mattress. The sight was so erotic it made him growl as he stepped up to slide his aching length against her damp feminine folds, coating his shaft and setting both their bodies on fire. He held himself back from entering her, but gripped her hips and watched as his thumbs caressed the smooth, pale skin of her derrière, watched himself slide between her legs over and over. "You gotta talk to me, Laura Leigh."

"Good," she sighed. "Really good."

"We'll do it the right way next time, baby, I promise," he said, sliding forward and back, doing his best not to plunge himself inside her just yet.

"Who says this isn't the right way?"

He groaned, fighting for control. "If I wasn't in love already…."

He started moving faster, and when he saw Lolly's fingers clutch at the sheets he panted, "Are you getting off on this? Because I sure as hell am." He leaned down, growling against her ear. "As soon as I feel you start to come, I'll give us what we've both been wanting."

She groaned and he felt her pelvis tilt backward, and a new surge of moisture seeped over him as he was now hitting her hot spot every time he pumped forward. "Laura Leigh," he coaxed, sweat starting to coat his skin. "I know how good this feels, baby. Let yourself go."

He felt her body tense, the first wave of orgasm gripping her. She called his name, but he was already positioning himself and sliding into home plate. He felt her internal muscles contracting around him as he pushed all the way in. It was tight. Damn, tight. And he wanted to stay just like that and enjoy the moment. But with Lolly still spasming around him, he wasn't going to last long.

He groaned as he struggled to pull out most of the way, and then grunted when he needed a little extra force to push in. Pulling out, he still felt her gripping him, and he knew he was going to lose it. So he started pumping, locking his hands around her hips and holding her in place. He felt his balls pull up. He felt Lolly coming around him. And then five years of tension exploded from his body.

He held his breath as he erupted in wave after wave after wave of release. His hips were tight against her ass. Lolly's body was bearing down around him and the pain and pleasure was so intense that he cried out, sucked in a breath, and cried out some more.

The words *'Holy Jesus'* seemed appropriate because he thought he was dying. Up on his toes, straining while the sensations continuing to rocket through his balls and cock were so intense he felt he was about to pass out. He moved his hands forward to the bed, hung his head over Lolly's back, and rode the crest of the wave until it overturned, wracking his entire body in pulsing spasms.

He went down to his elbows, his knees starting to buckle. Lolly crawled forward and he followed her down, landing on her back. His mouth was open against her shoulder blade, his breathing hard. He tried to speak, but he couldn't drag in enough air. Finally he was able to roll to her side and then onto his back, his legs still hanging off of the bed, his intake of air limited to short, desperate breaths.

He laid an arm over his eyes and felt the moisture. He had wanted to wail during his release. Hell, for all he knew he'd done exactly that. The longing he'd built up and stored had finally found release through every possible means. Through sex, through sound, through his pores, and even through his eyes.

Goddamn this woman.

"Lolly," he croaked. He willed himself to roll toward her. To move farther up into the bed and gather her in his arms. He held her there, unmoving, until more strength returned. Then he brushed her hair back from her face and told her he loved her. At least he hoped he did, because the darkness came upon him fast, pulling him under. Before he knew enough to resist, he was asleep.

CHAPTER THIRTY-THREE

Brooks was half-asleep when Lolly climbed back in bed. He hadn't opened his eyes but continued to dream even though he'd been aware of the shower and had formulated a plan in case Lolly attempted to leave the room. The fact that she'd come back to bed had him grinning blindly as she snuggled up against him. He threaded both arms around her, pulling her close and kissing the top of her head.

That accounted for three-quarters of his joy. The last bit was because he knew without a doubt his pecker was still in fine working order. After whatever the hell he'd gone through last night, he wouldn't have been surprised to find the thing broken in half.

Lolly must have noticed it too, because the most perfect woman in the world stroked a tentative hand down his hard-on, flawlessly bringing him awake. God, he loved her. With his eyes still closed, he hummed his appreciation as she continued, his body rejuvenating, energy stirring his limbs and mind. He hauled her on top of him, moving them both to the center of the bed. Her knees straddled his hips, her hands braced on his chest. He opened his eyes to find damp hair falling over him while Lolly positioned herself over his erection. Then, ever so slowly, she dropped her hips back and he found his way home.

His hands clasped her knees, his thumbs rubbing up and down her thighs. She sat back on him and he rewarded her by lifting his pelvis and rotating his hips. He pulled his knees up and placed his feet flat on the bed. She tossed her hair out of her face and looked down at him through dark sapphires, her lids already starting to get heavy.

She bit her lip as she circled her hips, grinding herself around his swollen cock. She closed her eyes, and he snuck his hands up her legs where the enticing triangle of dark curls sat against his body. His thumbs uncovered her most sensitive spot. His right thumb stroked low and found its mark. Lolly leaned back, exposing herself to his fingers while still circling her hips around his shaft.

"Brooooks," she sighed, eyes closed, head back. "That feels soooo good."

"For me too, Laura Leigh. For me too."

Goddammit, he wanted to put his mouth on her. Somewhere. Anywhere. But it felt too good having his cock stretched taut, jammed to the hilt inside her and being manipulated by her rotating pelvis. So he bit his lips and focused on the erotica in front of him.

Their tempo changed little by little—she started moving up and down; he started moving in and out. When she leaned forward to brace her hands on his chest, he captured her wrists, extended her arms over his head, and placed her hands on top of the headboard. Then he raised his head and captured a stiff nipple with his teeth. He latched on and sucked. Lolly moaned and increased her tempo, intentionally rubbing herself against his torso.

He had a lot of energy and he was dying to show Lolly how much he appreciated this kind of physical activity first thing in the morning. So he slid down the bed, under her body, allowing his cock to fall out of heaven so he could put his mouth directly under her sweet, sweet core. He pulled her hips down, tilted his head back, and indulged.

Dear God, the taste of her turned him on like nothing else. His hands gripped her hips, forcing her down on his face, making her ride him so his mouth could make love to that sweet bud at the top of her apex while his finger stroked her deep inside.

And oh, she liked it. He could tell she liked it, even as she shrieked when he inserted his thumb and slid his fingers further along her backside, massaging the sensitive nerve endings. "Dear God that's good," she said, moving slower and slower, then stopping while she let his hands and mouth do all the work. He sucked and manipulated until the heavy panting turned into one—long—wail of release as her body tightened and shook, cum easing down over his hand.

He moved that hand between his own legs and spread Lolly's essence over the head of his cock and down the shaft, leaving his mouth to extend Lolly's orgasm as long as she wanted to go. When she collapsed, he rolled her over to her back and crawled up her body.

"You don't have to do anything," he said, spreading her legs with his knees and kissing the tender spots around her collarbone. "Just let me see how far we can take this."

Lolly threw her arms over her head, welcoming him to her body. He laid his hips down against hers, rubbing himself on top of her pubic curls, then into her damp heat, sinking deeper along the length of her body. He rubbed himself between her folds again and again, shivering at the sensation. "Oh, Lolly DuVal," he uttered, low and serious. "Forgive my language, but you are one…great…lay."

He pushed himself inside, sliding in deep and long, moaning his appreciation. His arms went straight, supporting most of his weight so he could look down between their bodies and watch. His intention was to keep it slow and steady so he could extend the pleasure and bask in the physical sensations of loving Lolly. But his body was greedy, wanting more intensity and craving the climax.

Like the night before, monstrous lust shot from his muscles to his nerve endings, shutting down the civilized part of his brain and turning him from Dr. Jekyll into Mr. Hyde. Thrusting deeper, harder, and faster, he moved them up the bed. Lolly braced her palms against the headboard, giving him more resistance. When she wrapped her legs around his back he slid deeper, cried out, and pounded his way home, the bed creaking violently beneath them.

Lolly watched the power of Brooks' muscled form strain every sinew from his forehead down, and from his toes up. She watched the energy converge and surge where their bodies joined. *God is an awesome architect,* she thought as she reveled in the power of Brooks' climax.

His arms broke down one at a time as he collapsed onto her body. She wrapped him up in her limbs, her fingers drifting over his shoulders and back. His naked body was magnificent, and it was all hers.

He rolled off too soon, leaving the bed, telling her to stay where she was. With her arms empty and her body craving his spent weight upon her, she rolled over instead of moaning her distress. Then she heard a soft buzz and wondered if he'd gone to shave. The memory of an electric toothbrush by his sink made her smile. He was brushing his teeth. She heard the water running. Soon enough, everything went quiet, and she felt the bed shift to her right. She rolled over and looked into his freshly-scrubbed face.

"I wanted to brush my teeth before I did this." He leaned in and kissed her, all minty fresh and cool. His body stretched out on the bed before wrapping her up in his arms. His tongue played across her lips before she opened up and let him inside.

They made out for the sheer pleasure of it, eventually turning it into a competition between tongues and lips, laughing out loud when teeth got involved. It was going to be great fun loving Brooks 'Golden Boy' Bennett.

"Best. Day. Ever," he said between kisses.

"Mmm," she agreed. "And it's just getting started."

ONE WEEK LATER

Duncan James stood in a hallway just off the main foyer of Raleigh's largest courthouse. He was dressed for court, though he wasn't scheduled. Beside him stood a bright-eyed Annabelle Devine in her signature white business attire, perfectly fit for court. Beside her was one very nervous Vance Evans. He was dressed in an unprecedented three-piece suit that put his impeccably dressed father to shame. The man was drawing looks from every female who walked by, and a few of the men as well.

The fact that Vance wasn't returning any of those looks spoke plainly to the stress he was feeling. They were all here to meet Piper Beaumont, a woman Vance hadn't laid eyes on since fourth grade. A woman who was about to be ambushed as far as Duncan was concerned. His colleague, Matt Collins, was standing in the center of the foyer waiting for Ms. Beaumont to come out of the courtroom where she was defending a young client. Matt had assured Duncan that Ms. Beaumont would be able to handle the spontaneous introductions. He went on to say that Ms. Beaumont could handle anything.

In short order, Matt's hand gestured toward them, indicating that he had Ms. Beaumont in his sights. Duncan, Annabelle, and Vance all moved just into the foyer to wait for Matt to announce their presence and bring Piper over for introductions. Duncan could tell there was a lot of momentum coming from the courtroom. He noticed what looked like a couple of parents with their college-aged daughter moving swiftly toward the front doors of the building, followed closely by a herd of dark-suited males.

And then came a bit of sunshine, Duncan thought. No, not a *bit* of sunshine, but the whole ball of fire come to earth in the form of one petite, curvy, outlandishly-dressed-for-court Piper Beaumont.

Duncan knew it was Piper because Matt had stepped directly into her path and was talking to her, apparently explaining that he wanted to make an introduction. Piper, in her bright-yellow garden party dress and three-inch yellow patent heels, handed her large yellow tote to one of the three, briefcase-toting male lawyers surrounding her. She turned her head to say something to all of them. They nodded, and off they went, full stride.

"Is that *her?*" Annabelle said, sounding overly delighted. She moved past Duncan as if compelled to take a closer look. Duncan, apparently under the same compulsion, moved in step behind Annabelle. Admittedly, he was just as intrigued. He only hoped his voice didn't come out sounding quite so delighted.

Matt Collins turned to indicate the two of them. "Piper Beaumont," he said. "This is my colleague, Duncan James."

Oh, Duncan thought as he took her hand. *Not a ball of fire at all, but a Kewpie doll come to life.* Yellow-blond curls, large blue eyes, and big pink cheeks. Forget her mouth. He couldn't chance another look at her mouth, for Christ's sake. He was standing next to Annabelle.

"Ms. Beaumont," he grinned. "It certainly is a pleasure to meet you." He cleared his throat and then remembered the woman standing to his left. "May I introduce Annabelle Devine? She's from Henderson. Like you."

"Oh, really? Henderson?" Piper asked Annabelle, as if Annabelle had come from the moon rather than just an hour's drive away. "It's got to be my favorite place in all the world. I grew up there. Well, I didn't grow completely up there exactly, but I was there through fourth grade."

"I lived there most of my life," Annabelle gushed. "I'm in Raleigh now, but my parents are still there, and I go back all the time."

"Oh, I've been meaning to go back. I keep tellin' everybody that the Research Triangle may as well be the Bermuda Triangle. Once I moved in, I never moved out. Except for college—I did manage to get out of the state for college. But that inexplicable pull, that force of the Triangle, had me back here before I knew it. How is ol' Henderson?" Piper asked. Her southern drawl became noticeably stronger the more she talked to Annabelle.

"Just as lovely as ever. You really ought to come back for a visit. The center of town has been transformed by a few boutique shops and two nice restaurants. There are a couple of small businesses, too. Other than that, I bet you'd find it just as you remember."

"Ms. Beaumont, the reason we're here," Duncan interrupted, "is to reintroduce an old friend of yours *from* Henderson. Maybe you remember Van—" Duncan looked behind him and saw nothing but empty space. "Wait. Where'd he go?"

The lobby area had cleared out as they'd stood gabbing. Except for the security detail, Matt Collins, Piper Beaumont, Annabelle, and himself were the only ones around.

Vance Evans had disappeared into thin air.

The Heroes of Henderson Series continues with Vance's story in

Bad Cop
Heroes of Henderson ~ Book 2

Coming soon

If you missed how Duncan James swept Annabelle Devine
off her feet, download my e-book

Playin' Cop
Heroes of Henderson ~ Prequel

(Originally published as *Keeper of the Debutantes* in
Countdown To A Kiss ~ A New Year's Eve Anthology)

OR

Catch up on all the action in Henderson last New Year's Eve with

Countdown To A Kiss ~ A New Year's Eve Anthology
by
New York Times Bestselling Author Colleen Gleason,
Holli Bertram,
Mara Jacobs
&
Liz Kelly

For information on new releases and sneak peeks
visit **www.LizKellyBooks.com**

Acknowledgments

I would like to acknowledge and thank my brilliant critique partners, *Tammy Kearly and Holli Bertram.*

Also:
Christy Crain, my mental health counselor and first reader.

Erin Wolfe, Victoria Shockley, and Patricia A. Thomas,
my invaluable editors.

Carla Christensen who sat next to me in 10th grade English class and introduced me to my first romance novel.

The 'Daughters-of-the-Heart' Research Team
(Who are far younger and sassier than I am)
Liz & Jody Cumberpatch
Kate & Mary Southgate Dickson
Molly & Abby Ford
Heather Hodge
Stacey Collins
Molly Wills

And My Biggest Fans & Cheerleaders
Harry & Jody Ford
Lynn Brilhart
The Spa Sisters & their handsome husbands
The B Team
The Jamiers
Ginnie Pitler

and
My siblings for always being so very entertaining.

About the Author

Growing up every summer in a place where *dancing and romancing* are literally part of its theme song, Liz Kelly can't help but be a romantic at heart. And since her favorite author, Kathleen E. Woodiwiss wrote some of the world's greatest romances, she's just trying to give the world a little more of that. (Okay, maybe a little sexier *that*, but we are now in a new millennium after all.)

A graduate of Wake Forest University, where she met her handsome golf-addicted husband, (who is now sporting dark glasses everywhere he goes) Liz is a mother of two grown sons (also sporting dark glasses) and a miniature Labradoodle named Isabelle. They live in the *Fountain of Youth,* a.k.a. Naples, FL where dancing and romancing continues on ad infinitum.